FIREWORKS

SARINA BOWEN

Tuxbury Publishing LLC

ONE

August, Twelve Years Ago

A SIXTEEN-YEAR-OLD GIRL stares out the window of her mother's beat up Dodge. They don't even make this model of car anymore. Nothing in this girl's life is new. Not her clothes. Not the threadbare duffel bag at her feet.

Only the scenery. That's always new, because they've moved five times in three years, each time into the home of her mother's latest boyfriend. Then—a few months later—they leave again.

This time, the countryside rolling past the car window is prettier than usual. So that's something. There are farmhouses and cornfields. Tawny cows graze beside a dark-red barn. In the distance, she catches occasional glimpses of Lake Champlain between the hilltops.

"The school is much better here," her mother is saying, the words squeezed around a cigarette dangling from her lips. "And the air is clean. You liked Vermont when you were little."

But our girl knows to make her own judgments. Her mother never tells the truth. And in spite of the scenery, she's already worried. They're heading for the home of her least favorite of her mom's ex-husbands.

Her mom has had five marriages. And five divorces. It's a staggering number for a woman who's only forty-six.

Skye is never getting married. She already knows better.

"Are you sure Rayanne won't be there?" she asks her mother. The last time they lived with Jimmy Gage, Skye had a stepsister. That was a dozen years ago, but it was the only time in her life she ever had a sibling.

"No, she won't." Her mom sniffs. "That fool ran off to California. But now Jimmy has a room just for you," her mother says, turning off the main highway.

This is no comfort, because Skye likes Rayanne a whole lot more than Jimmy, her mother's second husband. She was five when they last lived with him. It was nice to have a seven-year-old sister. Wonderful, even. But she'd been afraid of Jimmy. He had scary eyes, and smelled of liquor and chewing tobacco. When Skye had said something he hadn't liked, he'd been quick to backhand her. She'd learned to keep her distance.

Maybe he's mellowed with age.

They turn off onto a narrower street, and Skye knows the trailer park is nearby. You can always tell. Even pristine Vermont has these roads— the ones with tires in the drainage ditch. Nobody takes pride in this stretch of land. They roll past a bathtub rusting by the side of the road. Then a sign comes into view: PIN VIEW PARK.

Our girl wrinkles her nose at the missing letter. "Last time we came here, he lived in a house," she points out. Sixteen year olds always point out the painful truths. It's their job.

Her mother turns into the trailer park, ignoring this bit of criticism. "Skye, look at the numbers," she orders. "Which one is thirteen?"

Lucky number thirteen. "That one," she grunts. Naturally it's the most tired-looking trailer in a tired-looking place. The front porch rests on cinder blocks, and the windows need cleaning. "She's a looker."

"You watch your mouth, girlie. At least you have a roof over your head." Her mother pulls into what passes for a driveway and gets out of the car. After slamming the door, she takes a moment to straighten her blouse and finger-comb her hair.

Skye doesn't make a move. She waits in the car, knowing there's no rush. Sometimes her mother pulls up to homes where they aren't as welcome as her mother expects. She watches her mom knock on the flimsy door. After a moment, the door opens and she disappears inside.

It's not a bad sign. But our heroine gives it a few more minutes just to be safe. And when no shouting comes from the house, curiosity gets the better of her. She pulls her duffel out and steps up to the door. Her mother stands just inside, speaking to Jimmy. The man's face is just as hard as she remembers.

And, yup—those scary eyes. He's wearing a trooper's uniform. That's new.

"Sweetie, come in here," her mother calls with artificial cheer. "That will be your room. In there." She points down a narrow hallway as Skye enters the trailer.

First she has to pass Jimmy Gage. But he doesn't step aside. She can feel the slow slide of his gaze down her body. "Somebody got awful pretty," he says under his breath. "Sixteen going on twenty-six."

Our girl doesn't have any idea what to say to that. So she says nothing. She squeezes by, holding her breath, and it's only two paces past him until she can turn into the musty little bedroom. There's a Kanye West poster hanging halfway off the wall. This little room was obviously Rayanne's.

Skye is still sad that Raye isn't around. She's entertaining, and Skye's only almost-sibling. On the other hand, there is no way the two of them could share this closet of a room. The twin bed barely fits inside.

From the kitchen comes Jimmy's voice. "How long are you staying?"

Our girl freezes in the act of setting the duffel on the bed. Jimmy's question is not a good sign.

"I'm not sure," is her mother's coy answer. "Just until I have a little money saved up."

He grunts in agreement. "There's some things I need you to do for me."

"I'll bet there are, sugar."

Our heroine does not want to hear any more. Leaving her bag, she slips out of the room, passing the two adults where they stand in the tiny kitchen. "Housekeeping things," he clarifies.

She's through the front door before she can hear anymore.

Stepping outside is a good decision. The air is sweet and cool, with a piney scent. Unlike some of the uglier trailer parks she's seen, this one is small. The single and double-wides are arranged in a half-moon, backing up to an old-growth forest. The ground is dotted with the season's first orange leaves.

Skye walks behind trailer number thirteen. There she discovers that when you turn your back on all the tin cans that people called home, only nature is visible.

Not bad.

She steps between two towering pines and walks into the forest. Her eyes are drawn upwards, into the canopy, while she takes slow steps through the woods. How many years does it take a tree to grow so tall? Seventy five? A hundred? If she only looks up, there is no trailer park, no unwelcoming ex-step-father. Only the colorful canopy against a blue, late-summer sky.

"Watch your step."

Skye chokes on her shriek of surprise. Her chin snaps downward until she finds the source of the voice.

Then she's even more startled, because it belongs to the most beautiful boy she has ever seen. With thick black hair and dark eyes, he smirks at her from a ridiculously large lounge lawn chair. It's sized for two people, and sitting right smack in the middle of a clearing.

"What are you doing here?" she asks stupidly.

He regards her in silence for a moment, which might be creepy on some boys, but not on him. His gaze is nothing like Jimmy Gage's. It's more friendly than leering. "Probably the same thing you're doing here," he replies eventually. "Getting away from all that." He tips his head toward the trailer park.

"Oh," she says, in another display of brilliant wit.

"Oh." He smirks. "You got a name?"

She can't answer for a second, because she's distracted by the cleft in his chin. She would like to measure it with her thumb. "It's Skye," she finally remembers to say.

"Welcome to the trailer park, Skye. I'm Benito Rossi."

Our girl smiles inside, because Vermont just got a little bit brighter. But her face is impassive, because she's an old hand at keeping her own counsel. "Do you go to the high school? It starts tomorrow, right?"

He nods. "Senior. Thank God. You?"

"Sophomore."

"Ah. Got a schedule yet?"

She shakes her head. Skye's mother can't be bothered to register her ahead of time. By the time her mother gets around to driving her there tomorrow, and filling out the paperwork, Skye will have missed the first

4

two or three periods already. "Is there a bus?" she asks, because her mother isn't good with details.

Benito Rossi nods. "Stops outside the park at ten after seven." He moves his long jean-clad legs to the side and pats the generous space next to him on the broad seat. "This is my double-wide," he says with a smile. "Trailer-park joke."

She smiles.

"Have a seat."

Skye would love to sit there next to this handsome creature on the chair's cushion and lean back to see the tree tops. But she's the new girl and has to watch herself. Boys make assumptions. Ever since Skye turned fourteen and grew B-cup breasts, men have stared, and boys have tried to help themselves.

At sixteen, she knows she's attractive. Once in a while she finds it useful. She knows the sophomore boys will give her whatever information she needs at school tomorrow. They'll offer her a seat because she's nice to look at, saving her the embarrassment of eating alone.

But most of the time being desirable is a drag. The lingering eyes on her chest. The smirks, and the uninvited hands on her bottom.

This is why Skye avoids the giant chair and sits on a stump instead. There's a sort of fire pit, too—a circle of rocks and a dug-out place where blackened coals crumble. "Is this your party spot?" she asks.

"No." Benito shakes his gorgeous head. "That would ruin it. This is where I go to get away from people. I like people but there's too many in my trailer. I have three older brothers and a twin sister..."

Skye gasps. "That *is* crowded."

He smiles again, and it makes her stomach dip and swoop. "One of my brothers is away at basic training, and my sister is staying with a friend this year. So there's just Mom and me and Damien and Matteo. Still crowded. We're not small people. A guy needs his own living room." He raises both arms like a king showing off his palace. "But if you keep my secret, you can use it any time. Just don't hide the remote." He winks.

Skye smiles in spite of herself. "I won't tell a soul," she says.

He tucks his hands behind his head. "Now what else do you need to know about school?"

TWO

Skylar

THE RENTAL CAR is a brand new Jeep Grand Cherokee in cherry red, and I love it desperately.

I'd never owned a car of my own. At the rate I'm going, I never will. When you live in New York City, and you're just scraping by at the Worst Job in Journalism, the idea of paying five hundred bucks a month for parking is laughable. Forget the cost of the car itself.

Hence my joy at depressing the accelerator on forty-five-thousand dollars' worth of four-wheel-drive luxury. It's *awesome*.

So what if I have to stay in the right lane because there's a kayak strapped to the top? The impressive stereo is blasting my favorite tunes, and the leather seats feel cool beneath my bare knees. Bonus— the car is roomy, accommodating my very tall frame without difficulty.

It even has that new car *smell*.

I need this—a brief escape from New York, after the woeful week I've had. Pity I have to spend my getaway in Vermont. In spite of Vermont's reputation for beauty, I'm not a fan. I was born there. I lived there twice when I was young.

The last time broke my heart.

I would never have chosen Vermont for a weekend destination, but my crazy stepsister asked me to come. Also, she paid for the Jeep because she needs me to bring her the kayak on the roof. I can stay at her place. So it's a free trip out of town.

My phone rings. And all I have to do to talk to my aunt Jenny is to tap a button on the fancy car's display screen. "Hello! Greetings from the Wilbur Cross Parkway!"

"Greetings from the boardwalk in Palm Beach. So how's the trip so far?"

"I'm still in Connecticut, Jenny."

"I know. But since you hate Vermont I thought I'd get the question in early. How did you talk your boss into giving you this little vacation? I thought he was the Ebenezer Scrooge of local news?"

"Oh, he is. But I'm currently the laughingstock of *New York News and Sports*. And YouTube. And probably Twitter." I can't even look at social media right now, it will only give me anxiety. "The station is getting a bunch of mail about my blunder. They don't want me on air until it blows over in two weeks or so."

I say that breezily. But the truth is that I'm terrified it *won't* blow over. My producer—John McCracken—wouldn't even let me take my work laptop home with me today. And that really freaks me out. Are they going to fire me? Usually the man wants that computer stapled to my hands.

"Oh, honey." Aunt Jenny sighs. "It could happen to anyone."

"But why the helipad did it have to happen to *me?*" Let's face it, you need some serious misfortune to accidentally sketch a perfect outline of an erect penis on live TV.

There I was, "drawing"—via the miracle of technology—with my finger on a digital street map of Manhattan, tens of thousands of viewers watching me trace the outline of an Upper West Side traffic snarl. In confident purple pixels, I drew a ring around Columbus Circle, to show the origin of the trouble. Then I followed the stretch of Broadway heading northwest to Sixty-first Street.

Now, Broadway happens to run at a very *perky* angle there. I outlined it, well, *thickly*. Then, speaking calmly into Camera Six, I outlined Columbus Circle *again*, because I was trying to make a point about how badly traffic had slowed.

Who knew that the result would look like a penis and a set of balls in profile? I was just doing my job. And my mind is never in the

7

gutter, so it never occurred to me that I was accidentally drawing a very ambitious erection on the traffic map.

However, there are five million YouTube viewers with gutter minds. That's how many hits the YouTube video has gotten in the last seven days. Or so I'm told.

Some of those five million views must be repeats, though I've only watched the twenty-second clip of my own humiliation once. Okay, twice. And on the second pass, I realized that it wouldn't have looked so sexual if I hadn't gone on to include the outline of Central Park as it plunged down like a set of trim abs. Or, if I hadn't capped the, um, *head* of the traffic problem at Sixty-first Street with a mushroom-shaped arrow.

If only. If only. Picturing it makes me want to bang my head into this very expensive steering wheel.

"I know how this plays out," Jenny says. I can hear the cry of a seagull near her, because the Jeep's speakers are top notch.

"How does it?" I'm eager to know, because I should be at work right now, scrapping for the next story. Since I work for assholes, whenever I get a line on something good, they never let me do the reporting. All my scoops are handed up to more senior newsies. They only let me cover the results of the dullest borough meetings. And traffic and weather.

"You're out of the office for two weeks, right? They probably miss you already. You practically hold that place together, right? Your boss will be weeping into the phone by Monday."

In my heart of hearts, I'm hoping she's right. It was a real shock to hear my sweaty producer say: "You have seventy-two vacation days saved up. Take ten of them starting tomorrow."

It's not a good sign. Nobody ever gets days off at NYNS. And when they do, they take their computer and work from the road.

"I hope you're right," I confess. "And I hope they took my computer just so I couldn't get any lewd emails." That's my favorite theory. And it's not like I want to hear from my new fans, either. Some women could probably laugh off this whole episode, but I am not that girl. I don't make sexual jokes. Ever. The whole thing makes me want to crawl under a bed and stay there.

But I can't. In the first place, it's hard to hide under a bed when you're six feet tall. Secondly, I *need* my job at *New York News and Sports*. I need to convince Sweaty McCracken that I'm a serious journalist. After this short trip out of town, I plan to march back into his office and demand my on-camera job back. I'm terrified to do it, but I will.

"Anyway—deep breaths. And call me when you get there," Jenny says. "No—I retract that request. I want you to have a great time. Don't think of work. Don't think of me. Just see the sights and let Rayanne entertain you."

"The sights?" There are no sights in Vermont.

"Mountains. Strapping lumberjack men. Good cheese. Whatever it is that Vermont is good for."

If only I knew. When I lived there as a teen, there was barely enough food, let alone good cheese. And don't even get me started on the men.

But I don't express these doubts to Jenny, because she worries about me. "I'll call when I can," I tell her instead. "Talk soon!"

"Love you!" she says. "Bye!"

I hang up with a smile on my face. Jenny is my only real family member. She and my crazy almost-stepsister in Vermont are my whole world.

She hasn't told me *why* she needs the little boat on the roof of this Jeep. I haven't asked, because Raye is always hatching a get-rich-quick scheme. They always fail, but that doesn't stop her.

Once upon a time my loser of a mother was married to Raye's creep of a father. Rayanne is a fun person, which is sort of a miracle because her dad is a scary lunatic.

We've grown closer these last few years as Raye—now thirty-one —has been trying to buckle down and make something of her life. She spent her twenties hitchhiking around the West Coast, tending bar and partying. Then the get-rich-quick schemes started. She's already failed at gourmet coffee roasting, mural painting, and stand-up comedy, in quick succession.

I hear all these tales on our semi-annual visits when Rayanne swings through New York to visit her crazy web of friends. And I've worried about her over the years.

But then she found yoga. I thought it would last a week, like the rest of Raye's obsessions. But no. Yoga is her life now. She's got a twice-a-week teaching gig at a resort lodge, and she's dreaming of opening her own studio.

I love Raye, but it hadn't been easy for her to convince me to do this favor. "Please, Skye?" she'd begged yesterday. "I'll rent the car for you. The kayak company will put the boat on top. You don't have to do a thing. I'll even pay for the gas."

That had all sounded like a lot of effort. "Why don't you just buy the boat in Vermont?"

She was quiet a moment, which is very unlike Raye. "I don't want anyone to know I've bought it. I'll explain when you get here."

At that point I was still unconvinced. After all, she was asking me to drive to the epicenter of my heartbreak. All the worst things that had happened to the teenage me had happened in the same corner of Vermont where Raye now lives. It isn't something I like to think about, let alone discuss.

So I'd been opening my mouth to refuse, when Raye interrupted me with the only argument that could have won me over. "There's a story in it for you. A good one. A career-making scoop."

"What?" I'd whispered. Raye isn't the sort of stepsister who pays much attention to my career. When we have our monthly chats, she usually asks me whether I've found any hot clubs she should check out next time she comes to the City with her friends.

(My answer was always the same: Aspiring journalists do not go to clubs. They go to work. They go to the over-priced gym, and they go home.)

"A *story*, Raffie! A good one." (That's her nickname for me. Like *giraffe*. I get a lot of tall-girl jokes.) "There's something happening at the border up here that you need to hear about."

"You mean...something illegal?" All the best scoops are about illegal activity. *Breaking News: Major scandal uncovered by our own Emily Skye! Film at eleven.*

A girl can dream.

"I'll tell you all about it when you get here," Raye had repeated. "I wouldn't tease you about this."

Fresh on the heels of my on-screen dick pic, I need a story. Badly. So here I am driving a kayak to Vermont.

"This better not be a disaster," I'd warned. "There are people in Vermont that I don't want to see." Like any of the Rossi family. And Jimmy Gage. And every single person I went to high school with.

The list is long.

"It'll be fine, Skye! I promise. You won't regret it. I'll take good care of you."

She probably shouldn't have added that last bit. Raye has never once taken good care of me. She's hapless, clueless, and luckless, and doesn't seem to mind that much.

I love her eternal optimism. She and I have been pasted with a whole lot of bull-shishkebab by our mothers and her dad. But unlike me, Raye is still a happy, childlike human who believes that good news is always right around the corner.

In contrast, I'm the doom-and-gloom sibling. Whatever I imagine can go wrong usually does, plus a whole lot of other things that I didn't predict. (Like the TV penis. Who could have called that one?)

If my short trip to Vermont actually results in a useful scoop, I'll be stunned. My plan, though, is to deliver the kayak to Raye, spend two or three days with her for the first time in about a year, and then get the heck out of Colebury.

At least I don't have to drive past our old trailer park on this jaunt. Raye now lives in a rental house in the center of Colebury. I assume I'll meet her there.

But no. When I stop in Massachusetts for a takeout salad, I find a text from an unfamiliar 802 phone number. *Raffie, it's me! Meet me at the Orange County Welcome Center off of 89*, she's written. *There's something I need to show you.*

My first reaction is a flash of annoyance. It's just like Raye to change plans at the last minute. But I've only agreed to a forty-eight-hour dose of Rayanne and her flighty ways. And you have to pick your battles. *Fine*, I text instead. *Reprogramming the fancy GPS. It says I'll get there at 8:15.*

Cool, she replies immediately. *I love you!*

You'd better! I don't drive to Vermont for just anybody.

She replies with the prayer-hands emoji, and then a unicorn. Pure Rayanne.

See? I can handle this. I can drive to Vermont like the adult that I am, to help out family. It's just another place in the world. I can go for the weekend and see Raye and experience a little closure.

Vermont didn't break me. It tried, but it didn't.

I'm still feeling pretty cocky when there are a hundred miles to go. But by the time the GPS counts down to thirty miles, I start to feel twitchy and sad. And it's all because of a boy who doesn't even live in Vermont anymore.

Benito Rossi.

Twelve years ago, I'd wanted him so badly that I would have done anything to have him, including most of the things my evil ex-stepfather accused me of doing whenever he got drunk. But Benito had friend zoned me for almost the entire time we'd known each other.

Then, for a few glorious days before I'd left Vermont for good, it looked as if my romantic dreams might finally come true. But no. At the last second, he ditched me in the most painful way possible.

My heart aches just thinking about it, even after all this time. It doesn't matter that I won't run into him. I'm still holding a grudge against him and the whole state where I fell for him.

When there are only a few miles between me and the highway exit, I ease up on the gas pedal. Now that I'm close, I can hear the echo of my teenage naiveté inside my head. It had been such a hard year. I'd been sixteen and nearly friendless. And every time I walked into school wearing thrift-store shoes, I felt shame.

But here's a comforting thought—if I *do* run into someone from high school, they might not recognize me. It's been years since I wore clothes from a secondhand store. For this trip I've chosen an outfit that I'll call, She's Headed To The Woods In Style. My silky purple blouse hugs my curves. Over that, I'm wearing a filmy cashmere cardigan. And my short skirt ends several inches over the tops of my cozy tall socks and kickass leather knee boots.

I look expensive. I look devastating. *Take that, Vermont.*

One perk of working in television is the hair and makeup department. The makeup girls are always good for freebies and demonstrations. And Taz, the hair guy, gives me a trim every three weeks for free, just because I'm not a snooty bitch. So tonight I'm rocking a long, swingy cut and expensive cosmetics that I didn't pay for.

Life could really be worse, I remind myself.

The disembodied GPS voice orders me to take the next exit. And I actually do it, because I really need to pee. The Welcome Center is just off the highway. The parking lot is nearly empty.

"You have arrived at your destination," the GPS voice says.

"That is not *even* true," I argue aloud, shutting off the Jeep in order to have the last word.

I hop out, grab my purse, and run inside the well lit building. I don't see Raye anywhere. I hope she's not late. My boots echo on the tile floor as I dash past a vending machine selling T-shirts that say "802"—Vermont's only area code—on them.

Now there's a piece of clothing I'll never wear.

I take care of business in one of the bathroom stalls, and, after washing my hands, I touch up my lipstick at the mirror. "Still don't like you, Vermont," I whisper into the stillness.

There is no sign of Raye when I come out of the bathroom. So I buy myself a package of pretzels and read posters about Vermont's agricultural history while I wait.

And wait.

Where in the helipad is she?

Just when I'm getting really steamed, my phone buzzes from yet another 802 number. *Come outside,* it says. *I'm really sorry I had to cancel on our weekend. Love you.*

A chill snakes down my spine. She wouldn't!

I run out as fast as my designer boots will take me. Raye isn't visible in the pool of lamplight outside the doors. And I don't see anyone in the parking lot.

Also missing? The red Jeep. My ride! It's *gone.* And in its place is, unbelievably, my weekend bag. It's sitting there on the pavement, with a piece of paper on it, weighted down by an unfamiliar object.

As I step close, I see the object is an old, battered phone with a scratched screen.

While my heart ricochets, I grab the phone and the paper, which turns out to be a note.

Skye—I'm so sorry to strand you like this. I couldn't think
of another way. I need help, but I can't have you mixed
up in this. The phone is for you to hold. It's a burner

phone—I pre-paid cash for it, and it can't be traced to me. Use your own phone to get an Uber into Colebury. Then go to the Gin Mill and ask the bartender to fetch Benito Rossi.

"What?" I inhale sharply. "No *way.*"

Yes, way. I know that seeing Benito wasn't in your plans this weekend. But did I tell you he's back in Vermont these days. No? Whoops! My bad.

Anyway, he's back. And he and I are going to have to have a chat later. But right now I need you to tell him something for me. Tell him this: The thing he's waiting for is happening sooner than he thinks. And I'm going to text you guys some evidence as soon as I have it. Skye—let him take care of you for a couple of days, okay? I'll use this phone to share information with you and Benito when I need to.

DO NOT text me from your real phone. They might be watching.

DO NOT text me at all, actually. Wait for me to reach out to you.

The key to my house is under the Buddha statue on the porch. I don't know if I'd stay there, though. People might come looking for me.

And don't panic. I'll be fine. I've got this.

I really do love you, but I know you're probably pissed at me right now.

—Raye

P.S. Benito has only gotten hotter in the last twelve years. Enjoy the view.

I let out a shriek of pure horror. "You scheming little witch!"

I read the note three times, growing more enraged each time.

Rayanne and her drama. I should have known. I love her, but she's selfish and a little cray-cray.

How dare she send me to find Benito! And what blabber is this note, anyway? *Evidence?* She's a yoga teacher. And Benito is...

Okay, I have no idea what Benito is. The last time I stalked him on social media, I discovered he was in Afghanistan, working for a defense contractor. There was a picture of him in a combat uniform in the desert. That might have been five or six years ago, though.

When I fled Vermont at seventeen, I used to stalk him online. He wasn't very interested in social media, so it wasn't very fruitful. But that was back when I used to spot him in crowds. Or I thought I did. My subconscious was still looking for the boy who broke my heart.

It wasn't until I saw that single photo of him thousands of miles away that I was able to stop looking for him. And I haven't thought about him much since. Except in my dreams, and they don't count.

Flipping Rayanne. She's off somewhere enjoying this. I don't know whether to punch her or worry for her safety. The cloak and dagger thing sounds serious. Except Rayanne is never serious.

The only thing I know for sure is that it's a bad idea to stand around all night at a rest stop. My jacket was in the backseat, and I'm already cold. The car keys were in that jacket—and the Jeep had one of those nifty fob-sensor ignitions—so she wouldn't have had to hotwire the thing.

I hate my life.

Grudgingly, I do as Rayanne suggested—I open the Uber app on my phone. When I left Vermont twelve years ago, there had been no such thing as Uber, and I'm a little startled that it exists here in the woods. To my complete surprise, I find that an available driver is only 0.1 miles away. The driver has a five-star rating so I quickly tap the screen.

Immediately, a set of headlights flares in a dark corner of the parking lot. I see the car ease off its brakes and drive toward me.

Okay, that's a little creepy. I peek at the phone screen to verify the driver's name and car model. *Damien R. Driving a black Toyota RAV4.*

Damien R? There's no way...

The black Toyota RAV4 stops in front of me. I open the back door and squint at the driver. "Damien R?" I say softly.

Benito Rossi's brother turns his head to study me. "You look familiar," he says. "Have we met?"

A beat goes by while I swallow my shock. "Nope," I lie. "I need to go to the Gin Mill."

He frowns. "That's so odd. Rayanne bet me ten bucks that my next ride would go to the Gin Mill."

"She cheated!" I yelp as I climb in and shut the door. "Don't pay up."

"Figures." He chuckles as he pulls away from the curb.

"Did you bring Rayanne here just now?"

"Yep. Ten minutes ago, maybe." He accelerates onto the highway.

"Do you know where she went, after?"

"Nope. I didn't ask."

"Didn't you think the Welcome Center was a weird request?" I squeak.

He shrugs. "I've had stranger requests. And Rayanne is kind of a character. Tonight she tried to tell me my aura is too blue and that I should drink ginger tea to try to stabilize my chakras. But whatever. She also gave me a tip."

This highly accurate portrayal of my almost-stepsister only makes me grumpier. And I'm so nervous that I can hardly sit still in the back of the car. I don't *want* to see Benito Rossi. Maybe I don't have to. I could get a motel room somewhere and wait for Rayanne to text me. I need to figure out what the hell is going on with her.

"Excuse me," I ask Damien. "Are there any new hotels in Colebury?"

"That depends on your perspective," he says. "They were new in about 1980."

Oh. Bummer. At least they'll be cheap.

A few minutes later, Damien exits the highway and drives for two more minutes on the state road. Then he pulls into the parking lot of a beautiful old brick building.

"This is the place?"

"Yeah. There's only one Gin Mill."

"Is, um, Benito inside, do you think?" Saying his name aloud is even harder than I expected.

Damien turns his head, looking startled. Then he snaps his fingers.

"I knew I recognized you. Our next-door neighbor! You and Benny had a thing in high school."

"We didn't," I say icily. One kiss does not a *thing* make. Even if it was the world's best kiss. "Does he work at this bar?" I peer out at the old mill building, beautifully redone into a bar. Even the exterior is about ten times classier than anything I remembered from my time in Colebury.

"Not usually," Damien says cryptically. "Just go inside and ask the bartender to grab him."

That's exactly what Rayanne's note says to do. Maybe Benito is a regular here?

But I'm sick of asking questions, so I get out of the car, shoulder my weekend bag, and wave Damien off.

After he pulls away, I look up at the building. It's tall, although I count only three floors. Each one would have high ceilings. There's a cute neon sign lighting up THE GIN MILL in vintage letters. I can hear music coming from inside, and the sound of laughing Friday-night partygoers.

There is nothing about this place that feels familiar. When I last came through Colebury, I'm pretty sure this building was vacant and sad. Now it looks fantastic and lively. And I feel a moment of unexpected rage. How *dare* Colebury have a hip new bar, and sweet-smelling nighttime air? How dare Benito Rossi return to Vermont and enjoy this town that tortured me?

And how dare Rayanne make me come back here and witness this!

I'm going to kill her just as soon as I make sure she's okay.

THREE

September, Twelve Years Ago

OUR GIRL IS SETTLING in at Colebury High School, if by "settling in" you mean learning all the ways there are to be snubbed by your peers.

Her clothes are all wrong, because her mother's last boyfriend lived in Georgia, where the weather was always warm. She doesn't have enough money to buy warm clothes at a decent store, so she's stuck with whatever Rayanne left behind in the tiny bedroom she's inherited.

And that's not much.

Skye's bigger problem is transportation. The high school is nowhere near the trailer park. The school bus stops at the entrance to Pine View Park at eleven minutes past seven o'clock. The trailer park is the end of the line, both figuratively and literally—and the bus ride is an hour long.

The first morning she's waiting when the surly driver pulls up. Six kids get on, but none of them is the devastatingly handsome Benito.

On the second morning, Skye is twenty yards away, waving and yelling "hold up!" as the last kid gets on.

The driver does not, in fact, hold up. As she pants toward the bus, the yellow doors are yanked shut, and the bus accelerates away from her.

Skye stands there, fuming, staring down the road. It's twelve miles to school. She has no friends to call, and no phone either. Her mother is at work already—putting in a six-til-noon shift at the all-night diner on the outskirts of Colebury. It's a job that Jimmy secured for her, demonstrating a surprisingly keen understanding of her mom. (The woman is famous for pulling the old "I can't find work" excuse.) It's quite possible that keeping her mother employed is Jimmy's way of showing the two of them the door as soon as possible.

But our girl can't worry about that right now, because she is stuck at the side of the road, a long way from school. Asking Jimmy for a ride isn't on the table, either. He has a creepy, lingering way of looking at her that she does not enjoy.

Hopelessness is setting in when the rumble of a motorcycle approaches. She moves off the roadway just as a shiny Triumph rolls into view, its driver hugging the bike with long, jean-clad knees.

The bike stops beside her, and the driver lifts his helmet off.

Benito. Even with his hair askew, he is too handsome for words. All of a sudden, our girl gets the flutters.

"Miss the bus?" he asks. He flashes her a quick smile.

"Yeah," she says, tongue-tied.

He shrugs off his backpack. From inside it, he pulls another helmet. "Hop on. You'll have to wear my backpack, though."

"Where'd you get this bike?" She's never ridden on a motorcycle before and has no idea what to do.

"It's my brother's, and he's in the navy. Quickly, okay? I need to get to school early. My sister is havin' some kind of crisis she expects me to solve before the first bell."

Skye manages to lift the helmet over her head, but she fumbles with the chin clasp.

"C'mere." Benito beckons, and then his big hands fix the strap. "Here." He takes the pocketbook out of her hands, zipping it into his backpack. He hands over the pack, which she shrugs on. "Climb up. Let's go."

She doesn't know how to get on the bike, so she throws a knee over the top and it works well enough. (Sometimes being as tall as a tree is useful. Sometimes.)

He reaches back and grabs one of her hands, pulling it against his stomach. "Hold on, Skye. Ready?"

She isn't ready at all. She's trying to get used to the sensation of being pancaked against Benito's tight body, with one hand on his six-pack. The engine revs, and self-preservation demands that she wrap her other arm around his body, too.

The bike shoots forward, and everything is breeze and sensation. She is flying, and she is holding tight to the most beautiful boy in the world.

Falling for him is as inevitable as the trees dropping golden leaves onto the roadway as they pass by.

They arrive at school fifteen breathless minutes later. When Skye climbs off the bike, a half-dozen girls stare in disbelief. She collects her bag, hands the helmet to Benito, and thanks him.

"Don't mention it," he says.

But everyone else does. Skye hears her name whispered throughout the hallways all week. And the next, too, because Skye misses the bus several days later. It isn't a ploy. Just more of her bad luck.

Once again he bails her out, and once again the senior girls go a little insane at the sight of their favorite bad-boy ferrying the quiet new sophomore girl around.

They hate Skye on sight.

Skye is used to being friendless at school. One whole school year is the longest she's ever spent in one place. That's too short a stay for the amount of ass-kissing and strategic maneuvering she'd need to do in order to climb the social ranks.

Screw that. It's easier to be alone. She doesn't have the money for the right clothes, and she doesn't have the energy for the abuse she'd have to take.

Unfortunately, she's going to take more than her share of abuse, but not at school.

The first night her mother works the late shift at the diner, Skye eats her microwaved dinner in front of Jimmy Gage's TV. It's a rare moment of solitude in the crowded trailer. But it doesn't last. She hears the door of Jimmy's car slam. As a patrolman, his hours are all over the map. Skye can never predict when he'll turn up.

She chews faster, considering an escape to her little room. But he bursts through the door a minute later. He smells like whiskey and cigarettes. He's probably been drinking at the bar with his pals.

"Look who it is. Little Miss Priss," he whispers.

Skye feels herself go cold everywhere. She's lived here two weeks, and every day this man leers at her. She'll only shower right after he's left the trailer—that way she knows he's not likely to come home again soon.

And she always keeps the flimsy door to her room shut. There's a lock, but it's flimsy, too...

A second later he lands on the other side of the sofa from her. "Whatcha watching?"

It's a cooking show. Skye is aware of the irony of watching gourmet cooking while eating a frozen dinner, but she doesn't feel like talking about it. Not with him.

"I asked you a question," he snarls.

"Just watching whatever's on," she mumbles. Having lost her appetite, she sets her plate on the end table. Then she hands him the remote. "Here. You pick." Skye already knows how to placate her mother's men. She's an old hand at living in homes where she's not entirely welcome.

He doesn't take the remote or even glance at it. "What do you get up to when I'm not here?"

"Um..." Skye doesn't like this line of questioning. "Not much?"

"You got a boyfriend?"

"No," she says quickly.

"Liar." He rolls his eyes drunkenly. "You're not your mother's daughter if you don't have a boyfriend in every town."

Skye's pulse doubles. She eyes the hallway to her room, but Jimmy Gage is in the way. There's only a few feet between the TV and the sofa. If she tries to run past, he could just reach up and grab her. She'll need to be more subtle about making her escape.

He doesn't shut up. "You let your boyfriend kiss you?"

"There is no boyfriend," she mumbles, unsure whether to engage at all. You can't reason with a drunk, angry man.

"You let him touch your pussy?"

The food she's eaten turns over in her stomach. "I'd better rinse this plate," she says carefully. Then she picks up the plate and rises.

He lets her take four steps before he grabs her wrist. "Such a pretty girl. Let me look at you."

She wrenches out of his grasp. "Don't touch me," she says clearly. Her heart is trying to beat its way out of her chest, but she walks calmly to the little kitchen area and puts her dish in the sink. He's not following her. Yet. But she can't risk getting trapped in this space, too, so she doesn't take the time to wash the dish.

As she heads down the hall toward her bedroom, she hears his foot-falls. She slips into the room, quickly shuts the door, and pushes the button on the knob to lock it. But there's no way the lock will hold if he wants to follow her in here.

She should have walked out the front door.

"Hey," he says. "I'm talking to you. Get back out here." He smacks his hand against the cheap, hollow door, and Skye jumps. Then he does it again. The door vibrates.

The lock will pop open if he does that a few more times. He probably knows that.

Skye turns toward the room's only window. The day was warm, so the window is partially open. She grabs the little metal clips that hold the screen in place and removes it quickly.

One thing about a trailer—it's not a big jump down to the ground. She's outside and moving toward the tree line before she hears his voice again. It's loud. "Hey little slut…"

Skye runs into the woods. She's not thinking about a destination, only that she needs to leave his sight. For the second time she stumbles into Benito's "living room," this time with wild eyes.

Benito looks up when she bursts into the clearing. Again he's sitting on the giant chair, but this time with a ukulele in his lap. Wordlessly, he pats the chair beside him.

And this time Skye doesn't hesitate. She sits down on the webbing beside him, hugging her knees to her chest, staring back toward the trailer and wondering if Jimmy will follow. She has no idea what she'll do if he chases her out here.

Benito doesn't say anything, and she appreciates the silence. The sun has already set, and the shadows are lengthening. The sky deepens. Skye's breathing eventually slows.

"Is he drunk?" Benito finally asks.

"Yep."

He slaps at a mosquito. Fall is coming, but it's still warm enough that bugs are a problem. Benito reaches down under the chair and pulls out a can of Deep Woods Off. "Can I offer you a sample of this fine cologne?"

And Skye smiles for the first time all week.

FOUR

Benito

I'M KNEELING on the rug, poking the logs in my fireplace. It's a kickass old fireplace that's set into the brick wall in my living room. I love this building. I love this room. But tonight I can't relax. I'm building a fire just to have something to do with my hands.

Usually I enjoy my nights off. But this one is bad timing. I'm *this* close to making a couple of big arrests. And I don't think I'll be able to get my mind off the case until these assholes are behind bars.

So tonight I don't quite know what to do with myself. Mostly I've been pacing the rug, waiting for the phone to ring. But it hasn't. I should call a fuck-buddy of mine and make plans. Or I should go downstairs to the bar for a beer. But even beer and sex aren't interesting right now.

I might as well have given the patrolman the night off and done the stakeout myself.

Leaving the fire alone, I do a loop around my generous living room, while my mind does another loop around the suspects. There's Jimmy Gage, who's moving drugs through Vermont and into the rest of New England. And his felon sidekick. I expect them to make another big buy next week.

And then there's Gage's daughter. The cop who's tailing Rayanne for me tonight is as sharp as they come. I haven't quite figured her out yet. I know she's is involved, even if I haven't worked out all the details. Tonight she's meeting somebody named Raffie.

Who is Raffie? That's what I need to learn.

I'm shit at taking nights off, obviously. Pacing my rug and thinking about the case. This is what I call relaxation.

Eventually my phone lights up with a text from Officer Nelligan. *Bad news. She gave me the slip.*

My reply is instant. *What? Where?*

Shit.

Nelligan: I've been watching her boyfriend's car outside the burrito place. But he came out alone and drove away.

Rossi: Did you go inside?

Nelligan: Of course. Can't find her anywhere. There's a back door to the alley, though.

Jesus. *Walk the area.*

Nelligan: Doing that now.

I let out an actual moan. On the one hand, I have the satisfaction of knowing that my gut instinct was right—Rayanne's mysterious weekend visitor is important. So important that Rayanne pulled off some kind of disappearing act.

On the other hand, I'm totally screwed. There's a very real possibility that Gage's organization is smuggling in a new packet of pure fentanyl from Canada earlier than I thought.

So much for my night off. I check the fire one more time and replace the fire screen. Then I grab my jacket and shove my feet into my boots. Rayanne is probably miles away from the burrito place by now. But I can't just sit here and do nothing.

My phone buzzes with another text just as I holster my gun. For a second there I get really excited that Nelligan has reestablished contact.

But no. It's a text from my brother. *Get down here*, it says. And by "down here" I can only assume he means his bar, which is directly below my apartment.

Can't. On my way out.

His response is a photograph. In the thumbnail-sized pic all I see is a woman standing by the bar down at the Gin Mill.

But then I tap on the photo, get a more detailed glimpse, and my pulse ricochets. "No fucking way," I whisper.

Years have passed since I've seen this face. But the same haunting light blue eyes look directly into the camera of my brother's phone. The same sleek blond hair cascades down her shoulders.

We're both twelve years older than we were last time we saw each other. But the only thing that really strikes me as different about Skylar is the tension in her mouth.

Jesus Christ. Skylar Copeland is downstairs in my brother's bar. And she's pissed off about something.

For a split second, my heart soars. *Thank you, Jesus.* I've gone twelve years without knowing where she was, or whether she's okay. On any given day of the last decade I would have given anything for the chance to hold her. Or, hell, just sit in the woods and talk with her.

Now she's here?

Just as I'm starting to process this, reality sets in.

Skylar Copeland is loosely connected to Rayanne Gage. And Rayanne is under police suspicion for assisting her piece-of-shit father. The whole case will come to a boil in the next five days.

This is when Skye turns up? Jesus Christ, *why? Any week but this one, lord.*

I can't believe I have to go down there and look into those sweet eyes—the same ones that always turned me into a goner—and play it cool and then quiz her about her stepsister.

There are nights when I hate my job.

Grabbing my jacket, I take a deep breath. *Stay loose, Rossi.* This girl broke me in two, and she'll probably do it again. But I'm going to have Gage's head on a plate before the month is out.

If my heart gets shredded again in the process, that's just my cross to bear.

FIVE

Skylar

"DON'T I KNOW YOU?" the bartender asks me when I approach the bar.

And I'm obviously wound up too tightly, because I snap at him, "No. Is that a problem?" I'm not a rude person, generally. It's just that I'm freaking out. I can't quite believe that the only boy—now a man—I've ever loved is nearby.

I'm so not ready.

"You look really familiar," he presses, peering at me from across the gleaming bar.

"I promise you we haven't met." But maybe he watches a lot of YouTube. If he asks me to draw him a penis on a cocktail napkin, I'm out of here.

"A good bartender never forgets a face," he insists.

"That's nice." It comes out as a bark. "Can you help me locate Benito Rossi?"

"Ohhhhhh, *shit!*" His eyes light up brighter than the neon sign outdoors. That's when he begins to smirk. "I *do* recognize you. From Benito's yearbook."

Whatever. "Is he here?"

"Probably. We'll know soon enough." He's slipped his phone out of his pocket and taken a picture of me.

"What's that for?"

"I'm summoning Benito for you. This will work like a charm." He taps his phone and then puts it away again. "Okay. Give it sixty seconds or so. What can I pour you?"

"Um." Of course he wants me to order a drink. I stare up at his menu board, my eyes unseeing. "What's good?" Like I even care. I'm too hung up on the bigger questions. Will Benito look the same? Will he acknowledge the awful thing he did all those years ago? Or will he play it down and pretend that it's good to see me again?

I don't even know what I want him to say. Unless he falls to his knees to beg forgiveness, there's no way this can go smoothly. Maybe he won't show his face at all.

In fact, I should be relieved if he doesn't turn up. So why does that idea make me almost as crazy as the thought of seeing him?

"...a pilsner with a fruity, hoppy finish," the bartender is saying. "Or the Shipley Cider. We're pouring their Early Season Amber tonight."

"Wait," I say as my brain trips over the name Shipley. "Like the Shipleys who grow all those apples?"

Mr. Hot-but-Smirky nods. "Those are the same ones."

I feel a tingle along my spine. Here I'd thought I could pop in and out of Vermont without running into my past. But I knew the Shipleys. When I'd gone to Colebury high, Griffin Shipley had been a senior and his sister May had been a freshman. I once visited their dreamy orchard. "Okay. I'll try the cider, please."

I can even hear Ruth Shipley's voice in my head. *Wool socks are magic.* I look down at the socks I'm wearing now. They're cashmere. I haven't thought about Mrs. Shipley in a long, long time. But I still carry her kind voice in my heart.

Revisiting your past is weird. Really weird. There are ghosts all around me.

A moment later a wine glass appears before me, with a gorgeous amber liquid inside. I draw a ten out of my clutch and put it on the bar. Then I glance toward the door again. Still no sign of Benito.

While the bartender makes change, I scan the crowd, trying to reconcile this scene with my life in Colebury. This place is full of happy, prosperous people enjoying craft brews and good company. Except for the flannel shirts and technical fabrics, I could almost be in

New York—but on a weeknight, when the crowds aren't crushing. This bar is really pretty cool.

No, it isn't, I remind myself. *Vermont is a horrible place.* I take a sip of my cider, and then notice how good it is—earthy and interesting, sweet and bitter and musky.

It's really too bad that I hate Vermont because this cider is flipping amazing.

These are my scattered thoughts as a second man appears behind the bar in my peripheral vision. He must have come through a back door somehow. I feel tingles on my scalp, because he's watching me.

Slowly, I turn to face him. And *holy shishkebab.* Six-foot-three inches of my high school heartbreak is staring intently at me.

All my blood stops circulating. There stands the man who basically ripped the beating organ right out of my chest and stomped it with a motorcycle boot. I need to look away, but I almost can't. My heart is pounding wildly inside my chest, and I feel the onset of a fight-or-flight response coming on.

Flight is sounding like a good option.

Yet, because I'm a big idiot, I keep on staring. And he looks *good.* When did his shoulders get so wide? His eyes are just as beautiful as they always were, so dark and brooding.

From the nose down, he's not the same, though. He isn't the clean-shaven high school senior who once kissed me. This version of Benito has a scruffy beard. And his hair is a little too long.

It does nothing to dim his attractiveness, though. On the contrary, the mountain-man look suits him.

This is information that I never needed, by the way. I could have gone my whole life without knowing that he grew up as hot or hotter than he was at eighteen.

Back then, my whole world orbited around this man. Even now I feel my world tilt subtly in his direction. He has his own gravitational pull. And he looks...devastated. For a split second I see hurt in his eyes when he looks at me. And then I blink and it's gone. His face is impassive.

But he's still staring at me.

Trying for casual, I lift the cider glass to my lips and take another sip. I study him.

"Skylar."

At the sound of his sexy rumble, my hand wobbles, and I actually spill a drop of cider on my wrist. *Smooth, Skye.*

He ducks under the bar, which puts him right beside me. I get a whiff of him, and it wrecks me all over again. Leather and pine needles. "Come over here and talk to me," he says in a soft voice that brings out goosebumps all over my body. Then he takes my wrist in one large hand and leads me across the room.

Everything is happening too fast. His hand is wide and warm, and my brain is all swimmy. If only I could go meditate for a half hour somewhere, to clear my head. But who am I kidding? A prepaid week at a yoga spa wouldn't be enough to restore my equilibrium right now.

Benito nudges me toward a booth, where I sit down hastily, tucking my duffel bag against the wall and setting my drink on the table. I'm breathing too quickly as Benito shrugs off his leather jacket and tosses it onto the opposing seat.

I have no choice but to look up. The first thing I see when I lift my chin is his black T-shirt. It hugs an impressive set of abs. I lift my gaze slowly, taking in a chest far more sculpted than even my fantasies and a muscular arm propped on the table.

Wow. He must have spent the last twelve years at the gym.

Then, when it can be avoided no longer, I look up into his face. And there it is—the cognac-colored gaze that had always regarded me softly. When we were friends, I looked into those big eyes a thousand times, and they never let me down.

Until the night when they did.

And it had been bad. At the moment when that beautiful man was supposed to turn up on my doorstep for the biggest night of my life, Benito hadn't shown. I'd sat on the porch in my fancy dress and I'd waited. Like an idiot.

I'd sat there for hours, unable to believe that Benito had abandoned me. And then finally I learned how deep his betrayal really was.

That night I left Vermont for good and never came back.

Now, twelve years later, Benito has spoken four or five words to me, and my stomach is lurching around, and my hands are sweaty.

This was a terrible idea. I *have* to get out of here, I decide. Abandoning my cider, I slip my bag onto my shoulder again and scoot toward freedom.

But no. Anticipating this maneuver, Benito Rossi folds his big frame into the booth beside me, blocking my exit with his muscled bulk. "What, no hug for your old friend?" he says.

As if. But now I'm trapped. The choices are A) stay put, or B) climb into his lap to make my escape. And the latter sounds far too appealing to be a good idea.

"Crumbs," I whisper.

"What's that Skyescraper?" he asks again, catching both of my hands in his. "Look, I'm surprised to see you, too. So why don't we start with an easy question. What the fuck are you doing here tonight?"

His broad hands give mine a gentle squeeze, and my heart skips a beat. *Stupid heart.* It takes me a second to remember that I hate that nickname. And now that flight is no longer an option, I go straight to fight. And that's easy, because suddenly I'm so hopping mad that I can't see straight.

"Don't *call* me that," I bite out. I *never* appreciated the fact that he'd given me a tall-girl nickname. Although, until the Night of a Thousand Disappointments, it was the only thing I *didn't* like about him.

Back then, I would have done anything to hear more of his deep voice in my ear. But now I just need to get away before he can bring any more of that ache back to the surface. I'd cried a river of tears for him, and I didn't want to turn the taps back on. So I tug my hands back from his. "There won't be a hug, and I don't want to chat. Just let me go."

"Nope," he says with a simple shake of his head. "First we're gonna have a talk."

First, I'm going to have an out-of-body experience. Because he's so achingly familiar, sitting right there beside me. When I was sixteen, I'd memorized the curve of his cheekbones, the masculine shape of his nose. I'd learned the precise form of his full mouth when he smiled.

And every time he touched me, I leaned in, not out.

"First I'd like to give you an overdue apology," he says in a voice that's way too calm. "I'm sorry I let you down on the last night of school twelve years ago. It's all my fault, and I've regretted it ever since. I'm sorry."

My jaw hinges open, because his apology is both unexpected and woefully inadequate. Does he know how much pain he caused?

Not that I think about it anymore.

Not usually.

"And now," he continues, "feel free to tell me why you disappeared for twelve years without a goodbye."

I can't do that, though. Because I refuse to let him know how deeply he wounded me. Which he should already know. He'd stood me up on the only magical night of my young life. Did I just slip his *mind*?

"Skye, I went half-crazy wondering what happened to you. So start talking."

My head nearly detonates. Because if he went half-crazy, it was probably just the guilt talking.

"No? Fine," he continues. "I get that you were pissed about missing the dance. But you didn't give me a chance to make it up to you."

"Wow." In the first place, I can't believe he'd characterize such a major betrayal as something that could have been easily fixed with flowers or another ride to school on the back of his bike. It wasn't only that I'd missed a party. He'd taken another girl instead of me.

Even now I feel a wave of humiliation. I can't go back to that moment. I don't want to think about this ever again.

In fact, I'm changing my plans. This setup of Rayanne's had a stink to it from the moment I'd read her weird little note. And just because she wants to send me on a wild goose chase tonight doesn't mean I have to participate.

New plan—I can go to Raye's place and find the key under the Buddha. I'll go there and regroup, and wait for Rayanne to contact me. If I decide that I need help, I can find Benito later.

"Excuse me," I say as firmly as I can. "I've heard you. You're sorry. But I did not drive two hundred and fifty miles to talk about grad prom." The name of that fateful dance rolls easily off my tongue, as if the whole episode had happened only ten minutes ago.

Ugh. I'm drowning here. He's too close. And his scent—a heady mixture of leather and the outdoor air—it's so familiar I want to cry. "It wasn't a big deal," I add, eyeing the edge of the booth. I'm just a couple of feet from freedom. "If you'll excuse me."

He frowns at me, pinning me with his chocolaty gaze. "It wasn't a big deal," he repeats slowly.

"Right." *Liar, liar, J. Crew skirt on fire.*

"If you didn't really care, then why did you take off like that? Not even a *note*, Skye. For twelve *years.*"

Hmm... He has me there. "I cared back then. But I don't anymore."

"I see," he says. And then we have a stare-down—his soulful eyes versus my looking-into-camera-number-four stare. And the crowded bar just falls away. In spite of my professional advantage, I am in serious risk of losing this contest and tipping headlong into that brown-eyed gaze. This is how he used to look at me—as if he could see all the things I hid from everyone else. And back then, I was okay with that.

No, Skye, I coax. *We're not doing this again.*

I break our stare-off. "Look, I gotta go. Could you let me through, please?"

"No can do," he says immediately. "Not until you tell me what you're doing here tonight."

"No can do," I echo, which brings out his husky chuckle.

The sound of his laughter is so familiar that it makes my hands shake. This is why I've avoided Vermont for so many years. Now I'll have the sound of Benito's laugh—and an updated image of his devastating face—in my head when I go back to New York on Monday.

Flipping Benito. I wish I'd never met him.

"Skye—are you here to meet your stepsister?"

My eyes fly to his. "Why? Have you seen her tonight?"

I brace myself for another devastating grin, but his face is serious now. "No, honey. Did you?"

The way *honey* sounds on his tongue makes it difficult for the rest of his words to penetrate. "Um, no? But if you move your surprisingly large, tank-like self, I could go outside and try to find her."

And wouldn't you know? That's when he flashes me the blinding smile, and no grade of armor is strong enough to withstand it. I feel my knees loosen as his broad, kissable mouth quirks, his chin cleft barely visible beneath the scruff of his proto-beard. "My 'surprisingly large, tank-like self'?"

Ack! "It's... You're...in my way," I stammer, giving his shoulder a shove. But it's like trying to move a wall. *Smooth, Skye.*

To my surprise, Benito slides his rocking bod out of the booth and stands, allowing me to slip past him. My heart gives one last lurch at the idea that I am actually about to walk away from him. "Thanks," I whisper, clearing the booth of my duffel bag, and heading for the door.

Don't look back, I order myself as I dodge bar patrons. The place is really filling up now. It's hard to make a sweeping escape when there are happy beer drinkers in your way. "Hey!" a man says, stopping me. "It's you."

I blink up at him for a second. But it's nobody from high school that I recognize. "Hi?"

"Nice penis," he says. "Top notch."

"Thank you," I say stiffly, because it's quicker than punching him. Then I dodge to the side and keep going. The door is in my sights. *Don't look back,* I remind myself again. A few more steps and I'll be gone, with nothing but a racing pulse and a bunch of regrets to remind me of Benito. *Don't look back.*

But I am *weak.*

Slowing my pace, I look over my shoulder to capture one final memory of Benito Rossi. It doesn't work. Something warm and hard collides with my back. And the scent of pine overtakes me even as I begin to pitch forward.

A strong arm curls around my waist, keeping me upright. "Careful, Skye," his voice rumbles in my ear. The arm supporting me is surprisingly strong. I hold my breath for a split second. But then Benito releases me. He steps around me, opens the door and holds it open.

Seriously? He can't even allow me a clean getaway?

What. A. Jerk.

I step outside. The cool evening air is a blessing, because I need my wits about me. I have to find Rayanne's place and see if I can make contact with her. With a deep, cleansing breath, I step across the parking lot.

Footsteps fall in behind me.

I walk faster.

So does he. Benito is following me, and I'm not going to take it lightly. "This is *bullshizzle!*" I say, whirling around.

"What was that, honey?" Benito asks. He crosses those muscular arms in front of his chest and frowns at me.

"I'm going to *kill* Rayanne. She's going *straight* to helipad. And you're next."

Benito's forehead crinkles. "You're not making a lot of sense, Skye. What's with the gibberish?"

"You can't curse on TV!" I squeak. I'm starting to panic. My stepsister has *left me here*, in my least favorite town on earth, with nothing but a spooky note and a random phone. She might be in trouble, but she might be pulling my chain. "You can't swear on TV. So I *never* swear. Not even when my nut of a sister ditches me in *Colebury flipping Vermont* with nothing but a phone, a change of clothes and forty dollars."

I'm so over this.

Benito's voice is soft and low, the way you'd speak to a crazy person. "And you think you might be on TV?" He steps up to me and puts a hand on my shoulder, the way you might do with a crazy person.

"Well, sure! Every day," I babble, because I'm getting a contact high off Benito's nearness. "Except this week, because I accidentally drew a penis."

"Come again?"

And now I've gotten too far off topic. I wiggle out of Benito's grasp. "Let me go, so I can hunt down Rayanne and kill her." My sister's place is only a half mile up this road. I can walk it.

"Not so fast," Benito says. All traces of humor are gone from his face. "Does Rayanne call you *Raffie* by any chance?"

"Yes?" That tingle is back along my spine. "Why would you ask me that? And how would you know?"

His lips press into a thin line before he asks me another question. "What does Raffie stand for?"

I roll my eyes like a teenager. "God, Benito! It stands for *giraffe*, okay? It's another tall-girl joke, because there aren't enough of those in my flipping life. Now *move*." I give his big chest a shove. And since the thirty-year-old edition of Benito is made from cinderblocks, he doesn't budge. But I dodge to the left and gain my freedom. Turning tail, I take off across the gravel parking lot and cross the street beyond.

SIX

October, Twelve Years Ago

AS SKYE'S year in Vermont wears on, avoiding Jimmy Gage becomes her new after-school hobby.

Luckily, it's football season and he's often too invested in the games to pay attention to her, and she's able to tiptoe into her little room, lock the door, and succeed at being forgotten. And some nights Skye is busy babysitting for the Carreras in trailer Number Two. She avoids Gage and earns ten bucks at the same time. It's perfect.

Other times? She's not so lucky.

Like tonight. Skye is distracted. She's leaning out her bedroom window, chatting with Mrs. Rossi. Benito's mom wears an apron, like a mom out of picture books.

"Is something the matter?" Skye asks, wondering why the woman is kneeling with a flashlight behind the trailer. "Did you lose something?"

"No, honey! I'm picking sage leaves. These and the chives are still good until winter," she tells Skye. "You should come over for dinner this weekend. Sunday, maybe? My boys should be home."

This is such a lovely idea that Skye is too busy thanking her for the invitation to hear Jimmy Gage come into the house. When she hears his chuckle, it's too late. He's already standing in her open bedroom doorway.

Skye bangs her neck against the window frame, trying to right herself quickly.

"Talking to your boyfriend?" he asks. He has a bottle of whiskey in his hand, and from the sound of things, he's already half in the bag.

She lives with a cop who drives drunk. This is why a sweet girl of sixteen is also one of the more cynical people on Earth. She notices things. And yet she is powerless to change them.

"No," she says slowly. "Mrs. Rossi is outside."

He snorts. "Nice try. Which one gets to fuck you? The one with the motorcycle? Or the one who drives the taxi?"

Skye fights off a shiver but says nothing. She's doing the math on how to get a drunk cop out of her doorway.

"You let 'em take turns? I bet you do. You're a dirty girl, ain't you?"

Dirty girl. No, she isn't. But there's no way to prove it. There will never be a way.

"Mom left you a meatball sandwich," she says. "I'm supposed to heat it up for you." Her mother doesn't cook, but sometimes she brings home food from the diner. Skye enjoyed her portion earlier, but suddenly it's congealing in her stomach.

"Well. Get on that, then." He chuckles.

She waits.

He slowly moves out of the way and goes into the living room.

With shaking hands, Skye microwaves the remaining meatballs and then arranges them in a hoagie bun. She wishes she could somehow slip him that drug that knocks you out for the night. But that's just a fantasy born from something she saw on TV once.

This little daydream distracts her, though, and that's an error. Gage comes up behind her, and Skye tenses. And when he puts his hand on her butt, she goes completely cold.

"You're a little whore, aren't you? Just like your mother." His chuckle scrapes her insides.

There is no air. He stinks of whiskey and humiliation. Her heart is galloping in her chest.

That bullying hand sinks a little lower, the thumb stroking the back pocket of her jeans. Her fingers whiten on the edges of the plate. "Here's your dinner," she finally says in a gasping voice. "Where do you want it?"

He chuckles as if she's just done something funny, and Skye feels her eyes start to burn. Holding her breath, she turns around quickly, wedging the plate between them and knocking his hand off her bottom. It's a risk, though. If he puts his hands on her again, they'll land on her front instead of her back...

After the longest three seconds of her life, Jimmy takes the plate. He hooks his whiskey bottle between two fingers and carries his meal toward the sofa.

Skye counts to ten as slowly as she can. When the TV sounds start up, she counts to ten again. Then she slips quietly into her bedroom and shuts the door. The lock is deployed, but she knows that it will be useless if he decides he's coming in.

It's cold tonight, and her jacket is out of reach—hanging on the back of the trailer's front door. So Skye scrounges through the tiny closet and puts on one of Rayanne's flannel shirts, then adds a sweater and a scarf, too. She doesn't wait for Jimmy's knock or his shouting. She's not going to feel that hand creep down her body again tonight.

Dirty girl, he called her. He's half right. She feels very dirty right now, thanks to him.

Armed against the cold, she opens the window all the way. Then she climbs out, dropping carefully onto the leaves and avoiding the stump below.

The stump was Benito's idea. He placed it there to help her climb back inside on nights when she needs to flee. She stands on it now and closes the window to make her escape route look less obvious.

Then Skye walks carefully into the darkness toward Benito's outdoor living room. She can barely see the chair when she arrives. It's covered with a tarp, and a rock in the center holds the cover in place. She removes the rock and the tarp and sits down.

Who knew that sitting in the cold woods alone at night would seem cozier than being at home? The air is crisp and still, and there are no bugs this time. Small mercies.

Not ten minutes later she hears footsteps and sees a flashlight bobbing in her direction. The approaching footsteps might have been terrifying, except she knows it's Benito. He's humming to himself, and she's familiar with the sound of his voice.

"Evening," he says mildly when he arrives a moment later. As if this were a perfectly normal place to be on a cold fall night.

"Evening." She hopes he won't ask why she's here, because she can't say it out loud. It's too icky. She feels gross, just thinking about Jimmy and his hand on her in the kitchen.

But Benito doesn't ask. He sets his backpack down beside her but doesn't sit. Instead, he wanders around the edges of the clearing, picking up little sticks and snapping them. Then he takes a few bigger logs from a collapsed stack at the base of a pine tree.

He arranges his finds carefully in the center of the fire pit. From his backpack he removes a section of newspaper. He balls this up and shoves it under his wooden structure. Lastly, he pulls a book of matches from his jacket pocket, lights one, and sets the whole thing aflame.

He kneels there a while, watching his fire catch, poking at it. The air fills with the scent of wood smoke, and the orange glow from the flames illuminates the clearing.

Skye can't take her eyes off Benito. The warm light makes his eyes shine. He's the most beautiful boy she's ever seen. But she'll never tell him so. She wouldn't even have the words.

Eventually, he's satisfied with his work. He adds one more log to the fire and then comes to sit next to her on the doublewide chair. He kicks his feet up and leans back, hands behind his head, eyes to the sky. "Marshmallows," he says quietly. "I'll try to remember to get some."

"Mmm," she agrees. Skye feels so much safer sitting next to this boy in the woods than she feels in her so-called home. He's right there beside her in the dark, but he doesn't touch her.

Mostly she's grateful for that. But she has the unreasonable urge to rest her face against his sweatshirt right over his heart. She wants to know what would happen if she tried it. Good things, maybe. He could put an arm around her, and they could sit just like that together and listen to the fire crackle.

But the risk is too great. Things are pretty nice as they are, and Skye knows not to rock the boat.

"My sister Zara lives with another senior girl," Benito says suddenly. "Jill Sullivan."

"I remember." Benito has told her this already. They talk all the time now. "Because there's more room for her at Jill's."

"That's not really why she lives across town," Benito says quietly. "Jimmy Gage is why."

"Oh."

Oh. Her heart dives again.

"He started harassing Zara last year. Gage would always try to get Zara alone. That's not an easy feat when there are so many of us. But he was relentless, so my brother Damien went to the police station and complained to the chief."

"And it didn't work?"

Benito shakes his head slowly, his eyes deep pools of empathy. "The chief didn't even write him up. And afterward, Gage threatened to torch our trailer if we complained about him again. This was five months ago— in May. Since then we've gotten twelve traffic tickets. Every cop in Cole-bury stops us. Mom is saving up money to move somewhere else, but it's gonna take a while."

All the air leaves Skye's lungs. She'll never be safe. And Benito might move away.

"I'm not trying to scare you," he says quietly. "But you need to know how it is. The chief thinks anyone who lives in the trailer park is trash who deserves what she gets. Since he doesn't care, Gage does what he likes. But that doesn't mean you have to take it."

Skye makes a polite noise to show that she's listening. But inside she's collapsing.

"Does your mom know the things he says to you?" he asks.

Skye shakes her head.

"You have to tell her."

Skye knows he's right. And she also knows it might not matter.

SEVEN

Benito
_____

SKYE IS STRUTTING AWAY from me. I give her a ten-yard head start before I begin to follow her.

Just then, my phone vibrates with a text. Ahead of me, Skye is looking both ways, preparing to cross the two-lane country highway.

The text is from Nelligan. *I called for backup and still can't find the suspect. I'm so sorry. She's in the wind.*

Roger that, I reply. *New development. I know who Raffie is, and I'm following her into central Colebury. Turns out it's an old friend of mine. Stay tuned.*

Stay sharp, is his reply.

Always.

But I'm a liar. Tonight has already knocked me on my proverbial ass. Seeing Skye in the Gin Mill was like seeing a ghost. A six-foot tall, long-legged, girl-of-my-dreams ghost. Who also broke my heart.

Our little chat in the booth was completely unsatisfying. And now she's striding across the road. She makes good time on those long legs of hers—the same ones that marched through my teenage fantasies the whole year we were friends.

Hell, she still walks through my fantasies. And I'd follow her no matter what. Case or no case. It's not even a conscious choice. Wherever she goes is where I need to be.

Apparently that's uphill toward town. I follow about thirty paces behind her. Meanwhile, my foolish mind can't help replaying the first time I ever laid eyes on Skylar.

At eighteen I'd been on the cusp of my last year in high school, imagining that senior year would be a snore, and feeling more than ready to leave for the military and see the world.

I'd been a dumb kid hanging out in the woods, thinking he had somewhere more important to be. And then she'd appeared—as if a wood nymph dropped from heaven into the forest in front of me.

It's no exaggeration to say that I'd never seen such a beautiful girl —in my town, in my *life*.

Stunned, I'd watched her approach, wondering if she was even real. She hadn't seen me, but even before I opened my mouth to warn her not to trip over me, my heart spoke up.

Mine, it had said. And I'd been pretty much gone for her from that day forward.

But at that point in my life, I'd already known that love at first sight was a curse. Everyone in my family knew it. My mother had fallen for my father from across a crowded dance hall in Montpelier, before she ever knew his name or heard his voice.

Nice story, right? Except that the man broke her heart on a weekly basis from that moment on. He gave her five children to feed and raise, and had been no help at all. He slept around, toyed with her affections, and then disappeared for months at a time. When I was fourteen he'd disappeared for good.

And yet if you cornered my mom right this minute, she might tell you she still loves him.

The heart is a fool, and love at first sight is a vicious bitch. She doesn't care who she burns or how much destruction is left in her wake. She will eat you up and spit you out.

Ask me how I know.

When Skye had come into my life, I'd wanted her from the first second. But we can't always get what we want. I realized right away that Skye hadn't needed a horny teenage boy trying to get under her skirt. She'd needed a friend and a protector

It had been easy to be her friend, and harder to keep her safe. Ultimately I'd failed at both, and that's how I lost her. I can't fail again.

But—Jesus Christ—the love of my life has the worst possible timing.

Pacing up the hill, I continue to keep my distance from her, because I need a minute to formulate a plan. Not only is my mind shattered by her sudden appearance in town, my strategy is blown, too.

I'm a hundred percent sure that it's Jimmy Gage who's flooding the local market with poorly cut drugs. Overdose deaths are suddenly up, because the man is careless.

I just can't prove it. Yet.

I've spent the last several weeks gathering facts, but I don't have enough evidence yet to proceed with a sting operation.

On Wednesday morning, I'd gotten a break I hadn't expected. I'd been hanging out at my sister's coffee shop and Rayanne had been sitting at a table nearby. I'd overheard her convincing someone named "Raffie," to drive a kayak to Vermont.

Who goes kayaking in March?

And my ears had really perked up when Rayanne had told Raffie that she didn't want anyone to know she was coming. I hadn't been able to tie Rayanne to her father's dealings, and, frankly, I hadn't wanted to because I knew what it was like to be painted with your father's sins, but the conversation had been damn odd.

Forty-eight hours ago I'd thought if I followed the lead—and Rayanne—I might crack the case wide open. But if Skye is Raffie?

I don't know what the hell to think.

I hadn't known Skye and Rayanne were close, or that they ever even spoke. I thought when Skye got out of Vermont she'd never looked back.

The sidewalk begins to level out at the top of the hill, and we come into view of Colebury proper. Skye knows I'm walking behind her. I can see it in the determined set of her shoulders.

She doesn't want to talk to me, but she's going to. Soon.

I have to figure out how Skye is involved in her step-family's drug business. I can't imagine she knows what they're up to. In the first place, I don't buy that Skye turned to a life of crime. But even if she had, Jimmy Gage would be the very last man on Earth she'd help.

She'd sooner run him down with her car then help him smuggle drugs across the border.

I know this in my gut, but I'm still on the job. And if she's not involved, she's in danger.

After our nice, brisk walk into Colebury, Skye skirts the perimeter of the town green. She takes her phone out of her pocket and peers at the screen, perhaps checking the address. It's dark in spite of the street lights. And most of the old houses that line the square aren't well lit. So it takes Skye a moment to get her bearings.

I can tell when she's figured it out. She straightens her spine and marches toward the smallest house on the block. It's obviously a rental—it has that under-cared-for look. I break into a jog to close the distance between us, so I don't miss any details.

I stop at the foot of the front walk and watch as Skye climbs three wooden steps and then stops. Without a search warrant, I can't follow her into that house. I can only observe. And what I see is Skylar going absolutely rigid as she stares at the front door.

Fuck. It's ajar. I can see light creeping out between the door and the jamb.

"Raye?" Skye calls in a quavering voice. She gives the door a gentle push. More light escapes. I get a glimpse of the mayhem inside —furniture knocked over, books strewn across the floor.

This house has been tossed.

"Raye!" Her voice goes up as she takes a step inside.

"Wait," I call after her. "Hold up."

She turns, showing me wide, frightened eyes. "Something's wrong."

"Then don't go in there. Come here," I say in my cop voice. Not that she knows it's my cop voice.

As much as I want to, I just can't march into that house. That's how good cases get blown, and that's how detectives get fired. Anything important I spot inside will be a waste of evidence.

On the other hand, if Skye walks into a dangerous situation while I'm standing out here on the sidewalk, I'll never forgive myself. I take a step forward—

She hops off the porch and comes to stand beside me, trembling.

Old instincts kick in, and I wrap an arm around her and pull her to my chest. I pull out my radio. "Nelligan."

"Sir."

"Get over to 15 Elmhurst. I'm standing in front. Your ETA?"

"Ninety seconds," he says.

"What was that?" Skye asks with wide eyes.

"A police officer is on his way," I say quietly. "Tell me where you think Rayanne is tonight."

"I...was meeting her," she says in a choked voice. "But she took my rental car and drove off. She left me a phone and a note and told me to go find you."

"To find *me*?" That makes no sense. "Where is this note?"

Rob Nelligan pulls up before Skye can answer. He hops out of the cruiser. "Evening, detective."

"Detective?" Skye says.

Nelligan gives me a questioning look. "Sir?"

I turn Skye to face the patrolman. "Rob is a Colebury policeman." Skye shivers, and I realize too late that her only experience with the Colebury police was Gage and sexual harassment.

Shit.

"He's one of the good ones," I add quickly. "If you're worried about Rayanne, you can ask him to do a welfare check. That means we'll go inside the house and see if anyone is there."

"Okay," she says quickly.

"What's your name, miss?" Nelligan asks.

"Skylar Copeland."

"This is your place?" he asks, even though he knows it isn't. Nelligan is a good cop.

"No." Skye shakes her head. "My stepsister's. I was supposed to spend the weekend here, but then she ditched me. The front door is open, though, and it looks like someone trashed her place. Raye isn't a slob."

"So you're inviting us inside to look for her," Nelligan clarifies.

"Please," Skye says. "I'm worried."

Nelligan trots up the walkway, identifies himself at the open doorway and then steps inside.

I give him a thirty-second head start, then I walk Skye up to the front door.

"You're a cop, too?" she asks.

"Yep. Different kind, though. I'll explain later." We step through the door. Rayanne's belongings are scattered everywhere. A gym bag is crumpled on the floor, its contents dumped out on the rug. A bamboo plant lies toppled on the coffee table, its water dripping everywhere.

The house echoes with silence, except for Nelligan's solitary footsteps upstairs. My gut says there's nobody else here. Still, Nelligan does a thorough check—I hear him finish upstairs and then watch as he comes down again and walks through the little messy kitchen.

"Nobody home," he says. "I'll check the cellar."

I follow Skye as she flips on all the lights and picks up a few items. I'm pretty happy not to find Rayanne's dead body lying on the floor. Given the people she's mixed up with, it's a very real possibility.

I'm not looking forward to explaining this to Skye. But my job isn't always a good time.

EIGHT

November, Twelve Years Ago

IT'S SUNDAY AFTERNOON, and Skye's mother is preparing to go to work. She's wearing her orange polyester waitress uniform.

Skye is in a dark mood. Gage isn't home yet, but Skye knows he'll turn up. He always does. "Why do you have to work six to twelve? He's terrible to me." She can hear how unattractive her whiny tone is. How shrill and desperate.

Her mother is unmoved. "Maybe don't sass people and you'd be easier to live with," she grumbles, tugging the too-short uniform skirt down. Her mother's life is a series of dead-end jobs and dead-end men. Skye is never, ever going to walk that same path. She will get through high school and work her way through college so she won't come home at midnight smelling like hash browns and bacon.

But some days just don't feel survivable. "I don't say a word to him," she tries. "He comes after me." She's afraid to bring up the time Jimmy Gage grabbed her ass. Her mother will assume she did something to attract his attention.

And deep in her heart, Skye is a little worried that maybe somehow it's her own fault. She might have given him the wrong signal. She won't make that mistake again. Skye doesn't ask her mother for new clothes anymore because wearing Rayanne's old too-big sweatshirts seems safer.

"You have a room to yourself, Skylar." Mom tucks her keys and a pack of cigarettes into her purse. "You have a roof over your head. Don't complain. And don't use my phone anymore. I don't have enough minutes."

"I was only calling Aunt Jenny."

Her mother sniffs at the sound of her only sister's name. They don't get along, which Skye doesn't understand. She'd kill for a real sister—for someone else who understood her. Skye calls Aunt Jenny when she's feeling low. And Aunt Jenny always reassures her.

"She said I could live with her if *he* won't leave me alone," Skye says, wondering if her mother would even notice if she left.

But this threat makes her mother's face get red with anger. It's much more of a reaction than Skye expected. "You ungrateful little *bitch*. You have a lot of nerve for someone who doesn't pay any rent."

"You don't pay it either! And yet I'm the one he calls a whore."

The slap comes so fast that she doesn't even see her mother's hand move. There's just a loud, ringing sound and sudden stinging pain on her cheek.

Skye lifts an arm up to her face, shielding herself, just in case her mother does it again.

A few seconds pass and she hears the front door open and then slam shut. And then she hears her mother's voice outside. "What are *you* looking at?

Her car starts up a moment later and then peels away.

Skye lets out a long breath. She shouldn't have baited her like that. But she's desperate.

Aunt Jenny's offer is real, but it's complicated by the fact that she lives in a one-bedroom apartment in the Bronx. "The schools aren't good here," Jenny had explained. "There are metal detectors on the doors, and the teachers have to be careful when they walk out to their cars at night. But we could make it work, Skye. If you turn up on my doorstep I'll know it's because your house is scarier than a Bronx high school."

Skye doesn't know what to do. She knows that if she escapes to Aunt Jenny, it's permanent. Her mother won't ever take her back.

There's a light tap on the door. Skye's blood pressure doubles because she's so jumpy. Jimmy Gage doesn't knock on his own door, so at least she knows it's not him.

She opens it to find Benito standing there. "You okay?" he asks between gritted teeth.

Skye looks him up and down. His hands are balled into fists, and his eyes look hot and angry. What is *with* everyone today? "I'm fine," she says quickly. Enough with the drama. "Something wrong?"

"Skye. There's a hand print on your face."

"Oh." She covers it quickly. "It's just, uh…" This is so embarrassing.

He sighs. "Look, you want to go to an orchard for a few hours? The Shipleys are looking for some help with the cider apples."

"Um, sure?" Getting away from the trailer sounds like a great idea. "Let me get my jacket."

———

Benito has the use of his brother Damien's taxi today, so they don't have to take the motorcycle.

Skye spends the car ride with an elbow propped against the door, chin in hand, staring at the outdoor scenery. She knows she's terrible company, and she doesn't mean to be ungrateful. But she knows Benito overheard the fight with her mom, and now it's harder to look him in the eye.

Still, she's comfortable with Benito. They've spent many evenings on the chair in the woods in front of the fire. She's not sure if Benito can actually hear her climb down from her bedroom window, or if he keeps a constant eye on the pathway into the woods, or if he just has some kind of sixth sense about when she needs company, but she rarely waits more than five or ten minutes before he appears with his ukulele and his calm demeanor. He lights a fire and strums the ukulele and pretends that it's perfectly normal for her to hide in the woods from a man who wants to…

Actually, Skye is still confused about what Jimmy Gage wants from her. He talks about teaching her a lesson and asks her who gets to touch her pussy and whose dick has been in there.

Spoiler alert: nobody's.

Every minute of his attention terrifies her, but she's starting to think that terror might be the whole point. The man has a gun and could ultimately get anything he wants from her. They both know it. The fact that he hasn't done anything other than say horrible things to her and touch her ass, only heightens her dread.

He likes that best, maybe. Her dread.

Beside her, Benito hums along with the radio. He's a quiet comfort, and she loves him so much. She'll never tell him, though. Too risky. Instead, she spends their evenings together entertaining him with school gossip. Skye is somewhat invisible at school, which means she hears everything.

The girls at school are still mean to her, but Skye doesn't complain to Benito about that. Boys don't like it when you complain. Besides—the two meanest people are Jill Sullivan and Zara Rossi—Benito's twin sister.

Skye knows that Zara hates her for taking up Benito's attention. And Jill hates her because Jill is also in love with Benito, and because Skye is a newcomer. It's the oldest story in the world.

But Skye doesn't have time to worry about Zara and Jill. She's too busy avoiding Gage and sticking close to Benito when she can.

"Lotta people will be here," Benito says as he turns up a long dirt driveway. "They do this at the end of every season, and the food is epic. All we have to do is move apples around so they can press a lot of cider at once."

"Cool," she says.

He parks behind a long row of cars. Then he snaps the keys out of the ignition and gives her forearm a quick squeeze before opening his door.

Benito is a toucher. He's always patting his buddies on the back or throwing an arm around his siblings. Skye loves the pats and squeezes she gets, although they're confusing.

How can one man's touch be terrifying, while Benito's is something she craves?

In the orchard, they're greeted by Ruth and August Shipley, and Skye can tell immediately that they're like parents from a storybook—smiley and warm. Mrs. Shipley is wearing a freaking apron and holding a plate of cookies.

Who does that?

Skye gobbles down the cookie she's offered and follows Benito into an orchard row. There are apples everywhere, and Skye has barely eaten anything today.

Their job is to kneel beneath the trees, gather up fallen apples from the thick grass, and then place them on a tarp.

"We let 'em get ripe enough to fall," Griffin Shipley explains. He's a fresh-faced senior with broad shoulders and an easy smile. "I'll sort them because I already know what I'm looking for."

It's true, too. Griff sorts the apples into two crates as quickly as Skye and Benito can harvest them. When the first crate fills, he hoists that giant thing on one of his broad shoulders and strolls off. His sister May takes his place. She's only a ninth-grader but her hands are just as fast as her big brother's.

May Shipley glances shyly at Skye from time to time, and she's always smiling. Surely there's a mean Shipley somewhere? This place is like being transported to the Land of Happy, Healthy People. It's kind of startling.

Skye plucks hundreds of apples from the ground, and then also from the trees. Some of the apples are a funny variety that has weird, rough skin the color of a paper grocery bag. They're the only thing on this farm that doesn't look like it's part of a storybook.

"They're not pretty, but they make good cider," Griff explains.

Whatever. Skye will pick apples for the rest of her life if it means working shoulder to shoulder in the orchard with Benito. Her hands are freezing and the light is already fading, but it's the nicest day she's had in a long time.

Then Ruth Shipley comes down the row to announce that dinner is ready.

Skye rises from a crouch beneath a tree, and Ruth frowns down at her feet. "Where are your socks, honey?"

"Laundry day," Skye says quickly. She doesn't have many socks, because you don't need them in Georgia, where she and her mom lived last. She doesn't have a winter coat, either, but that's a problem for another day.

Ruth just smiles and tells her to leave the apple crates where they are and make herself a plate of food.

———

Zara Rossi spends the afternoon in the cider house, feeding apples into the water bath whenever Mr. Shipley tells her to. It's a wet job for a cold day, but there's a perk. Griffin appears every ten minutes or so with a new crate of apples and a smile.

Griff is a football player who's going to Boston University next year. Half the high school is in love with him. But a girl can dream.

When it's finally time for dinner, Zara's hands are raw and red from all that cold water. She's shivering when she comes out of the cider house. The first thing she sees is Ruth Shipley fussing over someone. "Take these," she says to Skye Copeland, pressing something into the girl's hands. "Wool socks are magic in this climate. Try them and they'll change your life."

"Thank you," Skye says as spots of pink stain her exquisite cheekbones.

"Now let's get you some food," Ruth Shipley says. "Griff! Will you make a plate for Skye?"

"I've got it," Benito says quickly.

"Good lord," Zara's friend Jill mutters from beside her. "Like she can't get her own food? Do her hands not work?"

"Seriously," Zara hisses. But she knows why people fall all over Skylar. The girl has the kind of rare, unholy beauty that other girls would sell their souls to have.

"I wish she'd just go back to wherever she came from," Jill grumbles.

So does Zara. In the first place, Zara can't stand how her twin brother looks at Skye—like she's a gift from heaven. Benito has it bad.

Jill can tell, too. Hell—anyone with eyes can tell. Whenever Skye shows up, Jill's mood turns sour. So that means Zara's life gets a little less pleasant. Jill wants Benito badly. It's dawning on Zara lately that her twin is the only thing Jill has ever wanted that she couldn't acquire.

Zara wishes her brother would just take Jill out on one date, or invite her to the Christmas dance or even fuck her in the back of Damien's car. *Something*. Maybe it would make Jill nicer.

If only.

"Come on," Jill snarls.

Zara follows her dutifully toward the food table. As a permanent guest in Jill's home, Zara is expected to do whatever Jill wants.

Jill craves attention in all forms. She views herself as Zara's benefactor. Jill feels entitled to Zara's loyalty. After all, Zara is merely the daughter of their housekeeper. Yet Zara gets to live in Jill's brother's room while he's in college in Albany. She gets to borrow Jill's clothes (at Jill's whim) and ride in Jill's white Volvo to school.

In return, Zara is expected to kiss Jill's ass twenty-four-seven, and to help steer Jill into the path of her uninterested brother.

Hard to do when Skye takes up all her brother's time. Benito is never alone, so they can't talk like they used to. This stupid year is killing Zara. She lives with the school mean girl. She misses her twin.

And who's fault is that? That turd Jimmy Gage—Skye's stepfather. The man threatened her family, and now prevents Zara from living in her own home.

That whole family can just fuck *right off*.

Zara is burning with rage by the time they sit down at a picnic table with Benito, Skye, and Griffin.

"Hey, Z," Benito says from behind his pulled pork sandwich. "How you been?"

"Cheeky," she snaps. Her brother doesn't even hear the sarcasm. Nobody in her family can see that she is drowning. "Look," she says to Benito. "You better have brought something in the trunk of the taxi for me."

"Demanding much?" her twin asks with a wrinkle of his nose. But he lifts his chin toward the driveway. "I did, though. You're welcome, and I love you too."

This makes Jill giggle. Because everything Benito says makes Jill giggle.

"Cool," Zara says, biting her sandwich and hating the sound of her own voice.

Maybe she'll get to talk to Benny later. The kids always get drunk in the woods after a day at the Shipley's. Since Griffin's parents don't want a bunch of teenagers getting bombed in their orchard, they'll take the party down the road a bit and build a bonfire.

Across from her, Skye is cleaning her plate. Zara notices this, but it only makes her angrier. That skinny girl can *eat*. Zara will simmer with teenage resentment, instead of coming to the logical conclusion, which is that Skye is starving because she's too stressed out when she's at home to eat.

Mrs. Shipley comes around as they're polishing off the dinner, handing out envelopes. Skye takes hers with a confused frown. "Thank you?" When Mrs. Shipley moves on, Skye peeks into the envelope. "Thirty bucks. This is a *paying* gig?"

The boys beam at her, like she's adorable. But Zara rolls her eyes. What does the poor fool think they're doing out here in the cold, if not for thirty bucks and pulled pork?

Except for Jill, who has all the money she needs. Jill is here for Benito. Not that he's noticed.

"Let's go hang out," Griff says from the next table. "I stacked the fire-wood already."

Zara shoots up from the table and hurries off to toss her paper plate in the compost bin so she can follow Griffin. But he's halfway across the meadow with another girl by the time she turns around.

NINE

Skylar

BENITO IS A COP. Now that's something I didn't see coming.

He stands beside me in the living room of Rayanne's house, holding my hand, saying nothing.

"Nobody's here," the other cop says after a very thorough check.

"I got that," I say in an almost normal voice. "But it looks like she's been robbed."

The cop exchanges a significant glance with Benito. And I am totally lost.

"No sign of forced entry," the cop says, tapping his notepad against his palm. "Can you be sure if anything was taken?"

"No." I shake my head. "I've never been to this house. Rayanne typically comes to see me in New York, but this whole visit is weird."

"Will you tell me about it?" Benito asks.

"Sure," I say with a sigh. Rayanne had told me to make contact with Benito, and now that I'm seeing evidence she's in serious trouble —and I've learned he's some kind of cop—it seems like the right thing to do.

Still, if this is some kind of prank, I will kill her with my bare hands.

"Unless I can help you two in any other way, I'll be going now," the uniformed officer says. Benito thanks him and the cop waves goodbye and makes a move toward the door.

"Come on, honey. Let's go," Benito says.

"Where?" I ask, and it comes out sounding a little breathy. I'm too old for Benito to be solving my problems for me. Although I'm still holding his hand, which I don't remember taking. But, damn him, it feels nice, if only because I'm terrified right now.

"You're coming with me," he says, and his voice is awfully authoritative. Or maybe that's just my desperation talking. But I follow him out onto the porch. "Back down the hill to the mill building. I need to ask you some questions."

I pull Rayanne's door closed, and the lock clicks behind me. Benito watches me closely, but he's not the only one with questions. "You're a *cop?*" I demand as soon as the officer's taillights disappear. "Really?"

"Yeah. I'm a detective for a special department of the state police."

"Wow." My mind has been blown too many times tonight, but if I had a few minutes to think about it, I'd probably decide that Officer Benito makes some sense, given his teenage penchant for keeping certain people safe.

Me, in particular.

"Here's the question of the hour," Benito says quietly as we leave the porch and head for the green. "Do you want to report your rental car stolen?"

"No," I say quickly. "Besides, it wasn't. Rayanne paid for the rental. Technically it's hers. It's more like she stole…my weekend." And my trust, which hurts worse. "She asked me to meet her at the visitors' center off of 89. But while I was inside the building, she took the Jeep and left me a phone and a creepy note."

Benito's expression is incredulous. "Creepy how?"

"I'll read it to you when we get back down this hill," I say with a shiver. The temperature has dropped a lot, and so has the adrenaline in my system. Suddenly I'm freezing in my skirt and my little cashmere sweater. So I pick up the pace.

Wordlessly, Benito slips his leather jacket off and drapes it over my shoulders.

I stop on a dime under a streetlight. "No," I say, shrugging it off again, eyeing his thin-looking black T-shirt. "It's yours."

He takes the jacket from my hand but doesn't put it on. Instead he shocks me by stepping into my space and wrapping his free arm around me in a hug.

Startled, I look him right in the eye. This is possible because I'm a six-foot girl in heeled boots. Our gazes are locked and level. Just like old times. And I feel the same flush of excitement I always did when he was close to me.

This is *not good*.

"Skye," he whispers. "I don't know what's going on with you or Rayanne. I don't know where you work or who your friends are. But I will keep you safe and out of trouble if I can."

I blink. It's hard to focus on what he's saying when our bodies are touching. He looks bigger and older but *just* the same, too. Except for that beard that briefly tickled my jaw. "What kind of trouble?"

"Doesn't matter." His voice is thick. "It never did. I'm here for that. I'm here for *you*."

My throat is suddenly tight. Twelve years ago, I'd never known what I'd done to deserve Benito. He was the greatest gift I'd ever been given. And he disappointed me in a very ordinary, teenage-heartbreak sort of way. He'd stood me up for prom. Big deal, right?

Yet it wrecked me because he was the best boy I'd ever met—before or since. The best *man*. He knew more about being a man at eighteen than most will ever know.

Now he steps back and grabs my hands—both of them—and balances them on his palms, inspecting them.

"What are you doing?" I manage to croak, in spite of the lump in my throat.

"Checkin' for a wedding ring."

My heart skips a beat. "As if. But you could just ask."

"Really?" He drops my hands. "Twelve years I don't hear from you. Information isn't very forthcoming. I didn't even know you and Rayanne still talk."

"Only once a month or so. She's half of my remaining family. It's just her and Aunt Jenny."

"Your mom—did she pass?" He lifts the jacket and arranges it over my shoulders again. And I let him.

"But you'll be cold."

"Nah." I get a quick smile. "I'm from Vermont."

He puts a hand on my back and we walk again, and, once again, I'm hit by how surreal this night has been. "My mom didn't die," I tell him. "I just don't talk to her anymore."

"Sounds like a reasonable choice."

"I haven't spoken to her since the night I left Vermont. She called me exactly once after she learned I had a TV-news job. She wanted money."

Benito makes a growly noise. "I hope you didn't give her any."

"Not a chance. Besides—the joke's on her. I have the worst job in television. I'm on the very bottom rung, and I get paid like shizzle."

His laugh is a bark. "The fake-swearing thing is hard to get used to."

"Whatever. I thought it would keep me from dropping an f-bomb or similar on-air. Turns out you don't need words to humiliate yourself."

He turns to look at me as we walk back down the same hill I climbed a half hour ago. "How's that?"

"Never mind. Too embarrassing." If Benito isn't one of the five million people who's already watched me draw a penis on the traffic map, I'm not going to enlighten him.

As we make our descent, I scan the parking lot for signs of a cherry-red Jeep, with or without a kayak on top.

No dice.

"Is there a parking lot in the rear?" I ask.

"Nope," Benito says, dashing my hopes. "The river runs right along the back. That's why my brother bought the place. There's a kickass terrace. Great for summer business."

"Your *brother*? Which one?"

"There's a lot you've missed, Skye." He takes a set of keys out of his jacket pocket as we cross the street. "Alec bought the old mill at auction."

"Alec..." He was the brother I'd never met while I'd lived next door to the Rossi's. "Wait. Is he tending bar tonight?"

"That's right. He tends bar most nights."

No wonder he looked so familiar.

"How about a glass of wine while we talk?" he asks me.

"Well..." I am truly stuck right now. "Sure. And I need to, uh, scare up a hotel room somewhere, too."

Benito gives me a dark look. "Sweetheart, you don't need a hotel."

"Yeah, I really do." I'm still hoping Rayanne turns up with a plausible explanation and a "just kidding," but I'm starting to lose hope. With her reputation for trouble, I might as well wish for a pink pony and world peace.

And I really don't want to spend the night alone in her ransacked house.

"Come on," Benito says. He pulls out a set of keys and walks to the far end of the building, away from the bar's entrance. He taps a security code into another door, and holds it open for me.

"What's this? I thought we were having a glass of wine?"

"We are. The mill has a second and a third floor. I bought in, so the second floor is mine. Come on up." And then he jogs up the steps ahead of me, while I admire his butt in those tight jeans.

It hacks me off that Benito still affects me. I *never* bother looking at men's hindquarters. It's like they're not even there. But Benito makes me think thoughts that I don't usually make time for.

Good thing I'm leaving Vermont as soon as I can.

I chase him up the stairs and follow him into an absolutely stunning loft apartment. "Wow," I hear myself say. "This is all yours?" I'm standing in a big living room with exposed brick walls and high, beamed ceilings. The tall leaded-glass windows curve at the top, where the brickwork makes an arch. There's even a fire crackling cozily in the fireplace, giving the wide-plank wood floors a rosy hue. "Benny, this is so much nicer than the trailer park."

He snorts. I watch him remove a gun from a holster at the back of his jeans. "This never moves from here, okay?" he says as he unlocks a cupboard above the refrigerator. His kitchen is one end of the long room. There's a black stone countertop demarcating the space.

"Okay," I say. "I'm never touching your gun. Or any gun."

"I just have to say it," he says. "My niece comes up here often and that's the only thing I ever really worry about."

"Your...niece?" Wow. "Who had kids?"

"Guess," he says with a wry smile.

"Alec?" I try.

Benito shakes his head. "Zara. Just one kid."

"Oh. Wow." Zara, who used to hate me. I hadn't thought about her in a long time. "So... you're Uncle Benito."

"That's right." He smiles, and I realize that it might undo me completely to see him holding a child. The news headline would read: *Tough Guy Holds Infant. Women Faint in a Twenty Mile Radius.*

Yup. Sounds about right.

I change the subject, though, because I can't talk about Zara. "Can you help me find a place to stay?"

He opens another cabinet, this one containing wine glasses. "You're staying here, Skye. With me."

"Oh." But that's too much like the girl I used to be—the one who let Benito solve all her problems. "Your girlfriend might not like it."

"No girlfriend."

I'm relieved, but also embarrassed. Because how subtle was that? "You really don't have to take the trouble," I say.

He sets two wine glasses on the stone countertop and sighs. "It's no trouble, okay? Jesus."

It is for me, I realize. Seeing him again actually hurts. It's like a dull ache right at my breastbone. You'd think twelve years would be enough to get over someone, but you'd be wrong. And the worst part is that I thought I *was* over him. I don't walk around New York brooding about the boy who stood me up when I was a teenager.

I *thought* I didn't, anyway. But now I'm wondering if some quadrant of my heart still echoes with this old wound. I'm not married. I don't even date.

Maybe this weekend has a higher purpose. Like God is telling me I'm in a rut, and that I need to move on. Destiny calls.

I usually only think about destiny when I score Chanel lipstick samples at Sephora. But even so, I make a decision, right here in Benito's groovy living room. I will enjoy this night in his company. I will remember the good times.

And when I go back to New York, I'll do so knowing that I looked him in the eye and survived it.

"You eat dinner?" he asks.

"I did. I promise."

"Glass of wine?"

"I'd love one," I say, because that's how I'm going to play this tonight. One heaping dose of wine and memories. Bring it on. "Don't you think all those nights on the giant lounge chair would have been better with wine?"

"You know it," he says, opening a kitchen drawer and removing a corkscrew. "I only have red."

"My favorite color." I am not much of a drinker but I like a glass of wine once in a while.

He pulls a bottle off a wall rack, and proceeds to open it, while I try and fail not to watch the muscles in his forearm flex. It's the same arm I used to try to ignore when we were seated side by side, and he was playing the ukulele and humming quietly to soothe me...

My stomach does another dive and roll, and I take a deep breath.

"This is so civilized," I say, forcing myself to make small talk. "I'm a little in shock. Where's the hidden keg in the shrubs? Where's the Deep Woods Off?"

His smile opens up as he crosses the room with two glasses. The scruff makes him look older, but the smile is still potent. So I smile back.

See? I can do this.

"I know this place lacks some of our former ambiance," he says, handing me a glass. "But try to put up with it."

"I'll do my best."

He sits down on one end of the charcoal-colored velvet sofa. Taking his cue, I sit beside him, but not too close. I'm sitting on his left side, which is exactly where I used to sit on our old chair.

I'm in a time warp, and I don't know if I even want out.

"Now," he says, sipping his wine. "Start at the beginning. When did Rayanne contact you last, and when did you decide to come to Vermont for the night?"

So I tell him the whole story again—including all my speculation. "I thought maybe she was starting a kayaking business or something. Like, kayak yoga. Is that a thing? I know there's yoga with goats. And on paddle boards."

His forehead creases with a frown. "Not to my knowledge. Will you show me the prepaid phone and the note?"

"Sure." I open my purse and fish them out. I spread the note out on the cushion between us, and Benito begins to read. That's when I remember the post script…

"'P.S.'" Benito says while my face heats. "'Benito has only gotten hotter in the last twelve years. Enjoy the view.'" He glances up at me.

Shishkebab. "Uh, I guess Rayanne admires you," I say, feeling my face flush. "But, come on. Are you paying attention? Did you notice the part about the phone and the texts and the *evidence*?"

His chuckle is noncommittal although I feel a tingle in places where I don't usually tingle. "Just seeing if *you're* paying attention. Now I have a couple more questions. When was the last time you spoke to Rayanne about me?"

"Um…" That's actually a harder question than you'd think. Rayanne knows how in love I was with Benito in high school. But we don't ever mention his name. Usually he only comes up when I'm trying to explain to Raye why I don't date. "Not recently."

"Would you say the two of you discussed me within the last three months?"

I shake my head. "No. Rayanne and I have barely spoken lately."

"Until the call on the ninth," he prompts.

"Right. When I read your name in her note, it floored me. I didn't know you were a cop, and I didn't understand her mention of evidence. Do you guys talk?" A weird little electric spark runs through me. Could Benito and Rayanne be *involved?* I'll die of jealousy.

He rubs the bridge of his nose with two fingers. Then he squeezes his eyes shut, as if in pain. "Look, a lot of what I do at work is secret."

"Okay?"

"The less you know, the safer you are."

"Oh." He isn't going to tell me.

"But I'm going to be transparent about one fact—Rayanne mentioning my name in your note is as surprising to me as it is to you. I haven't spoken to her—except for a wave hello in the coffee shop—in months."

"And the, uh, evidence she mentions?"

He shakes his head. "Collecting evidence is something I do all the time. But she's not involved in that, and I don't know why she's making it sound like we're collaborating. Zara takes Rayanne's yoga classes sometimes. That's as close as the Rossis get to a friendship with Rayanne."

"Oh. Okay." I feel a wave of inappropriate relief.

"So if you can think of a reason why your stepsister is mentioning me, I want to know right away."

"She hasn't mentioned you before," I admit. "Except, uh, when I used to talk about high school."

"Okay." He doesn't ask me about that, thankfully. "Here's another question, and it's pretty important. When's the last time you saw or spoke to Jimmy Gage?"

The moment I hear that name, my stomach clenches. It's been forever, but it doesn't matter—I can still see his weasel face in my mind's eye. I'm still afraid.

I must look it, too, because Benito reaches across the cushion and grabs my hand. "Just tell me, okay?"

"Well..." I clear my throat. "The last time I saw him or spoke to him was my last night in Vermont."

His eyes widen. "Twelve years ago?"

I nod. "Yeah. I was waiting on the porch for you to come and get me. You didn't, but he did."

Swear to God, Benito's face goes ashen right in front of my eyes. He lets go of my hand. "What happened that night?"

I must not be a very nice person, because there's a small part of me that wants him to worry. I always hated facing Gage alone, and that night Benito forced me to do it. Except Benito looks like he wants to throw up right now, and so I tell him the truth. "He was mean as a snake that night. But nothing out of the ordinary happened."

His eyes fall shut and I watch him take a breath. "I'm sorry I put you in that position. I know you don't believe me, but I really am."

"Thank you," I say softly. What's the statute of limitations on heartache? I don't think mine is over.

That night Gage came home and found me sitting there in my borrowed prom dress and shoes. I'd felt so small and so alone. "I don't know who you're waiting for, but that kid on the motorcycle isn't coming," he'd said. And then he'd twisted the knife even further...

Every time I think about that pathetic girl on the porch, I get angry. But I'm not just angry at Benito, I'm also angry at myself. I'd fallen for him. I'd given away so much of myself that he was able to level me in a single night.

"Skye," Benito whispers. "What else happened that night? Why did you leave and never come back?"

"Nothing," I choke out. "I was just *done*. I locked the bedroom door and packed my bags. Then I climbed out a window and hitch-hiked to the bus station in White River Junction."

Benito takes a gulp from his wine glass.

"Why are you asking me about Gage, anyway?" it occurs to me to ask. "I don't want to think about him."

"Ah, well." He sighs and sets the glass down. "Unfortunately it's my job to think about him. I'm investigating Gage for drug trafficking."

"Oh no," I whisper. Benito only nods. And because I'm not a stupid girl, my next question hurts. "And you think Rayanne is mixed up in it?"

His expression is grim. "I can't rule it out. And I wouldn't even mention it to you, except you have that phone, and instructions to watch it. That's not the behavior of someone who isn't involved."

I pick up the burner phone and turn it over in my hands. I wake it up with a press of my thumb, but the screen shows no new texts. "Her note says the phone is untraceable."

"That's probably true," he says. "If I had a warrant I could try to discover where she purchased the sim card, and ultimately find the number."

"So I guess I'll wait for her to message me? That's either dire or melodramatic." I sure hope it's the latter.

"Yeah. You'll let me know if she contacts you?" he asks. "It's important."

He seems awfully serious. "Does Rayanne know you're a cop? You don't look like one."

"Sure," he says easily. "I mean—I don't drive a cruiser, and I don't wear a patrolman's uniform. But it's a small town, and it's not a secret that I work for the state. That's why I do most of my drug busts in towns where nobody knows me. And that's why I have longer hair and I don't shave very often." He passes a hand over the scruff on his chin, and suddenly I'm itching to examine its texture with my fingers.

And I hate the thought of Benito mixing with druggies and dealers. "Is your job always dangerous?"

"No, baby." He smiles. "Careful, though. A guy might think you cared."

I hide behind my wine glass because I do care, darn it. Not that I want to. But I promised myself I'd be cheerful about seeing him. Just this once. I lift my glass and touch it to his. "It's good to hear that you're doing well."

He tips his head to the side and considers me. "Likewise."

We sip. And the wine is tasty. There isn't much wine in my life because I don't have enough money nor anyone to drink it with. I work a lot of hours. I don't leave the office until eight most nights. And I don't have a lot of friends because I never developed that skill. Growing up, I was always just passing through. I missed my window for learning how to make lifelong friends. And even though I've been at my current job for five years, it isn't a very social office.

We're all too terrified of being the next in line to be fired.

The first third of my wine disappears pretty quickly, and Benito tops it up. "I had a thought," he says. "You should tell Rayanne that she has to text you every twelve hours just so you know she's okay. That way you won't worry as much."

"That's not a bad idea," I admit. I pick up the burner phone and start a text message. *Raye—if you don't text me every twelve hours I won't go along with this weird scheme.*

I take a sip of wine and wait. She answers barely two minutes later.

Told you not to contact me! I will text you tomorrow morning and night, but otherwise leave me alone. Okay?

Fine, I reply, as Benito leans over my shoulder to read along. *But if you miss a text, I'll send the police after you.*

Not cool, she says. *Chatter about me on the police scanner could get me killed.*

"By who?" I ask, turning my chin to see Benito.

His big dark eyes are right there. "I don't know," he says.

"Yes you do," I whisper.

He gives me a patient smile. "Forgive me for not providing you with a powerpoint presentation of the county's alleged criminal network. Don't ask questions I can't answer."

"Okay," I say, and then sigh. Both he and Rayanne are trying my patience.

"You must be tired, and in need of some distraction," he says. "Want to watch a movie on TV?"

I look around the living room. "Where are you hiding it?"

"Well…" He rubs the back of his neck. "It's in the bedroom. But since you're staying over, we're headed in that direction eventually anyway."

"I'll sleep on the couch," I say quietly. That's what people do when they visit, right?

"Skye, we used to sleep on a patio chair surrounded by snow. If you're against sleeping on the other side of my king-sized bed, I'll take the couch. But I know you're not afraid of me."

Of course I'm not. But my *Embrace the Memories Tour* has its limits. Curling up next to Benito might break me.

No. I catch myself. It won't break me. Maybe I need to feel this ache one more time before I can let it go for good.

"I'm not afraid of you," I assure him. "Even if you're twice as large and an officer of the law, I can still take you."

He grins at me over the rim of his wine glass. "Come on. Let me show you where the bathroom is. Then we'll watch a little TV to get your mind off Rayanne until we can learn more."

TEN

Skylar

WE'RE SITTING on Benito's bed, which is neatly made. I'm wearing a Natori nightgown that seemed perfectly modest when I thought that only Rayanne would see it. But now I feel naked. And unless I'm crazy, Benito's eyes keep finding their way over to my side of the bed.

There's a comedy on TV, but I can barely pay attention. I'm too busy processing everything that's happened in the last three hours. Rayanne's disappearance. Benito's reappearance.

It's trippy to be so close to Ben. Every time he laughs at the TV, the sound echoes inside my chest. I'd spent so many hours sitting beside him just like this. I know the sound of his laugh as well as I know my own.

On the screen, two characters are exchanging sexually charged banter. The woman is fashioned to be sexy and slick, with shiny lipstick and a low-cut top. Half-hour comedies don't have time for subtleties. She cocks her hip and makes a comment, and the laugh-track rewards her with laughter.

When I was a teenager, I'd watched women on shows like these and figured I someday might achieve similar confidence. I'd known I was a bit of a late bloomer in the sex department. But I'd thought it was a matter of styling. If I could afford slick clothes and hair products, the confidence would fall into place, too.

Apparently it doesn't work that way.

I'm no longer the frightened child I was at sixteen. But men still baffle me. It's not like I can't appreciate their finer points from a distance. I admire handsome faces and strong bodies as much as the next girl.

Yet I've never mastered the art of getting what I want, because I can never figure out exactly what that is.

Case in point—my first boyfriend. He'd been my professor for Investigative Journalism. I'd thought the man was a genius, and maybe he was. He had bylines in every major news publication.

By November of my junior year, I was smitten. I had it bad for his big brain, and also for his wavy hair and intelligent eyes. I spent each lecture entranced, taking him in as he paced the lecture hall. And I was always first in line for office hours.

Then, one cloudy day as I put on my coat to leave after a meeting, he kissed me.

At first I was astonished by the smoothness of it. He just pressed me up against his office door and plundered my mouth. After a moment I got into the swing of things and kissed him back.

"Thought you needed that," he said after the second best kiss of my life. He was super smooth, and I was speechless. Still stunned, I rode the subway home to Aunt Jenny's apartment just trying to understand it.

So the next week I went back for more. We talked for an hour about the journalistic tradition of unnamed sources. And then he beckoned to me. I walked around the desk. He pulled me into his lap and we went to town.

Then he put his hand up my skirt.

Again I was stunned. It was the first time I'd ever let a man do that. His fingers stroked me between the legs, and I whimpered into his mouth and tried not to panic.

I was ticking off all kinds of first-times with him, but I didn't want him to know it. And I liked his touch. Nobody had ever made me feel so desirable. Even though I didn't know what the hell I was doing, professor Smooth didn't seem to mind.

He *really* didn't mind. A few minutes later I found myself elbows down on his desk blotter. My panties dropped, and I heard his zipper unzip.

He opened the desk drawer for a condom. Later I would wonder about that placement. But never mind. I was about to join the club. I was going to learn all the secrets that other girls knew.

Trying to keep my breath even, I stared down at that blotter, noting that he had a Friday appointment with his podiatrist. I was nervous, and maybe that's why it hurt so much when he pushed inside a minute later.

I hated every second. But I'd heard other girls say that first times aren't really so great. Maybe it would get better.

So of course I went back. He was still a genius and I still loved the way it felt when he locked his office door and kissed me. Like the sun was shining only on me.

Unfortunately, the sex didn't feel any better on subsequent occasions. Apparently I'm not a very sexual person. I never saw fireworks.

We carried on like that for most of the year. And then one day I was early for office hours. And there were three people leaving his office together, smiling. A woman, a preschooler clutching her hand, and a toddler on her hip.

Professor Smooth had a wife and two boys. They looked just like him.

Instead of walking into his office, I walked past his door, stunned. Later I Googled him. The first ten pages of hits were all bylines. But I found the wedding announcement eventually.

Of course I never went back to him. I deleted all his emails, and ignored his subsequent texts.

Ultimately it was a fine lesson in investigative journalism. Until that rude surprise, I saw only what he wanted me to see, and I did everything he asked.

Since then I've dated a couple of other men. But I never again found a man who seemed worth the trouble. Even if they seemed nice, I always wondered what they were hiding. And as for sex, I still don't know what all the fuss is about.

The only man I've ever really loved is sitting beside me on the bed. No wonder Vermont still has such a hold on my soul.

The comedy we're watching ends right about the same time I finish my second glass of red wine. We drank the whole bottle. I'm a big girl, but two glasses is a lot for me, so I feel pleasantly tipsy around the edges.

"Hey, where's your ukulele?" I ask suddenly. It's nowhere in the room.

"Haven't played in a while." He takes my empty glass from me and carries it into the kitchen. When he returns, I barely notice the uke in his hands, because the sight of him entering the room floors me all over again. I mean, the man was only gone for thirty seconds. But that face and those broad shoulders and...

I've still got it bad for him. Staying here tonight is either a really bad idea or an important moment in the process of getting on with my life.

It could really go either way.

"It's been a while." He sits down on the bed again, cradling the instrument. "My fingers are going to feel stupid. That year when I played a lot of ukulele for you, that was pretty much the high point of my musical career."

For me. I wonder if he meant to say that? He strums slowly, and simple chord progression makes the hair stand up on my arms. "Why did you stop playing?" I whisper.

Benito shrugs. "Joined the army. Got too busy. Honestly I was never much of a player until I spent a lot of time sitting by that fire with you." His fingers change position on the guitar's neck, and he strums again. The chord vibrates in my belly. "I liked the way you listened."

"I loved listening," I admit. His music was a calm, peaceful thing in my hellish life. Nothing bad ever happened while Benito was playing music.

His hands go still on the strings. "Loved playing for you. Also, I needed something to do with my hands." He strums again.

"Why?"

He laughs, and makes a chord change. "Horny eighteen-year-old boy sitting close to the prettiest girl in Vermont? I spent every night trying not to reach for you. The ukulele gave me something else to focus on. And I needed that. Badly."

My heart rate doubles. Because Benito never said a single thing like that when we were teens. I'd found him inscrutable, even though my whole psyche orbited around him.

Even now I feel my world tilt subtly in his direction. Twelve years later and he still has his own gravitational pull.

And he's sitting beside me strumming a Clapton tune, like he didn't just admit something important.

"Why didn't we?" I blurt out.

"Hmm?" The chords he's playing run over me like water. I can feel them everywhere.

"Why didn't we ever..." It's not easy for me to say. I'm twenty-eight years old, and I've never figured out how to talk about sex, or even how to enjoy it. That's probably why I rarely have any.

And suddenly I feel really sad about it. Maybe it's the two glasses of wine talking, or maybe it's the maelstrom of sentimental feelings hitting me tonight.

Benito has stopped playing the guitar, in favor of watching me. "There are about a hundred reasons why we didn't have sex," he says with a sad smile.

"That's a lot of reasons," I say, wondering if I should retreat from this topic. The old Skye would have. But the new one shouldn't. I promised myself I'd look the past square in the eye tonight. "Why don't you share the top ten?"

His smile widens. "You were sixteen, for starters. I thought maybe you didn't want your first time to be on a discarded patio chair behind a trailer park."

"You didn't ask," I point out.

"Fair point." He runs his palm up the strings of his instrument, and I can't tear my eyes away. I wish that hand was on me. "Also, there was a certain uniformed police officer who wouldn't like it. And I had to be careful. My whole family was always on the lookout for him."

"Oh." Now *that* makes a whole lot of sense.

Although I'd have never thought Benito was intimidated by Jimmy Gage. He never *looked* scared. Not once. Benito was my rock.

"You know, he used to accuse me of it," I say, realizing too late that I really don't want to talk about Jimmy Gage. "He would ask me which one of the Rossi boys I was..." I clear my throat. "When I didn't answer him, he said that maybe I let you all take turns."

Benito flinches. "I knew he said that shit to you. I could hear him talking to you sometimes. I never wanted to make your life harder, Skye. You weren't ready. I could never touch you, because it was too complicated for both of us. Didn't mean I didn't think about you way too much."

"You did not," I whisper. "No way."

"Way," he says, smiling. "But I should remind you that you never asked. You never said, 'Hey, Benito, put down that ukulele and do me.'"

I actually snort with laughter. "That doesn't sound like anything I'd say."

"No." He shakes his head. "It doesn't. And I couldn't afford any misunderstandings. My only goal was to keep you safe. And if I thought for one minute that I might scare you off, then it wasn't worth it. If you were afraid to be alone with me the way you were afraid to be alone with *him*, I couldn't risk that. I was happy to wait. For you."

"Oh." That sounds so lovely that I just bask in it for a minute. I don't even let myself get mad that he *didn't* actually wait for me. I push that thought aside.

"So that's why I played so much ukulele." He strums again. "To hide my boner. It was a year of untucked shirts and strategically placed objects."

I laugh, because boner is a funny word. Although my eyes feel a little hot. I never knew I had such an effect on him. And part of me really needed to hear this. It's healing to know a nice boy wanted me, and then didn't make a big deal about it.

"And when we slept by the fire on my doublewide chair," he adds. "I had to keep you away from my lap. I had it so bad. I ached."

Past tense, my brain points out. But I want him to ache for me right now. "Teenagers," I say, and then laugh again to cover my yearning.

He reaches over and smooths my hair with his hand. It's the way he used to touch me—warm, but not sexual. I miss him so much. "We should get some sleep," he says.

"Okay," I agree, even though I'm not the least bit drowsy.

"I'll sleep on the couch if it would make you more comfortable."

I shake my head before I can even think about it. The truth is that sleeping beside Benito always gave me great comfort. And my heart still wants him beside me.

"Then I'll be right back," he says.

A few minutes later he's shut off the light, and he's pulling back the covers on his side of the bed. He gets in, and for a moment we lie there in a heavy silence. I feel the weight of all our history pressing down on us. "This is so much more comfortable than the lawn chair," I whisper.

He laughs, and the tension is broken. "What's that old saw? Living well is the best revenge."

"I hope that's true," I whisper. "The other kind of revenge sounds fun, too, though."

"What's the other kind?" he rolls onto his side to ask.

I roll, too. We're facing each other in his bed, and I am thrilled by this moment of quiet intimacy. "My foot on Gage's windpipe," I say. "Except I don't want to go to jail. Okay—Gage in an orange jumpsuit. Oh—and the prisoner in the next cell never shuts up. He's constantly asking Gage which of the guards gets to take turns with him in the showers. Just a drumbeat of humiliation for the rest of his days."

Benito blinks. "You are not to be messed with."

"I'm not," I agree, even if it's all bluster. My fear of Gage is still bone deep.

"Goodnight, Skyescraper," he says. Then he gives me a teasing grin.

"Goodnight you jerk."

His smile comes closer, and I realize that he's going to kiss me goodnight. And before I can brace myself, warm, firm lips meet mine.

It could have been a chaste kiss. Perhaps Benito meant to give me a peck and pull away. And if my brain were in charge of this situation, maybe it would have been. But no. Twelve years of closeted heartache seize the moment. Something inside me rears up to meet his kiss. I fit my mouth against his, as if to reclaim what I'm owed.

Benito makes a low noise of surprise. He leans in, tilting his head to join us more perfectly. Soft lips caress and then meld to mine.

And suddenly I'm the shameless girl I always wanted to be. I kiss the stuffing out of him. I part my lips and taste him, as if I do this every day. He tastes of toothpaste and Benito. His fingers sift through my hair as his tongue makes a slow slide against mine.

I'm a livewire. I'm a buzzing, crazy mess. I kiss him again and again and then...

His phone rings.

Benito pulls back quickly. "Jesus Christ," he curses, rolling off the bed. "God, I'm sorry. That was..." He makes a noise of dismay as he lunges for the phone on top of his dresser. "Rossi. Talk to me," he barks into the phone. There's only a brief pause before he says, "Where? Okay. I'll be right there."

He drops the phone and then yanks down his flannel pants. My eyes practically pop out of my head as his muscular thighs appear and then disappear into a pair of trousers.

"The Orange County sheriff's office found an abandoned Jeep," he says as he pulls a sweatshirt over his head. "The car is not in good shape. I'm checking it out."

Those words finally break through my kissing haze. "What?" I leap out of the bed. "I'm going, too."

"No," he says harshly. "No way. I'll text you if I find out it's hers. Give me your phone."

I unlock it and hand it over.

"There," he says as he texts himself from my number. "Now I can't lose you so easily again."

Yikes.

"Get some rest," he says, jogging out the door of the bedroom.

I catch up to him in the kitchen where he's holstering his gun in the back of his trousers. "Benny! You can't just leave me here!" I picture my stepsister's body in the woods and shiver.

"Yeah, I can. Later, Skye."

He disappears out the door, and it closes with a bang.

Several heartbeats thump through my chest before I can even react. "You...!" That's as far as I get, because I don't have a substitute curse word for *bossy asshole*.

Stomping back into the bedroom, I find my phone. I pull up Uber for the second time tonight and summon a car.

Then I start searching for an internet feed of the county police scanner. Wherever the cops are headed, I'll follow.

But I am foiled by the police scanner. I can't find an online broadcast for the Orange County sheriff's office. And then my phone rings with an 802 number.

"This is Damien Rossi," a voice says when I answer. "Calling on behalf of Uber."

"I know who you are, Damien," I say to Benito's brother. "Are you downstairs? Do you happen to know where Benito went?"

"All I know is that your ride is canceled," he says. "Benito said not to pick you up again in Vermont."

"What?" I shriek. "He doesn't control Uber. And neither do you."

"Yeah? Well I'm the only Uber in eastern Vermont," Damien says. "Sorry I can't help you."

Then he hangs up on me.

Outraged, I open the app and peer at the map. And...there aren't any little cars showing on it. I make the range wider, to show more of Vermont.

Still nothing.

"This is bullshizzle!" I shriek. I'm stuck here. And I'm furious. Also, I'm a little bit drunk on red wine and on kissing Benito for the second time in my life.

I spend the next twenty minutes pacing Benito's beautiful apartment. I open drawers and closets, hunting for...

Okay, I don't know what I'm hunting for. But I'm trapped here and curious about Benito's life. My search is unsatisfying, though. I believe he'd said that Zara was living here until recently. That must be why his closets are fairly empty. I find some ski equipment and a pair of snowshoes. The medicine cabinet contains antacids and lip balm.

In the spare bedroom there's a couple of baby toys that must belong to his niece.

By the time I go back into Benito's bedroom, my conscience is taking a toll. So I stop snooping and climb into his bed. I'm not relaxed, though. Rayanne is in danger.

After forty-five minutes, my phone lights up with a text from him.

The Jeep is orange, not red. It has Vermont plates, and is registered to an Orange County farmer.

That's not it, I reply.

I agree. Just thought you'd want to know.

I did want to know, and it was nice of him to tell me. Finally I'm able to close my eyes and tell my body to calm down. Except that kiss woke up parts of me that I didn't even know were there. And the bed smells of Benito. I lie on the pillow, sucking in oxygen and trying to think of a single reason why Benito and I shouldn't have more of those kisses when he comes back home later.

Oh, right. Because then he'd expect sex. And I'm not good at sex, and I don't particularly like it.

Still. For him I'd try. If I weren't upset right now. Everything is so confusing. I'm worried about Rayanne, and my heart is on fire.

So are my loins. That kiss! It still rings through me like a bell. I can feel the vibration in my chest.

But somehow I still fall asleep.

————

My dreams are sweet. *Really* sweet. I dream that Benito and I are tangled up together in bed. *I love you*, he whispers to my dreaming self. *I love you, Skye. Just you.*

And here in dreamland, sex is fantastic. Everything is white, like we're making love on a cloud in heaven. Benito's kisses are magical, and his hands can't stop touching me. I see *all* the fireworks. Benito's naked body is hard and warm. I caress his ass while he moves against me.

Then scruff tickles the skin of my neck, and Benito lets out a low moan. So that's what his beard feels like. And his T-shirt is tangled up in my hand. But I swear he wasn't wearing a shirt a minute ago.

My eyelids flutter open, and it's mostly dark in the room, except for a gray streak of predawn light from the window. And Benito's scruff is real. He's here in the bed with me, holding me against his body.

I slam my eyes shut again. I need to get back to the dreamy, sexy place I was before.

Except this place is nice, too. I'm pancaked against his hard body. I'm not sure how I got here, lying on my side, my face tucked against his chest. And—this is embarrassing—one of my legs is thrown over his muscular thigh. And one of my hands is parked right on his muscular butt.

"Skye," he murmurs right into my ear. "Sweetheart. Tell me you're awake." A big hand sweeps down my back.

"Nope," I whisper, and he chuckles.

"Which is it, honey? Please be awake, because I'm loving this."

"Shh," I order. It's dawning on me that my subconscious has taken control of my actions. When Benito got into the bed with me, I must have rolled toward him. And then sometime in the night I began to have sexy dreams about him.

I should be mortified. Plastering myself to Benito isn't something I'd do. Except I'd done it. And he feels so flipping good.

"Skye," he whispers, and it sounds like a prayer. A hot, open-mouthed kiss lands on my cheekbone. "Give me your mouth, sweetheart."

It's as easy as lifting my chin and fitting my lips against his. He groans as his mouth strokes mine. We don't waste time with pleasantries. The kiss goes deep and hot right away. It's a kiss that knows exactly what I was dreaming.

Benito's tongue claims mine. There's heat pouring off us, and my brain is on fire.

He rolls me onto my back and leans into the kiss. His weight on my body is delicious. I lift my knees, hugging his slender hips, holding him close, so he won't leave me. He plunders my mouth with deep, wet kisses. And then he grinds his hips—just one slow thrust of his body against me.

"Oh," I sob into his mouth. I want this. I wanted it when I was sleeping, and now I want it even more now that I'm awake. My nightgown has ridden up, and my panties are drenched. That never happens.

So *this* is what all the fuss is about.

Benito worships my mouth while his whiskers abrade my lips in the best possible way. I feel wild and loose. My hands are hungry, wandering things. I touch his arms, his back, and then reach under his T-shirt. His skin is so soft. I want to feel it against mine.

I've gone from asleep to heavy-duty making out in about two minutes. It's amazing. And it leaves me no time to think. I can barely process the slide of his tongue against mine and the dragging kisses that merge from one right into the next.

It's on. I want this. I grip his rock-hard body and try to catalogue every new sensation.

Benito doesn't rush, though. He kisses me thoroughly, like he's got all morning. And I guess he does, since we're here in his bed together. It's me who's impatient. I want to know if he can make me feel things nobody else can.

So it's me who works her hands up under his T-shirt to touch more of him. And it's me who reveals that ridiculously cut chest.

Wowzers. Even if sex ends up disappointing me, the view here is loads better than with any other guy.

Benito sheds his T-shirt and then scans my body with hungry eyes. I always wanted him to look at me like that—like I was sexy and exciting, and not just a scared waif who often needed his help.

Meanwhile, my hands have taken on a life of their own. I can't stop exploring the line of hair that begins at his sternum and runs down his belly. When I was sixteen, I ached to touch him here. And he seems to like it. When he leans down to kiss me again, his mouth is both soft and demanding at once.

I lose myself in those kisses. I forget to be nervous, even as the nightgown I'm wearing disappears with a whoosh over my head.

"This okay?" Benito asks hastily.

"Yes," I slur. And then I can't speak at all, because his hot, eager mouth is on the move. He kisses the underside of my chin, and then my neck.

Goosebumps break out everywhere on my skin.

He presses on. His tastes my collarbone, then he kisses his way across the swells of my breasts. And when he sucks one of my nipples into his mouth and I gasp so loudly, I'll probably be embarrassed about it later.

But *wow*. I have never been so turned on. The feel of his lips on my breast is exquisite. I thought my boobs were only good for holding up jewel-toned blouses on camera.

How wrong I was. Each swipe of Benito's tongue across my nipple makes me sink more deeply into the bed. I run my fingers through his hair and make a whimpering sound that I don't even recognize as my own.

And then Benito *moans*. It's a rich sound from his chest, and it resonates deep inside mine. I'm gripping his quilt and gripping his head and making shameless sounds. And I'm wondering if it's possible that he feels as crazy right now as I do.

ELEVEN

Benito

THIS SHOULDN'T BE HAPPENING. I shouldn't be worshiping Skye's body with my mouth. The timing is terrible and there are too many things left unsaid between us.

Also, I'm investigating her sort-of-sister for—

I can't remember what. *Christ.* Her nipples are pebbled, beckoning to my lips. I caress them with my tongue as she gasps again and again. And she shivers as I kiss my way down her body. I feel wild, filling my hands with her tits, pushing her back against the pillows. Her skin tastes like everything I've ever wanted.

The heat in her eyes? I put it there. She's like a gift that was never mine to unwrap. But now she's looking up at me like I hung the moon and stars. I can't stop.

And, damn it, she started this. I think she did. It's difficult to say who rolled toward whom, and whose hands wandered first.

All I know is that the last scrap of fabric standing between me and heaven has got to go. I tug her panties down and toss them over the side of the bed. Then I'm living out my best fantasies—Skye is naked on my bed. I slip a hand down her sleek torso. When my fingertips brush the small V of hair between her legs, Skye holds her breath.

"Skylar," I pant between kisses on her stomach. Words aren't really working for me right now, but apparently her name communicates enough. Skye's legs relax, falling open for me. When I slide my hand over her pussy, I find so much heat and slickness. I moan, and she tips her head back and gasps.

I'm such a goner. Her chest heaves as I stroke her. And her fingers dig into my arm when I tease her. I prowl down her body again, feeling crazy. I've always wanted to spend a whole goddamn night exploring her. But right now it's a struggle to go slow. I kick my boxers off while Skye watches me with a hungry gaze.

Propping myself on my elbows I dip my chin and take a first, slow lick at the honeyed center of her.

"B-Ben!" she shouts, her fingers landing in my hair. "Oh G-god," she pants as I begin dropping tender kisses on her pussy. Her hips lift as she tries to move closer to my tongue.

I'd chuckle but I'm too turned on. My skin is on fire, and my cock is leaking against the bed. I force myself to take my time with her, licking and gently sucking on her sweet flesh. Skye is moaning and writhing under my attentions, and I'm actually shaking with need.

"Please," she begs, as all her muscles tighten up in my arms. She's straining for release.

I want to be there when it happens. I'm too greedy. So I sit up between her legs and give myself a single, slow stroke. I'm impossibly hard. She watches with lust-darkened eyes.

"This okay?" I rasp. I lean over toward the nightstand and tug open the drawer. There's an open box of condoms right inside.

Skye doesn't say anything. So before I tear a condom off the strip, I check her face. Something has gone wrong. Her gaze is locked on the open drawer, and the condoms. Her eyes are wide with surprise. And every muscle in her body is tense.

"Skye?" I say. My voice is husky, but her alarm helps to clear my head. "What's wrong, honey?" I drop the condoms back into the drawer.

"Nothing." She shakes her head quickly. But she won't make eye contact.

"Hey." I stretch out beside her. "Look at me."

But she doesn't. She gives me a little push instead. "Get the..." She clears her throat. "Let's do this."

"Not until you tell me what's wrong." That comes out as a growl, even though I don't mean it to. I'm all keyed up.

"There's nothing wrong," she snaps.

Oh, hell no. "This is me, okay? You don't get to do that."

"Do what?" Now she turns to me, looking alarmed.

"*Lie.* Something just freaked you out, and I need to know why." Skye had a really rough time of it as a teenager. And now I'm mentally slapping myself for assuming she was down for sex without really asking.

She shakes her head. "I was just...reminded of something stupid I did once. It's fine. Everything is fine."

But she doesn't look fine. She looks the opposite of fine. I know fear when I see it. She's already gathered a sheet to cover her nakedness. She's in retreat.

And I need to cool off. I skim one of my shaking hands across her hair as a show of affection. But then—still breathing hard—I get up off the bed and steer my worked-up self into the shower.

How did I just let that happen?

Under the warm stream of water I curse myself for being so rash. The year I was eighteen, I was a paragon of fucking virtue. No matter how badly I wanted Skye, I never let myself reach for her like I wanted to. I spent an entire year hard for her. But I didn't break the seal.

Now I'm thirty and obviously far dumber.

Nice going, Rossi. You dumbass. I wash my hair instead of banging my head against the tiles like I want to.

When I emerge from the shower, the bed has been made and the bedroom is empty. For one long beat, I panic, thinking Skye is gone. But then I hear the water running in the kitchen and relax again.

Skye and I are going to have a thorough chat. Very soon.

She's avoiding, me, though. When I go into the bedroom for clean clothes, she sneaks into the bathroom for her own shower.

And, lord, she's in there forever. I wait on the living room sofa, and at least a half hour passes before she emerges freshly dressed in another short skirt that will probably melt a few more of my brain cells. Her long legs are clad in socks that don't cover her smooth knees. Her sweater looks soft and clings to all the right places.

When she gives me a sweet, tentative smile, I return it instantly.

God, I feel eighteen again. I'd forgotten how it feels to have a brain clouded with equal parts lust and affection. It's a miracle I could function at all. I remember so keenly how it felt to have her clinging to me on the back of my bike, her arms hugging my chest. It was wonderful, horrible torture.

"Benny," she says softly. "You don't have a coffeemaker? I looked everywhere."

"There's a coffee shop about twenty paces outside the door," I explain, my gaze lingering on her sweet face.

I'm so fucked.

"We might need to visit, then," she says. "I'm no fun without coffee."

I stand up. "We will. But first, could you come here a second please?"

"Why?"

"Just get your gorgeous, stylish self over here for a second. No harm will come to you."

Slowly, she draws nearer, her eyes wide.

"Closer." I open my arms. "Can I give you a hug please? It won't take but a minute of your time."

"Well sure. If you insist."

She steps into my space and I gather her up in my arms. I put my chin on her shoulder and sigh. She feels so good, and it takes about two seconds until she relaxes against me.

"That's better." I have to say it at a whisper because I don't trust my voice. "You don't have to ever be afraid of me. Not for one second."

"I wasn't afraid," she whispers.

"No? Then what happened there?"

"I can't talk about this with you." She pulls back and gives me a sheepish smile.

"Sure you can."

She shakes her head and smiles. "Too embarrassing."

"No such thing," I say. "Come here and sit with me like we used to. I need to ask you something, anyway."

She sits, and I sit right beside her, and I take her hand in mine. "Listen—I wish you hadn't stayed away for twelve years, but I understand why you did." I stroke her palm with my thumb and choose my words carefully. "Right after you left, I spent weeks trying to figure out who your aunt Jenny was, so I could call you and make sure you were okay." I squeeze her hand. "When I became a cop, I suddenly had the tools to find you. But I didn't use them."

"Why not?" she asks, then looks away, like she wishes she hadn't asked.

"Because I thought maybe you wanted to stay hidden. I knew how hard it was for you here, and I didn't want to make you think about Colebury again if it brought you pain. And it's not like I could call you up and tell you that Gage was gone. I want more than anything to be able to say that. But he's still here."

"I know. But that's not your fault." She squeezes my hand back.

It is my fault, I mentally correct her. But that conversation will come later. "Anyway, I had this idea that you were out there in the world somewhere having a great life that was no longer shadowed by that prick."

"I'm doing well," she agrees.

"I hope so. Except when I was picturing your wild, happy life, that included lots of fantastic, headboard-banging, unruly sex with someone who loves you."

She goes still beside me. "Not so much," she says slowly. "I haven't had fantastic…" She clears her throat. "But it's not because I'm traumatized or anything."

"It's not? Why then?"

"Um…" She shakes her head. "I just don't like it very well."

"Like what? Sex?"

Her cheekbones pink up as she nods her head. "I don't take to it. Sometimes I ruin the mood, like I did with you. Or—usually—I just sort of grit my teeth."

"You…grit your teeth." I know I'm repeating her again, but I really don't understand. "You weren't gritting your teeth a while ago when I had you moaning in my arms."

"Well..." She blows out a hot breath. "That part was pretty great. The lead-up can be nice. Maybe that's what all the songs are about. But the rest..." She takes her hand from mine. "It's a disappointment —like those fancy desserts that look beautiful in the glass case but taste like nothing but empty calories. You know how that is?"

"Um..." I'm stumped. "Fancy desserts and energetic sex are two of my favorite things."

"Oh. Well." She picks some invisible lint off her sweater. "To each his own, I guess."

"Help me understand," I insist. "Which parts don't you enjoy?"

"The sex part."

The sex part. Now all I can think about is sex. Sliding inside her. Making her moan for me. *Shit.* I give myself a mental slap. "Can I assume you've done a thorough study of it? With people who love you and want you to enjoy it?"

She frowns. "Not super thorough, no. Just enough to know that it isn't for me. I never see fireworks. I don't think I'm a very sexual person. "

I flash back about twenty minutes to Skye gripping my hair while I pleasure her with my tongue. *Not a sexual person* my ass.

And I know I can't just let it go at that. Not a chance. After all this time, I can't be so close to Skye without having our moment together.

Or more.

"Right, okay," I say casually. "I'll have to take your word for it. But only after one more little experiment."

"One more...what?" She looks at me with wide eyes, like a doe's.

I clear my throat and consider how to phrase this. "I want the chance to prove you wrong. One chance. One night."

"One night," she says slowly. "For..." She doesn't even finish the sentence. Sixteen-year-old Skye never said the word sex, and couldn't refer to it without blushing. It appears that twenty-eight-year-old Skye is the same.

"Fireworks," I whisper, trying not to scare her. "With me."

"Oh." Her mouth forms a perfect O, and I just want to kiss it. "But we should be focused on other things. Like finding Rayanne."

"That's a good point," I concede. "I promise we'll get to the bottom of that situation. And then I'll get my chance. Say yes."

"Maybe," she says. "Can I think about it?"

"She has to *think* about it." I tip my head back on the sofa and smile at the ceiling beams. "Sure, sweetheart. Now let's go have coffee."

TWELVE

November, Twelve Years Ago

AFTER THE SHIPLEYS' outdoor supper, all the high school kids move on toward the bonfire in the woods.

Skye walks slowly beside Benito, wishing they could just go home. The other girls probably won't talk to her. Skye doesn't mind much at school, but at a party it's just awkward.

Benito stays by her side, at least until his friends pester him to come throw a football around with them.

"Dude, come on," the Shipley cousins urge. But he hesitates.

Skye knows what she has to do. She gives him a smile to say she doesn't mind. "I'll hang here," she says.

That's when Jill Sullivan pipes up. "She can come with us."

"Of course," Zara adds with an evil smile. She hooks her arm in Skye's and sets off toward the other side of the fire.

Skye isn't fooled. Jill and Zara wouldn't suddenly decide to be her besties. But she allows herself to be led away. She'd rather be insulted for an hour than cramp Benito's style.

"Where'd you live before Vermont?" Jill asks her.

"Where *didn't* I," Skye grumbles. "Last stop was Georgia. Before that, Kansas City."

"Army brat?" Jill asks.

"No. Just brat."

Jill laughs, but Zara makes a face. "Well I've spent my whole life right here," she complains. "Nothing ever happens." Her eyes flicker toward Griff Shipley as she says it.

"Moving every few months is a drag, though," Skye assures her.

"Then why do you do it?" Jill demands.

"My mom breaks up with whichever loser she's dating, and we have to leave."

"Classy," Jill says.

Skye only shrugs, because she's right.

"Let's drink already," Zara says. She digs into her purse for the bottle of rum her brother gave her. Jill has brought red plastic cups and a gallon of freshly pressed cider she brought from the Shipleys' cooler.

Skye doesn't ever drink. The New Girl can't, really. Too dangerous. But Benito is close by, and he won't let anything bad happen to her. So she takes the cup that Zara offers her.

The cider is sweet, and the rum is strong. It blurs Zara's evil smirk, and it mutes the cold seeping through her thin clothing.

She finishes the cup, and lets Jill pour her another.

Meanwhile, Benito tosses the ball around, and then drinks a beer with Griffin and his cousin, Kyle.

"You tapping that new girl?" Kyle asks.

"No," he says quickly. "She's only sixteen." That's not the real issue, of course. But he isn't willing to say more.

"You *want* to, though," Griffin says with a grin. "Who wouldn't?"

Benito is guilty as charged. Now he scans the faces around bonfire, looking for Skye's shining hair. But she isn't there. "You kids have fun," he says, tossing the ball to Griff.

"Thanks for bringing the beer!" his friends call after him.

"No problem!" He circles the bonfire, looking for his favorite girl. But there's no sign of her. Panic makes his pulse thrum as he wanders through the trees, stumbling past couples making out on the pine needles.

If anyone is taking advantage of Skye, he's going to lose his mind.

And then finally he spots her, slumped against a tree trunk, Jill and Zara standing over her, laughing.

"Hey there," Jill Sullivan says, standing straighter. "What's up, Benny? Want a sip?" She offers him a silver flask containing God knows what. The Sullivans have money, so it's probably her daddy's liquor.

He sees an empty rum bottle cast aside on the ground.

His eyes dart to Zara, who's smirking, and Skye, who's looking up at him with a lopsided smile on her face. There's a fuzzy look in her eye.

"What did you do?" he barks at Zara. "What did you give her?"

Zara's expression hardens. "It's just alcohol. Nobody's dying. She has the tolerance of a toddler, turns out. Not very sexy if you ask me."

Skye drops her chin in an attempt to disguise her injured expression.

"Why are you such a bitch?" he snarls at his sister.

"Why are you so boring all the time now?" she spits back.

Benito will have to deal with her later. "Come here," he says to Skye, offering her his hand.

She grasps it with icy fingers, pulling herself up slowly. "I'm cold," she whispers, shivering.

He can't even look at Zara as he tucks Skye against his hip and guides her slowly toward the car, one arm wrapped around her. She doesn't even have a real coat.

"I don't feel so good," she says as they approach his brother's taxi.

"I'll bet."

"Just..." She shoves him away suddenly, then lurches toward the tree line. Doubling over, she heaves into the grass.

"Hey," he says as she gags. He gathers her silken hair in one hand and holds it out of the way. "You're okay..."

"I *know* that," she barks, straightening up. "God. Just give me a minute here." When she turns to face him there's anger on her face.

He takes a quick step backward, although the fire in her eyes shouldn't surprise him. It must take real grit to survive in that hellish household where she lives.

Benito gives her space. She's sick, and it's his fault. Zara is angry at him for God knows what. This year she's been sucked into Mean Girl hell by that flake she's staying with.

He should have known they'd fuck with Skye. He should have prevented it.

Skye brings out a fierce protective streak in Benito. He always knew it was there. He'd take a bullet for his mom, his sister or any of his brothers. But, man. Skye makes him crazy. At least once a day he has to take a few calm, deep breaths to avoid going postal on her idiot mother or that scum of a cop Skye lives with.

He watches Skye pull herself together. Her back to him, she spits. She wipes her mouth on a scrap of something she's found in her pocket. Then she straightens her spine and stands tall.

She's a quiet girl, but she never looks beaten. That's why the other girls are intimidated by her. It's not just her pretty face. It's all that silent dignity. "Okay, sorry," she says. "We can go now."

Her walk is still a little unsteady, but he doesn't comment. He just tucks her into the car and then gets in on the driver's side and starts the engine. But he doesn't drive away just yet. "Need a minute?"

"Probably a good idea," she sighs.

It's so dark that the sky above them is filled with stars. Benito reaches across the seat and takes her cold hands. And when Skye's fingers close around his, it's enough. There's so much more he wants, but somehow this is still wonderful.

She doesn't seem sick anymore, but she starts to nod off. So he starts toward home. When they pull into Pine View Park, it's quarter past eleven. Skye's mom's car isn't there, and Benito knows it will be another hour before she shows up after her diner shift.

Unfortunately, the temperature outside is plunging fast. He sits there in the car with the sleeping Skye for a few minutes, but the chill sets in immediately. "Come on," he whispers. "I can make a fire."

Skye startles awake. She squints at the darkened trailers and groans. "I just want to go to bed."

"I'll bet. But your mom isn't home yet."

Skye gets out of the car. She walks toward her trailer.

Benito follows her in a hurry. "What are you doing?"

Her eyes flare, and she raises a finger to her lips. "The TV is off," she mouths. "It's dark. He's asleep already."

She might be right, but he can't just let her go in there alone—not like this. He follows her up the makeshift steps. She turns around, eyebrows raised. "I have to be sure," he says at the barest whisper.

Skye hesitates. But then she unlocks the door with her key and steps inside.

It is quiet. And Gage is audibly snoring from one of the bedrooms.

"See?" Skye mouths.

He does. But drunk girls aren't very quiet. And Skye is obviously inebriated. Benito has ugly visions of Gage finding her in this state and...

He can't even finish the thought without feeling nauseated.

Skye tiptoes into her bedroom with Benito on her heels. "Get ready for bed," he says right into her ear. "I'll wait here until you're tucked in."

She gives him an angry frown, but he doesn't care. He sits on the bed, reaching over to unlock her window in case he needs to make a quick escape. He could always listen from outside, he supposes.

Skye spends some time in the bathroom. As he suspected, she isn't very quiet.

But Gage's snores don't cease. He might have hit the bottle pretty hard himself tonight.

Eventually his favorite girl returns wearing a giant North Carolina T-shirt and sleep shorts. She locks her flimsy door, and Benito stands up so she can get into her twin-sized bed.

"How are you going to get out of here?" she whispers as she climbs into bed.

"The window. Duh."

She smiles up at him. "You're insane."

"That's probably true." He puts a hand on the side of her face, his thumb stroking her cheekbone. He doesn't usually allow himself to touch her like this, but Skye lying down in bed is doing crazy things to his body. And she's leaning into his touch. "I'll leave after you fall asleep. How's your stomach?"

She makes a face. "I'll live. I'm never drinking again."

"We all say that at one point." They're whispering so quietly that Benito has to bend down close to communicate. He wants to climb into that bed and hold her, but he won't do it. He looks around the darkened room to distract himself. "You're a big fan of Kanye?"

"That's Rayanne's. You must know her."

"Sure. Nice girl."

Skye grins sleepily. "Nice isn't the word I'd use. Fun. Crazy. Lively."

"Yeah," he whispers. "True. But how do *you* know her?"

"We lived with Gage before—when I was five and she was seven. She made him bearable."

"I'll bet." It's hard to imagine Gage being anyone's dad. No wonder Rayanne got the hell out of here right after graduation.

"I think he put up with my mom so that he'd have someone to take care of his kid," Skye whispers. "Not sure why he puts up with Mom now. Except..." Skye clears her throat, and her eyes dart toward the wall—the one separating her little room from the other bedroom. She makes a face and changes the subject. "What are you doing after graduation?"

"Joining the army," Benito whispers. "They'll help me pay for college later."

"*Oh*," Skye says slowly. "That's...soon."

"Yeah," he admits. Graduation is six or seven months away. They stare into each other's eyes for a long beat. Benito can't imagine just walking away and leaving Skye here.

Saying goodbye? Unthinkable.

He shoves that thought aside for now. He hears the sound of a car on the gravel drive outside. Skye's eyes widen. It's probably her mother.

"It's okay," he mouths.

And it is. They listen in silence while her mother enters the house. A sink runs in the bathroom, and the toilet flushes.

Skye holds his hand. The trailer settles into silence again.

Benito waits a little longer, so her mom will be asleep when he sneaks out. He strokes Skye's hair, and her eyes flutter closed. Her breathing levels out.

Benito waits ten more minutes. Then he leans down and places a single kiss on Skye's hairline.

But that's all. Just the one. And then he jumps out the window and goes home.

THIRTEEN

Skylar

I NEED COFFEE VERY BADLY. My brain sure isn't working. If it was, I wouldn't have rubbed my naked body all over Benito's and then panicked when he decided it was time for sex.

Ugh. I can't believe that happened. He's been *so* nice about it. And now he says he wants us to try again sometime? The man is obviously a glutton for punishment.

"Do you have a jacket?" Benito asks, shrugging his on.

"No," I say with a sigh. "Rayanne drove off with it."

"You can wear mine. Or you can borrow a zip up sweatshirt to wear over that sweater. I'd offer you a pair of sweats in place of that little skirt, but I don't think Skye 2.0 would be seen in public in those."

"Skye 2.0?"

He grins, and I feel fluttery again. "You look fancy, honey. I liked the other Skye just fine. But this one doesn't wear sweats even to a coffee shop on a Saturday, does she?"

"No," I admit. Not that there's anything wrong with sweats. But I always dress well, and I don't usually ponder my motive. After all— style doesn't need a reason, right?

But suddenly I have the nagging suspicion that I've spent the last twelve years trying not to look like a trailer-park kid. That's a long time to be running away from my past, isn't it?

This keeps happening—I've been back in Vermont for less than twelve hours, and I've already had a dozen brain-exploding moments. I don't know how many more I can take without doing lasting damage.

"Here—how about this?" Benito hands me a flannel shirt that's lined with fleece. "To keep you warm. What else can I give you? Hat? Gloves?"

"I wouldn't say no to gloves."

He finds me a pair. I watch Benito holster his gun, and then we walk downstairs together. As we step out the door, I notice that the air is crisp and scented with pine and wood smoke.

I feel a little tug of sentiment that I never expected to feel. Vermont smells nice. It's about the only nice thing I can say about this place.

Oh, and Vermont gives good scenery. Forget the Green Mountains —I mean the hot guy in the leather jacket who puts a hand on the small of my back as we cross the gravel parking lot.

It's a short trip. Benito wasn't kidding when he said the coffee shop was right outside. The shop is called the Busy Bean, and when Benito opens the door for me, I fall immediately in love. The interior is adorable, with comfortable, mismatched furniture and a long counter stacked with luscious baked goods.

There is also a seriously cute guy wearing a baker's apron behind the counter. And he's talking with…

Uh-oh.

Oh, *shishkebab.*

The moment I identify her, Zara Rossi turns her head and spots me, too. And just as my inner sixteen-year-old starts to flinch, some-thing unexpected happens. Zara's mouth falls open. She takes in me and her brother. Benito pauses, putting an arm around my shoulder.

And then? Zara's eyes *get wet.* Or maybe I'm hallucinating, because she quickly looks away.

It's the weirdest thing I ever saw in my life.

"BIMBO!" someone shouts, startling me. When I look down, there is a small person with very red hair hugging Benito's knees.

He leans down and scoops her off the floor. "Hi, Nicky. Say hello to my friend, Skye."

The small person considers me with a brown-eyed squint that is so much like Zara's that it's eerie. "Huhwoh," she says coolly.

I laugh. "Wow. I thought cloning was illegal."

"Right?" Benito kisses her on the head, and I can practically feel my ovaries dance a jig.

"What did she call you?" I ask. "Did she say, *bimbo?*"

"I'm pretty sure it was Benbo," he corrects.

"BIMBO!" the toddler yells. Then she grins evilly.

I love her already.

Benito gives me a nudge with his free hand. "Let's order some coffee. My sister doesn't bite."

I'm not so sure that's true. But Zara has wiped her eyes after that strange attack and is plastering what is supposed to pass for a smile on her face. So I step forward.

"Skylar," she says with a sniff. "I'm so happy to see you."

Okay, that's even more unexpected than almost having sex with her brother. "You too," I say stiffly.

Her smile gets more realistic. "I'll bet. Now what can I get you?"

"This is your place?" I look around at the dark wood and the pretty old windows. "It's really nice."

"Thank you! My business partner and I worked hard at it. I'd introduce you to Audrey Shipley, but she's on maternity leave."

"Shipley," I repeat slowly. "I don't remember an Audrey."

Zara's smile turns wry. "Nope. She's a flatlander. Showed up here three years ago to fall madly in love with Griffin."

"*Oh.*" It used to be Zara who was madly in love with Griffin. I guess if you leave a place for twelve years, a few things are bound to change.

"Audrey's the best," Zara says easily. "It's her kickass recipe for pumpkin muffins that we're serving today." She jerks her thumb toward a display of fat muffins with cream-cheese frosting. "The pretzel bagel with smoked salmon is also great. And we've got choco-late chip banana bread if you're into that. But personally I don't think chocolate chips belong in banana bread."

"Want it," the toddler on Benito's chest says.

"You already got yours," Zara says. "Skylar?"

"The, uh, pumpkin muffin, please. And a large coffee. Thank you."

"Double that order," Benito says, taking out his wallet.

Zara waves his money away. "Special occasion."

"Wait, what?" Benito gasps. I assume he's just kidding around until I get a look at his face. "Who are you, and what have you done with Zara? Or is there something wrong with the muffins? Bad batch?"

"No! Jesus." She bites her lip. "Don't look a gift horse in the mouth."

"Thank you," he says. "You're my favorite sister."

And his *only* sister. She moves away to pour our coffee without comment.

"Usually you pay, huh?" I ask, still finding her behavior strange.

"Sure. If you have four brothers who really like baked goods, you kinda have to put your foot down. Between Zara and Audrey they're related to half the county."

"Good point." I look around again. "This place is great. And that baby is seriously cute."

"*Not* baby." The little girl pouts. She doesn't think much of me. It must be genetic.

"I know you're a big girl," Benito says. Then he pretends to stagger under her weight, which only makes her giggle. My ovaries start twerking again. Even when Benito was a teen-aged motorcycle-riding bad boy, he was still sweet. Picturing him with kids was never that hard.

I'm in deep, deep trouble here.

Zara sets two full mugs and two plates down on the counter. "Trade you," she says, holding out her arms for her daughter. "I have to run upstairs and hand her off to Alec."

"Mom's not babysitting today?"

"Not 'til later. She's getting her hair done." Zara takes her daughter and leaves the shop.

I watch her go, a million questions in my mind. Like—how is she still so beautiful? What redheaded man is her baby's father? And how did everyone grow up to be functional adults, owning coffee shops and bars, while I'm still struggling with my first job out of college?

Revisiting my past is trippy.

Benito somehow carries all our goodies over to a cute little sofa facing a marble-topped table. On my way to join him I pass a support beam that functions as a blackboard. Some amusing person has chalked the following sentiment up there: *If you love someone, set him free. If he returns with a cup of coffee, he's a keeper.*

Benito sits down and pats the sofa cushion beside him. When I sit, he puts an arm around me. "You good?"

"Yep. Just taking it all in."

He grins, and then hands me a mug of coffee. "Must be weird seeing all of us again. And if you'd asked me nine months ago who Nicole's daddy was, I couldn't have told you."

"I wouldn't have asked," I say quickly. "I'm not nosy."

Lies, lies, lies! I'm totally nosy.

He smiles, as if he can hear my thoughts. "No—I meant I couldn't have told you because I didn't know. Zara had a fling with a professional athlete. Then they went their separate ways for two years. It was all kinds of drama. But then he came back this past summer and now they're going strong together."

"Wow." I take a big bite of the muffin and then moan. "Oh my God. This is so good."

Benito chuckles. "I can tell."

"No really." I take another bite, and it's just as amazing.

"Jesus, honey." Benito shifts in his seat. "I'm getting all riled up over here. You keep making that noise, we're going to have to finish breakfast naked."

"What? Oh." I suppress a shiver when I realize what he means, and on the next bite I manage not to moan again.

"Look." Benito watches me with warm eyes. "I'm sad to say I have to go to work for a couple of hours. You can hang out here or at my place." He puts a set of keys down next to my phone on the coffee table.

"Okay," I say around a bite of muffin. "You don't have to do that, I could, uh..." I try to think of somewhere else I could go and come up blank.

"Please. Take my keys. The front door code is May Shipley's birthday." He rattles off a date. "Six digits. And will you let me know if you hear anything from Raye? If she texts you, try to ask questions. If I could find her and question her, this whole situation could be cleared up."

"But she doesn't want that," I argue. "And anyway, I know she's not into drugs." Is she? Are there yoga instructors who do drugs? "Is it pot?"

He shrugs, unreadable.

"Ben!"

"You don't want to know. I need you to trust me. Can you do that?"

"Yes." I always have before. "But if Rayanne is somehow involved, please remember that it might not be her choice."

"I get that. I really do. Let me do my job and find her again." He eats the last bite of his muffin, drains his coffee and stands up. "Text me when she makes contact with you."

"Okay."

"I probably can't answer you right away if I'm on the job. But text me if you need anything at all. The Wi-Fi password in the coffee shop is *busybean*. In my apartment it's on a sticker on the bottom of the modem. If you have any questions about my place, ask Zara. She lived there last summer."

"Thank you. I will." It's a lie, though. If I was drowning I wouldn't ask Zara for a lifeboat. She'd probably run me over with it.

Benito kisses me on top of the head. "Be well. I'll be back in time for a late lunch. I hope."

"I'll be fine," I say, and give him an awkward wave. Then I stare at his butt as he walks away. He really fills out a pair of jeans.

Good lord. Even if sex is not my thing, I can still enjoy the view.

I finish my excellent coffee. Zara may be a bitch but she makes a nice cup of joe. The coffee table has a daily edition of *The Colebury Standard*. Since I've got little else to do but worry, I pick it up, sit back on the sofa and scan it.

For a local rag, it's not bad. I'm something of a newspaper connoisseur at this point. This year I've sent résumés to every news outlet in New York and New Jersey, hoping to land a better job. I'd love to work for a struggling local paper as long as they let me do some real reporting.

Let's face it—I hate doing the traffic and weather in low-cut tops. But jobs are scarce, and I don't have great bylines to prove my worth. Every time I apply for an opening, the job is always filled internally. I am rarely even interviewed.

This week's local news is pretty grim. The lead story is: "Twelve Overdoses in One Month: New Vermont Record." There's a photo of a smiling farm boy who died just last week. He was found on the floor of his parents bathroom after shooting up. There was fentanyl as well as heroin in his bloodstream.

"*Fentanyl is really lethal,*" the local drug-awareness counselor says in a quote. "*Even experienced drug users have a high risk of accidental overdose.*"

Sadly, it's not the first time I've read this story. It's a national pattern. First-time users get hooked on prescription painkillers. When those get too expensive, they switch to street drugs like heroin and fentanyl—a synthetic drug that's made in a lab, so it's super strong. Pure fentanyl is so potent that a dose the size of a peppercorn is enough to kill several people.

I skim the article again before letting the newspaper slide off my lap. Is this what Benito is working on? Is this what Jimmy Gage is doing these days?

The burner phone chimes from inside my bag, and I actually jump, because the sound is unfamiliar.

Checking in. Nothing to report, Rayanne has written.

Well that's just underwhelming. I could sit here for days at this rate. *You need to tell me what you're doing,* I text back. *Benito thinks maybe you're involved with something bad. So if you'd just explain yourself he won't keep thinking up ways to find you.*

Nice try, she replies immediately. *But we're doing this my way. I don't trust anyone.*

Not even me? I ask. That's low.

I trust that you care about me. But you think I'm a screw-up just like everyone else. If I told you the whole story you'd tell Hot Cop, and that would get me killed. I know what I'm doing and I don't have time to listen to your arguments.

Well, darn it. For once I don't have a comeback. *I hate this. Be safe.*

I will. Raffie?

Yes?

Did you do him yet? Was it hot?

And now I'm mortified, because Benito will see this message. And even if he wouldn't, I still wouldn't know how to answer. Because the truth is that I came close and then bailed. *I don't know what you're talking about,* I reply.

She sends me an eggplant emoji. And then a laughing emoji. Rayanne is the worst. But she's all I have.

I'm grumpy now, and grumpiness requires a second cup of coffee. I pull a five out of my wallet, but leave my handbag on the sofa. That's something I'd never do in New York, but the seven other customers in the Busy Bean are too busy with their own conversations to steal my Kate Spade.

The cute guy is minding the counter. "Can I help you?"

"Could I have a cup of coffee?" I slide my five toward him.

"Sure." He pushes the money back. "But Zara said your money is no good here."

"Why?" That makes no sense.

He shrugs. "Enjoy it, because I never heard her say that before." He refills my cup with a smile.

I can't imagine why Zara suddenly wants to buy me coffee. It's the weirdest thing.

But I have bigger mysteries to solve. So I go back to my seat and drink my coffee while pondering Jimmy Gage. From a comfortable seat in the world's coziest coffee shop, I can think of him as a puzzle to be solved, and not the scariest person in my former life.

Staying away for twelve years means that I don't have too many facts, though. I know that he's no longer a cop. Rayanne told me he lost that job a couple of years ago when the Colebury police chief went to jail and the new guy cleaned house. That's really all she'd told me because she knows I don't like hearing his name. But she assumed I'd like hearing that he got fired.

She was right. I did like it. But now I wished I'd asked more questions.

Paging Dr. Google.

I pull out my phone, but a search on his name isn't very illuminating. There's only a one-line mention of his departure from the police force. And when I search the Vermont Department of Corrections for his name, I come up dry. So he hasn't ever been incarcerated.

If I had my office laptop I could perform a background check. But I don't, thanks to McCracken.

All I have are more newspaper articles on the internet about New England's fentanyl problem. There are plenty of these, and I spend the next two hours reading about the flow of drugs from the big East Coast cities. Dealers drive it into Massachusetts, New Hampshire, and Vermont, touring the smaller towns like a low-budget rock band playing smaller clubs. By driving the drugs into rural areas, dealers can charge two or three times what they can on the streets of a big city.

Maybe Jimmy Gage saw a business opportunity? An ex-cop would already know all the lowlifes in this area. Even without his badge, they might still be afraid of him.

It's all speculation on my part. But that man is capable of *anything*. And the newspaper is full of dying kids.

I stand up, drain the last of my cold coffee, and put on Benito's fleecy shirt. It's time for a walk.

"Need anything?" Zara asks when I carry my cup and plate to the bussing station. "You can stay as long as you want."

"No thanks," I say, giving her a wary smile. I want to believe that anyone can grow and change. But this girl hated me back in the day. "I'm going outside to get a little exercise."

"Have fun," she says with a friendly wave.

I don't trust it.

Outside, I cross the parking lot and run upstairs to put my bag in Benito's apartment. Then I tuck my wallet and his keys into my pocket and leave.

I head uphill like I did last night. The idea of entering Rayanne's ransacked house isn't quite as scary in the watery March sunshine.

When I reach the house, the key is still under the Buddha statue, just like she'd said it would be. I open the door. "Hello!" I call hopefully.

Silence.

I walk in and close the door behind me, surveying the mess. It's startling to see my stepsister's belongings tossed around. But Rayanne doesn't have a lot of clutter in her life, so it won't take me long to clean up. I move around the living room, placing all the yoga magazines in a tidy pile on the coffee table. The yoga mats and blocks are easily stacked.

The only broken thing in this room is some kind of diffuser for essential oils. She'll have to replace that. But I take the time to tidy up her books, straightening them on her shelves. Their covers feature yogis looking calm and enlightened. And—fine—they look just a bit smug. Whatever.

I move lovingly through the house, straightening up Rayanne's possessions and looking for clues. Where is my stepsister, who tossed her house, and why did she want that kayak?

Upstairs, Rayanne's bedroom floor is covered in clothes, and the drawers are all open. But I don't pick up the clothes because I spot something on top of the dresser. It's a laptop. I tap the keyboard a couple of times, and the screen blinks to life. It's not even password protected.

Benito seems to think that Rayanne could be involved in something illegal. But *come on*. No password?

I stand there in her messy room and open the browser, pulling up a map of the state of Vermont. If I were a kayaker, I guess Lake Champlain would be the obvious destination. It's huge, and has great access to New York State.

Would a drug dealer care about water travel, though? To get to New York you can drive over a bridge or take the ferry. And the amount of drugs a girl could fit into kayak is smaller than in a car.

I really want to believe that Rayanne is innocent. But who goes boating in fifty-degree weather? It's something to consider.

The jerk who ransacked this house has knocked Rayanne's garbage over on the kitchen floor. Apparently my sister likes kimchi, bananas and whole-wheat tortillas. It's starting to stink already. So I gather up the garbage and shove it in a fresh bag. Then I take the whole mess out the back door.

Outside, I scan the garage. There's a pickup truck parked in there, facing out. But no room for trash. Turning, I locate two metal trash cans against the back wall of the house. One is full already, and smelly as heck. But the other one is empty except for a cardboard box in the bottom. Before I can drop the trash onto it, the photo on the box catches my eye.

I grab the box out of the can—is this is some classic investigative reporting, or what? Then I dump the trash and read every word on the box, which once contained an action camera—the kind that you can strap onto a helmet. The very enthusiastic packaging explains all its uses. *Skiing! Boating! Wherever life takes you!*

The camera is waterproof and it comes with both a chest strap and a helmet attachment. *Interesting.* Rayanne has a sporty boat and a sporty camera. Either she's giving up yoga to make river-rafting videos, or there's something else she wants to film...

The sound of knocking stops me cold. Three distant, muffled raps, probably on Rayanne's front door. "Raye!" a gruff voice says. "You in there?"

It's not an exaggeration to say that I am suddenly frozen with fear. Because that voice belongs to Jimmy Gage. And I'm the idiot who'd left the front door open for him.

Later, I'd realize that darting toward the back of Rayanne's property line would have gotten me out of there quicker. But I'm sixteen again and terrified. I'm like a bunny trying to make itself invisible to the wolf, cowering against the back of the house, clutching the cardboard camera packaging.

The only act of self-preservation I manage is to crouch down, hiding myself from view of the kitchen window.

"Hey, Rayanne? Where are you?" My body flashes hot and cold as his voice advances toward me. I hear his footsteps on her kitchen floor, and I couldn't breathe even if I wanted to.

"Sparks, she's not here," he says from a terrifyingly close distance. The wall is the only thing separating us. "Place is fine. Why would you ask?"

Terror creeps down my spine, and I feel sick. How many people are in Rayanne's house?

It takes me another minute to realize he's having a phone conversation. "She's just not home. Her truck's in the garage. Maybe her hippie friends took 'er to a yoga retreat. And since when do you ask the questions, fuckwad? My kid is a flake, but *you're* a meddling asshole. Just do your job and keep us out of the fucking papers. You're wasting my time right now."

The back door creaks open and then immediately bangs shut, and I startle like the virgin in a horror movie.

But then the sound of Gage's voice dampens, as if he's facing away from me. "I'm going to grab lunch, and afterward..." His side of the conversation recedes. Still, I nearly swallow my heart. I think he might be leaving.

I wait, listening to my heart pound. But Jimmy Gage does not reappear at the back door, or anywhere in the yard. At some point I hear a car start and drive away, but I don't look. You couldn't pay me to move from this spot.

The silence deepens. Eventually it's replaced by other neighborhood noises. The chatter of a pair of joggers running down the block. A truck rumbling past. Gage is gone, but it takes me a little while longer to move. I basically scramble to a section of wall that has no window and stand up. I shake out my legs and then finally bolt toward the property line. A row of pines conceals a neighboring house. I run through the yard and then down the driveway, finally arriving at a sidewalk.

Slowing down, I try to stop acting like a crazy person. I walk down the sidewalk, wondering where to go. I feel exposed. I turn on my phone and send a text to Benito with shaky fingers. *Call me when you can*.

I would give anything right now to climb onto that giant old lounge chair in the woods and lay my head on his shoulder—the only place in Vermont where I'd ever felt safe.

FOURTEEN

Benito

I'M SITTING on the tailgate of a pickup truck, surrounded by roofing equipment. The truck is parked in an empty parking lot beside a now defunct big-box store in a Vermont town that's seen better days. I'm drinking coffee and waiting for the dealer to show up.

He's five minutes late, maybe because he had to pull over and shoot up to keep himself on the level.

I can wait. I'm patient like that.

After another ten minutes, a junker of a car winds its way toward me. My pulse kicks up a notch, but I won't let it show. I've done this dozens of times before, and I'm trained for any contingency.

There are two men in the car, which is one more than I'd hoped to see. The passenger gets out, and he's the guy I was expecting. So that's not so weird. I glance at the other guy without staring.

White. Thirties. Scruffy beard. Patriots cap.

I drain my coffee as the dealer approaches. Like I don't have a care in the world. "Thought you were gonna stand me up," I say calmly. "Coffee's gone and I need something with more of a kick."

The skinny dude gives me a weak smile. "Show me some skin."

I slip a twenty out of the pocket of my flannel shirt. "Here."

He takes it from my fingers. Then he gives me a weird little smile. That's the first indication that something is wrong.

My senses dial up immediately. I'm aware of everything around me. The other man in the car never shut off the motor. But now I hear the engine change its tune. Like he put it back in gear.

"You gonna give me the stuff or what?" I ask.

"Here's what's gonna happen," the dealer says. "Slowly reach for your wallet. Hand it over."

"Oh man," I sigh. This tool just bought himself a longer stay in prison. "And what if I don't?"

"You will." He shifts his jacket a little to show me a pistol that's pointed at me.

"Jesus." The weapon adds more years to his sentence. "Maybe don't point that thing at me while I get my wallet?"

"Just do it now. With one hand," he adds.

"Fine. Just take my whole wallet, okay? I don't need to spend all day with your gun pointed at—"

"FREEZE. VERMONT STATE POLICE!" my team shouts as they pop out of the shuttered storefront. "ON THE GROUND! HANDS OVER YOUR HEAD."

The second he whirls in the direction of the bullhorn, I kick my would-be attacker in the nuts. He goes down like a tree in a windstorm.

That's when his friend guns it, trying to drive away.

My guys let the accelerating car get well clear of me before they shoot out a tire. Meanwhile, I've got cuffs around the perp, who's moaning about his balls on the cold asphalt.

He has a reason to moan. Instead of merely selling drugs to an officer of the law, he's amped that shit up to armed robbery.

"You good?" a deputy asks me.

"Yup. Search 'im."

So I've had worse mornings. As a member of Vermont's drug task force, I frequently drive to towns around the state to buy drugs from small-time scumbags. These two will be arrested. At which time they'll be interviewed extensively to see if they can provide information about bigger, scummier scumbags.

When we drag this much manpower out for a bust, we're hoping to move things up the chain. We want this guy's supplier more than we want this guy.

That's the game. Little busts, followed by lots of questions, followed by more little busts. We inch our way up the chain until we can get to the guy who's bringing all the drugs into Vermont.

That guy is Jimmy Gage. I'm close to getting direct evidence against him. So close.

Meanwhile, these two perps are shoved into the backs of two different police vehicles for their rides to the station, so I'm done for now. I hand off my wire and the video device concealed on the pickup truck. Then I shake a few hands and get gone.

There will be paperwork.

But first, it's time to check in on another project.

———

That goes less well.

"Bring me evidence," Colebury's police chief barks from beneath his unruly mustache. "If you don't have video, the D.A. can't build a case. And if you can't build a case, you're just wasting my officer's time."

I know this. And he knows I know this. But the stubborn old fool won't give me any more manpower. I don't work for the town, I work for the state. My job is to help guys like Lewis stem the flow of drugs into their counties. But cooperation takes two.

Some guys are more cooperative than others.

"I'll get that video," I say carefully. "But I'll get it faster if you give me Nelligan full time."

"No can do," he says immediately. "You can't steal my officer to work a case in another county."

I feel a splash of anger hit me. *Careful*, I warn myself. My temper was a problem when I was younger. But now I'm better at not losing my shit when guys like Lewis won't do the right thing. The man is so short-sighted.

We both know that Gage is breaking the law right here in Colebury. Just because he's picking up his drugs from fifty miles north of here doesn't mean I'm pillaging his resources.

"I'm going to lay waste to the dealer network in Colebury," I say quietly. "He's moving lethal stuff through your town. I can stop him faster with your help."

His shrug is completely indifferent. "The week after you nail Gage I'll have fresh faces peddling heroin in the alleys. And there's no shortage of fucktards lining up to buy that shit and jam it into their veins."

And there it is—the reason he doesn't care. Law enforcement needs to see opioid addiction as a disease, not a moral failing. But some of these guys just can't view it that way. They think users just deserve what they get.

I can't make him care. So I try another tack.

"A Colebury girl is missing. I think something is going on inside the organization."

Lewis nods. "If a missing-persons report is filed, Nelligan can investigate. Let me know if she turns up. Let me know if that camera of yours spots a Colebury resident climbing out of that lake. Then we can search her house and tap her phone and her whole damn life. Until then, good luck to you."

Fuck. I want to break something. Instead I say, "Thank you sir." It's my only line. I have no leverage over this man. I'm too new at this job and my case is still developing.

Irritated, I go outside.

My job is complicated. And since last night, my life is also complicated. And one of these things looks like it's gonna calm down soon. But now it's time for lunch.

I check my texts and spot Skye's request for me to call her. *I'm free now. Can I take you to lunch?*

Her reply is almost instantaneous. *Can you come get me?* she asks. *I'm up the hill in Colebury.*

Sure. Where?

She starts tapping her response right away. *There's a street that runs behind Rayanne's street. I'm there.*

That's a strange choice. But maybe she took a walk? *Be there in two minutes,* I reply, because Colebury is a small town.

Sure enough, when I coast past a tiny neighborhood playground, her head swivels from where she's seated on a bench, her back to me.

And I'm floored all over again. Seeing her again is a shock to my system. Countless nights I've had dreams just like this—that I'd look up to finally see her face.

Ten years ago, when the ache was still fresh, I used to look for her in crowds. I wondered where she was, what she was doing. I wanted to know if she had friends, and if she ever thought about her difficult year in Vermont.

I'm in a dream state even as Skye moves quickly on long legs toward the car. She slides into the passenger seat and then slams the door. "Thank you," she says, exhaling.

"Don't mention it. How do you feel about burritos?"

"I saw him."

"Who?" It takes me a beat, but all at once I understand. "Seriously? You saw Gage?"

"Well, I *heard* him. I was in Rayanne's house, looking around. I went out the back door to throw something in her garbage can. And he came in the front door, talking on the phone. I heard his voice. It was definitely him. I *know* what he sounds like." Her voice is shaking.

"Okay," I say, pulling over and putting the car in park. "Are you all right?"

She gulps. "Yeah. Of course."

But that's the same answer she always used to give me. And when I look closer, she's too pale. "Take a deep breath, honey. Can I pick up some takeout food and drive you home?"

She nods quickly. "Okay."

I clasp her hand in mine. "Do you have any idea what Gage was doing at Rayanne's place?"

"Looking for her." She swallows hard. "He told whoever was on the other end of the phone that she was just flaky that maybe she went away for the weekend."

I chew on that for a minute. I still can't figure out exactly how Rayanne is involved. But if Gage doesn't know where she is, maybe she's not in as deeply as I thought.

Or maybe she's trying to get out.

"God, I *hate* feeling like this. It's like..." Her voice is panicky. "I heard his voice, and I'm sixteen years old again and cowering in that bedroom. *This* is why I don't come back to Vermont."

All I can do is reach across the gearbox and take her other hand, too. "I get it," I say.

She's silent for a moment. "I'm so *angry*. That's what I didn't expect. All this rage." She won't look at me. She's staring out the window.

And I can barely breathe. Because it's a cruel trick to have her back and to know that the same evil man is still standing between me and Skye, and between Skye and happiness.

"I'm going to get him," I promise. "I'm going to lock him up. For you and Zara and everyone he's ever harmed."

She lets out a breath. "He was gone from my life until I came back here."

My stomach dives. "You can get on the train to New York tonight. I'll find the Jeep, and I'll find Rayanne." I am making a shitload of promises right now but I mean every one of them. "You can go home."

She turns her chin to look at me, and her eyes blaze with anger. "I want to see her. And I want to help you get him."

"You can't help," I say quickly. That's not even a little bit practical. "But you can stay as long as you like. Let's have some lunch and figure a couple of things out."

"Okay," she says. Then she gives me a tiny smile. "You're the only good guy on earth, Benito. Swear to God."

It's not true. But I sure like hearing it.

FIFTEEN

Skye

_____

BEN STOPS at a little roadside food truck called Sally's Soups. I fidget in the front seat for the entire six minutes that he's out of the car.

Calm down, I order myself, but it doesn't really work. Until I'd heard Gage's voice, I was able to convince myself that Rayanne was a drama queen who'd made my weekend awkward on purpose.

All it took was sixty seconds of terror to remind me that some people in the world are just scary.

"Hey." Benito's voice is gentle as he slides into the driver's seat and hands me a warm sack. "Hang on to this for ten minutes, and then you can choose between clam chowder and chicken tortilla."

We end up going halfsies, splitting both soups while sitting on Benito's sofa. There are fresh rolls and butter, too. After eating, I feel almost restored.

"Better?" he asks, handing me a cup of peppermint tea.

"Yeah." His presence is more impactful than the soup. I keep this to myself, but it's true. He was always able to make me feel safe, even sitting in the woods in the wintery breeze.

The brick walls and shining floorboards of his apartment are about a million steps up from our old hangout. Benito's place feels impenetrable, although my better mood has more to do with the hot cop beside me than the deadbolt on his door.

"I need to ask you a few questions," he says. "About the conversation you overheard."

"All right."

"Do you know who Gage was talking to? Did he use a name?"

"Um, I feel like he did use a name. But…" I'd been so terrified, I hadn't taken much in. "I wasn't trying to eavesdrop."

Ben gives me a smile. "I get that. Just tell me what tone he was using. Was he happy? Mad?"

"Gruff," I say slowly. "His tone was sort of bitchy. Like he was talking to a subordinate." As soon as I start talking, more of it comes back to me. "The guy was asking questions about Rayanne, and Gage didn't like it. He was sort of telling the guy to mind his own business and get back to whatever it was that Gage needed him to do."

"And the name?" Benito presses. "Was it long or short?"

"Not long. Just…" I wrack my brain. "One syllable. Not *Mark,* but something abrupt like that."

"Like…Sparks?"

My head jerks back with recognition. "Yes. Sparks. How did you know?"

"Just a hunch." Benito picks up my hand and gives it a squeeze. "So Sparks was asking Gage questions about Rayanne?"

"It seemed that way—like he wanted to know where she was. But Gage was just trying to shut him up. That's how it sounded anyway." I tell Benito everything else I can remember about the conversation, which isn't much. And then I tell him about the text conversation Rayanne and I had earlier.

He listens while he strokes my hand. Even after I stop talking, his long fingers press against mine, and his thumb slides sweetly against the back of my hand.

Maybe sex always lets me down, but hand-holding is pretty great.

When I check Benito's face, there's a distant look in his eye, though. He's not concentrating on me at all. He's thinking. "It doesn't look great that Rayanne won't ask for my help," he says eventually. "If she's trying not to get killed, there are better ways of doing that."

"I know," I say miserably. "She's afraid of something. Would Gage implicate his own kid?"

"Maybe, if it kept him out of jail. Or maybe she's afraid of someone else. Like Sparks," Benito muses. "Can I see the texts she sent?"

I hesitate.

"You want to help her, right?" he asks. "I wouldn't ask if I didn't think it was important."

But I've already told him everything we said to each other. Except the last bit...

"Skye," he whispers. "Help me out here."

I dip into my bag and hand him the phone. He opens the text messages and scans the conversation. Then he laughs out loud.

My face is bright red. "Stop, okay?"

"Your stepsister has boundary issues."

"I noticed."

He drops the phone into my bag and grins at me. "You didn't answer her question."

"It's none of her business."

"Why is she asking, anyway?" His big brown eyes bore into mine.

Because she knows you're my biggest regret. I won't admit it, though. "Because she's nosy," I say instead.

Benito leans forward. He slides one arm under my knees and lifts me onto his lap as if I'm weightless, not a six-foot giant. Strong arms wrap around my body and warm lips kiss the underside of my jaw.

I break out in goosebumps everywhere. The good kind of goose-bumps—not the hiding-next-to-the-garbage-cans kind.

"You can tell her," he whispers as his lips trace my cheek. "Tell her I'm going to lay you out on my bed and turn you into a moaning, shuddering wreck the second I get the chance." He kisses a sensitive spot beneath my ear, and I give a little shiver of longing.

Then he sighs and tucks my head against his neck. "But first, I have to go back to work."

"You do?"

"Yeah. I have to interrogate the asswipe I arrested this morning. My goal in life is to get one of these guys to hand me information I can use against Sparks or Gage or whoever is fucking up the drug supply around here."

"It's the fentanyl, right? Someone is killing people."

He chuckles, and since my ear is pressed to his body, I hear it in stereo. "You are the little investigative journalist, aren't you?"

"Do I look little to you?" I ask, wrapping my arms around his neck. I don't like to seem needy, but he just said he was going back to work. I hate this idea.

"You look like everything I ever wanted," he says, stroking my hair. "And I can't believe I have to go right now, because it's seriously tempting to stay here and get started on our other project."

"Project?"

"Naked adventure? Sexperience? Call it whatever you want." He slides me back onto the sofa with a groan. "You are not easy to walk away from. But I'm going to do it anyway, before my dick gets any harder. Later, honey. Text me if you need anything. Or call me here…" He slides a business card out of his wallet and sets it on the coffee table. "Someone will answer the station phone and fetch me out of the interrogation room if you tell them it's important."

"Bye," I say softly, wishing he wouldn't leave.

He shrugs his jacket on, then pauses with one hand on the door-knob. "You're going to be fine here alone. You know that right?"

I nod, trying to look brave.

His eyes soften. "Lock the deadbolt behind me, okay?"

"Will do."

"Good. Now go watch some TV, or download a book. Distract yourself. I'll be back before you know it." He winks, then opens the door and disappears.

I don't watch TV or read a novel.

Instead, I call another junior reporter at *New York News and Sports*. He's my rival, I suppose. But he owes me a favor. Everybody there does, actually. "Hey, Hooper," I say when he picks up. "It's Skye."

"Hey!" he practically shouts into the phone. "You're not at work! And you're always at work!"

That is true. "They made me take two weeks off."

"I heard. But it still seems weird. The place is already falling apart. McCracken is complaining about your absence. Apparently nobody can edit scripts and fetch coffee at the same time, like you can."

I bristle. "I'm sure you could if you put your mind to it."

"I'm *joking* Skye." He chuckles. "But come back soon, okay? This job is better when there are two dogs to kick instead of one."

I'm sure that's true. "I need a favor. Could you do a search for a Vermonter named Sparks? I'm interested in arrest records, convictions, that sort of thing."

"Sparks. Just Sparks? Got a first name?"

"Nope." I should have tried to get that out of Benito. "But how common could it be?"

He sighs. "You wouldn't believe all the shit I'm supposed to do today."

"Five minutes, dude," I prod.

"What's in it for me?"

I actually gasp. "Are you kidding me right now? I saved your butt just last week getting you some research at *midnight*. Don't be like that."

There's a silence, and I feel self-conscious. I don't usually stand up for myself at work. But I'm having a really intense time right now, and it's making me raw. I have a lot less patience for this kind of malarkey than usual.

"Listen," he says. "I'll look up your guy. But all you gave me was a single name. And they won't even let me do the traffic while you're gone."

Hmm. That's interesting. "Who's got traffic and weather?"

"Smythe."

"Oh." Smythe is slick in a way that Hooper isn't. Hooper won't get any on-camera work until he gets contact lenses, a better haircut, and learns a few things about personal hygiene. "Well. Maybe next week you too can draw a penis on air. Thanks for this favor," I say stiffly.

"Sure," he grunts. Like I'm supposed to feel bad about this. But Hooper took ten days of vacation over the holidays and I covered his work without complaint.

Maybe that was a mistake.

Some days I hate people. I really do.

We sign off. And I get busy with more research on the opioid epidemic. It keeps my mind off Rayanne. Somewhat. I glance at her phone every five minutes or so just to make sure she hasn't texted.

At about seven o'clock, there's a knock on Benito's door. And—damn it—tingles race up my spine. One scare and I've turned into the world's biggest chicken.

"Skylar?" comes a voice. It's unfamiliar, but it's also female.

I walk over to the peep hole and look through. On the other side stands a tall, pretty woman with dark hair, and she's holding a plate.

Feeling sheepish, I swing the door open. "Hey. Sorry. I was just…"

Cowering in a corner.

She smiles at me. "I'm May Shipley. I live upstairs."

"May Shipley?" But this is a tall, smiling woman. Not the skinny little girl I remember kneeling in the grass picking apples. I give my head a shake. "Come in. Sorry—you look so different. I met you once a long time ago at your parents' orchard."

"Oh yeah? I remember that, too. We didn't speak, though. You were so beautiful and I was a little afraid of you."

I open my mouth to speak, but nothing comes out. Because that makes no sense.

"It's true," May says with a friendly grin. "Can I give this to you?" She holds out the plate. "Benito just called to say that he's hung up at work, and that you were here alone."

I take the plate, which is loaded down with spaghetti and meatballs. My mouth waters as the scent of homemade tomato sauce rises up to meet me.

"We would have invited you upstairs for dinner earlier, but we didn't know you were here. Did you eat?"

"No! Wow. This looks great," I say. "Thank you. I really appreciate it." And I do. Except now I'll have to figure out some way to pay May back for this favor. I don't really like owing anyone. Nonetheless, I grab a fork out of Benito's drawer. "Can I, uh, offer you a glass of…" I open Benito's refrigerator. "There is literally nothing in here except a half empty bottle of wine and a bottle of mustard. It's a sad bachelor's fridge."

May just laughs and pulls up a bar stool. "I don't need a thing, and I don't drink anyway. Recovering alcoholic."

"Oh!" I slam the fridge. "Sorry." It's amazing to me that May could grow up, abuse alcohol and then give up alcohol all in the time I was gone. I feel a little like Rip Van Winkle. I don't know why I expected the entire state of Vermont to stay the same as it was while I was away.

She shrugs. "No big deal." She watches me take a bite.

"This is really good," I babble. I'd never make this dish for myself or even order it in a restaurant. It's too carby. The camera adds ten pounds, and the producers at NYNS are ruthless when any of the on-air talent gains weight.

But man, it's tasty. *Just this once*, I tell myself. *It's okay.* Besides, May is watching me.

"I know you're probably wondering why I'm just sitting here like a lump," she says. "But we're all terribly curious."

"Curious? About me?"

She grins. "Of course! You disappeared completely. You didn't even come to the last week of school. And Benito was *heartbroken*. He didn't come to a single bonfire that summer. He just mowed lawns and waited to ship out for basic training. Everybody was talking about it."

I put more spaghetti in my mouth so that I don't have to say anything for a moment. *Heartbroken.* There had been a time when I'd wished Benito had felt heartbroken when I'd left. But I knew he had Jill Sullivan to keep him warm.

The memory makes me feel a little sick. So I change the subject. "What do you do these days when you're not making excellent meatballs?"

"I'm a lawyer. And I'm helping Alec start up another business next door. There's a tasting room and a brewery for non-alcoholic beer." She tells me a lively story about how it all came to be, and I keep eating spaghetti while I'm listening.

And then I tell her about putting myself through college waiting tables in New York City, and sleeping on Aunt Jenny's couch. "It took me seven years to graduate. So I've been working at the TV station for five years. Aunt Jenny retired to Florida, so at least I have a bedroom now. New York is super expensive."

I picture my apartment, dark and quiet without me. Although it's quiet most of the time. I never have anyone over. This is the most social I've been in months.

"You know, the Colebury housing market is a lot tighter than it used to be," May says. "Alec and Zara are riding the wave of gentrification in the river valley. Their businesses make people want to live nearby."

"This spot by the river is really nice," I agree. Then I remember that I hate Vermont.

"Totally!" May says, standing up and stretching. "And it's even better in the summertime. Hey—if you need anything, knock on our door upstairs. In fact, let's plan a night out, the four of us. Soon."

The four of us. She makes it sound like I'll be sticking around for a while. An unfamiliar wistfulness comes over me. "Thank you. That sounds like fun." Although I know I'll be back at my desk in New York soon enough. I have a job and a life.

Okay—it's a cruddy job and a quiet life. But a girl can't just pick up and move to Vermont because everyone is suddenly more friendly than they used to be.

"Thank you for dinner," I add. "I really owe you one."

She waves a dismissing hand. "See you soon, okay? Maybe tomorrow at the thing for Audrey and Griff? Night!" She gives me a friendly smile and turns toward the door.

I show her out, feeling wistful and unsettled. Then I go back to my plate and polish off every last drop of that dinner.

Many hours later, I wake up slowly in the gray light of dawn. I'm in Benito's bed again. I'd fallen asleep here with the TV on, alone. I'd managed to stay awake until Raye texted with her nighttime check-in. *Still here. Nothing to report.*

I'd tried a different tactic to get her to spill. *You promised me a story. I could be working on it instead of doing nothing in Benito's apartment.*

Hey, enjoy it, she'd said. *And don't be nosy. I see right through you. You'll get your story, but not until it's over. Stay out of it or you'll be sorry. That's not a threat, it's just a fact.*

If you're in trouble I'd take the risk anyway.

She'd replied with a heart emoji. And nothing more.

After that, it had been impossible to stay awake. My eyes had closed during a late-night talk show host's monologue.

Sometime in the night Benito came home again, turned the TV off, and fell asleep beside me. I can hear his steady, even breathing. Waking up beside him in bed ought to be weird. And lord knows I made it awkward yesterday by trying to sex him up before either of us was awake.

This time, I merely roll onto my side so that I can admire him covertly. He's lying on his chest, his face turned toward me. Those dark lashes fan out to nearly touch his cheeks. His muscular back rises and falls with each breath.

He's so, so beautiful.

At sixteen, I'd always wanted to wake up next to Benito. When I fell asleep in my bed at night, I'd wished he was next to me. I would have followed him anywhere. But that's not how it turned out.

I watch his sleeping form, and I wonder why.

SIXTEEN

December, Twelve Years Ago

WINTER SETTLES ONTO VERMONT. There's a Christmas dance at school. Skye has seen the posters and noted the date. It's the kind of event she usually skips. The New Girl doesn't ever have a boyfriend to take her to the dance, and she's wary of boys who think the New Girl is up for anything.

She can't help listen to the gossip, though—who's taking whom to the dance, etc. Griffin Shipley has invited Tiffany Douchet. It's all over school, and Skye can't help noticing that Zara Rossi looks even angrier this week than usual.

Meanwhile, Jill Sullivan has been campaigning for an invitation from Benito, and it's painful to watch. The girl's unrequited eagerness reminds Skye of her own crush on Benito. Skye hides hers, though, whereas Jill is willing to position herself in front of Benito at every opportunity.

If Jill's strategy actually works, Skye will be crushed.

On the afternoon of the dance, she sees Benito putting beer into the back of Damien's cab. "Hey," she says casually. Or at least she hopes it sounds casual.

"Hey," he says, flashing her a smile. "You going to this dance tonight? I get the car. Happy to bring you with me."

Her heart leaps for a second, but he hasn't actually asked her to be his date. "Nah," she says. "It isn't really my thing. You?"

He shrugs. "Sure. The dance itself will be lame. Bunch of guys want to have a bonfire later, though. Could turn into a fun night."

"Cool. I'm staying in, though. I have some TV to catch up on." Also, Skye has no dress. She's already worn everything in Rayanne's closet, and there aren't any dresses at all. Skye can't spend her babysitting money on a dress, either. She's saving up for a bus ticket to Aunt Jenny's.

Benito closes the trunk of the cab and then leans against the bumper. "Your mom working tonight?" he asks carefully.

"No," Skye says quickly. "She has the night off."

Benito nods, satisfied. "Okay. Good deal."

Skye's heart gives one more flutter. That's Benito for you. He won't let anything bad happen to Skye. But neither will he make a grand gesture and invite her to the dance.

Shy girls like her don't end up with the Benitos of the world, anyway.

Later, she spies out the window as he gets into the cab and starts the engine. He's wearing khakis and a nice shirt under a leather jacket. He looks even more beautiful than usual.

Benito drives away, and Skye tries not to feel bad about it.

The following Monday, she eavesdrops on all the gossip. May Shipley got drunk at the bonfire and barfed, and her brother had to clean her up and leave early. But Griffin and Tiffany are dating now. They hold hands in the cafeteria at lunchtime.

There's a rumor that Zara hooked up with Tommy Boyer and gave him a BJ in the woods.

Worst of all, there's a rumor that Benito and Jill Sullivan spent some quality time together in the back of the taxi cab. Skye doesn't know what to think of this rumor because Benito hasn't really glanced in Jill's direction since. Even more telling? Jill has been spreading the rumor herself. It smacks of wishful thinking.

Whatever, Skye tells herself. It's none of her business.

And anyway, during Christmas break, Skye spends a lot of time with Benito. He invites her over for movie night a couple of times. Benito's mom makes buttered popcorn and pigs in blankets, and they all crowd around the TV to watch DVDs which are fetched from the town library's collection.

It's magical to hang out with the Rossis. Skye has always wanted a big family. They argue and tease each other. Matteo teases Damien. Damien teases Benito. Benito steals popcorn from Zara and Matteo.

There's nary a sentimental word spoken among any of them, but Skye still feels safer and happier right here than she ever does at home. And when the brothers call each other a "stupid goober" there's no malice in it.

Skye knows malice really well. In fact, the only true malice during movie night is from Zara, and it's aimed at Skye. Even though Zara glares at her constantly from one end of the sofa, Skye still enjoys herself. Every time something funny happens on screen, Benito laughs, and the sound of it warms her frightened little heart.

Luckily, Jimmy Gage works lots of overtime during the holidays, because the chief is on vacation. That suits Skye just fine. He also goes up to some cabin at Lake Memphremagog for ice fishing. She prays for him to fall through the ice and never come back.

But he does come back, just in time for New Year's. And that night her mom is on shift at the diner until midnight.

Skye hides in her room, lights out, pretending to be both asleep and invisible. But Gage starts drinking and then ranting about something. Apparently rants are no fun without an audience, because he gets up and kicks her door. "Where's the dinner?" he hollers. "Lazy little bitch like your mother. What's a man supposed to eat? You in there?"

Her heart begins to hammer in her chest. It's eleven-thirty. Skye's mom will be home soon, but plenty can happen in half an hour.

She should have left through the window already. But it's cold outside, and she thinks Benito is out for the night. The Rossi's trailer is dark and quiet.

And Gage is still standing there, yelling through her door.

"You got a boy in there?" he asks, thudding the door again. "That why you don't answer?"

The door visibly bends under the force of his blows.

"Let me hear you," he says. "I'll bet you're a screamer. Maybe he's fucking your face right now. Are you on your knees for him?"

Skye curls up in a ball. If she moves around her room to put on warmer clothes, he'll hear her. And the window will squeak if she raises it.

"When is it my turn?" he rasps. "You know I'm gettin' in there. You're gonna scream for me, too. Sometime soon. You're a dirty girl, Skye. Or you will be when I'm done with you."

He rattles the doorknob, and Skye can't even breathe. Her throat is hot and her eyes are burning with fear and anger.

"Open up, you little whore," he says.

And then Skye sees the telltale flash of light outside her window—the kind that comes from headlights turning toward the trailers at this end of the row.

Please be Mom, she begs the universe. If her mother steps through the front door, Gage will back off.

Ten heart-stopping seconds tick by. And then her prayers are answered, at least for now. Her mother's footsteps stomp up onto the tiny porch. She's always tired after a long shift.

Gage's voice can be heard talking to her. He's still complaining, but now to her mom, who shuts him up by handing over some diner food, if Skye has interpreted things correctly.

She wipes her scratchy eyes and clutches her pillow, wondering how much more of this she can take.

SEVENTEEN

Benito

WHEN I WAKE up to see Skye beside me in the bed, all I can do is smile. How many times have I slept alone, wishing she was there?

Too many.

"Hi," she whispers, blinking at me.

"Hi honey," I rasp.

One of her hands lands on top of my head, long fingers trailing through my hair.

My body reacts as if she stroked my cock instead. Heat sizzles down my spine, reaching my erection, which is trapped against the bed. I let out a low groan of need.

Her fingers freeze in my hair. "Everything okay?" she whispers.

"Yeah," I tell the pillow. *Fuck*. It's going to be another long day of wanting her. "Coffee would help."

"If you had a coffee machine like normal people, I could have taken care of that for you already."

What else will you take care of for me? I roll over and smile at her. "I'll buy a coffee maker today. What's your favorite brand?"

"Any kind, as long as it works," she says, stretching her arms up over her head and yawning.

God. I just want to climb on top of her and kiss her stupid. I glance downward. Even though I'm covered by both boxers and the bed sheet, there's no mistaking my hard cock pointing up at her.

Skye follows my gaze, and then her eyes heat and her cheeks pink up. Then she jerks her chin upwards, as if caught staring. "Can I jump in your shower?"

"Can I jump in with you?" Whoops. That just slipped out. "Kidding. Go ahead."

She swings her feet off the side of the bed, but I realize I have one more thing to say. So I catch her smooth hand in mine before she can make her escape. Her hand closes around mine unconsciously. She looks down at our joined hands, and then gives me a hot smile that does nothing to calm my body down.

"Sorry," I whisper. "Realized I forgot to tell you something. Even though it's Sunday, I have to go to work for a couple of hours."

"Oh." The disappointment on her face is hard to miss.

"But then I'll come back. We'll buy a coffee machine, and—if it's okay with you—we'll swing by a party."

"A party?"

"It's for Audrey and Griffin Shipley's baby's christening. But that's just an excuse to throw a party in this space that's being renovated into a brewery. It's right next door. We don't have to stay a long time. Do you remember the Shipleys?"

"Sure," Skye says. She's still holding my hand. "We picked apples at their place. They were super nice. And I caught up with May last night. The Shipleys are *still* super nice."

"Mostly," I agree.

"Mostly?" her eyebrows arch in curiosity.

"Well..." I chuckle. "There was this rough patch when Griffin broke up with Zara and we all hated him for hurting our sister."

"They were together?" Skye's eyes are wide. "I missed a lot of gossip."

I laugh, because it's true. "Briefly. But now Griffin is married to Audrey, Zara's business partner. And Zara is in deep with her professional hockey player baby daddy. But May Shipley is living with Alec upstairs. Did you follow all that?"

Skye blinks. "Wow. Small towns."

"I know."

"How come you're the only single Rossi?" Her blue eyes study me.

Because I was waiting for you. "I'm not," I insist. "Damien is single. And Matteo is probably single. Although who knows. He moved to Aspen, and we never see him."

"Oh. Huh."

"Now go do whatever it is that takes you a half hour in the bathroom."

She gives me an eye roll, then pads off toward the bathroom.

I lie in bed, picturing her naked under the spray. But I'm a gentleman. So when she emerges wrapped in nothing but a towel, I don't gawk. I head into the shower myself, instead.

After a pit stop at the Busy Bean for coffee and excellent pastries with Skye, I take my leave. At the Colebury station house, I sit down with Nelligan. The two of us do some brainstorming.

"Let's just say I'm right," I propose. "Rayanne got tricked into driving drugs down from Gage's fishing cabin into Colebury. Now Rayanne wants out, so she wants to prove that her father or Sparks is the trafficker. And that's why she's AWOL."

Nelligan nods because he's heard most of this before. Our interest in Rayanne started a few weeks ago, when I was casing Gage's fishing cabin. I saw Rayanne inside, sitting on the sofa, reading a book in front of the picture window.

It's not illegal to read a book at a fishing cabin. But she'd driven her father's car up there. And Lake Memphremagog has the unique feature of lying half in the US and half in Canada. The border isn't as tight there as in some other spots.

Furthermore, Fentanyl is highly portable. There's a Canadian law that prohibits the postal service from opening envelopes below a certain weight. So it's actually possible to ship a fortune in Fentanyl via ten or twenty ordinary envelopes.

I think Jimmy Gage has someone in Canada who's collecting Chinese fentanyl in small batches, then ferrying it across the border. Gage is dealing it widely, but doing a sloppy job of cutting it first.

I know I'm right. I only need to prove it.

My phone buzzes with a message. "Sorry, I gotta check it," I say.

"Dude, I know."

But the text isn't related to our case. It's from my fuck buddy. *Where've you been?* she asks. **Working? Want a new photo?**

"Fuck."

"Any news?" Nelligan asks.

"Nope." I shove the phone in my pocket without answering. "Just, uh, a social message."

Nelligan snorts. "Don't let me keep you from your weekend plans."

I shake my head, because I've had a permanent change of plans with regard to that particular friend. I should really call her up and break things off when I get a chance. "Where were we?"

"You were guessing that Rayanne has become a one-man sting operation," Nelligan prompts.

"She's trying to be." The idea that Rayanne's hoping to take down her father is the only explanation that makes sense.

"Your friend Skylar brought her a kayak," Nelligan muses. "So Rayanne thinks the handoff is happening on the water."

"She has a waterproof camera, too."

"But Sparks and Gage are here in Colebury," Nelligan says. "Or they were yesterday around six."

"What were they up to?"

"Eating fast food with their cars parked side by side, the windows down so they could talk. But then they both went home."

"Shit," I said. "I need to track those cars. If even one small-time dealer would just give up either of their names…"

"One small-time dealer with a death wish," Nelligan adds. "Would you give up Sparks's name? That fucker is mean."

"No. But I'm not a drug-addicted sleazebag."

"No. You're merely sleazy." He grins.

"Pot. Kettle," I grumble. Besides, I'd rather be done with hookups and bachelorhood. If only I can convince Skye to stick around.

"Let's go beg the chief for more resources," Nelligan says. "If Sparks or Gage heads up north, we'll be ready."

"Let's," I agree.

EIGHTEEN

Skylar

IT'S SUNDAY AFTERNOON. I should be headed back to New York after a weekend with Rayanne. But I'm still in Vermont. In fact, I'm wearing Benito's bathrobe, lying on his bed, waiting for my laundry to finish drying.

Rayanne texted at noon to check in. I did my usual begging. *Please tell me what you're doing. How does this end?* Etc.

No whining, she'd replied. *You're not the one huddled in a Jeep in the woods, waiting for assholes to show up.*

Just call me and tell me why you're doing that.

She hadn't replied. I'd spent the next ten minutes trying to decide if her message gave me any clues to where she was. The revelation that she's in "the woods" is no help because most of Vermont is in the woods.

Benito came home a little later with an espresso machine under one arm and a bag full of groceries under the other. I made us sandwiches while he unpacked the espresso machine and made cappuccinos.

I almost cut my thumb off slicing tomatoes, because I couldn't stop watching his forearms flex as he tamped the grounds in preparation for brewing a shot. Moving around the kitchen with him was far too stimulating. I was almost relieved when he'd said he had to pop out again to hand off some documents to the Colebury police.

Now I'm alone again and washing my meager supply of T-shirts, underwear, and socks. If I'd known I'd be overstaying my welcome in Vermont, I would have packed accordingly.

Benito's bed is really comfortable. These are very silky sheets.

Maybe it's because I'm a little bored, or because I'm mostly naked right now. I'm just lying here on Benito's bed, listening to the dryer turn. Yet I feel an unfamiliar hum in my body. My breasts feel heavy against the quilt.

So I roll onto my back. But that's no better. When I close my eyes, I can picture Benito's lips on my naked breast.

The hum gets stronger. There's a new sort of electrical pulse in my bloodstream. And it's focused on my naked breasts and my restless thighs.

Okay, maybe there's something wrong with me. Rayanne is missing and my life is in turmoil. And what am I thinking about? Benito's hands on my bare skin. When he slipped his fingertips down my belly, landing exquisitely on my—

The phone beside me rings, and I sit up quickly, as if the caller can read my private thoughts. Unfortunately, the number showing on my phone begins with 212—a New York number. "This is Emily Skye," I say, giving my on-camera work name. "Can I help you?"

"Skylar," the deep voice on the other end booms. "I need you in the newsroom tonight to cover for Smythe."

It's McCracken, my producer. He doesn't even bother to identify himself. "But you told me to take two weeks off," I argue.

"We're short-staffed," he grunts. "Need the help."

I'm trying to process this strange directive when Benito's face appears in the doorway, and he smiles at me. The smile doesn't help my executive function. So it takes me a second to respond to the producer on the phone. "I couldn't possibly come in tonight," I say carefully. "Or tomorrow. You gave me the time off. You *insisted*, actually. So I left town to see my stepsister, who needs my help."

"Your sister? Are you pulling my chain? You never visited this sister before. You're always right here at your desk where I need you."

This is true. But what has that ever gotten me?

"I don't see how that's relevant." For once I let myself sound mad.

"I followed your instructions, and I am unavailable. I'm also more than two hundred and fifty miles away from the office. Tell Smythe he can't go to the hockey game with his buddies this time."

While I say this, I'm conscious of Benito's eyes on me. Maybe I'm getting all this courage from him. I don't want him to hear me behaving like the doormat my colleagues expect me to be.

But it's possible that Benito isn't listening. His eyes have gone dark, and his gaze drifts down my body.

I tug the bathrobe a little more tightly around myself, and I almost miss what the boss says next.

"Get your tight little ass back to New York City. You're always telling me how badly you want to cover news items. I'm not impressed right now. This isn't the holidays."

"No kidding, I always work the holidays," I sputter. But he's already hung up.

I give a little shriek of rage and slap my phone down on the bed.

"Things aren't so good at the office?" he asks, entering the room.

"It's just the usual bullshizzle. The producers want perfect obedience, and yet they're constantly contradicting themselves."

"That sounds...shittastic," he says, sitting next to me on the bed.

"Nobody ever quits," I point out. "News jobs are scarce. I stick around hoping that something will change for the better. Rayanne offered me a story."

"A what?" Benito asks, covering my hand with his.

"A story. A lead. She said..." I frown at him. "Are you listening?"

"No," he admits with a shake of his dark head. "I'm sorry, but my IQ is compromised right now, because you're wearing my bathrobe and you're essentially naked on my bed." He reaches up and closes the robe where my boobs are in danger of spilling out.

I look down at his hands near my body, imagining them opening the bathrobe instead of closing it. And...

The buzzer on the dryer sounds.

I shoot off the bed. "Laundry's dry. Now when does this party start?"

"It's starting now. Are you ready?"

I give Benito a look. "Do I look ready?"

"You look ready to..." He rolls his eyes toward heaven. "Let me know when it's time to go. I'm going to wait in the living room..." He walks out the door, adding something under his breath. It might have been, "...and ice my crotch."

Whatever. I can't worry about those hot looks Benito gives me. And I can't worry about my body's strange reaction to him. I can't even worry about Rayanne right now, because I have *got* to fix my face. It's quite possible that everyone who ever snubbed me in high school will be at this party. I cannot look like that scared teenager from the trailer park.

So I spring into action. I put on my closest-fitting cashmere sweater—this one is blue, and it brings out my eyes—and my shorter skirt. I blow out my damp hair, thanking the lord above that I brought my own hair dryer and round brush on this jaunt.

Then it's time to do my face. I go for a smoky eye—but it's subtle. And I use my favorite Urban Decay mascara, because it makes my lashes look long enough to reach the moon. Lastly, I add my favorite Chanel lipstick in *Cécile*.

"Ready!" I finally announce as I trot into the living room in my high heeled boots.

On the sofa, Benito makes a show of looking at his watch, as if a great deal of time has elapsed. Then he turns his chin and looks at me. "Holy fuck," he says, his voice strained. "I guess that was time well spent."

His gaze burns me. He doesn't even stand up—he just sits there, appraising me.

"Are we going to this thing or what?" I squeak. I may have spent ten extra minutes on my appearance hoping that he'd notice. And yet I'm not all that comfortable with the obvious results.

"I suppose," he grunts, getting off the sofa. He walks around behind me and sets his leather jacket on my shoulders. "Here, honey."

"What about you? Do you have another jacket?"

He shrugs. "Don't need one. I'm from Vermont."

"You're too much of a bad—" I almost slip up and curse! What's gotten into me? "—a tough guy to feel the cold?"

"I'll just stand next to you," he says, opening the door. "That'll keep me warm. Now let's go eat some barbecue and admire a new baby."

Downstairs, he holds the door open for me, and then leads me in the opposite direction from his car. "Wait. Don't we have to drive?"

He shakes his head. "It's right next door. My crazy brother is opening a beer-tasting room with a couple of other businessmen, including Griffin Shipley. We can just walk through the woods. Here..."

Benito slips my hand into his. Long fingers close around mine, and he leads me across the gravel parking lot to a wet path through the woods. It's March, so everything is slowly melting. There are still piles of snow between the trees, but they're uneven.

I inhale the scent of pine and mist, and my heart beats faster. It's like stepping backward in time. Trees, fresh air, and Benito's nearness.

"What are you doing?"

Whoops. Busted. "Sniffing the air like a weirdo."

"No place smells better than Vermont."

"I guess."

"You guess?" He stops walking. "Don't you like Vermont?"

"Nope. Can't say I do."

He puts a hand over his heart like I've wounded him. "Wow. Okay." He takes a comical, shaky breath. "Let me just try to recover from that."

"Look," I tell him. "I literally ran away from here. It doesn't leave a girl with fond memories."

He takes a step closer. "So it's like a phobia. You see maple syrup, you break out in hives?"

"Something like that," I agree. This is one of the sillier conversations we've ever had.

Benito snaps his fingers. "I've got it. We'll just give you some Vermont aversion therapy."

"And what would that entail, exactly?"

"I'm afraid you'll have to milk a cow, and then scrape shit off your shoes."

I giggle.

"Then you'll drink some very craft beer and eat a tub of Ben & Jerry's."

"That might work," I admit. And now I'm craving ice cream.

"Also?"

"Yeah?"

He comes closer, his free hand cups my chin, and I only get a split second glimpse into his big brown eyes before they fall shut as he kisses me.

And *oh* his kiss. It's slow and teasing. It's both too much and not enough, so I lean in for more. Benito makes a sound of approval, then parts my lips with his tongue.

I wrap my arms around his neck, as if I really know what I'm doing. Even I can handle a kiss in the woods.

Or can I? As he licks into my mouth, I feel my body melt into his. When Benito strokes my bottom with his hand, I feel it *everywhere*. My knees get squishy and my tummy flips. And as our tongues slide together, I actually sway on my feet.

"Easy," he says with a chuckle against my lips. "How does anyone walk in heels, anyway?"

But it's not the heels that are putting me off balance. I take a deep breath and steady myself. "What did you do that for?"

"Aversion therapy." Benito smiles. "And because I had better self-control when I was eighteen than I do now."

He's smeared himself with my Chanel lipstick, so I cup his chin and wipe it off with my thumb.

"I'm not afraid of a little lipstick," he whispers. "You can mess me up any time you want, honey."

Honey. I like the sound of that too much. Every time he says it, I light up inside. And I feel dizzy from his kisses. The scent of pine trees and the feel of his whiskers against my skin has put me on some kind of emotional overload. "Let's go to this party," I suggest. Although I'll need my game face for that.

I think I left my game face in the missing Jeep, along with my jacket.

He takes my hand and leads me farther down the path. Our walk through the woods is over just minutes later, as we emerge in front of a big, brick building. There's a sign overhead reading, *The Speakeasy*. And when Benito opens the door, I see a groovy party space with fairy lights wrapped around rustic wooden beams, and candle sconces on the walls.

At one end of the big room there's a table laden with food, and also a bar. And at the other end there's a platform, where a banjo player, a fiddler, and a guitarist are tuning up.

"Wow," I can't help but say. It irks me that Colebury is so much cooler than it was in high school. I always thought I'd left behind a backwater of a town for better opportunities. But I keep finding things to like about this place, darn it.

"There's going to be contra dancing," Benito says.

"What's that? Is that like a square dance?" I vaguely remember being made to learn that during gym class at the high school here.

"Sort of. Are you game? No pressure."

"I don't think it's my thing," I admit. "I'd have to learn it all over again."

"Then let's find you a drink, before my family swarms."

"Do they have Shipley Cider?" I hear myself ask. I might as well get one more taste while I still can.

"You can bet on it. In fact..." Benito gives me a cheeky smile that makes his brown eyes sparkle. "You should try their award-winner. It's called *Audrey*."

"It's that good, huh?"

"It's a great beverage," he agrees, his brown eyes sparkling. "And some would call it *inspirational*."

"Really." I swear I can't look away from this man. I couldn't tell you who else is in this room right now, because only one person here interests me. "Well then, I've got to try it."

"Coming right up," he says.

NINETEEN

Benito

─────────────

I FETCH a pint of *Audrey* for Skye. It's a terrific cider, and it's won awards. Also, people claim that it's an aphrodisiac. That's probably not really true, but a guy can dream.

"Here, honey," I say, handing it over. "Drink up."

She takes a sip and watches me with those bright blue eyes. I feel a familiar tightness in my groin, and it doesn't have a thing to do with cider.

We could have just stood there for the whole evening staring at each other, but I hear my mother let out a shriek from across the room. And when I look up, she's locked onto us like a heat-seeking missile.

That's when I realize that I've made a severe miscalculation. I should have warned Mom that Skye had come back to town. Furthermore, I should have let on to my family members that Skye isn't here in Vermont just to shack up with me.

But it's too late now. As she comes barreling toward us, with a look of ecstasy on her face, I can almost hear her planning my wedding.

This is going to be awkward.

"Oh, thank you, baby Jesus!" Mom skids to a stop in front of Skylar. "*Honey*. I can't believe my eyes! You are six inches taller and twice as beautiful as you were at sixteen. And you were already a very pretty, very tall girl then." She claps a hand to her heart.

"Hi, Mrs. Rossi," Skye says shyly. "It's good to see you."

Mom isn't done, though. She has to reach up to clamp her hands onto Skye's shoulders. "It's *great* to see you. A revelation! I can't believe Benny didn't tell me you were coming! This is so exciting. And when I asked him if he was coming to Sunday lunch today, he said he had to *work!*"

"I *did* work," I grumble. Poor Skye is literally getting hug-mugged by my mother. "Maybe loosen your grip a little? There's a fine line between welcoming and psychotic."

That does the trick because Mom has to let go of Skye in order to smack me on the arm. "Behave! And I need more details. How did you two reconnect?" she crows. "This is so exciting."

Skye shoots me a glance over my mother's head. "It was an accident, to be honest," she admits. "My crazy stepsister, um, abandoned me for the weekend. And Benito has been kind enough to entertain me instead."

I hear Zara's quiet laughter nearby. "Is that what we're calling it?" She's enjoying this. If she loved me, she'd rescue us.

"You must come for dinner! You and Benny. Tuesday night at my place." Mom's breathless excitement is making me twitchy.

"That would be lovely, if I'm still in town," Skye says sweetly. "What can I bring?"

"You don't have to bring a *thing!* Just your beautiful self. You know, Benny has been moping around here for more than a decade wondering what became of you."

Just shoot me already.

It's obvious that Skye has no clue what to say. "How about I bring dessert? Do you like tiramisu?"

"I *love* tiramisu!" my mother gasps. But what she really means is, *How many grandchildren will you give me?*

Zara snickers behind me. And I think I hear Damien's chuckle, too.

"Well," Skye says, gulping air. "I think I hear the band starting up."

"Dance with me?" I ask.

Her blue eyes sparkle at me. "I love contra dancing!"

"Do you now? Let's do it." I squeeze her hand.

"Don't forget—Tuesday night!" my mother reminds us. "Seven o'clock!" She gives me a pointed look that says, *We'll be speaking more about this later.* Then she lifts her chin and walks away, undoubtedly toward her bridge-club ladies. Time for gossip.

Skye takes a deep drink of the cider in her hand. "Wow. This is..." She takes another sip. "Really interesting. So earthy. Was your Mom always so intense?"

"Oh, sure she was," Zara says, appearing by her side with laughing eyes. She's got Nicole on her hip, but she wraps her free arm around my shoulder. "It was refreshing to watch you be tormented for once. Did you enjoy your turn?"

"It was totes fun," I mumble. "Where's the guest of honor?"

"Right there," Zara says, pointing out Audrey near the dessert table. "Are you going to hold the baby?"

"No, holding me!" Nicole yells, stretching her arms out for me. "Bimbo! Bimboooooo."

Heads turn everywhere to see why a toddler is yelling "Bimbo" at the top of her lungs.

"I'm right here." I grab her from my sister. "No need to shout."

Zara and Skye both cackle.

Then Zara turns to Skye. "Listen," Zara says. "Twelve years ago I never got the chance to—"

"Whoa." I interrupt my sister. "Can we go five minutes without talking about high school, please?"

She pulls a face. "I'm only trying to apologize."

"There's really no need," Skye says quickly.

"Actually—" Zara starts to argue.

We are saved by Audrey, who approaches with her newborn son, who's wearing a fuzzy brown one-piece with bear's ears on the hood that's covering his little bald head.

"Baby," Nicole says, pointing.

"Shouldn't I hold him?" I ask her.

"No! Me."

Skye smiles, and I swear I can practically see hearts in her eyes, like a cartoon character in love. "Well, can I hold him, then? I'm

Skylar, by the way. I guess I should have said that before asking to hold your newborn."

"Oh, I've heard *all* about you this week," Audrey says, handing the baby into Skye's waiting arms. "I'm Audrey Shipley." She takes Skye's half-empty cider glass to give my girl full use of her hands.

"Aren't you just amazing," Skye whispers to the baby. There's a note of awe in her voice that I've never heard before. "How old are you?"

"He's seven weeks," Audrey says. "He's August Griffin Shipley the fourth."

"That's a lot of names for one little cub," Skye says, rocking him as lovingly as if he were the Christ child. As I've said before, love at first sight is totally real. And I think Skye just fell head over heels for an infant in a bear suit.

"We call him Gus," Audrey explains.

"Mmm. You know that old story about Rip Van Winkle?" Skye lifts her chin and smiles at Audrey. "When I left Vermont, Griffin Shipley was about to become a college kid, and May was a skinny ninth-grader."

"Wow." Audrey laughs. "Tell me tales! Was Griffin awful?"

"I wasn't!" Griffin insists, stepping into our circle and putting an arm around his wife. "I was a perfect gentleman at all times." He winks.

"Yeah, I was the awful one," Zara says.

"I didn't live here long," Skye says, carefully avoiding the subject of who was or wasn't awful. "But still—this weekend has been a real time warp. Congratulations on your little boy."

"Thank you!" Griffin crows. The big man has been beaming nonstop since the day of his child's birth—anyone can see how happy he is.

The band launches into a fiddle tune, signaling the start of the contra dance.

"You promised me a dance," I point out to Skye. "Even if it was just an evasive maneuver, I want it."

"Okay, bossy." After one more snuggle, Skye trades Audrey back —handing over the baby and taking her cider glass.

"Have fun!" Audrey encourages her. She gives Skye and I one

more measuring glance, because small towns run on coffee, pastries and gossip. "Nice to meet you, Skylar."

"Good to see you again," Griffin adds. Because he really is a gentleman.

"Food," Nicole says in my arms.

"I'll hook you up, baby girl," Zara says, taking my niece back. "Let's go make you a plate."

———

The contra dance starts slowly, with the caller giving out lots of instructions. Skye and I get a refresher on allemandes and see-saws and promenades. When the caller teaches us the "gypsy and swing," he says that we're supposed to stare into each other's eyes. Like that's a hardship. Hell, I practically fall in headlong every time I look at her.

Skye doesn't seem to mind, either. Her gaze lingers. And every time the dance calls for us to touch, I feel the heat between us.

Contra dance isn't meant to be erotic. But there's no denying the crackle that happens when our hands brush and our eyes meet.

"You know," I whisper to Skye as we promenade, "my mother fell for my father at a dance. And then quickly had five children." I leave out the ugly parts of that story, but there were nice parts, too.

"I can't imagine how that happened," she says, and then flashes me a hot smile with rosebud lips.

Maybe I'm not the first man to get turned on while learning a move they call the Mad Robin. But I probably won't be the last, either.

When it's time to speed things up, the caller arranges us into long lines, and the fiddler tucks into his tune. The banjo dives in, knuckles flying, pounding out a rhythm. The whole room moves in time with the beat. It's really cool, except for the fact that I lose Skylar. This dance takes her down the line without me, looping among other men.

I'm watching her silk hair flying when I almost lose the thread entirely, turning to my left instead of my right, and crashing right into May Shipley. "Jesus. Sorry," I sputter.

She laughs and bumps my hip with hers as a punishment. "Must be hard to do this with your tongue hanging out like that." She yanks me back into position so I can meet the next partner in time.

It's Daphne Shipley. "Another one bites the dust," is all she says to me.

So it's official—I'm the least subtle person in the room. But it doesn't matter, I suppose. I only need my poker face for drug busts.

———

Eventually we pause for food. Skye's cheeks are pink, and she complains of thirst. So I get her another cider and a glass of water.

"Where shall we sit?" she asks, handing me a plate of barbecued ribs with all the fixings.

"With Alec and May?" I point to a table. "Mom is on the other side of the room, gossiping with Ruth and Grandpa Shipley. Sit down before she sees us."

We sit down and tuck into the barbecue. We're joined by Roderick —baker extraordinaire—who works for my sister and Audrey at the Busy Bean.

"Don't I know you from somewhere?" Roderick says to Skye. "It's been bugging me since you came into the coffee shop on Saturday. I've seen you before."

"She lived here for a year during high school," I offer. "Twelve years ago."

"That's not it..." Roderick's forehead wrinkles. "Actually, you remind me of this girl I saw on YouTube."

"Here we go..." Skye says under her breath.

"Yes!" Roderick snaps his fingers. "It was a weather report! I swear she was your twin! The girl drew..."

"A penis," Skye says with a sigh. "That was me. But it was a traffic map, not the weather."

"Yeah!" Roderick says. "Traffic. Right! It was epic. I'm a fan of penises in general, but this one was stellar."

"Wait, really?" my brother Alec snorts. He pulls out his phone. "I need to see this."

Cringing, Skye turns to me. "Do me a favor? Don't Google it."

"Okay," I say immediately.

"I'm serious. Do me the favor of not looking it up." Her blue eyes beg me.

A moment later, Alec lets out a hoot of laughter. So now I'm desperately curious. I mean—drawing a penis by accident? How is it a penis and not, say, a long oval? "Were there pubes?"

"No—but there were balls," Roderick says.

Alec lifts his eyes from his phone. "That is undeniably a *dick*. Central Park is well-endowed."

Skye looks like she wants to sink into the floor. "Let's check out the dessert offerings, shall we?" I ask, standing up suddenly. I don't want her to feel embarrassed.

She gets up and takes both our plates.

"I'm sorry," I say, as we head over to the food. "My family is good at finding sore spots and then poking them."

"Don't be sorry," she says with a sigh. "Several million people have already seen it."

"I won't watch," I promise her.

She stops. "Really?"

"You asked me not to. So I won't."

She blinks. "Thank you. You can be the one person who doesn't see me make a fool of myself."

"No problem, honey. Everyone has their moments. But mine aren't captured on camera."

"Must be nice."

After that, we eat some brownies that are so dark and delicious they make me want to cry. "Listen, let's do a quick circuit," I suggest. "If I say hello to some people, then I can cut out early."

I introduce Skye to Father Peters, who performed little Gus's baptism. And to the Abrahams—Griff's neighbors.

"You know," Skye says. "Go ahead and mingle. I don't need babysitting. I won't go off into the trees and get drunk."

I snort at that memory. "Good to know, honey. But that's not why I keep you handy."

"It isn't?"

"No." I catch her chin in my hand and our gazes lock. "I just don't want to let you go. You've been giving me the 'fuck me' eyes all night, and I like it."

Skye's eyes flare, but she shakes her head. "I'm not."

"You are." Every time she looks my way there's a new heat in her expression. "It started this morning, and it hasn't stopped since."

Her mouth falls open. "That's impossible. Never in my life have I given anyone the..." She clears her throat.

"I know you can't say it," I say with a chuckle. "But if you're going to look at a man that way, at least own up to it. I practically need a cold shower every time I catch you undressing me with your eyes."

"You have a very large ego." Skye lifts her chin. "Maybe it's all in your imagination."

"Yeah? Prove it." I take her glass from her hand and set it onto a table. "One more dance." The band is playing a slow song right now. It's sort of a bluegrass version of "Hotel California."

Skye lets me lead her out into the sea of dancing bodies. When I put my hand on the small of her back and pull her close, she sighs. "We shouldn't tempt me," she whispers. "I thought the first priority was finding Rayanne."

"Oh it is. But you're the one who wanted to give her time. Meanwhile, you and I have other work to do." I slide my hands around her waist and step into her personal space.

And when her smooth hands land on my body, I know she can't even pretend to hide it anymore. As we begin to sway, her blue eyes flare with longing. I turn Skye gently in a circle, and she studies my lips with a hungry expression. And when she raises those pretty eyes to mine, I can tell she's plotting to remove every item of my clothing. With her teeth.

"That's right," I whisper. "You can look at me like that all you want." Leaning in, I drag my lips along her cheekbone in a slow kiss. She lets out a hot breath, and I smile into her hair, my hands dancing down her back, and then up again.

"Oh jeez," Skye groans, and then steps back an inch. "People will stare."

It's a fair point. I feel a little crazy right now, and I'll never hear the end of it from my siblings if I maul Skye in the middle of a party. So there's only one thing to do. "Come on." I take her hand and give it a little tug. "Come with me."

"Where?"

Without answering, I lead her off the dance floor, drawing her outside through the nearest exit. Since my brother's new joint isn't open yet, the parking lot isn't lit, and it's dark outside the building. I waste no time pressing Skye up against the wall and finding her hot mouth with mine.

She moans into the first kiss, and her fingers grip my shirt.

It takes all my willpower to kiss her slowly. I want to paw her like a beast. But I can't take that risk. Skye wants me, but she's skittish. I still don't quite understand it, but I want to.

My pulse is pounding in my ears, but I'm gentle when I tease her lips apart and deepen our kiss. She moans again as I slide my tongue over hers, and the sound vibrates in my chest and tightens my groin.

God, this woman could rip my heart in half again. I know it and I don't even care.

I thrust my cock slowly against her body as I kiss her again. Skye makes a new, desperate noise and pushes her breasts against my chest. Her fingers are in my hair and her torso molds to mine.

"Sweet girl," I whisper against her lips. "You need something from me?"

She blinks at me in wonder.

"You can't say, it, can you? You can't say—take me home and fuck me."

Her head gives a tiny shake.

I let my hands drift down her curves, and she shivers in my arms. "But that's what you need, isn't it? Kiss me again if I'm right."

Skye leans in immediately, her lips fitted to mine, her whimper loud and astonished as I claim her mouth and stoke her body like a campfire.

And I'm relentless. Bracing her against the wall, I kiss her with everything I've got. Every broken promise between us is cast away into the dark, damp night. All the lonely nights I've needed her are like fuel on these flames.

A few short minutes later we're panting and desperate. Skye feels shaky under my touch, and I'm so heated up that I can barely string words together. "Let's go," I croak when we come up for air.

"Your jacket..." Skye gasps. "It's inside."

"We'll get it tomorrow." I tug her off the wall and head into the woods, where it's truly dark. But there's just enough of a moonglow to show us the snow at the edge of the trail. The damp, pine scent is my new favorite aphrodisiac. We cross the woods in record time, and then we're practically racing up the flight of stairs to my place.

I have never opened a door so fast, not even when trying to run down a perp. Two seconds after reaching my floor, I've pulled us both into my apartment and kicked the door shut. Her hands are on my body as I kiss her hungrily. I fumble for the hem of her sweater and tug it upward, walking her backward at the same time.

She nearly bumps into the sofa, damn it. At the last second I yank her back onto the right path. I should slow down so I don't maim us both. But I can't seem to find the willpower.

Pausing in the hallway, I kiss her deeply, taking sip after sip from her mouth. My hands wander under that short skirt that's made me nuts all night. And when I find the skin of her upper thighs, she moans into my mouth.

My whole body is on fire. My hands are stupid, clumsy things. But somehow I find the zipper on her skirt and tug it down until the fabric falls away.

Meanwhile, she's unbuttoning my shirt. I let her get about halfway down until I just reach up and shrug it over my head, then fight my arms out of the sleeves. It's not graceful, but neither of us cares. I steer her into the darkened bedroom. Unless I'm crazy, I'm finally about to do something I've craved my whole life.

Even in my horny, desperate haze, though, there is still a part of me that needs to protect Skye. "Tell me to stop," I beg between kisses. "If there's some reason you don't want this tonight, speak up now."

She finds the bed with the backs of her knees and topples onto it. Then she pulls me down with two hands and kisses me desperately.

TWENTY

Springtime, Twelve Years Ago

BENITO WATCHES March melt into April. The snow doesn't disappear all at once. For weeks, there are dingy little piles in the shadiest spots.

But he feels it coming. He can see the buds on the trees. And when he drives his bike to school every morning—with Skye seated behind him —the wind smells green.

Her embrace makes him feel crazy. But not as crazy as the knowledge that graduation is just weeks away.

He's been looking forward to graduation for years, and now he sees the error of his ways. The nearer it looms, the less excited he is about enlisting in the army. They'll help pay for college, though, and he can bank his paycheck, too. It's always seemed like a win-win.

Except. It's dawning on him that he'll leave everyone he cares about behind. His mom will be there in the trailer, still worrying about their evil neighbor. And Zara doesn't have a post-graduation plan in place, so he's going to worry about both of them.

He tries to talk Zara into enlisting, too, because that would solve at least one problem. "You're already a badass," he reasons. "This would just make it official."

"Are you *high?* I fucking hate authority," is Zara's quick response.

Well, there's that.

Worst of all will be leaving Skye behind. He can't think about it without feeling a dull ache right behind his breastbone. Skye's not even seventeen. She has two years of high school left. Jimmy Gage shows no signs of letting up on her. And he's untouchable. How can Benito just get on a bus and leave her here?

The fear isn't totally selfless, either. When he thinks of long months away from her, he feels bleak.

That must be why he's spending so much more time in their outdoor living room, strumming his brother's ukulele and watching for her smile. He lights a fire nearly every evening of March and April. They sit and chat and listen for the first peeper frogs of the season.

In May they don't need a fire anymore. It's a warm Saturday afternoon when Skye turns up chattier and more bubbly than usual. "Aunt Jenny told me to come for a visit this summer," she says. "I mean—most people don't summer in the Bronx, but I'm going to start a new trend."

The ache in Benito's chest gives a quick stab and then eases again. Because if Skye's in New York City, she won't be anywhere near Gage when Benito ships out to basic training. "Are you thinking of staying past the summer?" he asks carefully.

"Maybe," she says immediately. "Unless I really feel like I'm underfoot. Aunt Jenny will let me, especially when I tell her how, um, bad it really is."

And it is bad.

"I just don't think I can survive this place after you're gone. I mean, there's Gage," she finally says. "But also…" She breaks off.

"What?" he whispers.

There's a look in her eye that he doesn't often see. It's *desire*. All his blood stops circulating. "I'll miss you too much," she whispers hoarsely.

Benito's had a lot of practice with exercising control around Skye, but he can't help but respond to the way she's looking at him.

"Hey," he says, because his ability to form sentences has suddenly slowed to half the normal speed. He pulls himself together enough to say, "Will you go to grad prom with me?"

"What?" she asks, her eyes unmistakably hopeful.

"Grad prom. Our school is too small to throw both a prom and a graduation party, so they do the whole thing on graduation day."

"Right," she says, licking her lips. "But do you mean…with a group of friends?"

"No, honey. You and me." He wants her safe with Aunt Jenny in New

York, but he'll be damned if he lets her leave without telling her how he really feels. "Let me take you out. We'll have one terrific night—a great meal, and the party. We can pretend that life is easier. Just once."

"Wow..." Her eyes get shy. "I'd like that very much."

"So would I. So it's a date?" He reaches over and grabs her hand, intending to give it a friendly squeeze. But the power of first love intervenes. Without even thinking, he tugs her closer and finally brushes a kiss across her soft mouth. It's the most natural thing in the world.

So natural, in fact, that Skye leans in for more.

Benito closes his eyes, because the sight of her loving expression is too much to process at close range. He needs to concentrate on the scent of her hair and the sweet exhalation that hits his lips just before he kisses her again. This time he presses his mouth firmly to hers, deepening the kiss just enough to get a hint of the sweetness he always knew was there.

It's like plunging into a cool lake on a hot day—it's still a shock to his system no matter how long he's looked forward to it. And yet. Because he's wise beyond his years, he kicks quickly to the surface. He makes the kiss a good one, but then he forces himself to pull away.

Skye blinks back at him afterwards, looking stunned. Her ivory skin is splotched at her cheekbones, and her lips are rosy.

"That'll have to hold us for now," he says, his voice a rasp.

She blinks one more time. "Right. I'm..." She puts her fingertips to her mouth and falls silent. Then she seems to shake herself awake. "I'm supposed to be babysitting for the Carerras in fifteen minutes."

"And I have work to do," he lies. But he has to put some distance between himself and that kiss. He knows the ukulele is an entirely inadequate barrier between what he wants and what he can have right now. "Later, Skyescraper."

She wrinkles her perfect nose. "Later, Rossi."

He walks away through the trees. And he doesn't look back so that she won't see how big he's smiling.

TWENTY-ONE

Skylar

_____

THE NIGHT WE NEVER GOT. Somehow, between the party and the bed, I lose my anger. My heart is ready to forgive Benito for his teenage betrayal. And my body forgave him last Friday night, about three minutes after I walked into the Gin Mill for the first time.

I'm flat on my back, holding Benito in a vise grip, taking every kiss and begging for more. I'm attacking Benito like a brazen hussy.

Do people even say *brazen hussy* anymore? Whatever. So long as Benito doesn't stop kissing me, I don't have to think.

We lost my skirt somewhere in the hallway, but I'm still wearing boots. I thrash a little, wondering if I can kick them off.

"I got you," he rasps. His hand slides down my leg to my boot, which he unzips efficiently. I arch my back, my chest rising and falling rapidly as he tugs it off, and then moves on to the other one. My socks are the next to go—both of them in quick succession.

Then soft lips graze my knee, and travel upwards at a teasing pace. My lady bits quiver as he approaches my panties. I actually squirm on the bed, unable to stay still. "Come here," I order. I crave his weight on top of me. I'm not in the mood to be teased.

"I like you bossy," he murmurs. Then he stands up and removes all his clothing. All of it, while I watch with a dry mouth. He lies down beside me on the bed, his head propped up in one hand. "What else are you going to order me to do?" Dark eyes look down at me, and there's humor in them.

And I love it. I love *him*, if we're being honest. But I'm in way over my head. I care too much and I know too little. I can't answer his question, because I don't exactly know what to do with a 100 percent naked Benito. Until now, sex was always something that was done to me.

And it was over so quickly that I never learned much about it.

Benito doesn't seem to notice or mind my silence, though. He reaches over and scoops my body closer to his. Then he takes one of my hands and places it on his chest.

Ooh. His chest. It's my favorite part of him. Actually, I really like his mouth and his eyes, too. But the chest is solidly in the top ten...

But Benito isn't done. Now he drags my hand slowly down his body. We pass a set of washboard abs, and the firm ripple actually makes me whimper with surprise, because he feels so good under my hand. A wave of heat rolls down my body.

A second later he places my hand *right* on his erection. It's an impossibly bold thing to do—the sort of thing that played through my teenage fantasies. No—it's hotter than my timid teenage dreams. But I always wanted him to treat me like a woman instead of a little girl who needed saving.

These are my thoughts as Benito removes his hand, leaving mine on his cock. I'm too captivated to take my hand away, so I leave it there like a dummy. I can't get over the hardness under my palm. So I close my fingers around it.

"Fuck!" Benito groans at the contact. His mouth finds the underside of my jaw, and his kiss explores my neck. I melt against the bed, stunned by how good it feels as his lips and tongue make love to my neck. *Stunned.*

I'm twenty-eight years old and I have embarrassing little sexual experience.

Benito isn't waiting for me to make the next brilliant move, though. He's reaching under my sweater, unclasping my bra. He moans, and that's when I realize I'm still clutching his penis like a stick shift.

Whoops! He knocks my hand away, though, because he needs me

to lift my arms to shed my sweater and bra. His confidence is enough for both of us, somehow. I kick off my panties as if I do this all the time.

And then I'm naked with the only man I've ever loved.

He whispers sweet things as he rolls onto my body. "Honey," and "so beautiful." I experience the hot press of his body against mine as another scorcher of a kiss finds my mouth.

My poor little brain has never processed so much sensory over-load at once. There's the firmness of his thighs between mine, and the gentle scrape of chest hair against my breasts. His fingers weave into my hair, which makes my scalp tingle happily.

And that's not even counting the warm slide of his tongue on mine, or the erection between my legs… I feel like an electrical circuit that's shorting out. My hips arch toward his, looking for more contact.

He gives it to me, dragging the base of his cock right across the epicenter of my desperation.

Holy macaroni. I let out a shameless moan as I reconsider the idea that I'm not a very sexual person. He groans in answer, and the sound spreads like liquid fire all throughout my overexcited body. Then his tongue strokes mine, and I taste beer and sex. And I like it a whole lot.

"Skye," he breathes against my lips. "If I grab a condom from that drawer, is that a good thing or a bad thing?" He kisses me deeply after asking the question, as if giving me time to ponder it.

His kisses are *so* distracting that I almost forget the question. His hand snakes down my body, teasing my thighs apart. And then his thumb brushes right over my clitoris.

"Oh," I gasp. And then I say it again and again as his fingers tease me senseless. I feel my body absolutely drench his hand with desire. I'm practically vibrating with excitement. And—yes—a condom would be a great idea right about now. But talking about it is too tricky.

So I just reach over and yank the drawer open myself. There. Message delivered.

Benito makes a happy sound. He kisses me very thoroughly one more time before finally sitting up. I hear the sound of a condom being ripped from the strip, and the drawer closing again. His back is to me as he suits up, and I close my eyes and take a deep breath because I'm having a moment of performance anxiety.

I open my eyes to find Benito looking down at me. "Come here, honey," he says softly.

"Mmh, what?" I stammer.

He moves until he's sitting beside me in the bed. Then he crooks a finger. "Come here." He grabs a pillow and shoves it behind his back, then leans against the headboard. His legs are bent in front of him.

I don't really know what he means for me to do, but I sit up anyway.

"Over here," he orders, and the bossy tone gives me a shiver. I like that he's in charge. Trusting Benito has always been easy for me.

He tugs my hand, indicating that he wants me in his lap. I throw a leg over to straddle him, and it's awkward for a second. But then we're face to face, and his warm brown eyes are right in front of me. And there's love in them. "Hey. I don't care what happens tonight."

"That is a lie," I whisper, glancing down at his very hard penis, which looks engorged to the point of pain.

He laughs. "Okay, parts of me care very much. However..." He runs a hand down my belly slowly, making me shiver, until his fingertips graze my mound. "My main goal is to make you feel good. It's something I've wanted to do for a very long time."

"Why?" I have to ask. Honestly, making me feel good is a whole lot of trouble.

He gives his head a shake, as if I've asked a ridiculous question. "Because when you look at me the way you're looking at me right now, I feel like a superhero."

"Oh." I'm pretty sure that Benito really is a superhero. But I keep this thought to myself, because he's still touching me, and it's very distracting. His fingertips dance across my breasts, then dip down to tease me. Just a brush across my lady bits, and I gasp at the daringness of it.

Then he ducks his head and finds my nipple with his mouth, and he sucks. Hard.

"Unggh." I arch my back to offer my breast. And this pushes my pelvis forward until I'm grinding on him. Holy moly. I feel amazing—

like I'm the kind of girl who can grip Benito's shoulders and moan just because it feels good.

He tortures both my breasts with his tongue. And then he tugs me forward until he can claim my mouth with his. Our kisses are deep and wild. He's holding me in a tight embrace. I've never felt so safe and loved as I do right now.

And I've certainly never been this turned on.

That must be why I push my knees down into the mattress and lift myself off his lap. Ben groans into my mouth. And then he takes himself in hand and teases me further, dragging his cockhead across the slick folds of my body.

Feeling brave, I trap him where I want him and then I just go for it —lowering myself down, taking him inside my body one thick inch at a time.

He lets out a whispered curse as I gingerly lower myself all the way down, until I'm full of him.

And then we're both quiet. We stare into each other's eyes, and I can't quite believe that we've actually arrived here. Benito inside me. I clench around him just to tell myself it's real.

"Fuck, Skye," he whispers. "I've been waiting for you. For this."

"Me too," I confess, although neither of us means it literally. But my heart has been waiting to feel like this—breathless and beautiful.

Of course, now he's expecting me to know what to do. And I don't know if I like being in charge.

Although it turns out that I'm not. Benito leans in to take my mouth in a kiss. And then he jacks his hips upward. All my nerves are dialed up to eleven, and it feels so urgently good that I need to move, too.

"Yes, honey. Just like that," he murmurs against my lips.

I feed on this praise, and pick up the tempo. So long as Benito holds me close, I can forget the rest of the world exists. There's just us and our heated skin and the delicious noises he makes as he exerts himself beneath me.

"So good," he says between kisses. "Take it just like that."

I don't want it to ever end. I'm a sex goddess! I was born for this. Except my body is crying out for release, and I'm starting to tire. I'm frustrated in the best possible way. I want fireworks, and this is as close as I've ever been.

"Come here." Benito wraps his arms around me, pulling me close. My face lands in his neck, and I can feel his rapid pulse under my cheek. Then he rolls us onto our sides, skimming a hand between our bodies. His fingertips worship my skin, finding the most sensitive part of me. I whimper with longing, and squirm against him. "Kiss me, honey."

It's easy to obey an order like that. Again I seek his mouth. It feels great on mine and tastes even better.

And then he takes over—touching me and kissing me and whispering the most lovely things. "Need you." "Beautiful." And finally, "Let go, honey. I've got you."

Let go. It's not something I do very often. But when Benito whispers it into my ear, I take a deep breath and let it all out—all the heartbreak, all my disappointments. I slam my eyes shut and just let myself experience everything at once.

He thrusts slowly, and then sucks on my tongue. That's when it happens. Fire and color and trembling release. It's bright and pure and a long time coming.

So to speak.

God only knows what sounds I make, but Benito's approval is immediate. As my body shimmies around him, he pushes me onto my back with a happy growl and pumps his hips.

That's when I realize he's been holding back. And I appreciate how careful he's been with me. Except the power of Benito *not* holding back is pretty awesome. The desperate noises he makes are raw and unguarded. Only moments later his muscles lock up tight and his body shudders over mine, his tongue a hot brand against my own. Then he makes a soul-deep sound of satisfaction.

Wow. Okay. I'd be impressed except I can't move or even think.

Neither can Benito. He collapses over me, then slides off, pulling me with him. I'm wrapped in powerful arms as one big hand skims down my hair. He takes a deep breath and exhales in a mighty gust.

We just lie there for a while, catching our breath. My body feels amazing—loose and well-used. All my anxieties have flown away.

But I am *very* emotional all of a sudden. My eyes get hot and I blink against unshed tears.

Do *not* cry, I order myself. *Don't wreck your only experience with awesome sex.*

Needing air, I twist out from under Benito and sit up, swinging my legs off the side of the bed to face away from him.

"What's the matter?" he whispers immediately.

"Nothing," I say in an almost normal voice. "I'm just…" I clear my throat. "You were right."

"About what?" His hand lands on my bare back, where it caresses me.

"When I was sixteen, I wasn't ready for this." I'd thought I wanted it. But I don't think I was capable of a sexual relationship that was healthy for both of us.

"Yeah," he says softly, his fingertips tracing my backbone. "I loved you, though. If Gage wasn't there to make your life a living hell, I don't know what might have been."

All this time I've been blaming Benito for standing me up for a stupid date. But he was there for me a hundred other times when I'd needed him. I reach a hand behind my back and give his a squeeze.

"You okay?" he asks.

"Absolutely," I say immediately. "Even if I don't know what it all means. And I don't know what to do now."

"You don't have to do a damn thing. All I ever wanted you to do was stick around."

Oh, man. "But I can't promise that."

"I know," he whispers. "Deep breaths. Let's sleep. Then let's find your sister. One step at a time, okay?"

"Okay," I agree. I get up and visit his bathroom, composing myself while I get ready for bed.

After that, Benito does the same. Except he comes back to bed naked, whereas I'm sitting up against the headboard, wearing my nightgown. "You don't need this," he says, gripping the fabric and tugging it upward.

"I don't?" I say, but I let him pull it over my head.

"No ma'am. We have this warm bed and these quality sheets. And I'm going to hold you like I always wanted to." He tugs on the quilt and then tucks me against his naked body. "Never got this night with you, but I've dreamed of it often."

I have, too. He deserves to know, but it would cost me too much. I'm still the cautious one. I don't know how to stop holding back. I don't know if I ever can.

Even so, I'm happy to be here. I roll over and wrap an arm around his fine chest. I kiss his neck. And it's so nice, I do it a few more times.

He turns his chin to give me better access. Then he runs a hand down my bare hip, and my lady bits wake up again and say, *Woo-hoo! We love sexytimes!* Because apparently I do. I'm not broken, after all.

I don't know the protocol, though. Benito probably needs his sleep. But his skin feels so fine against mine that I feel the need to suck gently on his neck.

And he feels the need to play with my breasts until they're heavy and pebbled again, and supersensitive. We move on to kissing, which we do until my lips are bitten and raw. And then Benito pushes me onto my back and grabs another condom out of the drawer.

I don't even blink this time. I'm just glad they're in there.

He makes love to me again, until we're both sated and exhausted.

Then there's more cuddling.

I guess Benito is not all that worried about getting enough sleep, after all.

———

As we lay together in the dark in the wee hours, I feel drunk on my own happiness. "How did you get this awful scar?" I whisper, tracing a jagged white line down his ribcage. The blemish only makes him look stronger and more beautiful.

Do I have it bad, or what?

"I got knifed by a teenager in Iraq," he says with a yawn. "That ended my tour in Iraq. But I was dumb enough to go back over to work for a military contractor, thinking that would be better."

"It wasn't?"

He shakes his head. "One thing I learned about war is that everybody always thinks he's the good guy. That kid who cut me imagined himself the righter of ancient wrongs. I was only offering to kick the soccer ball around with him."

I trace the scar again. "But everybody can't be the good guy."

"No." He brushes my hair off my face. "But that's why I catch bad guys in Vermont now. My odds of knowing who's a dirtbag and who just needs help are so much better at home. In the military you have to take it on faith that you're shooting at the right people. I don't really want to shoot at anyone." He thinks that over a second. "Well, almost nobody."

I lay my head down on his chest and listen to his heart thump. Best sound ever.

TWENTY-TWO

June, Twelve Years Ago

ZARA IS WEARING a nice dress for grad prom. It's better than she can afford, and it's the nicest dress she's ever owned. Her mom gave her some of the money, and her mom's friend altered the dress so that it fits perfectly.

Still. It's not the perfect dress. There was one she liked better, but it cost twice as much. And now, as Zara rides beside Jill Sullivan toward the pre-party, Zara can't see how beautiful she is. She doesn't know that eighteen is stunning in its own right, or that her shining dark hair and olive skin make her glow with a beauty that doesn't need designer labels.

It's the rare eighteen-year-old who understands that, though. Zara isn't alone in her failure to appreciate the perfection of being eighteen. None of them do.

For example, Jill Sullivan's thoughts are similarly irritable at the moment. Her dress cost a small fortune in Vermont terms. She made sure to tell Zara several times that she paid full price—two-hundred-fifty dollars—in a Boston boutique on a shopping jaunt with her mother.

But her shoes are all wrong. If she could have just gotten the Prada heels, too, it would have made the whole outfit.

Jill and Zara are both going stag to grad prom. They told all their friends that tonight was meant for spending together as a class. But each of them is really going stag because the right boy didn't ask.

In fact, Jill turned down an invitation from Bill Hurley. She doesn't regret it, because she doesn't want to hook up with Bill Hurley, even though he's reasonably attractive. But he's no Benito Rossi. So what's the point?

All anyone can talk about is Benito's date. He asked *her* to grad prom. After a whole year of telling people that they're just friends, he up and announces that she's his date.

Jill feels a little sick just thinking about it. In two hours she'll have to watch Benito hold Skye in his arms during the slow dances. And Jill won't be able to boast afterward that she and Benito hooked up, because this time nobody will believe her.

In her dreams they do, though. Every night.

"Slow down," Zara hisses beside her. "Cop car!"

Jill's angry thoughts have given her a lead foot, and she's speeding, damn it.

"Oh, shit," Zara says, her voice low and scared.

Sure enough, there are blue and red flashing lights behind them. Jill pulls over immediately, saying a silent prayer in her head. *Please don't let it be the scary cop.*

In the passenger seat, Zara is openly panicking. "*Why* were you speeding?"

"I was going forty-five!" Jill argues, her eyes in the rearview mirror. Even as the cop's door opens, she can see those mean eyes.

Fuck.

Fuck fuck fuck.

Zara pulls her cell phone out of her bag and begins texting madly, her fingers flying over the keys.

"What are you doing?"

"Texting Benito that *he* pulled us over. He told me to tell him if we're ever stopped."

Jill rolls down her window and smiles, hoping to look friendly and guileless. "Hi officer. Is there a problem?" The cop's boots are audible on the pavement as he approaches, and she feels each footstep in her gut.

"Ladies," he says with a slow grin. "Why don't you step out of the vehicle."

"Step out?" Jill asks. "Why?"

"Because I told you to," Gage snaps. "That's reason enough, aint it?"

Zara knows this is bad. Her hand is shaking as she releases the door to step out of Jill's white Mustang. They're over on the shoulder, so she's already scuffing her mom's best pair of heels. Mom will lose it if she ruins them.

"Don't we look nice tonight," the cop says, making it sound sinister. "Going somewhere special?"

"To grad prom," Jill says. "My boyfriend is waiting."

Zara has to give Jill credit for that bit of improvisation. There is no boyfriend, of course. Zara feels naked in her sexy new dress. And they're on a lonely turn of the country road that leads to the pre-party at Brent Hickey's place.

She doesn't even know if her brother got the text she sent. He might still be at the florist picking up the corsage he bought for Skye, or maybe he's back already, and they're off somewhere staring into each other's eyes like they do.

"You were speeding," Officer Gage says. "Doin' forty-two in a thirty-five."

"Jeez," Jill whines. "My dad will kill me if I get a ticket."

"What do you think?" Gage asks, turning to Zara. "Should I let her off? Hi, neighbor. How come you haven't been around so much lately?"

Zara's insides clench. "I don't know," she ekes out.

"No?" he asks, patting his gun holster. "I'm not sure if I should let her off. You want me to?"

"S-sure," Zara says lightly. "I don't know how it works." She's getting freaked out by the hard look in his eye, though. And all that attention.

"You got a date tonight, too?" he asks.

Zara shakes her head, and then wonders if she should have nodded.

Gage laughs. "How 'bout I make you girls a deal. No ticket."

"Thank you," Jill says quickly.

"I'll let you off, if the Rossi girl *gets* me off. She can come right over here and get down on her knees for me in the pretty dress."

Jill gasps, and Zara's hands get clammy. Her heart is racing, too.

Zara is known for her smart mouth. Her family says she has the sharpest tongue in Vermont. But not when Gage talks to her like that. She knows she should argue, but she trembles instead.

"What?" he sneers. "Like that's something you don't do? *Please*. Bet you get down on your knees every weekend."

She is frozen in place, staring down at the gravel just in front of his boots. The cop isn't wrong. At eighteen, Zara has given a generous number of blowjobs already. Not one of the recipients terrified her, though.

This isn't the first time Gage has said terrible things to her. This is, however, the first time she thinks he'll actually make her do it. In front of Jill, no less. The whole town will know by tomorrow. They boys at school already call Zara a slut. But this will be much worse.

Zara sucks in a breath. Her throat and eyes are stinging but she will *not* cry. He wants that too much. She may have to blow him, but she is not going to give him *any* fucking tears.

Just as she's making this small but important decision, she hears a faint buzz. It's not the rapid beat of a June bug's wings, but something better.

Benito is approaching on his motorcycle.

Jill turns her face toward the sound, too. She's as tuned to the Benito channel as anyone. And there he is a moment later, flying toward them with a corsage box held awkwardly in one hand even as he steers his Triumph.

He wastes no time parking behind the cruiser and marching forward like a soldier. "Problem?" he asks with as much gravitas as a guy holding flowers in a box really can.

"No problem," Gage says easily. "You can just move right along."

Benito shakes his head. "Can't do that, sir, until I know my sister and her friend are on their way. Has there been trouble?"

"Not yet," Gage growls. "But there will be if you don't *get*."

Benito walks up to Jill and hands her the box. "Here, honey. Hold this for me." His hands are free. He stands between Zara and Jill and flexes his fingers. He doesn't say a word, though. He just lifts his chin and looks *right* at Gage.

Zara is trembling. She knows something bad is still going to happen, and yet she's filled with relief. Because she needed Benny and he showed up. And she's not on her knees pulling out Gage's gross old-man dick while he sneers at her.

"I'm responsible for these two," he says to Gage with the steely calm of a CEO addressing his board room. "So whatever's wrong, I can help."

"Yeah?" Gage snarls. "You gonna suck my dick, too? Because that's what your slut of a sister was about to do when you drove up."

Oh shit. Zara notes the way her brother stops breathing. And she watches him curl his hand into a fist. Her brothers have thrown a lot of punches for her these past few years. But never at a cop.

No, Benny, she prays. *Keep it together.*

And maybe he would have if Gage hadn't kept running his mouth. "I heard you enlisted," Gage says. "Sad to hear you're leaving the neighborhood. After you go it will be just me and Skylar all alone in the house together. Won't that be fun?"

Then he *laughs*.

Benito's fist flies through the air and into Gage's nose. Jill and Zara both scream as Gage dodges the worst of the impact and then punches Benito right in the kidney.

The sound of pain her brother makes will stick with her for at least twelve years.

TWENTY-THREE

Benito

THE DAY BEGINS WITH A GASP.

Skylar sits straight up in my bed, the covers falling away from her glorious, very naked body. "Rayanne didn't text!"

"What?" I'm distracted by the profile of her perky breasts. My blood stirs. Again.

"I turned the volume up really loud, but Rayanne didn't check in at midnight." She's already grabbed the burner phone off the nightstand to check. "There's nothing here. Something's wrong."

Oh, shit.

Sitting up, I wrap an arm around Skye. "Okay, let's think." I pull her against my chest and kiss her neck. "Send her a message right now."

"I can't," Skye whispers. "She told me that was dangerous."

"In the daylight it might not be a big deal, if she's trying to hide in the car." I point out. The sun is already burning away the darkness, at least in the Eastern part of the sky. "Let's get up, get some coffee, and figure out what to do."

She leans her head back against my shoulder. "God, if something has happened to her…"

"Maybe not, though," I stroke her bare hip. "Maybe she just fell asleep, you know? Let's not panic just yet."

"Okay. But I feel so guilty. She's out there somewhere, hiding from *something,* and I'm here..."

"Having really good sex with someone who loves you?"

Skye turns sharply, her blue eyes wide with surprise. *"Benny,"* she whispers.

"What? I'm not supposed to say that? Sorry, honey. Some things are true whether it's convenient or not." I count them up on the fingers of one hand, held out in front of her. "Global warming. Neurotic families. I accidentally bought whole bean coffee instead of ground. So we can't make coffee this morning after all. Four—your stepsister is a flake who's doing things the hard way. And Five—I loved you from the first day I met you. That's never going away."

She grabs my hand and pulls it to her tummy. As if stopping my counting might shut me up. *As if.*

"Look, I know you're stressing," I tell her. "Go do whatever it is that takes you half a fucking hour to get ready to go to the coffee shop. Or— wait—I could just stumble over there and buy coffee and bring it back."

She whirls on me. "You go in there with sex hair and buy two of everything and the whole town will know we stayed up all night."

I chuckle, because that sounds about right. And I really don't see the problem.

"Twenty minutes," she says, sliding out of my arms. "Twenty-five if I have to deploy the extra-strength concealer." She walks away from me, her perfect ass drawing my eye down to long, smooth legs.

I let out an unmanly groan of longing. She doesn't even break her stride.

———

When Skye emerges, I take a two-minute shower and tame my sex hair. So it's twenty-seven minutes later when we enter the Busy Bean together. I must look perky in spite of my lack of sleep, because my sister takes one look at us and bursts out laughing. "Wow," she says. "I was going to ask why you two disappeared early last night, but maybe I won't bother. Coffee?" She reaches for two mugs.

"Oh hush," I say quickly, because Skye looks like she wants to hide under a table. I do feel good, though. I'm not sure I could conceal it even if I wanted to.

"It's the cider," Zara says, oblivious to my girl's discomfort. "That stuff has magical properties."

"I'm buying a keg of it," I decide aloud. "What smells so good? Can we have two of whatever that is?"

"This morning we have a quiche with leeks and Swiss cheese. If that doesn't float your boat, there's always the muffins or Roddy's bagels." She pours us two cups of coffee.

Still blushing, Skye orders a mini quiche.

"Make it two," I say, digging a twenty out of the computer case I carry when I'm headed to work.

But Zara pushes my money back, and once again I'm stunned.

"Seriously?" My next comment is only half joking. "Is there something I should know? Are you ill?"

"I'm fine." She shakes her head. "We'll talk later. Enjoy your breakfast. I'll bring it over in a minute."

Skye has already claimed the same sofa where we sat last time. *It's our spot*, my subconscious suggests. If only. Skye still doesn't expect to stick around. But right now her head is spinning. She's worried about Rayanne, and she's not thinking clearly.

There's some work to do there, but I like a challenge. If I'm patient, I can make her realize that a second chance is a rare and special thing. There are obstacles—jobs and lives. But those things could work themselves out.

There's no way I'm letting Skye walk out of my life a second time. It's not happening.

Skye's body language, though, suggests otherwise. Her back is as straight as a board, and she's texting Rayanne on the burner phone. I peek over her shoulder. ***Where are you? Check in or I'll ask Benito to declare the Jeep stolen and every cop in Vermont will be on your tail.***

She presses send, and then stares at the phone, hoping for a quick response.

There isn't one. Wordlessly, I hand over her coffee mug.

I sip my coffee and check my own messages. There's one from Officer Nelligan. ***Sparks hasn't been seen in twenty-four hours. I*** *couldn't find him last night, and he's not with Gage this morning. I'm thinking he's slipped out of the county alone.* "Shit."

"What is it?" She looks over my shoulder, too. "Where could he be?"

I quickly tuck my phone into my pocket. No sense in worrying Skye. "Let's eat, honey." My sister is approaching us with two plates. "And let's talk about our plan for the day. I have to go and meet with my boss in Waterbury. My apartment is yours, of course. But maybe you can hang out with Zara when she leaves later."

"Sure thing," Zara says, depositing two plates and two silverware rolls on the table in front of us. "Yoga was canceled again. So I was thinking of heading into Burlington to do some shopping."

Skye's eyes widen, and then just as quickly narrow. My sister is making the effort of the century, but Skye doesn't trust it. "I need to find Rayanne, frankly. I'm worried about her."

"Ah," Zara says, a hand on her hip. "Okay. Do you want me to figure out which Rossi can loan you a car?"

"No fucking way," I say around my first forkful of excellent quiche.

Now both women are squinting at me. "Why shouldn't she drive around if she wants to?" Zara asks.

"Reasons," I sputter. I can't sit in the middle of my sister's coffee shop and discuss an investigation.

My sister rolls her eyes. "You two can hash it out. But come to me if you want help," Zara says with a cheeky smile. "I'm no longer a bitch, but I'm still resourceful."

She walks off, and Skye's gaze follows her, looking puzzled.

"You cannot drive around the county looking for Rayanne," I say after she's gone.

"Maybe I need to look *outside* the county," she says, pulling her own phone out of her bag. "Ah. My colleague finally got around to running a search for me. John Oscar Sparks, age twenty-six, convicted in 2015 on weapons charges... Oh, *shinola*. He is a bad dude!"

I actually grab the phone out of her hands to see what she's got. And it's all right there—Spark's sordid past and three last known addresses. "What are you doing?" I yelp, making heads turn around us. I drop my voice. "Don't look him up. Your job is to stay the hell away from this guy, and let me do my job."

"It's not working," she returns at a whisper. "If you tell me you're going to drive around the northern part of Vermont looking for Rayanne today, then take me with you. Otherwise I'm going to look for that Jeep myself."

"In what car?" I fire back.

She bites one kissable lip. "There's a perfectly good pickup truck in Raye's garage. If you'll go up to the house with me for five minutes, I could maybe find the keys."

"There are a whole lot of problems with this idea. So many that I don't even know where to start."

"So that's a no?" she asks, her tone dry. "I'll ask Zara for help, then." The look she gives me is full of heat and challenge. I'm so fucked. I just want to kiss that smug expression off her pretty face.

"Back up a sec," I say. I reach for my mug and take a pull of my sister's wonderfully strong brew. Also, I've hoovered half my quiche into my maw already and I might need a second one after this one is gone. "In the first place, before you tackle the world, eat your breakfast. All-night sex can really fire up the appetite." I point at her plate.

Her eyes widen a trace, and she glances around as if concerned about being overheard.

"Now let's think this through. You're more useful to Rayanne if you stay where there's ample cell phone coverage. Driving around all day won't solve anything. There are hundreds of little roads. Where would you even start?"

"On a lake," Skye says simply. "Especially one bordering Canada. I thought I'd drive up to Lake Memphremagog and look around."

I nearly choke on a bite of quiche. Because that's *exactly* where I think Rayanne has taken drug deliveries before. I have a camera on Gage's fishing cabin there. But I don't think Skye knows about that place.

"Jimmy Gage has a fishing cabin up there," she says.

Fuck.

I take a sip of coffee and try to remain calm. "But you hate Gage. If you think he's at Lake Mem, shouldn't you drive in the complete opposite direction?"

She crosses her arms in front of her chest. "Nice dodge, officer. I notice you didn't confirm or deny that the cottage still exists. So that makes me think it does."

It would really be more convenient if Skye weren't so smart.

"And you're right—I don't *want* to see Gage again. I'm frankly terrified of him. But I can't sit around doing nothing, waiting for this Sparks guy to find her. He was incarcerated for weapons charges! You have to get him, before he gets Rayanne."

"I'm trying. But you're not helping me by driving off looking for trouble." There's something else nagging at the back of my brain. "Hey—where did you see this truck, anyway?"

"It's in her garage."

"Color?"

She shrugs. "Black? Navy? Who cares?"

I do. A whole lot. And I have a full-on tingle down my spine now. I pull out my computer and flip it open.

"What's the matter?" Skye asks.

"Probably nothing. I just want to check something."

Now, there are lots of ways to figure out if Rayanne owns the same model of truck that nearly hit Zara's car in the Gin Mill parking lot. But sometimes the quickest solution is the simplest one. I open up Facebook and type in Rayanne's name. This won't be the first time I've scrutinized her social media profiles. She doesn't employ good privacy techniques. Rayanne is an open book.

I head right to her photo albums and start scanning for a pickup truck. And it's right fucking there—in the background of a photo where she's holding up a big striped bass. Half the license plate is visible, too. It starts with ABX, but the other digits are obscured. The plate is yellow, not green like we have in Vermont.

Holy shit.

"Your sister owns a truck with New York plates?" I ask. In my investigation, I could never turn up a vehicle registered to her.

"Maybe? Rayanne moves around a lot. She's only been back here a year and a half, right? She was in Buffalo for a while."

I actually knew that. I'd found a record of her renting an apartment there when I did a deep dive through her credit history last month.

"Why do you care?"

I turn to look at Skye, who's looking at me with big, trusting eyes. There's really no easy way to say this. "Let me show you something." I've looked at it so many times myself that it only takes me a second to find the image on my computer. "This is a still shot from a security video shot on the night when Zara was almost killed by an erratic driver."

Skye leans in to look at the photo, then leans out again in a hurry, as if it might bite her. "You think that's the same truck? You think *Rayanne* almost hit Zara? She would never do that."

"I don't think anything," I say quickly. "But I've been looking for a match to this plate forever. The image is crappy and the shadows obscure the spot where the plate would say *Vermont*. But it's possible that this is a New York plate, and a partial match with Rayanne's truck. Look—they're both Ford F150s."

"That's the bestselling vehicle in America!" Skye squeaks. "It proves nothing."

She's right. Except I've tailed Rayanne in her dad's car several times. If she has a truck in her garage, she never drives it. And why is that?

"Maybe not," I say slowly. "But I still need to show this to the Colebury officer assigned to this case, and he'll probably check it out." My voice is calm, but inside I'm shouting. Because I know on a gut level that Rayanne's truck will match. We didn't find any plate in the Vermont database that was a decent match. This has to be important.

Skye pinches the bridge of her nose. "This is ridiculous."

"Maybe," I say just to placate her. "If the truck has no damage to its body, then she'll be instantly cleared."

"I didn't see any damage."

"Good," I tell her. But after the truck cracked the door off Zara's car, it fishtailed into a streetlight pole on its way out of the lot. Even if someone tried to repair it, the evidence will still be there.

"Can't this wait until after we find her?" Skye asks. "She doesn't even drink, Ben. She likes tea and kombucha. She couldn't have been involved."

In the next couple of seconds, I have two very startling realizations. The first is that this may be a big break for me. It doesn't matter if the car accident is unrelated to the drug case. If a judge gives the Colebury police a search warrant for the unsolved hit-and-run, we might be able to search Rayanne's home as well as the truck and the garage. And if she can't be located, the warrant could be expanded— to her phone records, her EZ Pass, and so much more.

This is big. It's a *huge* stroke of luck.

My other realization, though, gives me the cold sweats. This is how I lose Skye again. It won't be her job or the two-hundred-fifty miles between our homes that takes her away from me again. If I lock up her only (sort-of) sibling, she'll leave me forever.

If someone locked up Zara, I'd lose my shit.

The situation settles over me like an eerie calm. I become aware of all the ambient sounds in the coffee shop—the low murmur of my sister's voice, and the tap-tap of the portafilter as someone ejects the spent grounds into the trash. I can hear my own pulse.

But this won't even be a difficult decision. I will absolutely go after Rayanne if it helps me lock up Gage and Sparks. Gage has tormented my loved ones and the community of Colebury for over fifteen years. And I will do whatever it takes to put him away.

I'm doing it for Skye, too. Even if she won't appreciate my methods.

"Listen." I lower my voice. "Nothing will be solved by worrying. I'd better get to work. Are you going to be okay?"

"I always am," Skye replies. But she won't look me in the eye.

This wasn't how I'd wanted the morning after our big night to go. I should be giving her deep kisses right now, and inviting her to be naked in my bed again when the day is done. But my life isn't a fucking fantasy. "Please don't drive off in search of Rayanne. Wait for her texts. Or go shopping with Zara. I'll call you as soon as I can."

She puts her hand on my wrist. "Will you let me know what happens with the license plate? If it's really a match?"

"I'll call you in a couple of hours, no matter what," I promise. "I just want one kiss before I go."

"Here?" she asks weakly.

"Yeah. A goodbye kiss. People do it all the time." I reach up and cup the side of her face, my thumb tracing her pale eyebrow. "Just a quick one. It'll have to tide me over until I can kiss you *everywhere* later tonight."

Skye studies me with her big blue eyes. I'm not the only one who's afraid of what the day might bring. "Have a nice day at work. I will miss you."

"Me too, honey." I lean in and give her a gentle peck on her perfect mouth.

Or, rather, I meant it to be a gentle peck. But when my lips touch hers, I feel our attraction sizzle and snap. And I can't resist deepening the kiss.

She grips my shirt and kisses me back. My Skye is a study in contrasts. She's reluctant and yet passionate. Shy, yet also hungry.

"Whew," she leans back suddenly, gulping oxygen. "That's quite enough of that."

I smile at her, trying to memorize the way she looks right now. I wonder how long it will take me to stop wondering if each time I see her might be my last.

Then I kiss her quickly on the forehead and get the hell out of there while I can still make myself leave.

TWENTY-FOUR

Skylar

———————

AS BENITO'S shapely backside exits the Busy Bean, I realize I've learned a *lot* in the last twelve hours. For starters, I didn't know that you could be angry with someone and still wish he was naked on top of you.

What is happening to me?

I had fireworks-sex all night long for the first time in my life. It was amazing, but now I'm about twice as confused about Benito as I was before. He's a good man. I trust him on a gut level. I crave him in ways I didn't know were possible.

And yet I'm upset that he thinks Rayanne could have almost killed somebody. It doesn't make a lick of sense.

I'm so twisted upside. I need my life to just slow down a bit, so I can think. But that's too much to ask, it seems. I'll have to settle for the rest of my quiche and a refill on my cup of coffee.

"Everything okay?" Zara asks, trotting towards me with a coffee carafe.

"It will be," I insist, holding my mug out.

"I get off at eleven today when Roddy comes in to take over for me." She fills my cup. "If you want to hang out, let me know by eleven."

"Thank you," I say, wondering why Zara seems so sincere all of a sudden. "It all depends if I hear from Rayanne. She was supposed to check in with me last night and she didn't. I'm freaking out a little."

Zara frowns. "Where is that girl, anyway? I got a text from the Green Rocks resort that yoga was canceled."

"She, uh, didn't say," I admit. "I was supposed to spend the weekend with her, but she left town suddenly."

Zara straightens up in surprise. "You didn't drive up here to see Benito?"

"Not exactly," I admit. "That part was an accident."

"Well, I'm sure he appreciates it, nonetheless." Then she winks.

After last night's extra-curriculars, I'm sure she's right. I have an involuntary flashback to straddling his lap, gripping his shoulders and…

Oh my. That's going to leave a mark on my subconscious. I lower my face over my hot mug of coffee for cover.

Zara laughs. "If there's anything I can do to help you get in touch with Rayanne, just say the word. Her house is right up the hill near mine."

"I know. Thank you." She turns to walk away, but I realize I don't have all the information I need. "Hey, Zara?"

"Yeah?" she turns around.

"Benito said he's trying to find a truck that almost hit you. What's up with that?"

"Oh! Crazy story." She sets the carafe down on the table and plops down in front of me. "It was August—the night of Audrey's wedding. My boyfriend had just pulled up over there…" She points outside, toward the Gin Mill building. "I'd opened the car door to step out, and this truck accelerates toward us and drives right *through* my car door. He just clips it right off. I was almost right under its tires. Except my boyfriend yanked me back into the car by my arm just before it sped by."

I flinch at the thought.

"They never caught the guy. It was probably a drunk driver. They swerved around the turn to exit the lot, and banged the back of the truck into the light post before turning out onto the road."

"Whoa. Where did the truck hit the post?" I ask. "Did he side-swipe it?"

"Sort of. It was more of a hip check." She shrugs. "I haven't ever seen the video, because I didn't want to relive it. But Dave still has nightmares about it." She sighs. "Welp. I'd better tidy up before the next wave of thirsty people." She gives me another unlikely smile and gets up to do her thing.

———

An hour later I'm walking back up the hill into Colebury. I don't want to see Gage again, and I sure don't want him to see me. So I'm wearing a Farm-Way cap and a hooded sweatshirt, both found in Benito's closet. The shirt says *Body By the Colebury Deli* on it.

I never, ever dress like a slob. But this is my disguise. I've got the hood pulled up, and all my hair is invisible.

As I approach Rayanne's house, though, there's a cruiser parked outside. The young cop from the other night is leaning against it, just watching Rayanne's house. His muscular arms are folded across his chest, and he wears a patient expression that gives nothing away.

"What are you doing?" I ask him as soon as he notices me. I push the hood off and remove the cap, so he can see who I am.

"Miss Copeland," he says. "I'm afraid I can't discuss it."

"Is someone in Rayanne's house?" I ask.

He shakes his head. "I wouldn't know. Haven't seen anyone, though."

I glance at the house, which looks about the same as it did the other day when I'd searched it myself. But I'm careful not to look at the garage, which is where I really want to go. If I walk in there right now, I'll only draw attention to it.

"You need anything, miss?" the cop asks.

"No, thank you," I say primly. "Just out for a walk, hoping my stepsister had come home. But I'll come back later."

"Okay, then," he says easily. His words give nothing away, but I notice that he's fingering a cell phone in his pocket, the way I'd do if I were waiting for a call.

Hmm.

"Bye now," I say, and keep on walking. I do a slow circuit of the little town green. When I'm on the opposite side of the square I take out the burner phone and text Rayanne. *Why didn't you check in? I'm worried sick. And now I think you're in a whole lot of trouble. There is a cop parked outside your house. RIGHT outside!*

The phone rings in my hand a few seconds later. The noise is so unfamiliar that I jump, and then scramble to answer. "Hello?"

"I'm sorry," she says immediately. "I fell asleep and forgot to text you last night."

"You *forgot*," I spit. "This isn't a game, Raye! I'm still in Vermont for the express purpose of worrying about you! And—"

"Hush," she demands, cutting me off. "I got played, okay? I've been hiding in this Jeep for three days, eating granola bars and shivering. And it was all a setup."

I take that in. "Who set you up?"

"An asshole named Sparks. He told me shit was going down here at the lake, but it was a lie. Nothing happened here. Except that I can't feel my toes."

"That sounds miserable. But you still haven't told me a single flipping thing about Sparks or the trouble you're in. And now Benito thinks you're a hit-and-run driver."

"Fuuuuuck!" Rayanne whispers. Then she lets out a heavy, knowing sigh. "After seven months he finally found the truck?"

My heart drops all the way to my two-inch heels. "Raye!" I hiss. "Tell me it isn't true." I'd walked up the hill to see the truck myself. I was positive I'd find it free of scratches or dents.

"I didn't hit Zara's car, okay? Sparks did that. But nobody will ever believe me."

"Sure they will," I argue. "Either you were behind the wheel, or not! It's not that complicated."

She groans. "We were both in the truck."

"Why?"

"Because of *sex*, Skye. We were having a sexual relationship. But then he tricked me into doing some things that are totally illegal. I mean—I picked up on the fact that he's a scary dude. But I thought I could let him do me without becoming part of the story."

It's my turn to let out a groan.

"Trust me, I know. Anyway. I told Sparks that night in my truck that we weren't having sex anymore, and I wasn't going to do any more of his dirty work. I was driving us away from the Gin Mill, and I was sober. But Sparks was wasted. He didn't like what I had to say, and he threatened me."

Oh no.

"I started the truck because I wanted to drive home. I was in a snit, so I accelerated like an asshole. That's on me. But then he grabbed the wheel and intentionally steered me into Zara's car door. He did it to scare me. And it totally worked. I screamed like crazy and then banged the truck into a post."

"This is the most effed-up story I've ever heard." Although it sounds like something that would happen to Rayanne. The girl has gotten into more scrapes than a clumsy kid in roller skates. "And you thought it was a good idea to leave the scene of an accident?"

"No! But I did anyway," she wails. "He was yelling, 'Floor it! Floor it! You're the driver, you stupid bitch.' That stunt was his way of buying my loyalty. That and telling me every day that he'd kill me."

"Who *is* he?" I demand. "And make it good, because I've had enough of not knowing a thing."

"He works with my dad." She snorts. "I just made it sound like they own a real business. But I guess they do. They buy heroin and cut it with fentanyl. And they tricked me into helping them."

"Tricked you?"

"Long story. But fentanyl is small. You can drive a hundred-grand-worth around under the spare tire of your dad's car, and not have a clue it's there. Ask me how I know."

I shiver. "That's terrifying."

"That's just the beginning," she says, sounding smaller and more scared than she did a minute ago. "I need out. I drove up here to take pictures of Sparks picking up this month's drop. He let it slip what day it was."

"But it didn't happen?"

"No. It was just a ploy to get me up here alone. Last night he was cruising this town in slow circles, looking for me. I saw his headlights four times. He's going to kill me, Raffie. I'm a dead girl."

"So turn him in!" I plead. "You must have the goods on him."

"Yes and no," she says quietly. "I need pictures. Because if I'm not convincing, I'm a dead girl. The only way this works is if he's in jail forever and I'm not. Even then it's a tossup. He could hire someone to kill me for him."

I shiver again inside my hoodie. "Why don't you just explain this to Benito, and let him hide you?"

"Because he doesn't run the world! The more help I am to him, the better this goes. I'm so close to proving what Sparks is up to. But now he doesn't trust me. He drove up here just to hunt me down."

I'm afraid for her, but she also sounds a little paranoid. "How can you be sure?"

"I put one of those Tile tracker things in his car. That's why I needed the rental Jeep—so he couldn't spot me. I watched his location do slow circles around the lake all last night. I was lying on the floor of the backseat, terrified that he'd look into the windows."

"Oh gosh."

"You can curse, you know. When people are trying to kill me, you can say *fuck*."

"Go back to the truck a second. What about fingerprints? His prints should be on the steering wheel of your truck." That's how it would work on TV, anyway.

"No dice. I have a fuzzy, sheepskin steering wheel cover."

"Why?" Of all the stupid things.

"Hello? Vermont? It's minus-twenty here in January. And fingerprints aren't going to save me. Nobody is going to save me except for me. But now you know why I left you at the rest stop. Sorry about that. I couldn't think what else to do."

I want to argue, but it's a waste of time. "What do we do now?"

"We? Nothing. You stay there and boink Benito Rossi. I need to find a new hiding place."

"Come home," I beg.

"No can do. If Benito has a brain in his head, there will be a warrant for my arrest before lunchtime. And now they'll be looking all over Vermont for a red Jeep with a kayak on top. Fuck my life."

I stop dead on the sidewalk. "Where will you go?"

"Not sure, but whatever it is, I'm not telling you."

"Raye! I wouldn't rat you out."

"I didn't say you would. But I don't want you to have to choose between me and hot cop. I've made some bad choices in the name of sex, and wouldn't expect you to be any wiser. And I'd ask you if he's good in bed, but we'll have to catch up some other time, because I'm running for my life, here. Later."

Just like that, she hangs up on me.

TWENTY-FIVE

Twelve Years Ago

ZARA ROSSI SITS STONILY in the passenger seat of her mother's car on the way home from the police station. She's already missed the pre-party. And now she's missing the grad prom, which ought to be devastating.

But it's nowhere near as devastating as the sight of her brother in handcuffs, his face bloodied by Gage.

She'd had to watch Benito marshal his temper about five seconds too late. She'd watched his expression turn from outrage to fear as the truth sank in—you don't pick a fight with a man carrying a club, a Taser, and a service revolver.

He hadn't fought back while Gage beat him.

Even now, Zara can't believe he just took it. Her strapping eighteen-year-old brother could have overpowered Gage's fists. But as Zara stood there, choking on her own fear, Benito stuck to defensive moves only. After Gage dropped him with the second punch, he rolled away from the swing of Gage's trooper boot. And when he struggled to his feet again, Gage made another run at him.

Zara almost threw up as Gage charged, swinging. Benito blocked his face with his arm and spun out of the way the best he could. Jill sobbed like the world was ending when Gage finally landed a punch to Ben's nose. The blood was instant, a gush down his face.

And the blood changed everything. Gage stopped, breathing hard, surveying his damage. Maybe that was the moment he realized beating the neighbor kid to a bloody pulp would look bad on his record. Or maybe he was just tired.

Jill's sobs were the loudest sound among them. They drowned out Zara's own quiet tears. But as Zara wiped her face, she saw that Jill was clutching her shiny red phone. It's the new kind—with a camera. Wordlessly, Zara slipped the coveted thing out of Jill's hand and took a quick photo.

It's her only act of bravery. And she's still too afraid to raise the camera and make herself noticeable. So the angle will prove to be awkward. But even so, it will prove be valuable. It will eventually convince a judge that Gage came unhinged.

A month from now, all the charges will be dropped.

But tonight all Zara sees is the devastation she's caused. Texting Benito to come to her rescue was the worst idea she's ever had. How did she *think* this would end? Seconds after Gage broke Ben's nose, he'd barked at Ben to put his hands behind his back.

And her brother did it, a leaden look in his eyes.

Then Zara was treated to a view of her twin in handcuffs—something she *never* ever needed to see. They're eighteen now. Her brother could be a felon for the rest of his life, and it would be Zara's fault. He might never get a decent job. The military might cancel his enlistment.

None of that will happen, but Zara doesn't know it yet.

Just as Gage pushed Benny's head down to force him into the back of the cruiser, her brother gave Zara one instruction. "Tell Skye I'm sorry."

And then he was gone, and Zara was left alone at the side of the road with a sobbing Jill, who was still holding a corsage box meant for someone else.

Zara's bad night wasn't over, either. She had to call her mother and tell her that her youngest son had been arrested.

That went over about as well as you'd think.

In her anger, Maria Rossi exceeded all of Zara's expectations. She was white with anger at the police station. And then a very rosy red color from shouting at Zara outside of it.

And now, as they drive home from the station, she's still yelling the whole way. The theme is, "Why didn't you call your mother? Or your uncle? Or just pay the damned ticket!"

Zara doesn't explain that Gage didn't want ticket money. What difference does it make now? She already knows that calling Benito was a dumbass thing to do. Her mom is terrified, and they don't have three-thousand dollars for bail.

"What about those bail bondsmen?" Zara asks. "We can go first thing tomorrow morning."

Her mother launches into another lecture about how bail bondsmen exist to take advantage of desperate people. Zara hears words like "usurious" and "vulnerable." And then her mother says, "And after we shell out for that, we have to move, too, you understand. We can't live next to that man. Not after this."

Moving is something else they can't afford. Which means Mom will have to borrow money from her brother, who will lecture *her* about it, too.

It's all Zara's fault.

When they pull into Pine View, Skye is sitting on her tiny front stoop, looking amazing in a sleek dress. She looks like a supermodel waiting patiently between takes at a cover shoot.

Zara is filled with horror. She's supposed to be the one who breaks Skye's heart by telling her what happened? Seriously? The night's devastations aren't over.

"Go inside," her mother snaps. She's still in a full-on lather. "Lock the door behind you. And don't you dare step out, young lady. Not for anything. Your night is *over*."

Zara gets out of the car feeling numb. Her mother is watching, so she goes into their trailer and shuts the door, just as she's been told. Her mother's car turns around and drives away. She'll drive to Uncle Otto's house and ask for bail money.

Her mother hates asking for help. She's going to blame both twins for this disaster. Zara is still wearing her dress. Her *new* dress that they couldn't really afford. It's all a waste.

And Skye is still sitting out there.

Zara goes into her bedroom and peeks out the window at her. She dreads telling Skye where Benito is and watching her cry. The light is gone from the sky, so her brother's date sits patiently in the dark, even though she must know the dance has already started. The pretty line of her long, elegant neck is unbowed.

Zara closes her eyes and rests her head on the window sill. Everything is shit. She's a high school graduate now with no good job and no obvious way to pay for college. If college would even have someone as stupid as her.

Mom said to stay inside. She'll wait until Mom comes home before breaking the news to Skye. She'll wait a little longer.

But then she hears a car approaching.

Zara opens her eyes in time to see Gage step out of the cruiser. Whatever he says to Skye makes her stand up fast. "No!" she yelps.

He laughs. And it's the cruelest sound that Zara has ever heard.

Zara closes her eyes again, wishing she were somewhere else. Anywhere else. But at least she doesn't have to break the news to Skye herself. It's done.

Benito can give his own apology in the morning.

TWENTY-SIX

Benito

"YOU WANT the good news or the not-so-great news first?" my boss asks.

"Uh, you pick," I say, taking a seat in front of Sergeant Chapman, the head of the drug task force.

"The not-so-great news is that the judge only gave your Colebury boys a limited search warrant. They can search the truck and the garage. If there's any evidence of collision on the vehicle, the judge will consider a broader warrant."

"Ah, that's okay. I still have a good feeling about this."

"Good," he says, crossing his arms. "You'll have an even better feeling when I tell you that a midlevel dealer in Burlington gave up Sparks's name last night."

I play that sentence back in my head, because it sounds too good to be true. "Are you serious?"

"Serious as an overdose. This was the dealer's third arrest, so he's looking at a shitty sentence unless he can plead it down. That's apparently enough incentive to cough up Sparks's name and a very few other details."

"Jesus. Can we convince him to make a couple of controlled buys for us?"

"If we ask nicely."

We both snicker. No perp wants to become our informer. It's

dangerous work. But if we've got him red-handed, then wearing a wire and buying drugs from Sparks is his only way to stay out of jail.

"You can watch the video of the interview as soon as we're through here," my boss says.

"I'll make the popcorn!" This is the break we were looking for. "I wish it had been me that busted him."

Chapman grins. "I'm sure you do. I know you have a boner for indicting Sparks and Gage."

"And you don't? They single-handedly changed the flow of drugs into Vermont. No—into the whole goddamn country."

"Of course I do. But for me it isn't quite so personal. Be cool, cowboy. We're gonna need to be careful with our evidence. Maybe you're too close to this one."

"No way," I insist. "I'm careful. Always."

"Good. Now go watch the video and tell me what you think."

"On it," I say. And then I get the heck out of there.

———

I watch the video three times, making extensive notes. Then I start making plans. First, a small buy from Sparks—with no wire, in case they frisk my favorite new informant. But we'll capture the transaction on video from a hidden camera. Then we'll go back for seconds, this time for a larger amount. Sparks won't roll over on Gage unless we've got a lot of evidence against him.

"Hey, Brooks?" I call out to our assistant.

"Yessir?" he asks, peeling a banana at his desk.

"Can you find out if our informant has any relatives outside of Vermont? Parents or siblings, maybe? Bonus points if he happened to go to high school somewhere outside the state."

"Sure. On it."

Maybe my perp is planning a trip to see his sister, and he wants to bring some inventory to push off on his lowlife friends...

I'm working through all the possible set-ups when my phone rings. And the caller is Skye. "Are you going to arrest Rayanne?" she asks without preamble.

"Me? No," I say. "But the Colebury police are probably looking at her truck. Why?"

She sighs, and I feel like the worst traitor. The first thing I did after leaving the coffee shop was to send the Facebook photo link to Nelligan so he could chase it down. I assume he took one look and filled out an affidavit for a search warrant. That's what I would have done.

"Have you heard from Rayanne?" I ask carefully.

"Yes. She's terrified. She wanted lake photos of some kind of handoff. But it didn't happen. She says Sparks sent her on a fishing expedition. And now he may be trying to kill her."

Good thing she can't see me flinch. Because Sparks is a nasty piece of work, and totally capable of murdering his business partner's kid. "Do you know where she is."

"She wouldn't say," Skye says immediately.

"Honey, if she'd just come in and talk to me, we could sort the whole thing out."

"I'm scared for her," Skye whispers.

"Me too. But in the meantime, I'm doing everything I can to lock up Gage and Sparks. If you got Rayanne to talk to me this could all be over sooner."

"Okay."

"Stay cool, Skyescraper." I know she hates that nickname, but I use it when I need to prevent myself from turning into a pile of mush. "I'll be hours here, okay? Catching bad guys is a lot of work."

"Be careful," she says, and I grin.

"I will. Go amuse yourself with something besides worrying about Rayanne."

We hang up, and I turn back to my computer with a grimace. It's time to write up a new investigative plan for one John Oscar Sparks.

I only pause in my work when my sister texts me.

Zara: *Skye and I are going shopping in Burlington. She wants to pick up a few things because she didn't intend to stay this long.*

Me: *Reallllly. Girls' day out? That's nice.*

Zara: *Right? Either she's figured out I'm not a horrible teenager anymore. Or she's just so bored that my brand of evil sounds better than sitting around waiting for your ugly mug.*

Me: *You kids have fun.*

Zara: *I'm going to get her drunk for old time's sake.*
Me: *Don't you dare!*
Zara: ***Insert evil laughter****
Me: *Bye, bitch.*
Zara: *Bye, ugly.*
Some things never change.

———

I don't get home until eight o'clock that evening, and I don't call first, either, because I was driving around the county checking out the known haunts of Gage and Sparks.

But I didn't find them.

When I walk into my apartment, I'm a little stunned. In the first place, it smells good. There's a whiff of curry in the air, and the smell of something meaty. "Wow," I say, sniffing the air as I drop my jacket onto the coat tree.

Skye turns around, a spatula in her hand. "Hi. I cooked. Sorry. I needed something to do with my hands. And I needed comfort food."

I cross the room toward her, putting my gun away in the cabinet over the refrigerator. As I come closer, I notice a few things. One— Skye looks amazing in my kitchen. I'll keep that thought to myself because it might come out sounding sexist. But nobody ever cooks for me except my mom on Sundays. I lead a bachelor lifestyle of takeout food and sad microwaved leftovers.

The second thing I notice is how Skye is dressed—in a new pair of dark jeans that make her legs look a hundred miles long and a tight little V-neck T-shirt that makes me want to investigate that V of skin with my tongue.

And—I'm ashamed to say that this final detail brings out my inner caveman—she's wearing one of my flannel shirts over the whole ensemble. That's almost more than I can take, honestly. I'm seconds away from suggesting that she strip down to *only* that shirt and come immediately to bed with me.

"Hi, honey," I say instead, because she's watching me with big eyes. "If I wanted to kiss you, would you stop brandishing that spoon?"

She looks at the implement in her hand like she's never seen it before. Then she sets it on the counter. I back her up against that counter and find her mouth with mine. It's just one kiss, but I make it a good one. She smells like dinner and tastes like heaven.

I make myself pull back, because I need a shower after a long day at work, and I'm not ready to unleash my inner caveman on my girl. "I love that you cooked," I say, my voice raspy.

"It's a curried lamb stew," she says shyly as her eyelashes dip.

I let out a little groan of happiness. "You cook a lot?" I'm still boxing her in against the counter, because getting close to Skye is one of my two life goals. The other one is seeing Jimmy Gage go to jail.

"On the weekends," she says softly. I'm happy to note that she looks as distracted as I feel. "Aunt Jenny and I used to cook together. It saves money."

"How is Aunt Jenny, anyway?" I ask.

"She's good. She moved to Florida a year ago. I've been down there only twice to see her, and just for the weekend. I still live in her apartment, though. It's rent-stabilized."

I run out of small talk and just watch her at close range. She looks like she wants to kiss me again. "Stop that," she says instead.

"Stop what?" I move back an inch or two, since I probably smell like too many hours in an unmarked vehicle.

"Stop looking at me like that."

"Like what?"

Her cheeks get pink and she doesn't answer.

"You mean, like I want to strip off your new clothes and fuck you on the kitchen counter? I don't know if I *can* stop. I want you no matter what room we're in."

"Dinner's ready," she says, blinking at me. "I already took half of it upstairs to May and Alec. But I was waiting for you to eat."

"Ah. Well we'd better enjoy it, then."

She blinks one more time. "Move your extra-large, extra-hot self out of the way so I can serve up the rice."

"Yes ma'am."

But now I'm thinking about sex. So even as we sit down at my kitchen table with a freshly opened bottle of wine and a dish of rice and lamb stew, I'm turned on. "Any new word from Rayanne?" I ask to get my mind out of the gutter. "Any idea where she went?"

Skye shakes her head. "She said she was making a point not to tell me. So I wouldn't be in the middle of it."

"Smart girl. So you went shopping in Burlington? How was that?" I wonder if Zara was able to charm her.

"Well," Skye sets her spoon down. "Your sister is being ridiculously nice to me. Like *really* accommodating."

"That's good, right?" I ask, spooning up a giant bite. "My God, this is amazing. I'm going to eat an embarrassing amount of this."

Skye gives me a smile. "Thank you."

"What else did you do today besides shop?"

"My bossy producer called like four times because he's short-handed and regretting his decision to send me away for two weeks." She rolls her pretty eyes.

"Sounds like a fun guy."

"He's a bully. And I made the mistake of telling him I was in Burlington. So he called back with the address of an affiliate station and asked me to just 'swing by...'"—she makes her fingers into air quotes—"...to edit a story."

"And you told him to fuck off, right?"

"No." She picks up her wine glass and takes a healthy swig. "I know I should have, but my job security seems shaky right now. So I went to the affiliate and apologized profusely. They let me use a producers' station and I wrote the danged story."

"Wrote it? Or edited it." I don't know how the news works. Is that the same thing?

Skye snorts. "They refer to it as editing, but I wrote the piece. Someone else will get credit. But I took their interview footage, wrote the script, emailed it back and it will run tonight."

"What would they do without you?" I wonder aloud.

"Write their own stories?" Skye guesses. "That's hard to picture. I have a coveted job in TV, but most days I think my life would be improved if I sold mascara at Sephora. At least I'd get an employee discount for my luxury cosmetics habit."

Laughing, I gulp my wine. Everything is bliss. There's good food, and Skye is telling me what's on her mind. There are people who would mock me for saying I fell for Skye in one afternoon when I was eighteen. But that one afternoon was followed by hundreds of hours of talking in the woods.

I've missed her so much. I love her wry view of the world, her practical nature, and the soft glances she gives me when she thinks I'm not looking. After dinner I'm going to show her exactly how much I missed her all day.

But first, more food. "How did you pick journalism, anyway?"

"Ah." She gives me a cheeky smile. "To change the world, of course. Ask me how that's going."

"How should it be going?" I ask instead. "What did you want to have happen?"

"Well, Aunt Jenny is a widow," she says, taking a dainty bite. "Her husband…"

"Fell down an elevator shaft," I supply.

Skye's eyes widen. "Good memory."

As if I could forget. "I remember every single thing you ever confided in me."

She gives me one of those soft looks that I like so much. "Well, Jenny spent years trying to get the city to acknowledge that his death in that building was needless, but she didn't get anywhere. And then the first year I lived with her we got a call from a guy at the *New York Times*. He was doing a piece about elevator deaths. So Jenny gave him an interview. And that guy published a big exposé about fraudulent elevator inspections. Heads rolled, and things changed." She shrugs. "I wanted to do that, too—to call out wrongs and make people listen."

I set my spoon down and sit with that a second. "Like dirty cops who harass sixteen-year-old girls?"

"Maybe," she says quietly. "I never really thought of it that way."

"I'm a cop. You're a journalist." I spoon up another chunk of spicy, salty lamb. "Maybe we're both still fighting a really old war."

"Well, that's depressing," she says, sipping her wine.

"No, it isn't." I shake my head. "Doing good work is never wrong. Although sitting here with you right now is even better revenge."

She smiles into her wine glass.

"Finish your meal," I tell her. "We have some business to attend to."

"Business?"

"Naked business."

Her cheeks pink up, but she finishes her stew. And when she eventually rises to clear the table, I stop her. "I'll clean up. You already did plenty." I stand up, too, but I leave the dishes on the table. "But the cleanup starts with me."

"What?"

"I need a shower."

"Okay, go ahead?"

"Not alone. I want company."

Her eyes flare. "In the shower?"

"Yes, miss. There's plenty of room for two in there. Pin up your hair or whatever and follow me. While I'm young, okay?" I beckon to her.

She gives me a pointed look. "What if I don't need a shower?"

"You do, honey. You just don't know it yet. Now let's go. I need help washing my back."

Skye rolls her eyes at this thin excuse.

"Let's go. We don't want to waste hot water." I go into the bathroom and turn on the faucet. Then I start to strip.

It isn't until I'm naked that she peeks around the corner. "I've never showered with anyone else before."

This makes me irrationally happy. "So you're a shower-sex virgin? Excellent. Come here." I remove my own flannel shirt from her shoulders and toss it out of the room. And then I undo the button on her tight jeans.

She bats my hands away. "I can unzip myself, you know."

"Yeah? Then you take care of that. I need something from the bedroom."

I make a quick trip to the bedside table for a condom, which I deposit on the sink console. Skye is already in the shower, and when I open the door, it's like all my teenage fantasies come to life. Skye is standing under the spray, the water running down her breasts as she tips her head back.

Jesus H. Christ. I'm dead. But my cock definitely isn't. One look at water droplets on Skye's nipples and I'm insta-hard.

Skye notices, too. I see her eyes widen, and then her shy gaze lifts to meet mine. "Let's see this back of yours that needs washing."

I turn around just to keep up the ruse, and I'm rewarded by soap-slicked hands running across my heated skin. "That's amazing, honey. Don't miss any spots."

She gives a little snort and keeps washing me. I lift my arms and tip my head in either direction so that she'll touch me everywhere. "Now the front," I tease, turning around, my eager cock pointing right at her.

I hold her gaze as those slick hands work their way down my body. The only sound is the thrum of the water and my own pulse in my ears as she comes closer to touching me where I need her. "Go on," I rasp. "Want you."

Her eyes darken as her smooth, soapy hand encircles my shaft. I let out a groan of desire, and her breathing quickens.

I shamelessly reach for her breasts. They're slippery in my hands. She makes a happy sound, and there's no longer any reason to pretend that this is a business visit to the shower. I push her up against the tile and kiss her neck. And I let my hand slide down her slick skin, until I find the juncture of her legs.

"Spread for me, honey."

She sucks in a breath and adjusts her stance, parting her legs. Her pubic hair tickles my palm as I begin to tease the softest part of her. I bury my face in her neck and taste her skin with my tongue.

The water beats down on us and I have never felt more alive than I do right now. I'm no longer in a hurry. I don't need this to be over. The limits of my hot-water tank aside, I have all the time in the world to kiss her skin and stoke her body with pleasure.

There is no better use of this night. Hell—there's no better use of my life.

These are my thoughts as I kiss my way down her body and sink to my knees. I grasp one of her legs and lift her calf onto my shoulder. "Lean back, baby," I murmur. "I'm going to make you feel good. Yeah —hold on like that."

Her hands grasp my shoulder and my hair as I nose into the center of her. She breathes in hot gasps as my tongue finds her clit. My kisses are slow and teasing. And in between, I mutter every dirty, lovely word I know. "Give it to me," I say. "Use me."

I give her my tongue, flattened against her clit. Her hips buck and strain for more. I missed out on twelve years with my girl, and I don't want to miss another second. My cock is painfully hard, but I could do this all night. Slowly, I slide a finger inside her for the first time.

Her response is a gasp and a moan. She grinds against my lips, and it's perfect. "That's it," I rasp. "Spread your legs wider. That's my dirty girl."

And Skye freezes.

I gentle my stroke, kissing her thigh. But her body doesn't ease. So I raise a hand to check the water temperature. It's still fine. Then I peer upward at her, tilting my head to avoid a face full of water. "You okay?"

She nods jerkily. And yet I know there's still something wrong. Skye removes her leg from my back and puts both feet on the floor. And when I get to my feet, I see that her eyes are red. She looks like a cowering animal.

"Hey," I say in a voice that's still rough with desire. I raise a hand to push the wet hair out of her face, and she actually flinches.

Oh, shit. I play back our last two minutes and try to figure out where I went wrong. *Use me. Wider. That's my dirty girl.*

Now Skye is hugging herself and looking embarrassed. "Sorry," she says as I shut off the water. "I just need a minute."

So do I. My head is suddenly in a hundred places. Reaching out of the shower, I grab a towel and then wrap it around her. "I triggered you somehow, didn't I?"

"Probably. I don't know." She sighs. "Yes. It's stupid."

My pulse is pounding in my ears, but for a different reason now. "Was it 'dirty girl'?"

She bites her lip and looks away.

Shit.

With shaking hands, I find a towel for myself and dry off enough so that I don't drip water everywhere. Then I tie the towel around my waist and leave the bathroom. Pacing into the kitchen, I open the refrigerator and stare into it for no particular reason. But it's that or put my fist through the wall.

Only one thought rings through my brain: I'm going to kill Gage. That motherfucker is a dead man.

TWENTY-SEVEN

Skylar

─────────

THAT'S TWICE NOW.

I sink down on the edge of the bed, Ben's towel wrapped tightly around me. And I wonder—how many times can I ruin sexytimes before he decides I'm not worth the trouble?

And I'm kidding myself if I say I don't really care. I care way too much, and I always have. Even if I leave here in a couple of days, and never return, I'll still care.

What have I done to myself?

Benito stalks into the bedroom with a pint glass of cold beer and a grumpy expression.

Oh man. "You're mad, aren't you?"

"Of course," he says, setting the beer on the dresser. "I'm livid." Then he kicks off his towel and I'm treated to a quick view of his muscular backside while he pulls on a pair of boxers. "But not at you," he adds. "You get that, right?"

He turns to meet my gaze, and I just blink at him. Because of course he's mad at me. Who else is there to be mad at?

"Skye, Jesus." He brings a T-shirt and the beer glass around to the other side of the bed and sits down on it, stretching his long legs out. "Come here, would you?"

I turn to face the music.

"Here. This is for you." I'm stunned as he drops the T-shirt over my head. "Put your arms through. There you go. Gotta cover you up a little so my brain works while I'm trying to talk to you. Now take a sip of this." He hands me the pint glass.

I lift the glass, and as it approaches my nose I get a whiff of cider. "Is this Shipley cider?"

"It's half Shipley amber, half beer. That's what makes a snakebite. If you like it you can keep it and I'll get another one."

"Delicious," I say. It has the fruity nose of cider, but with the bitter kick of beer. "I didn't know you could mix them like that."

"The Brits invented it. It's sort of a compromise between beer and cider."

"It's delicious. Let's share." I take another sip and hand it back.

His brown eyes smile at me, and then the smile fades. "We need to talk for a minute."

Well, crud. I was afraid of that.

"I'm sorry I triggered you," he says. "I can tone down the dirty talk."

"But..." I'm speechless for a second. "You didn't do anything wrong. I don't have to be so sensitive."

His expression gets even sadder. "You're not, Skye. Someone taught you to feel shame. And I could fucking kill that guy. Come here, would you? Just for a hug." He hands me our glass and opens his arms.

"Sure." *Twist my arm.* I set down the glass and wiggle closer to him. His bare chest smells like soap and clean man. "We can still, um..." I clear my throat.

He chuckles, and I feel his abs tighten with the motion. "Someday I want you to enjoy finishing that sentence. But today doesn't have to be that day."

"Okay?" I take another sip of the snakebite and lean back against his solid warmth. This is how I always imagined cuddling in bed with Benito would be. It's good to know that I was right.

"Look, I've been to all kinds of training seminars, and there was this one about sexual abuse that really stuck with me."

"Now there's a cheery topic," I grumble.

"Hear me out, okay? Because this woman was smart. She was trying to explain to a room full of grumpy cops what it's like to grow up with a sexual abuser. She said that sex is like a private room in your soul. Kids don't go into the room, because they're too young to notice it. And then teenagers explore it at their own pace."

I relax against him, listening. And he strokes my hair while he chooses his words.

"She said that sexual experience is supposed to be like a room that's yours to decorate however you want to. Without anybody else's interference."

"Your own private sex room? Sounds kinky."

"I know, right? But she did a good job making us listen." He chuckles at the memory. "She said some people move right in and install a hot tub and a velvet swing. But some people are more cautious—beige carpeting and hospital corners on the bed."

"So you're saying that second thing sounds like me?"

He shakes his head. "No. You didn't even get a chance. Gage beat you to it. He busted open your safe space and flipped over the furniture and smeared shit on the walls."

"*Oh.*" I've heard worse theories.

"It's just a lecture I heard once. It doesn't make me an expert. I should probably just shut up. But I'm thinking that listening to Gage could put anyone off of sex. He used to call you a dirty girl, didn't he?"

An involuntary shiver runs down my spine. "Among other things."

"He called Zara a whore. I heard that one myself." Benito takes a deep drink of our snakebite. "Anyway. I don't actually know how to help you. Or if you need help. But I can be infinitely patient. If I say anything you don't like, just tell me. I won't be offended."

My heart is in so much trouble. This man is going to break me.

Benito passes me the glass, but I set it on the table beside us. And then I turn in his arms and kiss his jaw. He smiles against my lips, and I kiss him three more times, each one softer and a little more sensuous than the last.

This is what I never knew about sex—that the little moments can be amazing. Before Benito, I was never comfortable enough with anyone to explore the texture of his whiskers against my lips. I never traced anyone's six-pack with my palm, and then ran a fingertip around the flat disc of his nipple.

Benito moans quietly and fits his mouth against mine. His kiss is searching. His tongue familiar. When he exhales, it tickles my upper lip. He kisses me deeply. Endlessly. Our kisses run together like episodes of a hot new show—each one a cliffhanger that requires another.

We're binge-kissing.

Yet Benito doesn't push me down on the bed, or even pull me into his lap. His kisses are deep and firm and fully committed. But his hand is lying uselessly on his thigh.

Touch me, my body sings. My breasts feel heavy and full. I brush them against his chest just for a little contact.

Benito smiles against my lips and then kisses me again. Slowly. Patiently.

So I grab his lazy hand and put it up under the hem of the big T-shirt he clothed me in. It lands on my hip and squeezes. Yes. *Finally*. I tug him down on the bed and throw a leg over his. I'm still naked from the waist down, and the simple act of parting my legs a few inches feels shameless. In a good way.

But Benito doesn't take the bait. He rests his head in one palm and smiles down at me. "You want something?"

"Ben," I whisper. "Come here."

"Why?" he teases, stroking the arch of my foot with his. He's touching my *feet*, and I swear I feel turned on from it.

The feet? Really? "You know why," I complain.

His smile widens. "Honey, someday I hope you can say it." He pitches his voice high in a poor imitation of me. "*Ben, please come here for dirty, naked loving.*"

That sounds so unlike me that I have to giggle like an idiot.

"It doesn't have to be those words," he continues. "It's okay with me if you never like the word 'dirty.' I just hope you can ask for what you need and not feel shame."

I trace his nose with my finger. There's a little rise in the center of it that makes him look dignified. I'd always wanted to touch it when I was sixteen, but never quite found the nerve. "It's true that I'm not a fan of the word dirty."

"Like I said, that's not the point. But do you know what dirty means to me?"

I shake my head.

"Funny, I'm not sure I do, either."

We both laugh.

"No—let me think." He leans down and kisses me once. "Okay, when I think dirty thoughts about you, I really mean that they're raw. Unfiltered. And when I use that word in bed I mean...*unguarded*. Whatever crazy thing I want is just for the two of us. It's not *bad*, it's just not fit for anyone else's eyes. Just yours."

"I like that definition," I whisper. But what I really mean is *I really like you*.

"Good," he says. "Because I'm having some nice, not-at-all-shameful, dirty thoughts right now."

Then he leans down to kiss me again. And I pull him close and beg him—wordlessly of course—for more.

This time he rolls on top of me and gives me the weight of his body. His tongue strokes mine, and his fingers weave into my hair. He takes his time with me, kissing me until we're both desperate. When I finally kick off his boxers and welcome him inside, I'm ready and willing.

Everything is perfect as we're moving together. Straining. Sharing every breath.

If there really is a private sex room in my soul, Benito has a standing invitation.

TWENTY-EIGHT

Benito

———————

THE NEXT MORNING I get out of bed *very* reluctantly. There's a naked goddess in my bed. Sleeping Skye hugs the pillow, her fine hair spread everywhere.

She looks as thoroughly debauched as I feel. I spend a moment just sitting on the edge of the bed, stewing in my own wonderment. I'm still a little stunned that she's here. It's almost like having an extended dream. Waking up beside her doesn't even feel real.

Other things do, though. Like the fact that I have to get to work early. So I head into the shower. And she's still sleeping when I get dressed and ready to go. So I leave a little note on the counter and a tiny gift beside that.

The gift is sort of ironic, and sort of not. It really depends how you look at things.

After holstering my gun, I take one more peek at her sleeping form. Because I just can't help it. Then I make myself leave.

———

Because the day started so well, what comes next is something of a disappointment.

I'm on a rooftop in Montpelier, manning a video camera that's trained on the parking lot below. My new informant—Wayne Browers

—waits behind a defunct pet store for Sparks to show up. Browers is only twenty-six, but he looks a decade older. His knit beanie is pulled down low over his brow. And his eyes are the deep-set kind that have seen too much.

Before setting up here, we searched him thoroughly—both his person and his car. Our sting operation only works if we can prove that any drugs Wayne Browers possesses half hour from now weren't present when we took our positions in this spot.

But there's already a problem. Sparks is late. And when the dealer is late, it's never a good sign.

At least our guy doesn't look twitchy. He leans against his beat-up sedan looking awfully resigned for someone who's about to entrap a potentially violent drug dealer.

And when another vehicle eventually rolls into the parking lot, it's not Sparks's car. It's a black Taurus that I've never seen before. *Fuck.* It comes to a slow stop as I hear my boss speak into the wire in my ear. "New subject approaching. I don't know this guy. Caucasian male, twenties, heavyset. Tattoo visible on his neck." My boss has a better view of the car's driver from his position inside the pet store.

"Copy," I say quietly. "No ideas here."

Then the man steps out, and I don't recognize him, either. But he strolls up to Browers and they shake hands.

They chat a minute. It looks pretty friendly down there. I prepped Browers for the possibility that Sparks might send somebody else. And it looks like Browers is holding up okay under this slight change of plans. As he'd been coached, my informant pats his breast pocket and then removes the roll of bills I put there earlier. He hands the money to Mr. Heavyset Caucasian. In turn, he's handed a small paper bag.

My guy peeks into the bag and nods.

A minute later the perp drives away. Again, Browers does exactly as we instructed him. He opens the trunk of his car where we can see him. He puts the bag into the trunk and shuts it. Then he gets into his sedan and drives slowly out of the lot.

Since I'm still up on this roof, it's someone else's job to tail him back to our meeting place. I put away the camera and leave the roof via the store below—it's a chain shoe store. I thank the manager for his help and then drive back to our point of rendezvous.

Another detective has already confiscated the drugs from Browers's car, and Browers will be free to go momentarily, until we need him again. "You done good," I tell him. "Who was that guy?"

Browers shrugs. "He said, 'I'm Dave,' and I didn't exactly ask him for no ID."

"Fair enough."

"He said Sparks is busy until tomorrow or Thursday. And I *tole* him I had more business to do maybe, and should I ask Sparks about it later this week? He says sure."

That's not necessarily a bad omen. And this job is rarely easy. "Any idea what Sparks might be busy doing tonight?" Our man Browers doesn't strike me as Mr. Insightful, but it never hurts to ask.

I get a shrug. "Cookin' up the next batch?"

It's as good a guess as any. "You know where they bag it?" I ask. It burns me that I can't find his cutting room.

Another shrug. "His car got a Smokey's sticker on it. Must be local."

"Yeah, okay." I chuckle because that's not bad detective work. Smokey's is a barbecue wagon often parked on Route 12. And anyway—I can run the plates on the Taurus as soon as I get back to the office.

My job is like a slow game of chess. Because we got him on film selling drugs, I can get a warrant to track Mr. Heavyset with a device stuck to his car. We can follow him digitally around the county until he inevitably links us with Sparks. Who then links us with Gage.

But please, lord, let it be soon.

"We done here?" Browers asks.

"For now. Thank you for your service." I remind him of his obligation to stick around and get ready to do this again in a couple of days.

And then I head back to the office to contemplate which chess piece to move next on the board.

TWENTY-NINE

Skylar

WAKING up alone in Benito's bed is a pretty great way to start the day.

I'm naked, which is not a usual thing for me. Even though I live alone now, I never sleep in the nude. I never saw the point. Note to self—it's decadent to feel my skin right against the sheets.

I get up slowly, pulling on Benito's bathrobe over my bare body, and that feels decadent, too. The apartment is silent as I pad into the kitchen to make coffee in the new machine. That's where I spot a note on the counter.

Skyescraper,

It won't be easy to reach me until the afternoon. You know the drill—if you need anything, ask Zara. To make things easier, I had this made for you on my way home yesterday. My place is your place. Make yourself at home.

Love you,

B.

Love you. I get a little stuck on that salutation for a moment. Those are words that nobody ever says to me, unless we're counting Aunt Jenny. I sure like seeing it, but I don't know what to do with it. We'd gone a decade without seeing each other. Now, after I've been here less than a week, Benito is whipping out the L-word.

It's possible that word doesn't mean to him what it means to me. And only five days in, how am I supposed to know?

Beside the note is his gift—a single key to his apartment. It has the shiny finish of a key that's just been cut, and it's on a key chain that I think is meant to amuse me. It's a plastic cut-out of Vermont, and it's printed with "I love Vermont."

Somebody is a funny guy.

This is way too much thinking before I've had my coffee. So I point myself in the direction of the new machine and the grounds I bought yesterday. I turn it on and figure out where to put the water and the filter. Then I hit the button and wait for the telltale sound of coffee flowing into the carafe.

My phone rings, and I have to run into the bedroom to find it. My heart does a little dance, wondering if it's Benito calling.

Stupid heart.

But no, the caller is Aunt Jenny. Of course it is. When I don't keep in touch with her, she worries. "Hello!" I gasp into the phone when I find it. "Hi. Sorry. I should have called. I've been busy, what with the on-air penis and my impromptu trip to Vermont."

There is a silence on the other end of the line, and I wonder if our connection has failed. "You're *still* in Vermont?"

"Yeah. Rayanne is in some kind of trouble. It's complicated."

"You're staying with her?"

Here we go. "Not exactly, no. Her house doesn't feel, uh, safe to me, so I've been staying with…" Aunt Jenny is going to lose her mind. "…Benito."

She lets out a shriek so piercing that it actually hurts me. And then she starts babbling. I hear "unbelievable!" and "miracle!" and a few other words that make me cringe. "When is the wedding?"

"Jenny!"

She giggles.

"Stop it, okay? For all you know he could be married."

"Is he?"

"No," I grumble.

She laughs some more. "Tell me everything."

Well *that's* not happening. Jenny and I are close, but there's no way I can tell my aunt about hot kisses in the woods and hot loving in Benito's bed. So instead I tell her about his cool apartment in the mill building. "The windows are taller than I am. And the rooms are huge.

If this place were in Manhattan, it would cost three million bucks." A cop in New York couldn't live anywhere near this nice, even if his family did own the building.

"Fancy," Jenny says.

"It's really beautiful. That's the funny thing—I thought everyone I met in Vermont would be sort of trapped in amber. But everyone owns a cool bar or a funky coffee shop, or they make award-winning cider. I'm a little irritated at all of them for being more interesting than I thought they'd be."

Jenny snorts. "You're the only one who's allowed to grow up and have an interesting career and shop at…wherever it is you shop these days. I never could keep track."

"They even have bagels," I whine.

"Really? Out-of-town bagels are a dicey proposition."

"There's this cute baker at the coffee shop. He can apparently make anything." My stomach rumbles. "But it's still not New York."

"Right," Jenny agrees. "I don't know how you'd live without rats on the subway tracks and bad service from the superintendent. You'd better not move to Vermont."

"I could never," I say quickly. "My job!"

"Your job is a fucking shitshow," Jenny says.

"Jenny!" Sometimes I think she's determined to say every curse word that I avoid, just to even things out in the universe.

She laughs. "Well it is! They walk all over you and you don't put up a fight. They'd shit themselves if you ever quit, though. You run that place and never get any credit."

Jenny is very loyal, so I hear this sermon a lot. But she doesn't realize how many hungry journalism graduates are standing in line for my job. If I made a fuss, they'd pluck another pretty blonde twenty-something out of the line and hand her my laser pointer. She'd be doing the traffic and weather faster than you can say "point your tits at camera six."

"So what's that stepsister of yours done this time?" Jenny asks.

"She's mixed up with some jerks. And is therefore hiding from the cops." That's as much as I'm willing to say, because Jenny worries.

She groans. "That child is a lost soul. I thought all that yoga would help."

"It has," I say, rising to Rayanne's defense. As I often do when we talk about her. "But men are scum," I add quickly.

"That's her line," Jenny says quietly. "And I know Rayanne is angry, and has every right to be angry. Growing up with a father like that..." She sighs. "But at some point we have to take responsibility for our choices. And it's taken Rayanne a nice long time to reach that point."

I agree, but saying so aloud would feel disloyal.

"Is Benito treating you well? I assume he is, if you're staying in his apartment."

"Yes," I say, and it comes out sounding dreamy. "Benito is a great guy. Seeing him again will give me some...closure." My voice actually cracks on that last word because I'm actually thinking *orgasms* as I say it.

Jenny snorts. "I hope you're having a lot of *closure*. Now I have to go play poker with the biddies."

"May all your cards be aces."

"I wish. Love you, Skye. Take care of yourself."

"Oh I will." It's the one thing I learned really young. "I always do."

We sign off, and I allow myself a nice hour of lounging around on Benito's sofa, drinking coffee, and eating a bagel that Roderick baked. They're even good the second day if you toast them.

It's tempting to file that wisdom away for later. It's just that I don't know what later means to me and Benito. And it's too big a question to solve while I'm naked in his bathrobe. So I get up and shower. When I check my email, there's a demand from my boss inside.

Skye—I need you to call City Hall and get a quote from the parks department on the proposal for reduced public swimming pool hours this summer. It's going into a noon segment about the mayor's address last night. And I may need you to edit an evening segment later. Stand by.

I read the message twice and then let out a little moan of dismay. Jenny is right, of course. I did this guy a favor yesterday, and now he's come back asking for much more. If I'd stood up to him yesterday, he might not have taken advantage of my vacation time again.

So I craft a reply. **I'm still on *vacation*, with limited internet** service. I can make the call to City Hall, and I will forward the results. But I can't possibly edit video for you without my office laptop. You'll have to take care of that yourself.

Then I hit send, feeling brave and a little reckless.

My victory is short-lived. As soon as I hang up with City Hall, there's an email waiting for me. McCracken says: **Your "vacation" is unfortunately timed, and let me remind you that it was caused by your own actions. I've arranged for you to edit at our Burlington affiliate. They'll free up a workstation for you this afternoon.**

He is unbelievable. And he'll never stop. The only way this gets better is if he gets either promoted or fired. Neither of those seems likely.

As I stare at our email exchange a final message pops up. It contains an address in Burlington. And nothing else. Not even a *thank you*.

I lie down on Benito's sofa and contemplate the thick wooden beams overhead. Someone put them up there over a hundred years ago. And then someone else laid thousands of bricks, somehow building a wall that was straight and strong and lasted a century already.

A bricklayer couldn't be called in to work remotely on his vacation days. Maybe I should be a bricklayer.

The burner phone chimes. For one little second I squeeze my eyes shut and don't reach for it. In the moment before I read Raye's text, I can still imagine that she might tell me everything is going to be okay. That Gage and Sparks are safely behind bars, and that she's been cleared of almost killing Zara.

But I know imagining it won't make it true. Benito may have superpowers but he only left for work a couple of hours ago.

When I peek at the phone, there isn't a message. It's a photograph of two men in an unfamiliar black car. The driver is a rough-looking guy I've never seen before. I zoom in and make note of a couple more details. There's a sticker for a BBQ joint on the back of the car. Also, in the background of the shot, I see something familiar. It's the curve of the red clay track down at the high school.

My pulse kicks up. Rayanne is near the high school. She's in town.

The burner phone rings in my hand, startling me. "Hi," I squeak after fumbling for the talk button. "What is this?"

"That's Sparks behind the wheel. But—shit. I need you to delete this. I'm cropping it a little differently. Delete it, okay?"

"Why?"

"Because it reveals too much! Jesus. I need you to give the cropped one to Benito. I'm trying to be helpful. He needs to know that I'm not part of their thing."

"By 'thing' do you mean the smuggling of fentanyl?"

"Sheesh. You're too nosy."

"I'm a journalist. You promised me a story."

"Yeah, that was a mistake. I thought it would take me twelve hours to hand over money shots of Sparks taking delivery of a drop, and Hot Cop would arrest him immediately. Boom. Crisis averted. But nothing is ever simple."

No, it isn't. "So why are you close enough to Sparks to get a picture of his car?"

"I'm staying with this guy I know. He's a hookup I met at goat yoga in Springfield. So today I'm just drinking my tea and minding my own business when that car pulls up outside the house, and Sparks and my father get out. I about shit myself thinking they knew where I was. But they went to the house on the corner to drop something off."

"What was it?" I ask.

"I don't know and that's probably a good thing," she says quickly. "Nothing good. But when I stopped panicking, I ran for my phone and took that shot as they pulled away. I haven't seen that car before, so I thought Hot Cop would like to know what they're driving these days."

"Okay." Maybe he will? I really don't know how tracking drug dealers works. But something she said is bothering me. "Your dad is in this car?"

"Yeah, if you zoom in on the photo, you can almost make him out."

"You thought your dad showed up to *kill* you?"

She's quiet a second. "I don't think my dad would do that. But he doesn't know that I'm willing to send him to jail."

"Oh." That's heavy.

"He never gave me a choice, Skye. He set me up. He made me part of his little smuggling scheme. I don't think he gets that Sparks *will* kill me. That man has no soul."

The same could be said of Gage. I honestly have no idea how Rayanne walks around knowing that her father is an evil cretin. No wonder she spent most of the last twelve years in other places. "Why did you come back?" I ask her suddenly.

"To Vermont?"

"Yeah."

"Because, unlike you, I actually *like* Vermont. It was my home for eighteen years. I thought I could come back and live my own life, you know? But it was a huge mistake. I regret it now. And as soon as I can figure out how to do it, I'm out of here again. As you should be, too. Just as soon as you get Hot Cop out of your system. I assume that's going well?"

I make a grunt of general acknowledgment.

"Good. Now promise me you'll delete the first pic?"

"I promise," I say immediately. "As long as you send me the other one." It's easy to delete a photo from a phone. But it's not possible to delete it from my brain. I already know I'll spend the rest of the day trying to decide whether or not to tell Benito that I know where Rayanne is staying. I can picture that intersection near the high school —there are only one or two houses with that oblique view of the track.

"You'll have it in two minutes. Bye, Raffie."

"Bye," I say. We hang up, and I wonder again how this ends.

I drove to Vermont five days ago thinking that my life was more or less in order. Now everything is a mess. Rayanne is hiding from the police, Benito is confusing the heck out of me with his hot body and his hotter kisses. And my job is worse than I thought.

Not only is that a lot to take in, but those things can't all turn out well at the same time. Either I betray Rayanne or lie to Benito. If I keep my job I lose the only man I ever wanted.

The phone chimes with a new text. It's the same photo, cropped down tightly to the roof of the car. There's nothing in the background now but some pavement and a strip of winter-browned grass and a melting lump of snow. It could be anywhere.

I dutifully forward it to Benito and delete the other one.

Then I try to figure out how I'm getting to Burlington this afternoon to do McCracken's job for him.

THIRTY

Benito

WHEN I PULL into the parking lot at the Gin Mill, I'm just in time to spot Skye exiting the coffee shop. I give the horn a little tap, and she glances up at me. And then her face breaks into a big smile.

And, *boom!* That smile vibrates in my body like a good clap of thunder. She pivots and hurries over to the car, and I roll down the window.

"You're here!" she exclaims. "It's not quitting time, is it?"

I shake my head. "No, but I'm between obligations. And I have something to celebrate, so let's go out for lunch. How about Worthy Burger?"

"Where?" Skye looks blank.

"Woman, it's time for some Vermont aversion therapy. Get in this car."

Her face breaks into another grin. "Let's make a deal. You drive me to the car-rental place on Whiting Road. I'll have lunch with you right after."

"You're renting a car?"

She rolls her pretty eyes. "I have to go back to Burlington for work. Don't judge."

"I would never. And I'll take you to the place. Let's go."

Skye climbs into the passenger seat, and I point the car toward Whiting Road. And then I tell her all about Worthy Burger, and why we should drive a half hour out of our way for lunch. "I can't sample their yummy beers, sadly, because the work day isn't over," I finish. "But the burgers are heaven. Oh—and there's bacon jam!"

"Bacon jam?"

"Trust me. And you have to try all their weird pickles."

"I can't wait."

When we were young, I never got to take Skye out. Neither of us ever had any money to burn on restaurant food. "There are a hundred places I want to take you. This is just the beginning. We have to eat Mexican food in Burlington. And Japanese eel in Chester."

Skye groans. "Well, thanks, because now I'm *starving*. What are we celebrating?"

"That photo you sent. I saw that same car this morning with a different drug dealer inside it. Basically Rayanne just handed me a piece of the puzzle. I can tie Sparks to the midlevel guy with that photo."

"See?" Skye says. "Rayanne is trying to help. She's not a criminal."

I reach over and squeeze her knee. "I know, baby. But Rayanne isn't out of the woods, yet. Where'd she get that photo?"

"She took it."

"Yeah, but where?"

There is a beat of silence in the passenger seat, so I glance to my right and find her looking a little uncertain. "I don't know," Skye says.

Hmm. I'll have to revisit this question later. "Where am I taking you? Here's Whiting Road. But I don't even know where there's a rental car place."

"Oh—Zara told me it's inside the Toyota Dealership. I called ahead to make a reservation."

Just as she says those words, the building comes into view. And I'm suddenly uncomfortable. *Very* uncomfortable. Because my recent hookup manages the service department at the Toyota dealership. Her father owns the place.

Jesus lord. How do I get into these situations?

I pull into a parking spot, where we can both see inside the giant glass wall of the showroom. It's a nice building, actually. It's recently built. I've never been here. Why would I?

"Be right back," Skye says, opening the door and hopping out before I can decide if I should say something.

Skye takes long strides toward the door. Inside, she asks for help from a dark-haired woman behind a reception desk. I don't see my hookup anywhere, thank God. I make a private vow to return those calls on my phone and officially end things when I'm back at my desk in a couple of hours.

The dark-haired woman directs Skye toward another desk, where a man waits, handing her a form. And I've almost relaxed when a door opens from the back, and Jill Sullivan steps out not ten feet away from Skye.

Oh my fucking God.

I have the brief, flickering hope that the two women won't remember each other. But who am I kidding? Jill's face falls the moment she spots Skye. She says...something. It might be, *Can I help you?* Or maybe, *Oh, it's you.* Because Skye stiffens.

Jill marches toward a board hung with different sets of keys. She stares at it for a second as if she can't remember what it's for. Then she grabs a key off the board, whirls around and tosses it onto the counter in front of Skye.

At this point I'm already out of my car and striding towards the dealership door. Jill's mouth is set in a grim line as I enter and cross the big room. And when she looks up and sees me, her face doesn't even register surprise.

"Hi," I say as gently as possible when I reach the women.

Jill is already locked and loaded and ready to fire. "*Now* I know why you haven't answered my texts," she snaps. "How gracious of you to explain that you'd moved on."

"Jill," I warn. "Jesus."

She's right to be angry, but only up to a point. Jill and I are just a booty-call to each other, and I was very clear about that right from the start. Skye blew back into town less than a week ago, and I've been a little busy trying to figure out how to keep her stepsister out of jail and put her ex-step-father *in* jail and keep my own head screwed on in the process.

Yet it's true that I haven't given Jill a single thought since Skye showed up. And it was rude to ignore her texts.

And maybe I *am* an asshole, because it's not Jill who I'm worried about right now. Skye won't even look at me. She signs her name at the bottom of a rental form with a violent stroke, and pushes it back toward Jill.

"I'm sorry," I try. It's not even clear to me whom I'm apologizing to. I'm sorry that I was dismissive of Jill. And I'm sorry that Skye is here to witness it.

"You're not," Jill argues. "If you were sorry, you wouldn't bring your all-time-favorite piece of ass into my store. And you wouldn't have the balls to look surprised that I'm offended."

"Hey, that's not what—"

"Save it," Jill snaps. "I should have broken it off with you already. It's not like you're interested in me unless we're both naked."

I can *feel* Skye's shock beside me. She takes a step sideways, as if she's trying put distance between herself and me.

"Well…" I choke out. *Shit!* No matter what I say, one woman will be mad. "I never lied to you," is what I go with.

"I suppose not," Jill concedes in a softer voice. "I only put up with it because you're so good in the sack. Kyla honey," she says with a sneer as she turns her gaze to Skye.

"It's Skylar," I correct through gritted teeth.

"Oh right. *Skylar.* Be sure to ask him to bring home a pair of hand-cuffs. He likes those a lot."

Skye lets out a shocked gasp.

Jill shrugs, then points at the back door. "It's the silver RAV4 right outside. Bring it back full."

Skye grabs the key and breaks for the door. Not like I blame her.

I'm left with Jill, who's also gritting her teeth and looking like she wants to punch something. Probably me.

"This didn't go down like you think," I tell her. I'd never pit two women against each other.

"Really? You didn't forget my number the second she showed up in town after ten years?"

"Twelve."

"But who's counting?" Jill asks, and her voice is sad.

"I never meant to be a dick."

"I know, okay? Jesus." Her eyes are getting red. "And I didn't mean to break out my eighteen-year-old mean girl again. But I was startled to see her, and I've been wondering where you were."

"Ah, well. I apologize." *Again.* "I didn't use my head. You and I probably should have just, uh, stayed friends."

Jill grabs a tissue out of a box on the desk and dabs her eyes. "We were never friends, Benny. I was just a girl who had it bad for you and never knew when to cut her losses."

Ouch. "I'm sorry, then, that I'm just a dude who never paid enough attention."

"Go." She sniffs. "Your girl needs you to do some groveling. I don't think she knew you really are a bimbo. Like your little niece says you are."

Ouch again. "Okay. We'll catch up later."

"No, we probably won't," is her response.

I go out the other door to look for Skye. But there's no silver RAV4 out there and no Skye. So I jog around the side of the building and look up Whiting Road.

The silver RAV4 is making haste up the street without me.

THIRTY-ONE

Twelve Years Ago

BENITO IS VERY LATE.

But Skye keeps the faith. She hasn't stopped thinking about the kiss they shared. The first half hour of waiting passes easily as she replays the softness of his lips and the heat in his eyes.

It had been magical.

She is wearing a dress that Jenny sent her. Shortly after Benito invited her to the dance, Skye had a rare opportunity to call her aunt. Skye's mom accidentally left her phone behind when she took her shift at the diner. So Skye helped herself to a ten minute call, even though her mom would inevitably notice that her minutes had been used up.

But Skye needed advice, and Jenny was happy to hear from her. "Let me send you a strapless cocktail dress from Ann Taylor," her aunt had said. "I bought it for my twentieth wedding anniversary."

"Oh, I couldn't possibly borrow it," Skye had said. She didn't want the responsibility. And anyway, prom dresses were supposed to be youthful and flirtatious. She doubted Jenny's dress would look like anything the other girls were wearing.

Then again, Skye could not afford a dress. She needs to hang onto her money for a bus ticket out of here.

"Sure you can. Keep it. I'm not wearing it again. It's too dressy for a day at the office." Jenny is an executive assistant at Deutschebank on Wall Street. "And it's not like I can wear it to my thirtieth anniversary."

"I'm sorry," Skye had said quickly. Jenny was a widow. Her husband fell down an elevator shaft while on a plumbing job in the Bronx.

"Don't be. Take the dress. Where can I send it?"

Skye had ripped open the padded envelope with some trepidation last week. But the black satin that tumbled into her hands felt like butter. And the dress was only a little too big. Skye solved this problem by spending twenty of her precious dollars on a black strapless bra with a little bit of padding right where she needed it. And then she'd splurged on the matching panties, unsure if Benito would see them or not.

Did Benito expect to? And did *she* want him to? Those were terrifying questions that she would have to think about later.

But first, the dance. It's starting at eight, and it's past eight o'clock now. Damien's taxi is parked in front of their trailer. But Benito's motorcycle had gone roaring away at six p.m., and hadn't come back yet. A half hour ago she'd heard an engine that had turned out to be Mrs. Rossi's car. Zara had gotten out of the passenger's seat, quite obviously in the middle of a fight with her mother.

Mrs. Rossi had been angry—chewing out Zara for something Skye couldn't get the gist of.

Zara's face had been as bright as her red dress as she'd stomped up to their trailer and had gone inside, slamming the door. Then Mrs. Rossi drove away again.

Skye has no idea why Zara isn't at the grad prom right now. But tonight Zara isn't her problem, because tonight she has Benito.

Doesn't she?

He'd said they were going out to dinner. She hopes she didn't get that detail wrong, because she's starving. And it's getting late.

Skye waits on the tiny stoop of the trailer with the black silk tickling her knees. Black isn't a prom color. But the dress is sleek and expensive, and for once she's certain that anyone who looks at her won't immediately think *trailer park*.

It's June, so the light doesn't start to fade until late. In fact, it's about nine o'clock when Skye has to stop pretending that things aren't going very, very wrong. But she won't leave her spot outside. If Benito suddenly arrives, she wants him to notice her strapless dress.

He's coming, she tells herself. *He got hung up somewhere.*

She waits. Her hunger becomes a dull ache that she can ignore, because her heartache is worse. Maybe something happened to him? No —that couldn't be it. Zara wouldn't be pouting next door if Benito was hurt.

Would she?

It's quite dark by the time Skye hears another engine approaching. But it's not the sound of a motorcycle. It's the police cruiser.

Skye's heart plummets as Jimmy Gage parks the car and gets out. She doesn't even move out of the way until his boots are crunching in the gravel.

"Well, lookie here," he says with a low chuckle that crawls up her spine. Skye stops breathing as he reaches out and traces a fingertip across her bare skin just above the bust line of her dress. "That's an awful pretty getup for sittin' around outside. Don't know who you're waiting for. Prom started a long time ago."

Skye says nothing. For once, Jimmy Gage speaks the truth. And her skin is crawling from his touch.

"I saw your boy on his motorcycle earlier," he says. "He was all dressed up and carrying flowers. I watched 'im give them to that Sullivan girl. They make a real nice couple."

"No! You didn't!" Skye actually snaps.

Then she wishes she hadn't. Because Gage laughs, and it's the sound of someone enjoying himself.

"I *saw* 'em," he says. "Guess he didn't want a trailer trash whore for his date. And why would he?"

Gage steps past her and into the house, laughing to himself.

She stands frozen outside, feeling naked in Aunt Jenny's dress. Naked and ashamed. Her sexy black underwear mocks her. What was she even thinking?

She's been traded in for a girl who drives her own white Mustang. Of course.

For the first time ever, Skye feels just like the foolish whore Gage always accuses her of being. She feels like a piece of trash. She wants to curl up in a corner somewhere and die.

But there aren't any corners. Gage is banging the kitchen cabinets. Then the TV goes on, tuned loudly to a baseball game.

Skye waits until he's visible on the sofa with a plate in his lap. Then she scoots like a mouse through the trailer to her room, where she shuts the door and locks it.

The dress comes off. She folds it back into the FedEx envelope and puts it in the bottom of her duffel bag. Everything else that goes into the bag is more practical: underwear, socks. Her most decent clothes. Two books she can't leave behind. Hair brush. Toothbrush. Her hard-earned money.

Packing takes barely ten minutes. She raises the window screen for the last time and drops the bag out first. Then she exits after it, taking care not to turn an ankle. She might have to walk for hours until she finds a lift to the bus station.

Damien's taxi is still out in front. She thinks about knocking on the door and asking for a ride. But she can't stand the thought of owing the Rossi's anything. And she doesn't want any of them to ask why she's not at grad prom. So she heads into the night alone.

The sky is dark but the moon is nearly full. The air is sweet and the peeper frogs are singing in the ponds. It's such a weird sound. She won't miss it, Skye decides. Vermont is a terrible place. And she's never coming back.

THIRTY-TWO

Skye

I DRIVE AWAY in an angry fog. I can't believe that I let myself be blind-sided *again* by Benito. Same guy. Same story. And I fell for it!

"I love you, Skye," he'd said. And I'd believed him. He forgot to add, "Oh, and I've been banging Jill Sullivan off and on since prom night."

I must be stupid, stupid, stupid.

When I think about the two of them together, I actually want to throw up. Handcuffs? I'll bet she never flinches if he calls her a *dirty girl*. I'll bet she never flinches at all.

Several miles pass while I wallow in my anger and sadness. It's not that I assumed Benito was celibate. That's a ridiculous idea. And I haven't been, either. But I know Jill Sullivan. She and I are nothing alike.

Is she the kind of woman Benito really wants? And, if so, when he tells me he loves me, does that even make sense?

When we're alone together, I feel like I know him. And I feel like I can trust him. When we're not alone together, apparently all bets are off.

I can't do this. I can't fall for someone who says he loves me, but also loves Jill Sullivan. Somebody said—was it F. Scott Fitzgerald?—that intelligence is the ability to hold two opposing ideas in the mind.

My heart is not very intelligent, apparently. I don't understand Benito, and apparently I never will.

Thirty minutes later I arrive in South Burlington without remembering the drive. When I step out of the unfamiliar car in an unfamiliar parking lot behind a building I've only visited once, I'm shaking. Everything in my life is unmoored.

Except my darned job. I still have that. So I trudge inside the offices of WBVT for the second time. I give my name to the receptionist, who waves me through to the news room.

Jack and Jordy—the same two reporters I met before—both look up when I enter. Jack has a sturdy look to him, with broad shoulders and dark hair, while Jordy is on the skinny side with black glasses and an earring. They both have beards, which seem to be mandatory on young men in Burlington these days.

"It's Emily Skye! She's back!" Jordy says with a smile that quickly fades. "Oh dear."

"Bad day?" Jack asks immediately. "Seriously, are you okay?"

"Why? What do you mean?" I do a quick inventory of myself. All the clothing is in place and I put on makeup earlier.

"You look..." Jack hesitates. "...like you need a stiff drink. That's all. Come sit." He rolls his desk chair backward, yanking out the empty seat and offering it to me.

"Uh, thanks." I take a deep breath and try to look less shell-shocked than I feel. "I've had better days."

"Is it work trouble?" Jordy asks. "Your boss is a dickweed when he calls."

"That is not at all surprising." I flop down in the chair. "He's a..." I can't say *dickweed*. "He's never a great guy. But today he's just baseline awful."

"So it's family?" Jack asks.

"Or men?" Jordy suggests. "Men are the worst."

"Dude, you're a man," Jack points out.

"Well, I didn't mean *me*. I mean everyone on Grindr. And I didn't mean you," he adds quickly. "Although you get my lunch order wrong about half the time."

"No," Jack argues. "The deli gets it wrong."

"But somehow they only screw up when you're the one who gets lunch!"

"Not my fault!" Jack yelps. "They're distracted by this face." He puts a hand under his handsome chin, and Jordy laughs.

Watching them clown around, I feel the tiniest bit better. My stomach gives a loud growl, though. Because lunch never happened and it's going on three o'clock.

"You're hungry?" Jordy asks.

"I could eat," Jack says.

"Pizza?"

"Falafel?"

"The deli? So long as you don't care if Jack brings you the wrong sandwich." He rolls his eyes.

"Falafel," I say, because they're waiting for me to say something. "I'll buy." I pull out my wallet.

"Nah—" Jack says, holding up a hand. "There's, like, four more people I gotta include. We have a running tab. It's a whole complicated thing. This way everyone gets fed."

"Here's something for mine, then," I say, pulling out a twenty. "I really appreciate it."

He pushes it back. "You're having a rough day. It's my treat." Jack gets up and heads toward the control room. "Back in thirty."

"Wait! I want—" Jordy starts.

"I know what you want," Jack says, exiting the room.

"Thank you!" I call just before the door shuts on Jack. "You guys are too nice to me."

"Nah," Jordy says. "We're easy. That's why we stay here at this little bumfuck station. It's not New York, but it's a nice place to work."

"You're lucky," I say with a sigh. "I'd better edit this thing for the bossman. Do you mind if I use that terminal again?"

"Go for it. Let me log you in." He leans over and taps a password into the computer. "All set."

"Thanks."

I have to open my phone to reread my McCracken's instructions. So I see that Benito has sent me a flurry of texts.

I'm sorry. Where are you? I want to explain.

Then, after my failure to reply: *Look, I know that was bad. But it was never serious with Jill. I don't love her, and never claimed to. It was just sex. Please call. I need to hear your voice.*

I feel cold inside when I read these words. Maybe another girl would understand. But I might be too broken inside to believe that the way he feels about me is different from the way he feels about Jill. *It was just sex*, he says.

That's the part I'll never be able to understand. It takes ten kinds of courage for me to be naked and vulnerable with him. I don't think I could experience that with someone I didn't love.

When I think about him getting out of bed with her and then getting into bed with me? *I* feel dirty. And not in a good way. That's probably not normal, either. And I don't know if there's a cure.

I close his texts without answering. And I get to work.

―――――

Forty-five minutes later I've edited tape for McCracken. I've written up his script from sloppy notes. And now I'm trying to eat falafel in a ladylike fashion although it's messy and I'm as hungry as a bear.

"Did you pass my stories to the copyeditor?" Jordy asks.

"Uh-oh," Jack says.

"Dude!"

"Dude," Jack repeats. "I'm sorry. We'll rush the job when copy comes back?"

"He doesn't come back until five," Jordy grumbles.

"I'll do it," I hear myself offer. Because, let's face it, I have nowhere else to go. I can't even think about Benito right now. It hurts too much.

"Copyediting?" Jordy asks. "Is there anything you can't do?"

"Not really," I confess. "I went to j-school at Columbia. Then I worked crew for two years until they let me write a few stories. Then I started getting on-camera work in traffic and weather. But..." I sigh. "That's not going well. I'm on a mandatory two-week vacation."

"Dude," Jordy says. "You're not on vacation if you're eating falafel with us."

"Eating falafel with you two is more fun than I usually have at work. They just don't want me on camera until..." Uh-oh. I didn't want to tip these two off to my penis video.

"I don't get it." Jack makes an empathetic face. "You should have gotten a promotion after that penis video."

"Wait, what? You saw it?"

"What do you take us for?" Jordy gasps. "Of course we saw it. It's an important addition to the genre."

"The...sorry?"

Jack lunges for his tablet and pulls up YouTube. "We have a playlist. All the best accidental penises on air."

"Don't forget to be inclusive," Jordy argues. "We have accidental boobs, too."

"Double hurricanes are usually the culprit there," Jack explains, while Jordy nods. "And sometimes bulbous mountain ranges."

"We have a complete collection," Jordy says. "Jack's is arguably the best penis. No offense—Skye's penis is pretty special, but Jack's is spectacular."

"I'm blushing!" Jack says. "Stop."

"Jack has a penis, too?" I ask without thinking.

"Show her, Jack."

Proudly Jack taps on the tablet screen, and a clip comes up of Jack doing the weather. "The low pressure system will move east between the Green and White mountains..." He draws a long, banana-shaped area on the map. It's large, but the shape is not well-articulated. *Big deal*, I'm thinking. But then Jack turns his body so that the, uh, banana lines up with his crotch. Then he gestures with his hand. "...the low pressure system will produce heavy rains throughout the weekend."

And then? An animated graphic of rain showers begin to spurt from the distant end of the shape.

A gurgle of laughter rises inside me, but I quickly choke it down. The result is a terrible burp sound.

"No, girl. Let it out," Jordy says, chuckling. "I mean, come on! Jack is blowing a load on screen. He looks pretty happy about it, too."

And then I just sort of explode. All the tension of the week erupts in a torrent of laughter. My stomach clenches so hard that it actually hurts.

Immediately, Jack and Jordy start laughing, too. Because I'm contagious. I'm *howling*. Actual tears spring into my eyes, threatening my carefully applied Urban Decay mascara. I can't even believe my own mirth. In fact, I raise my head and look at the screen again, just in time to see Jack finish his drawing again and then turn to put himself in a compromising position...

I die all over again. I laugh until there's nothing left.

And then the door flips open and a woman in an impeccable suit steps forward. "What the fuck is this?" she thunders.

I've worked at a TV station long enough to know the sound of the producer's voice when he's on a rampage. Or when *she's* on a rampage, in this instance. Instinct kicks in, and the laughter dies in my throat. I don't want to get Jack and Jordy in trouble. But maybe I already have.

"What the hell is so funny that you didn't think to show it to me?" she bellows, pulling out a chair and plunking down in it. Then she reaches over to Jack's fries and steals one. "Seriously. I'm reading about drug overdoses and you didn't think to share?"

"It's just Jack's penis," Jordy says defensively. "You've seen it before."

"Wanna see Skye's?" Jack asks. "And don't eat my fries, bitch. Why did you ask for a salad if you wanted fries?"

My jaw unhinges.

She waves a perfectly manicured hand dismissively. "I didn't want an *order* of fries. Other people's food has no calories. And I've already seen the Emily Skye clip. The ball-sac is my favorite part. Nice to meet you, Emily Skye. I'm Lane Barker."

"N-nice to meet you, too," I stammer. I don't know what to make of Lane Barker. She's about ten years older than I am, and with the sort of fierce expression a woman needs to succeed in TV. But she's not yelling at Jack and Jordy, who are clearly goofing off.

Jordy clicks the tablet off, and the screen darkens. "That never gets old. Jack got ten thousand Twitter followers from that one. What was your social media bump, Skye?"

"Uh..." I really haven't looked at social media in a week. At first I was too embarrassed, but then I'd been too busy. I pull out my phone and open Piktogram, which is where I have my largest following. And then I gasp. "Holy macaroni!" I actually rub the screen with my finger to see if there's something distorting the number. But no. It's real. I have thirty *thousand* new followers.

"Wowzers," Jordy breathes. "You're an influencer!"

"Quick, post a selfie!" Jack says. "You need to interact with your new fans." He grabs my phone and hands me a coffee mug that says WBTV on it. "This'll be a road-trip shot. The caption will be: 'Just hanging with the news crew in BVT! Met some cool guys.'" He points the camera at me. "Look alive, Emily."

"My real name is Skylar," I say, giving him a practiced smile.

"You look too stiff," Jordy says. "Think about Jack's penis."

I giggle immediately and that's when Jack snaps the picture. "Money shot!" he yells. "Ooh, can I pick the filter?"

"Sure?" I never post on social media because I'm always too busy working.

"So does anyone want to report the news?" Lane asks. "I suppose we could just show a half hour of selfies later and then get fired. It's your call, though."

"I'll get out of your way," I say quickly. "I've overstayed my welcome."

"Not so fast, missy," Lane says. "Let's talk first about why your boss shipped you to Vermont."

"That penis video," I grumble. "The station was getting comments."

"Those comments are going to show up no matter what," Lane points out. "They probably get mail on a daily basis about your shirt and your bra size and your lipstick color. And no rational human thinks you were intentionally drawing porn on live TV."

I can only shrug. I think my boss putting me on paid leave was just a fit of temper that he regretted about fifteen minutes after I left.

"You got a big boost on social media and a lot of attention," she muses. "Maybe somebody got jealous."

"Nah!" I laugh. "I'm not important enough to make waves."

"Really? Columbia journalism degree, good technical background, camera-ready face and a big following on social media? I'll bet your phone extension at work lit up with job offers this week."

This stops me cold. "What?"

"Maybe your boss wanted you out of the way so nobody could steal you."

My first thought is, *that's ridiculous.* But McCracken had been so weird about not sending my laptop with me. My laptop is where my work email account lives. "But who would steal me?" I squeak. "I've been applying for jobs and nobody cares."

Lane's smile turns a little wicked. "I'd steal you if I had an open job. You're a multitasker in news production. A small newsroom needs that skillset. If you're only applying for investigative news spots in major markets, it'll be harder for you to find a job. Or it would have been before last week." She shrugs. "If you decide you like Vermont a whole lot, give me a call. We aren't hiring right now, but we sometimes need subs. I'd hire you knowing you'll probably quit in two years for a job in a bigger city. All the good ones do." She flips a business card onto the desk in front of me, then rises to her feet with a sigh.

"What are we?" Jordy yelps. "Chopped liver?"

"Thank the lord you're both unambitious," she says. "I have to beg for the work to get done, but at least you show up every day. Let's go, boys. No cookies unless I have your stuff by five."

"Cookies?" I can't help ask.

"She makes really good cookies." Jack grabs his computer keyboard and wakes up his machine. "Better get crackin.'"

What planet have I landed on? There are no cookies at *New York News and Sports.* We snack on veiled threats and fear.

"Nice to meet you, Skylar," Lane says. "Don't lose my number."

"It was lovely to meet you, too," I reply. But my mind is churning. Could I really find a better job? And is it possible to experience career growth from accidentally drawing male genitalia on air? "What a strange world we live in," I whisper to myself as I shut down the computer that Jack and Jordy allowed me to borrow.

"True story," Jordy says. "I hope we see you again. You're fun, Skye."

"No, you're fun," I insist. "I think I needed to see a newsroom where people aren't afraid of each other."

"Oh, I'm afraid," Jack says. "Jordy gets really pissy when you get his lunch order wrong."

My phone chirps, but there's no message. Then I realize it's the burner phone. *Call me*, is all it says. Yay. Time for more drama with Rayanne.

"Where're you headed?" Jack asks.

"I wish I knew," I tell them as we all shake hands one more time.

I head outside, pausing in front of the building to call Raye. She answers immediately. "Raffie, I'm leaving."

"You're leaving where?"

"Here. Vermont. I just need to go somewhere alone and ride this out. Yoga hookup man says I'm stressing him out. His chakras are out of alignment because I'm afraid for my life."

I'm immediately offended on Rayanne's behalf. "I thought yoga was all about generousness of spirit."

"He's a man, Raffie. They believe in generosity as long as it involves their dick in your hooha. But the minute you're not fun anymore, that's it. We're disposable."

Given the day I've had so far, it's not easy to refute that point. "Where will you go?"

"Not sure. I'll drive the rental Jeep out of town after dark. I'll return it somewhere there's a bus station and then just get on and go."

I try to take that in. Rayanne was always a traveler. She thrives on the chaos of not knowing where she'll end up. "Can I see you first?" She's the exact opposite of me. And I will miss her crazy self.

"You can," she says slowly. "But Raffie, I need cash."

"Oh."

Oh. So that's what this call is really about. "How much do you need? I'll hit the ATM."

"How much can you spare? I figure I can use my own card once on my way out of town. But after that it would leave a trail. Whatever cash I can gather is all I'll have to live on until I can find someone to hire me for cash."

"But…" that sounds impossible. "Where will you sleep?"

"As long as I'm still breathing, I don't care. Much."

It sounds like a terrible plan. Our family specialty. "Okay. I'll check my balance and see what I can do."

"All the banks have a daily ATM limit, anyway. There's only so much damage I can do to your savings."

"You're leaving tonight?"

"Yeah." Her voice is sad. "I have to. Yoga man is uneasy, and if I stay I'll probably sleep with him again even though I'm mad."

"Why would you do that?"

"What do you mean *why*? Angry sex is the best kind."

That makes absolutely no sense to me at all. But it's off topic, so I press on. "What color is the house?"

"White with blue shutters. It's on the corner of..."

"I know which corner," I snap. "What time?"

"Whenever you're ready."

"I'm in Burlington. And I still have to make a tiramisu." Tonight was the night we were supposed to have dinner with Benito's mom. There's no way I'm going to that now. But I said I'd bring dessert, and I always keep my promises.

"Oh. Well. Don't let saving my ass get in the way of your dinner plans."

God, people are testy when they're making bad decisions. "I don't have dinner plans anymore. But I promised someone a tiramisu. And you said you were leaving under cover of darkness. So I've got hours, right? I'll text you before I get there."

"Thank you," she says. "I'm sorry to be such a jumpy bitch. Both Mercury and Venus are in retrograde."

It would be convenient if I believed in astrology and could blame my troubles on the planets. "It's fine. See you in a bit."

We disconnect, and it then it hits me. I don't have any reason left to stay in Vermont, either. I came here for Rayanne. Somewhere along the way I told myself I could get closure with Benito.

And I guess I have. Today we came full circle. He doesn't belong to me, and he never did.

I walk around the WBTV building to find my little rental car. The sight of it fills me with thoughts of Benito and Jill in bed. He never mentioned her. Not once.

I've been waiting for you, Skye.

It makes me cringe to remember how those words had made me

feel. Elated. Special. But everything he'd said sounds different to me now. He'd probably said all the same things to Jill Sullivan.

He probably whispers that he loves her as he peels off her clothes.

And—this is what's giving me the sick feeling in the pit of my stomach—he probably calls her his *dirty girl*, too. Only she's okay with it. Maybe she loves that.

Sex with skittish me, versus sex with Jill Sullivan? That's not a competition I can win.

I've been waiting for you, he'd said. But if he had Jill, he obviously hadn't been waiting for me. That claim was just the murmuring of a horny man in the heat of the moment.

"Well, Benito," I say to myself. "Waiting suits you. So you can wait some more."

Another twelve years sounds like a nice, round number.

THIRTY-THREE

Benito

_____

THE AFTERNOON IS A BLUR. After I watched Skye drive off to Burlington without talking to me, I got called back into my boss's office.

My head is in a hundred places, but they need me here at work. We've traced the black car with the BBQ bumper-sticker to its owner. We've run his sheet and tracked down all our confidential informants to try to figure out how important he is. And everyone tells us that Gage is getting ready to make a new buy.

"I heard Gage'll have a lotta product next week," a Barre dealer tells me. We call him the jack-o'-lantern, because of his smile. "K2 _and_ smack."

Ugh. Like I don't have enough to worry about without our boys branching out. "Did he tell you personally?"

"He tole a guy who tole my guy."

"And that guy is...?" I try.

He just gives me that jack o' lantern grin and says nothing.

"Thanks for the heads-up. You know where they're cutting it, at least?" I get the usual head-shake. Then I give the guy his twenty bucks and wish him a good week.

We used to try to nab the jack-o'-lantern but he always figures out who the undercover cops are and shows up clean. So we switched tactics. Every week we pay him for gossip instead.

It frustrates me to hand money to dirtbags for information. So I walk away before I can let my attitude show. I check in with Sergeant Chapman, who tells me the Colebury police found the black car and Gage. He's sitting in a bike shop on Route 11.

"Officer Trache is on him right now," I'm told. "Go get some food and take a nap because we might be sitting on him all night."

"Yessir." I hang up, but I don't take his advice. Instead I drive to the Gin Mill and check the lot.

No silver RAV4.

Shit.

Although the coffee shop is officially closed, I let myself in with my key and find my sister sitting at a table, doing her books and looking tired. I ought to feel sympathy, but I'm too irritated with her already. "How could you send Skye to the Toyota Dealership?"

When Zara looks up at me, her expression is nonplussed. "She asked about rental cars. What's the big fucking deal?"

"Jill Sullivan works there."

"So what? High school was a long time ago. And if I were Skye, I'd want to know that her tormentor schedules oil changes at Daddy's car dealership. Skye's a TV reporter, Benny. She can hold her own against Jill."

I cross the room and pull out the chair across from her. "Well, I was there, too."

Zara studies me. "Still not seeing the problem here. Aside from putting Jill into a time warp, who cares?"

"Jill cares! I haven't returned her texts in a few weeks."

My sister puts down her pencil. "Her texts? Why was she texting you?"

"To arrange the next book club meeting." Shit. I'd just assumed my sister already knew all my shenanigans.

"What?" Zara gaps at me. And then her eyes narrow as she catches on. "Wait. You and *Jill?*"

"A few times," I grumble. "She asked."

Zara rolls her giant brown eyes toward heaven, which is a move I've seen countless times. Zara probably rolled her eyes since the day my mother brought us home from the hospital and put us to nap in the same crib. "How *could* you?"

"What do you mean? I didn't know Skye would walk back into my life."

"No! How could you bang Jill Sullivan, of all people?"

"Why do you care? It was casual. I thought she knew that."

Zara is already shaking her head. "You're a fool, Benny. Some other woman could have kept it casual. But not her. She's wanted you since she was fifteen. And she's had a rough couple of years. Her husband threw her over. She sold off her designer shoes and got a job. And then here comes the love of her teenage life and says, 'Hey baby, let's keep it casual.'"

"What?" I yelp. "The love of her…come *on*, Zara. Don't fuck with me. Jill already yelled at me at the dealership. Then Skye took off like a bottle rocket on the Fourth of July. I don't know where she is, and she won't answer my calls."

"Oh, Benny. You are such a dumbass. When you break Jill's heart, you could at least notice."

I put my head in my hands. "Do you have any more coffee? I'm having a really shitty day. And it's far from over."

"There's iced in the reach-in," she says. "The machines are off already."

"I'll take it."

She kicks my leg under the table. "Pour it yourself. I'm trying to add up columns here."

"Fine. But then I'm not paying."

"Fair enough." My sister goes back to her ledger.

I gulp down a large iced coffee and eat two leftover mini muffins. I never ate lunch, so I'll need to grab some real food soon. "Tonight I'm probably sitting in a car watching drug dealers."

"Wear your vest," Zara says without looking up.

"Always. But I don't know where Skye is, and I'm afraid she'll take off without saying goodbye."

"Oh." Zara puts down her pencil. "Would she do that?"

"I don't know what's in her head," I confess. "Jill made it sound like a big deal. I don't think Skye got the right impression."

"Well, maybe Jill never did, either. To her it was a big deal. She's probably speed-eating a tub of Phish Food ice cream right now, because you just made it abundantly clear that she'll never be your first choice."

My groan is loud. "I never would have made my little offer if I thought this would happen."

"What's that thing you always say? Everybody thinks *he's* the good guy."

"Well, that is fucking humbling."

Zara just grins.

"You want to hear something amazing?"

"Always."

"Skye and her nutty stepsister broke open my case this morning."

"Really? How?"

"With a photo of a car that links Sparks, Gage, and a third dealer. My guys found the car and tailed it to a motorcycle repair shop. We'll get the warrants we need and decide when to bring them in. I'm hoping for a big bust. It could even happen tonight."

Zara flinches. "You know I hate this part."

"I do." So does my poor mother. Speaking of which... "Can I ask a favor?"

"I suppose."

"Skye and I were supposed to have dinner with Mom tonight. But now that can't happen for a variety of reasons. Any chance you could offer to bring Nicole over there instead?"

"You want me to smooth Mom's ruffled feathers with smiles from a chubby two-year-old?"

"I've had worse ideas. And I think she was making chicken piccata. You love chicken piccata."

"You make a good point. I'll call her." Zara smiles.

"Thank you. And thanks again for suggesting the goddam Toyota dealership." I get up and push in my chair, taking care not to leave crumbs on the cafe table.

"Whoops," Zara says playfully. "If you kept your dick in your jeans, we wouldn't be having this conversation right now."

"Woulda shoulda coulda. Where should I put these dishes?"

"Leave 'em," she says. "Get some real food before your shift, okay? And wear your vest."

"Always." I kiss the top of my sister's head and get the heck out of there.

And there's still no silver RAV4 in the parking lot.

THIRTY-FOUR

Skye

RAYANNE DOES yoga to find her inner peace. But my inner peace responds better to desserts.

I find the ingredients I need for tiramisu at an upscale Burlington grocery store—mascarpone cheese, fresh cream and lady fingers. I'll be making an eggless tiramisu, because I don't really have time to make the traditional kind.

Also, eating raw eggs squicks me out.

Before I point the RAV4 back toward Colebury, I stop for two more things: a thousand dollars in cash, and two double espressos from a Starbucks drive-through. But I don't drink the coffee. I place it carefully in the car's cup holders.

And—this is sad—I actually experience a twinge of disloyalty for buying espresso from a chain, when I could have bought it from Zara.

That's why I need to leave Vermont. It's been less than a week since I came back here, but it's already far too real. I'm not a member of Zara's family, and I never will be. I can't stick around playing house with Benito and pretending that I belong here.

I never did, and I obviously never will.

Still, I won't let Mrs. Rossi down. I said I'd make tiramisu, and I will. Then I will hand that dish to Benny's mom, kiss her cheek, and drive away again.

I have an apartment in New York, and a job. And I need to figure out if any headhunters came knocking while I've been away. There are so many mistakes I've made, they're too numerous to count. It's time to buckle down and figure my shizzle out.

When I pull into the Gin Mill's nearly empty lot, I'm relieved to see that Benito's car isn't there. It's late afternoon, and the coffee shop is closed, while the bar has yet to open. I hate that I've already learned the patterns of this place.

I tap in the code for the downstairs door—the one that's May's birthday in about a month. I won't be here to wish her a happy birthday.

But you don't care, I remind myself. *It's not your family.*

Right.

In Benito's kitchen, I discover that he does not own a lot of bakeware. But there's a casserole dish that will suit my needs. I whip my cream and sugar together with a little vanilla. This takes some effort because Benito doesn't have an electric mixer.

See? This place isn't so great. I'm just going to keep telling myself that.

I blend in the mascarpone cheese and set the whole creamy mixture. Then comes my favorite part—dipping each ladyfinger in espresso, and filling the bottom of the dish with a layer of cookie goodness. I spoon the cream on top, and the sweet scent of it fills me with longing.

Hang in there, I coach myself. Let's not get sentimental over something that's really too fattening. Besides—tomorrow I'll be back at Fairway, stocking up on healthy groceries in New York. All by myself.

Yikes. I'm practically wallowing now. It's not a good look on a girl.

After I carefully arrange the layers, there's nothing left to do but shake fine cocoa powder over the top in a tidy layer. I've made a beautiful dessert that's meant to be shared among friends. And maybe it will. But not with me.

Tucking the dish into the freezer to chill, I start packing all my belongings. Not that it takes very long to remove all my makeup from Benito's bathroom and my limited supply of clothing from his room.

I take a quick glance around, looking for anything I might have left. But it looks like I was never here at all. And I don't allow my gaze to linger on the bed. That way is darkness. Sleeping next to Benito was all I'd ever wanted. The sex had been great, but the best part had been hearing his even breathing as he'd slept and feeling the heat of his body seep into mine.

It had been my first time sleeping beside a man, and the way I'm feeling right now, it might be my last.

My last act in Benito's apartment is to write him a note.

Dear Benny,

I have to go. I know I'm leaving without a proper goodbye again. But it's best for everyone if I just slip out of town. I've got work to do, and so do you.

Seeing you again has been

It's a struggle to finish that sentence. I think about it for a long time. How nice am I willing to be? How honest?

Amazing, I write eventually. And it's true. But it's still not enough to make me face down all the ways that he and I are different. I can't linger in his aura and hope that eventually his definition of *I love you* will match up with mine.

My life is so much different than yours, and I have to get back to it.

I can't stop the platitudes from flowing onto the page. Honestly, it gives me pause that I'm having so much trouble explaining why I'm so upset with him. I'm a flipping writer, for flip's sake.

It's crazy, but I actually walk back to the bedroom and stand in the doorway. And I make myself picture Jill in that bed with Benito. And it hurts just as much as I thought it would.

I'm glad he can't see inside my head right now, because it's full of ugly, jealous thoughts. Maybe other women aren't quite this crazy. It's not like I assumed Benito was a virgin. But why did it have to be *her*? I thought I was so much older and wiser than my sixteen-year-old self. But how many times can I repeat the same mistakes?

I turn away from that bed. I get my bag, and my tiramisu in Benny's dish. I cover it with plastic wrap and prepare to head out.

My last act is to leave that *I Love Vermont* keychain next to the note I left him.

I don't love Vermont. That hasn't changed.

The door clicks with finality as I close it behind me. And nobody sees me climb into the car and drive away.

———

Ten minutes later I'm standing in the kitchen of Rayanne's yoga boyfriend's squalid little house across from the high school running track. It smells like incense and cooked beans.

"Where is he?" I whisper over the cup of tea that Rayanne has poured for me. "Isn't he going to come out and say hello?"

She shakes her head. Rayanne looks really tired. But I guess that's what happens when you accidentally become a conduit of fentanyl for drug dealers. She's thin—maybe from stress or maybe from all that yoga—and looks older than her thirty years. "He's embarrassed to throw me out. He's worried about karma." She rolls her eyes. "Men, Raffie. They're all children."

I bob my head in agreement, even though this isn't my area of expertise. "Why do you keep finding new ones, then?" Given the way I feel right now, I doubt I'll date anyone again. But Rayanne keeps going for it. "I mean, first Sparks and now yoga guy?"

"I make poor life choices. But, in my defense, Sparks has some killer tats, and Yoga Guy is very bendy."

"But still." Now I understand that sex can be pretty great. *Thanks Benito.* But it's still not worth the heartache. "Here." I reach into my purse and pull out the thousand dollars that I was able to withdraw at the ATM on my way here.

"Thank you," she says in a hushed voice. "I hope this doesn't hurt you too badly."

"It'll put a pretty big dent in my designer-cosmetics budget," I admit. "But as long as I don't get fired, it'll work out." And I'm not as worried about losing my job as I used to be. It's dawning on me that McCracken is too lazy to find a replacement for me. And also that I'd be difficult to replace. Not that I'm brilliant—I'm just willing to put up with a lot.

For now. It's dawning on me that maybe it doesn't have to be that way. That Burlington studio was eye-opening for me. Maybe I would like to work in a smaller market where the boss appreciated me, instead of a major market where everyone was trying to eat each other alive.

"You've got that faraway look in your eye," Rayanne says. "Everything okay?"

"It will be," I say slowly. "Tonight I'm going home to New York. What if we drove out together?"

She gives her head a sad shake. "I gave you enough trouble already. How are you going to get home?"

"I have a rental, too. I'll call and ask them if I can return it in New York." I sip my tea, and Rayanne is quiet. And I wonder when I'll see her again. "You'll call me, won't you? When you land somewhere?"

"Yeah. I promise. I'm not taking any phones, though. I don't know enough about who can track what these days. I don't want them with me."

"Okay," I whisper.

She gives me an eye roll. "Don't *worry*, Raffie. I always land on my feet. I left Vermont when I was eighteen with fifty dollars in my pocket. I spent ten years as a nomad. I can do it again."

"Why are we like this?" I ask. "Both of us alone?" I'm not a nomad, but I'm as skittish as she is in so many ways.

"Daddy issues and mommy issues," she says immediately. "We've got the full menu. It's hard to trust people when you've had parents like ours. I mean—I didn't have a mother, and now I'm turning into yours."

"Don't say that!" I yelp. I wouldn't wish that on anyone.

"Fine. Unlike your mother, I learn from my mistakes. No more relying on men."

"That seems like a fine plan." I only spent five days relying on a man, but that seems like plenty. "I don't know if I got closure or not, Raye. But it's time to go home."

"I won't even ask you if he was good in the sack. Because we can't rely on that to see us through."

"Right," I say. Although sexytimes aren't even the best thing about Benito. It's when he looks into my eyes with his big brown ones and smiles like I matter to him.

If only it were true.

She gives me a pat on the butt. "Go on, then. Point your car toward New York. You look a little wistful. Blast some music. Plot out your next big story."

"I don't *have* a next big story. You promised me one."

"Sorry." She sighs. "I thought I could hand you and Benito photos of a big drug deal going down. But the joke—as usual—was on me. And it's too dangerous for both of us to keep trying. Go home. You won't have me to complicate your life for a while. Be grateful."

I'm not, though. "Okay. I have to make one stop first. I owe Mrs. Rossi a tiramisu."

"What? You and your unbreakable promises. We should just eat it. Besides, what about our vow never to set foot in a trailer park again?"

She has a point about that. "If I'm only there for one minute, it doesn't count."

"Take care of yourself, you hear me?" Rayanne leans in for a fierce hug.

I wrap my arms around her skinny body and fight tears in the corners of my eyes. "You too."

She sniffs. "Go now. I'll be ten minutes behind you."

And so I do it. I go outside again where darkness is falling. I get back into the rental car, which smells pleasantly of espresso and cocoa. And I head toward the one place I thought I'd never return.

THIRTY-FIVE

Benito

NO MOTORCYCLE REPAIR shop needs so many cameras. But this one has six. That's a pretty good clue that they're not just shining fenders in there. The second clue is the black Taurus with the Smokey's sticker parked outside for the last seven hours.

Surveilling this place is unfortunately difficult. It's on a wooded lot with a long driveway. Very little of the building is visible from the two-lane road. And if we parked a vehicle out there, it would be as good as posting a sign reading: *"We're here to surveil you."*

As a result, I'm currently propped in a low fork of an old tree. My ass is numb, and my fingers are getting there. Another officer is waiting behind a nearby tree, similarly uncomfortable. And a third one sits on a fire tower a couple hundred yards away, with a camera.

Furthermore, I've got the Vermont State Police tactical unit standing by, because Sparks's arrest is high risk. But no pressure.

On the plus side, I've got a warrant for one John Oscar Sparks burning a hole in my pocket. I could use it right now. But first we need to learn what he's doing in that building. We've never known Sparks to hole up with a motorcycle club before. And if I'm very, *very* lucky, there's a special reason he's there.

"Unfamiliar vehicle entering the Pine View trailer park." This bit of information is delivered into my earpiece by Nelligan, who's sitting at the entrance to Pine View, watching for any activity from Gage. Tonight we're watching everyone.

I touch the microphone button. "Copy."

"Silver RAV4 with Connecticut plates. The driver is your friend Skylar."

My pulse rate doubles. Because that makes no sense. "Passengers?" I ask quietly. Perhaps Rayanne is visiting her father? Strange timing, though. And I can't imagine Skye would willingly go anywhere near Gage.

"No visible passengers," Nelligan says. "Driver only."

Shit. I could ask Nelligan to follow her up there and watch. But if Gage is at home, he'll see the officer. Nelligan's job is to watch for Gage leaving Pine View via the only exit road. Not to show his face and tip off Gage that we're watching.

I don't know what to do.

And I don't have any time to decide, because I hear motorcycles approaching.

"Two bikes," says our officer in the fire tower. "White males. No visible weapons, but plenty of storage."

"Copy that."

Two dudes just stopping by for a little bike repair at six p.m. In the dark. That would be weird, but not illegal. Although the tingling at the back of my skull says otherwise.

The guys roll up the long drive and then turn their bikes around in the gravel circle in front of the shop. They park facing outwards. That's what I'd do if I thought I might have to make a sudden getaway.

"Can't read the plates," my earpiece says.

And I can't either. It's dark, and they're facing the wrong way now.

The bikers dismount without removing their helmets or goggles. There's no way I can ID their faces. One of them unzips a saddle bag and pulls out a large shipping envelope and tucks it under his arm.

This is the fun of twenty-first century narcotics police work. There's no aircraft full of pot and no tractor trailer full of coke. Pure fentanyl is so strong that you can put enough of it in an old FedEx envelope to kill the population of a medium-sized city.

The door to the bike shop opens as they approach. A yellow rectangle of light shines out, and Sparks is silhouetted in the door before the two bikers disappear inside.

The door shuts.

I listen to the thump of my heart and breathe. I feel it in my gut that those guys are making a drop. That bulky envelope will not turn out to be full of documents. This is really it.

"Tactical team to positions," I whisper. "We're going to wait until Gage leaves with the drop. The couriers are a lower priority."

"Copy," my boss says from a mile away. "We'll take the bikes on the highway."

The door opens again not five minutes later. Nobody even breathes as the bikers come out, each of them with a canvas bag. Money takes up more space than fentanyl. They zip their spoils into the saddle bags, start the bikes and drive back toward the road.

A long minute ticks by.

"Tactical unit in position," someone says into my ear.

"Copy. Waiting on the suspect." We don't know his schedule. More patience is required. I can't stamp my feet, so I squeeze my cold toes inside my boots as I watch the door. As the minutes tick by, I try to relax my eyes.

Then the lights flip off inside the building.

"Stand by," I murmur to my team.

The door opens, and two men come out. Sparks and a bearded guy I haven't seen before.

"Two suspects," says the officer on the fire tower. I'm surprised he can make them out in this light.

I make myself wait another moment, until Sparks has bleeped the locks on the black car, and the bearded guy is locking his shop door. "Police! Hands in the air!" I shout as I step toward them.

The two men bolt in opposite directions, and I take off running after Sparks. The first thing he does is drop the envelope. I actually have to leap over it in pursuit.

Sparks reaches the tree line before I do. So I snap on my headlamp to follow him. Behind me somewhere, the tactical vehicle accelerates up the drive and then brakes hard. But in their armored vehicle, they're prepared for an armed standoff, not a foot race.

I'm gaining on Sparks because I have a better visual. With my light on his back he's literally running into his own shadow. And now there's more of us. I see more headlamps illuminating the edge of woods.

Sparks dives behind a fallen log, and I hear him fumble for what is inevitably a weapon. "Gun!" I yell as I cover my headlamp and duck behind a tree. It's not really wide enough, but it's all I've got.

He fires three times, and only one of them comes close to me. But it buys Sparks a moment. The next sound I hear is him crashing farther into the woods. "He's on the move."

One of the tactical guys turns on a flood lamp. The tree trunks break up the light into slices, but it's enough to see Sparks's form crashing through the woods ahead and to the left. I can feel the tactical team fanning out as I move forward.

And then? Sparks trips and goes down. His weapon discharges again.

"FREEZE! Drop your weapon!" the nearest tactical guy calls as they close in.

I arrive at Sparks's side five seconds later. But I'm not the first. One officer is already bagging his gun and the other applies a nice tight pair of plastic restraints to Sparks's wrists.

My earpiece is full of instructions my boss is dishing out. "Take care—look for any signs of tearing on the packet. If it's damaged, wait for assistance. And wear a mask and gloves when you touch it." We don't need any of our officers OD'ing on a stray microgram of fentanyl. "Pick up the bikers. What's your ETA? Nelligan, status update at Pine View."

"Quiet," he says. "Nobody leaving or arriving. I got a visual of Skylar Copeland talking to a neighbor girl."

I don't understand that at all. "Let's pick up Gage," I chime in. I can't stand the idea of Skylar near his home.

"No, I want to see where he goes when he's shitting himself," my boss says. "There's more evidence to find," he says. "Speaking of which, what's in the bike shop?"

"Bikes," someone reports. "No cutting agents or bags. Just greasy tools."

Shit.

My night is far from over. And what the hell is Skye up to?

THIRTY-SIX

Skylar

_____

TWO SECONDS after my rental car climbs the winding road into Pine View, I know that I've made a miscalculation.

The Rossis' trailer is not the Rossis' trailer anymore. It can't be. Where Mrs. Rossi had once hung lace curtains in the window, there are now broken blinds slanting sadly behind the dirty glass.

Come to think of it, neither Benito nor his mom had said she still lived in the same spot. I'd just assumed it, and now I'm feeling pretty stupid. I'd come to my least favorite place in the whole world for nothing.

My headlights illuminate Gage's trailer next. I notice thick curtains where there never were curtains before. Maybe he's gone, too? I wonder if he's been alone all these years. I hope so. I hate to think that there's a string of girls like me who took his abuse.

I pull the car around to the other side of oval, where a teenage girl is checking her mailbox. She gives my rental car an anxious look. Then her eyes flick toward Gage's place.

And I know what her look means. He still lives there. And she's afraid of him.

Furthermore, I know this girl.

I roll down the window so she can see my face. "Hi," I say softly. "Misty? I'm Skylar. I used to babysit here when you were four."

She cocks her head to the side and studies me. "Skye! I remember. You used to let me chew gum."

Something clicks in my memory—sharing a couple pieces of bubblegum that Benito had given me. "Yes! That was me."

"I thought you were so pretty." She gives me a shy smile. "I guess you still are. What are you doing here?"

"Well, that's the problem. I wanted to give something to Maria Rossi, but…"

"They're gone," she says. "A long time ago. I think I was in first grade when she moved away. She lives in Eastwood now—the really nice trailer park." Misty's eyes flick up to Gage's place again. "I should get inside."

I'm inspired to do something nice for her. "Look, let me give you something." I grab the tiramisu off the passenger seat and get out of the car. Misty is halfway to her door, so I follow.

"Come on in for a sec," she says. "Mom won't mind."

"How is she?" I ask. Mrs. Carrera was a quiet woman who took in sewing while her husband worked three jobs.

"Tired, mostly," Misty says. "My dad died a year ago."

"Oh honey, I'm so sorry," I breathe. "What happened?"

She makes a face. "Overdose."

"Oh," I say, and wish to God that I hadn't asked. This poor girl. "Here," I say. "This is for you. I have to go back to New York tonight, and I won't have time to track down Maria. So you should share it with your mom when she gets home. It's tiramisu."

"Omigod," she says, looking down at my cuisine. "I love tiramisu. But…this is your dish."

"Oh!" I say. "Keep it." Now I owe Benito a dish. I'll send him one from Macy's.

"Let's eat some right now," she says, turning toward the kitchen counter. "I'm getting two bowls."

"Great idea," I say, throwing all my calorie-counting cautions to the wind. "What's that saying? Eat dessert first in case you die."

She giggles and opens a drawer full of spoons.

And the dessert is awesome, as always. The two of us eat tiramisu seated at Misty's little table. The trailer seems smaller than my New

York apartment. I don't want to be a snob, but I'm pretty happy at how far I've gotten from this place.

Crummy job or not, my life is awfully nice. Lonely, but nice.

Outside the window, headlights flare. Both Missy and I look out. She pushes aside the lace curtains and my heart rate doubles. It's Gage. He's fitting two duffel bags into the trunk of a running car.

Just like that I lose my appetite. My neck feels sweaty and my pulse is too fast. Twelve years later and he still has the same effect on me. One glance and I'm trembling.

"You know to watch out for that one, right?" I whisper.

"Yeah," she says heavily. "The second I see him, I bolt."

"Smart girl." I make myself peer at him out the window. In the porch light, I can see his hair is gray now, and it's thinning on top. He's skinnier, too.

Good, I think. I hope he doesn't feel as invulnerable as he used to.

"I wonder where he's going?" Misty whispers. "There's *another* suitcase." Sure enough, he's shoving a bag onto the back seat, too. "I hope it's far, far away."

This wakes me from my little reverie. I wonder if Benito knows that Gage is taking a trip? That seems like something that would interest him. I pull out my phone and open up the texts. Benito's words are still there, begging me to call him. I never answered.

So this is going to be a bit of a non sequitur.

Gage just put three bags in his car. By the time I've tapped it out, there's more to add. *Now he's driving out of Pine View.*

Like I will be, soon. I don't add that. I'm the worst kind of coward.

In my defense, I've been on emotional overdrive for five days. I don't trust myself at all right now. I want to throw myself into Benito's arms. And I also want to punch him.

That can't be healthy.

Gathering up my empty bowl, I carry it to the sink and rinse it out. "Thank you for chatting with me," I tell Misty.

"Thank you for this yumminess," she replies. "It's great to see you again, if only for a second. You look..." She cocks her head again and thinks it over. "Sleek. Fancy. Not very much like Vermont."

"Wow, thank you." A week ago I would have accepted that as

proper and inevitable. But right this second it makes me a little sad. Like I never had a chance of fitting in here.

It's probably just the hormones talking. I don't even like Vermont. Right?

I tell Misty how grown up and beautiful she is, and then I make a promise. "If I swing through town again, we'll have coffee," I say. "Love to your mom, okay?"

We hug, and then I step outside. I open the car door and toss my bag onto the passenger seat.

But then I hesitate.

The moon is rising. It's big and bright and low in the sky. Now that Gage has left the premises, I don't have to be afraid of this place. So I stand here and sniff the clear air.

Driving away feels like quitting. I didn't help Rayanne. Not much, anyway. And I don't feel any less tangled up over Benito.

When he finds that note, he's going to be so pissed. The other complicating factor is that I still love him. Standing here in the cool evening air, I can admit that to myself.

I shut my car door without climbing inside. And I let myself think about Benito for a minute.

As my eyes grow even more accustomed to the dark, I feel like I'm standing in a theater after the performance is over. Our year together played out just a few paces away. The trailers where we'd lived are shuttered and silent. But I can almost hear the echo of Benito's voice, telling me jokes in the woods. And the sound of the ukulele.

I follow my memory around the gravel loop, my high-heeled boots crunching against the surface. The last time I'd walked here, I'd worn ratty sneakers and second-hand jeans. I'd been frightened all the time. It had been a hard way to live.

That girl is still part of me, even if I like to pretend that she's not. I'm still hungry for love and eager to prove myself worthy of it. Sometimes I'm too hard on myself for all the things I didn't get right.

Maybe everybody is. Even Jill Sullivan.

I draw closer to the darkened theater of my early life. Stepping onto the winter-browned grass, I walk between the two trailers and head slowly for the tree line.

It occurs to me that walking in the woods at night should have made sixteen-year-old me jumpy. But I'd never felt safer than when I sought out Benito beneath these trees.

Once again, I inhale the scent of damp pine needles. And it smells like home. My whole life is defined by things that happened in this place, whether I want it to be or not.

I creep forward, unsure whether I want to see the clearing where Benito and I spent so many hours together. If the tattered remains of our chair linger there, my heart will break all over again. It might be like viewing a dead body—I prefer to remember this place as alive.

I keep going anyway. As I get closer to the clearing, I see a light. Squinting, I try to make out its source. It's diffused—as if something big and angular is blocking it.

I'm tiptoeing now, and I can see the big, angular thing is a shed— the kind you can buy pre-built. Moonlight glints in its single window. The door must be facing the other direction. And it's dark inside.

The light I saw, though, is coming from the interior of a car. It's parked adjacent to the shed on a narrow dirt road that hadn't been here twelve years ago.

My pulse kicks into overdrive. Because there's someone standing next to the shed in the darkness. And it's *him*.

Gage.

Fear climbs up my throat. I freeze there, watching. He's moving slowly around the shed's perimeter, and making a fair bit of noise as he kicks small branches out of the way and mutters to himself.

He thinks he's alone. And soon he will be.

Staying calm, I choose my path. The little road is my best bet—I'm less likely to trip or break any twigs and give myself away. Even though he may drive back down it momentarily, I'd hear his car start first. That will give me plenty of time to take cover in the woods while he passes by.

I take quiet steps, crouching down behind his car as I reach it, using it as a shield until I reach the far side of the road and duck behind a large tree.

I pause, taking stock of the situation. The car door is standing open, and the dome light reveals a suitcase on the back seat. There's something sticking out of it. A piece of paper.

It's *money*.

The reporter in me sits up and licks her chops. Gage has a suitcase full of cash, just like in the movies. He really is a drug dealer. And he's getting out of town.

Benito isn't going to get his man.

Just go, my inner frightened child urges me. *Gage is right there. He has scary eyes.*

But if I go, he'll get away with it. He'll take his cash somewhere and buy a new trailer, move in next to another teenaged girl. And he'll bully anyone who crosses him.

I smell something sharp and astringent now. The scent of my pine forest is gone, replaced with the smell of gasoline.

Oh my God. Gage is going to burn that shed. He's destroying evidence.

My inner reporter is practically frothing at the mouth now. I can't take out my phone and take pictures, because he'll see the screen's light.

What to do? I have about sixty seconds to figure it out. Maybe less. I squint at the car again. The keys are on the seat.

I must be insane. Because I crouch down and move toward that car. It only takes a second. My hand closes around the keys just as I hear the sound of a match being struck.

Shishkebab. This is going to happen fast.

I don't look at Gage. I dart back into the shadows and then move as quickly as I dare down the road.

Behind me I hear cursing, and my heart rate doubles. I drop down into a squat and hold my breath. But I don't hear the car's engine over the thumping of my pulse in my ears. And there aren't any footsteps coming this way.

I risk a look over my shoulder. Could it be that lighting a shed on fire isn't easy? I can't make him out on the other side of the car, but I hear him moving around.

Silently I rise to my feet again. I'm still clutching the keys, so I take one step toward the tree line and drop it at the base of a tree trunk. Then I creep forward down the road.

Whump. I hear the unmistakable sound of a fire starting. And then I hear Gage's fast footsteps. The sound fills me with as much fear as I have ever known in my life, even though I know he's headed to the car. He slams the car door a moment later, and I run for it, knowing that he'll have a busy couple of minutes looking for his missing key.

But I hadn't counted on the headlights.

The sudden illumination fills me with the sick taste of horror. My shadow leaps wildly in front of me as I lunge for the tree line to hide myself. But the branches there only slow me down. I can't run, and I know he's seen me. I hear the car door open again, and he gives an angry shout.

And I can *feel* him coming for me.

Terror swallows my heart. I leap out of the trees again and move as fast as I can down the narrow little road. The headlights show me that it curves back onto the Pine View access road.

Up to the trailers or downhill? I have almost no time to decide. The safety of my car is uphill, so that's where my feet take me. During the next two seconds, I question all my life choices. I should have asked Zara where her mother lives. I should have said goodbye to Benito. I should have called Aunt Jenny more often.

I never should have come back to Vermont at all.

He's coming hard and fast. The pounding of his footsteps is closing the distance between us. I don't know if I can make it. My lungs are burning and he's so close. I don't want to die. If Gage catches me, I'll never own a pair of Louboutins. I'll never know if Benito really loves me.

Benito's warm brown gaze appears in my mind's eye. *You got this,* says his smile.

Go go go. I won't give up, but I don't like my chances. My chest is on fire and my denim skirt prevents me from lengthening my stride completely.

But aging ex-cops get tired, too. I can hear Gage's labored breathing. He's only a couple of yards away now. And I didn't spend the last twelve years working my tail off so I could die in Pine View.

I dig deep and put on a burst of speed. I can see my car. I believe I'm going to get there.

That's when I trip.

It happens so fast that I don't even understand it. One second I'm running, and the next the gravel road rises up and smacks me in the chest. I draw a shocked breath and it comes out as a scream.

Even so, I'm already scrambling to my feet. I almost make it when an iron-like arm wraps tightly around my neck and head. "*You.*" His voice is a scrape as he forces me to bend forward in a headlock. "What the fuck? Princess Skylar shows her sweet face." Hot breath sprays my temple. The familiar smell makes me recoil. Whiskey and anger. "Where's my fucking key?"

"Don't know," I rasp. "I dropped it."

Pain shoots through my neck as he gives it a rough squeeze. "Try again, you little slut. Is it in your pocket?" He unlocks one of his arms only to place it on my butt.

"Get your..." I take a deep breath. "...FUCKING HANDS off me!" I yell as loud as I can. I hope Misty can hear me. I hope she calls 911. It feels really good to yell the f-word. It fires me up. "FUCKING FUCKER!" I add, because I'm out of practice for swearing.

"Mouthy bitch," he grunts while I consider my next move. His hand creeps across my bottom. "You'll be sorry, you bitch," he whispers. "Gonna be fun to finally show you how sorry."

But I'm busy putting all my weight on one leg, and lifting the other foot a few crucial inches. These suede knee boots have a two-and-a-half inch stacked wooden heel. "FUCK!" I yell as I bring it down hard on the top of his foot.

"Arraaaah!" he yells right in my ear. "Cunt *bitch*!" He grabs for the length of my hair to yank it, but I'm in motion again. Making a fist, I karate chop his crotch on a downward stroke, connecting on the first try. Gage bends forward into the pain, just like they'd told me would happen in all those self-defense classes Jenny sent me to. So I follow with an upstroke to clock him in the temple.

My head shot isn't quite as effective as my crotch punch. Gage sways, but doesn't topple. I feel a ruffle of panic in my gut. I shove him away from me just as a pair of headlights pops into view at the top of the access road. The car hurtles forward at an unsafe speed.

Holy crap. If this is one of Gage's buddies, I'm so dead. And now Gage has a firm grip on the back of my skirt. Panic screams at me to run from him. But self-defense training has other ideas. I grab his arm, lift my boot, and scrape it harshly down the inside of his leg, putting all my weight into the job.

Gage screams just as the car skids to a halt and the door flies open. "POLICE! Hands up."

Free now, I leap away from Gage and stick my hands in the air.

Gage doesn't. He bends slowly forward until he collapses into the dirt.

"Does he have a weapon?" asks the police officer. I can't see his face because he's silhouetted by the car's headlights.

"I...I don't know," I stammer.

"Skylar, move away from him. Get behind me."

The cop knows my name. As I move around the circle of light, I realize it's the same guy who checked Rayanne's house on my first night back in Colebury. "Hands on the ground in front of you," he orders Gage.

Gage does not comply.

"NOW!"

Gage moves his hands forward, flat in the dirt. Finally beaten.

Another car comes roaring into view, a single flashing light stuck to the roof. It too stops suddenly, and a man leaps out. "Skylar," he barks.

Benito. I feel all my cells exhale.

"Are you hurt?"

I shake my head like a drunk. I'm experiencing a sudden loss of muscle control. "I stomped his foot and punched his nuts. I threw away his keys so he couldn't drive off with the money."

"You are a goddamn miracle." He's beside me, pulling me into his arms. I sag against him. "What's that smell?"

"A burning shed. He replaced our chair with a shed! And then he torched it." I lift my head off Benito's shoulder, and it takes colossal effort. "Actually, the car and the money might be singed, too. Not sure."

A young voice rings out in the night. "Is Skye okay?" It's Misty, and she's crying. "I heard her scream, 'Get your fucking hands off me.' I called 911," she sobs.

"I'm fine!" I say quickly. Poor Misty.

"You said *fuck?*" Benito asks.

"Special occasion," I mumble. I straighten my spine and step away from Benito. "Misty, it's okay. I promise. Thank you."

And it's true. Time slides forward. My heart rate comes back into the normal range. Gage is wearing handcuffs. More cars pull up the hill, and more personnel get out. "My boss is going to need you to make a statement," Benito says gently. "You're part of the biggest drug bust in Vermont."

The biggest drug bust in Vermont. Now that's a scoop. "Excuse me a second?" I say to Benito. "Can I get my bag from the car?"

"Did Gage touch the car at any point?"

I shake my head.

"All right. Help yourself."

I climb behind the wheel of my rental car and find my phone. But I don't call McCracken or anyone else at *New York News and Sports.* They won't appreciate what I've got. Instead, I find the business card that Lane Barker gave me. Her cell phone number is on it, so that's what I dial.

"Barker," she answers immediately. "Who's calling?"

"It's Skylar Copeland. We met today at…"

"I remember," she says quickly. "What do you have?" She answers like a real news hound, and I know I'm in good hands.

"The biggest drug bust in Vermont. And the kingpin torched a small building in the woods to destroy the evidence. How fast can you get a van to Colebury?"

"Fast enough. The state troopers will be too busy to pull us over. Hanging up now to summon the van. Standby for more instructions."

The line goes dead. But I know I just got the biggest scoop of my career.

THIRTY-SEVEN

Benito

THERE IS nothing like the mayhem of a good bust. My boss has called in every special team that Vermont has—the Tactical Unit, the Clandestine Laboratory Enforcement Team, the Crime Scene Search Team. Okay, he lets the SCUBA guys and the canine teams sleep. But Colebury is swarming with Vermont's finest, and they're all dedicated to sealing this case up tightly.

"Look at this!" a crime scene investigator says, waving me over to Gage's car. We've got floodlights back here already, and photos have been taken. The investigator opens Gage's suitcase with a gloved hand, displaying bundles of hundred dollar bills. "Someone was on his way to South America, probably."

"He'll have to settle for the Southeastern facility!" someone else says.

The wreck of Gage's shed is still smoldering. My greatest regret in this case was failing to find his processing place. Before he incinerated it, the shed was probably a bastion of fingerprints and drug residue. I'll be praying hard that the crime scene guys can still find traces of narcotics in the wreckage.

We don't need the fingerprints. Gage owns this property and Skye saw him torch it. His prints will be all over the car, too. Thank goodness.

But I never found this spot because we missed the primitive little road he cut back here. I want to kick myself. My failure was assuming that I knew this spot already. The sergeant was right. I really was too close to this one. In so many ways.

Even so, when I walk back to the circle of trailers, I get a clap on the back from Sergeant Chapman. "Nice police work, Rossi." He chuckles. "You won't retire now that you got your nemesis, right?"

"No sir," I answer, even though he's joking.

"Good man. Because some other cockroach will skitter into town to take his place."

"I know." That's the job. It's like that old arcade game—Whack-a-Mole. But the more often we whack the moles, then fewer overdose deaths we'll see. It's a reality that I can live with.

Skye is leaning against her rental car while a colleague interviews her. I lurk nearby, keeping an eye on the two of them. After tonight I might have trouble letting her out of my sight. It gives me the cold sweats to think of her in hand-to-hand combat with Gage.

In fact, I had to let Nelligan cuff him earlier because I didn't know if I could get that close to Gage without thumping his skull against the ground and then stepping on his kidney.

I'm not a violent man most days, but I might not be able to resist when it comes to Gage. The world would be better off without him. But I'm going to have to settle for sending him away for life in jail.

He lawyered up before we even got him into a cruiser. The physical evidence will do him in. I'll make sure of it. Either that, or Sparks will rat him out. I hope.

Maybe I'll go to church this weekend. My mother will be thrilled.

A van crests the hill, and there's a satellite dish on top of it. *Fuck.* The TV-news is here to ask a lot of questions and get in the way. It's already pretty crowded, so the news truck has to wedge itself onto the grass at the center of the trailer circle.

A cameraman climbs out of the van. And then a woman in a suit pops out, too. Lane Barker. I recognize her from her reporting days. Now she's the producer. Her eyes scan the crowd, landing on me. Oh great. But her gaze keeps sweeping. "Skylar Copeland!" she barks. "Let's do this."

Skye pushes off the car, to the surprise of my startled colleague. "Just a couple more questions…" Rick tries, but Skylar is already crossing the space toward the news van, where Lane is holding out a sheet of paper to her.

"What did you get off the police scanner?" Skye asks.

"Police action at a motorcycle repair shop on State Road Eleven," Jane rattles off, handing Skye the pad. "At least one arrest confirmed, no suspect yet named. How long do you need?"

Skye glances around the space, looking right past me. She's all business. "I'm good to go. We can set up in front of the suspect's trailer. It's that one." She points at Gage's place. "Unless we could get closer to the raging fire. That would look great on camera…"

"No chance," I hear myself say. "And that's a restricted area."

"Of course it is," Skye grumbles. "The trailer it is, then. Let's go…" She glances at the camera man. "Sorry, I'm Skye. Your name is…?"

"Warren," he says.

"Nice to meet you, Warren." Her gaze snaps toward Misty. "Hey, is your mom home yet?" she asks the girl.

"Yeah. I called her home from work."

"Ask her if you can be on TV. Lane, do you have a release form?"

"On it," she says, diving back into the van.

Skye marches toward the trailer, and the cameraman hurries after her.

And I'm spellbound. I should be doing ten different things right now, but I drift closer to watch Skye work. The cameraman fiddles with his equipment. He hands Skye a microphone. He turns on a bright light, and Skye's golden hair shimmers in the sudden brightness.

"We have ninety seconds," Lane calls, scurrying over. "There's dirt on your shirt."

"Oh, geez," Skye says, brushing at it with her free hand.

"Is that a bruise on your neck?" Lane squawks. "Jesus."

My blood stops circulating. Gage bruised her neck?

"Quick, your jacket," Skye says. "Hold this." She thrusts her microphone at the camera guy and then shrugs off her sweater. She's wearing nothing but a tiny tank top underneath.

The entire Colebury police force turns to stare. But all I see is an ugly purple bruise across Skye's collarbone.

I feel murderous.

Lane drops her suit jacket onto Skye's shoulders, and my girl shrugs it on in a hurry. The sleeves are too short, so she pushes them up while Lane buttons the jacket, concealing the bruise.

"Thirty seconds," the camera guy says, handing back the microphone.

"No problem." Skye tucks in an ear piece. "Testing sound? Can you hear me?"

"We're good with sound" someone calls from the van.

"Six, five, four…" Lane counts down with her fingers.

Jesus Christ. If you want something done in a hurry, call some newsies. Skye dons a professional smile as Lane finishes the count-down. "This is Emily Skye, reporting from the Pine View trailer park in Colebury Vermont. Police are on the scene tonight to arrest ex-policeman James Gage in alleged connection with other arrests in a major drug sting operation. Given the sudden spike in overdose deaths from fentanyl, police have been heavily focused on the Colebury drug trade. This could be—to quote one officer on the Vermont State Police Task Force—Vermont's biggest drug bust."

My jaw unhinges. I don't know whether I'm more annoyed that she quoted me without my permission or that she said that it *could be* Vermont's biggest drug bust.

It totally is.

And I want to haul Skye out of that spotlight, check that bruise on her body, and then kiss the hell out of her. But it will have to wait.

"Police took Gage away in handcuffs. And in a moment we'll hear from at least one other Pine View resident about Gage as a neighbor. Now back to Charlotte on the news desk for more."

The light winks off and Lane Barker lets out a little shriek of excitement. "And there's still nobody else here! Kiss my ass, NBC! I smell an award for this one."

"I need more," Skye says. "We need to know what was found at the scene on route eleven."

"Press conference *tomorrow*," my boss says hastily. "And not a moment sooner."

"Can you confirm that John Oscar Sparks is in police custody?" Skye asks.

"Who's asking the questions here?" grumbles the sergeant. "You come over here and finish telling my deputy what you saw."

Skye hands off the microphone, looking reluctant. Then she removes Lane's jacket, and reaches for her sweater.

"Hold on," I say, aiming my flashlight at the purple flesh on her collarbone. "Could this be broken?" I touch the spot gently and she flinches. "After you're done here, I want to get you checked out."

She pulls the sweater over her head, and then blue eyes flash into mine. "I'm okay. Really."

"Yeah, I can see that. But..." I pull her against my chest and kiss her forehead. "You gave me a scare. I can't lose you. Not ever again. I may not let you out of my sight. What were you doing here, anyway? That's the part I don't understand."

"I was leaving," she says. "I was going to drive back to New York tonight. I was bringing a tiramisu to your mother..."

"What? She moved ten years ago."

Skye yawns. "I figured that out, thanks. But then I was chatting with Misty, and I saw Gage drive away. I thought he was gone. That's why I texted you."

"Thanks for that. Now let's back up to the part where you were going to New York."

"Well." She clears her throat. "I panicked. Flipping Jill Sullivan, you know? It was like reliving my worst nightmare."

"Really?" I would have thought Gage was her worst nightmare. And Skye is fading before my eyes. Her eyelids droop. "Are you okay?"

"Adrenaline crash," she says. "And I never ate dinner."

I tuck her against my side and pull out my phone, touching Zara's number. "Hey. Are you still with Mom?" I ask when she answers.

"Just about to leave. Why?"

"Is there any way you could leave Nicole there and meet us? Skylar needs some company and I'm going to be working all night."

"Company?"

"She subdued Gage in a fistfight before his arrest, and she's a little banged up and underfed."

"Jesus...bleeping Christ."

"Pretty much. She needs the emergency room and a snack."

"I'm not going to the hospital," Skye murmurs against my shoulder.

"Pizza and a stiff drink, then," Zara improvises in my ear. "Where is she now?"

"Pine View Circle."

"Gross. I'll be there in ten."

"I have one more segment to film," Skye says with another yawn. "I'm going to interview Misty."

"Make it snappy. Then let us take care of you."

"If you insist," she says, and I hug her a little tighter.

THIRTY-EIGHT

Skylar

WE GET some film of Misty and her mom. And then Lane declares me done for the night. "Thanks for the scoop, kid. This is going to be big. Come to the press conference tomorrow?"

"I wouldn't miss it," I promise her.

"Your dickweed of a boss is going to shit himself over this. I might be getting you into trouble by letting you cover it for us."

"He might not even notice," I point out. "And it's my story."

"That it is," she agrees. "Later, Skye." She hops into her van and they drive away.

The place is still crawling with cops and firemen. After I refuse again to go to the hospital, Benito finds a fire department EMT to look at my bruise.

"That's gonna hurt awhile. Use ice," the EMT says.

"Could it be broken?" Ben presses.

"Probably not. But if she's still in significant pain after a couple of days, she can get an X-ray."

"Fair enough," I mumble. I'm practically asleep on my feet.

Zara arrives, and I let Benito put me in the passenger seat of her car. It's only a few miles from here to the Gin Mill, but they might be right that I shouldn't drive right now.

Before we can leave, though, Benito opens the car door and leans down. "Honey, Rayanne was just arrested at the train station in White River Junction."

"*Oh.*" Oh no.

"Sweetheart, did you know she was running away?"

"Yes," I admit. "I saw her earlier."

He closes his eyes. "You should have told me where to find her. If she came in willingly, it would be easier to make her case."

"I didn't…" *Trust you.* "I didn't want to make that decision for her. You both put me on the spot."

"Right," he says. "But now there's no way for me to be involved with her case. It's my own sister she allegedly endangered. That's a conflict of interest. And we've already arrested our drug trafficker and seized his loot."

"You still need whatever evidence she has," I remind him. But there's a new bubble of hysteria rising inside me. I could have just told Benito where to find Rayanne. I could have let him talk her into surrendering herself. "She doesn't belong in jail."

If I'd just trusted him, this could have been prevented.

"Leaving the scene of an accident can be either a felony or a misdemeanor. Tomorrow we'll learn more," he says, kissing my nose. "It could turn out okay."

"All right," I say, but my teeth begin to chatter.

"Go get some rest," he says.

"I'll take care of her," Zara says. "Let us go, okay?"

He shuts the door.

I'm trembling as Zara pulls away. Because now we're starting down the access road, where I ran away from Gage. I can still hear the sound of his pounding footsteps behind me…

I shiver.

"Five minutes," Zara says soothingly. "We need to get some food in you. And maybe hot tea. The tequila will have to wait for another time."

She's being really nice, but I don't know if I can eat. I didn't know it was possible to feel so afraid after the fact. "I feel…nuts," I whisper, shivering again.

"It's shock. It will pass. I had the same thing happen to me the night of my hit and run."

I wince. Zara deserves to know how that happened, and yet I can't talk about Rayanne right now. I'm barely holding it together.

We arrive at the Gin Mill, where the parking lot is full of bar customers. Somehow I cross the lot on my own power and walk up the flight of stairs necessary to reach Benito's place.

Zara opens the door with her own key, and I make a beeline for the bedroom. All I want is the bed.

No—a shower first. I want to wash Gage off me.

So I wash my hair. I scrub the night off my skin. The hot water feels amazing as long as I keep it off the tender bruise on my collarbone. I'm just going to ignore the pain. Gage tried to get me, and he failed. What's one more bruise? He left plenty of those on my heart.

I wrap myself in Benito's bathrobe, and then head into the bedroom. I hadn't planned on staying here tonight. But now all I want is the comfort of Benito's bed.

And, whoops, my duffel bag is in the back of my rental car, which is still at Pine View. So I open and shut Benito's dresser drawers until I've located a giant Army T-shirt and a pair of flannel shorts with a cinch waist.

I shed the robe and change. The T-shirt smells like Ben. I wish I didn't find that so comforting, but I do. I climb into his bed, where the scent of him is even stronger. I pull the comforter over me and sigh. Everything will be okay if I never leave this spot. I'm pretty sure.

My limbs still feel shaky and weird. But as I lie in Benito's bed, I begin to drift, and the spasms of fear become more intermittent. I doze. Maybe half an hour later my eyes fly open when Zara enters the room with a tray.

"Ben had some of my mother's homemade soup in his freezer," she says. "Try a little of this."

"I'm not very hungry," I say from the safety of the covers.

"Your body can't shore itself up on nothing," Zara insists. "Sit up. Humor me."

Because she's being so nice (again!) I actually do it. I take the tray and lift the spoon. The soup has a tomato base with a hint of peppery spiciness. And there's pasta and white beans in it. "Okay, this is good," I admit, spooning up some more. "Thank you."

"You can thank Mom sometime."

"She moved."

Zara smiles. "Of course she did. She's very happy in the new trailer park. It's a bunch of gossipy women. The play bridge and trade secrets. Nicole is sleeping over there tonight. In the morning they'll all feed her too much sugar and spoil her."

That sounds orders of magnitude nicer than the old place. "I went to Pine View tonight because I was trying to take your mom a tiramisu. That's how I ended up fighting off Gage."

Zara flinches. "You're braver than I am."

"Well, I started out trying to be brave. But then I wished I hadn't. You know what? He did it again. He threatened to... *force* me." I put down the spoon on the tray with a clunk, because the memory steals my joy.

"Oh *sweetie*." Zara's big brown eyes are so much like Benito's.

"The thing is? For once I didn't believe him. Like—you're trying to flee the scene of a drug-dealing operation, but you pause in the driveway for sex? It doesn't make sense. But I was still terrified. He's all about the fear, you know?"

"Well, it's very effective. I was terrified of that man. Still am."

"Really?" That stuns me. "You always seemed fearless to me."

"Totally an act." Zara smiles. "I'm glad to hear that I fooled one person. "Oh! I forgot your tea." She gets up and runs out of the room before I get a chance to say that I don't really need tea.

Having Zara wait on me is pretty weird, anyway. I don't know what to think about that.

She returns a minute later, though, looking grumpy. "Okay, look. I know you're fragile right now. But what the hell is this?" She holds up a piece of paper—the goodbye note I left on Benito's counter.

I wrote that note four hours ago, tops. But it feels like another lifetime. "That's personal," I say

She makes a face. "No kidding, but I'm from a family of five kids. We forgot the meaning of 'personal' two decades ago. And I *cannot* allow you to ditch Benito in a note. Jesus." She tears the letter right in half.

Now this is the Zara I remember. "Omigod. You're scarier than Gage."

"Not by half! But I can't take another twelve years of Benito moping. If you two don't work out somehow, that will be sad. But you have to give it a try! No two people get as moony around each other as you two. You don't throw something like that away."

I open my mouth to protest that I'm never moony, except I think she's right. About me anyway. But that's the whole problem. "Benito isn't moony. And he doesn't mope over me. He has dirty sex with Jill Sullivan instead. Just like the last time I left."

Zara tilts her head and thinks that through. "I'll give you that the whole Jill thing is stupid. He doesn't care about her and shouldn't have bothered. But what do you mean about the last time you left?"

"Before! In high school." Not that I really want to get into it.

And Zara still looks blank. "Ben and Jill didn't make the beast with two backs in high school. In spite of my fervent prayer that he'd make her easier to live with."

"He didn't? But what about..." It's embarrassing to reveal that I still feel the sting twelve years later. "Grad prom. He took her and not me."

Zara's jaw flops open. "No!"

"Yes."

"No! He really did not. I promise. I was there when the whole thing went down. And Benito didn't get near that dance."

"Yes he *did*," I argue. And then—for the first time ever, I stop to consider my source. It was Gage who had told me why Benito stood me up.

I let out a gasp.

"He got arrested, Skye. He spent the night in the holding cell."

My lungs seize up, and my eyes fill with tears. Because now I realize that Jimmy Gage did even more damage to my teenage psyche than I ever imagined.

"Oh my god," Zara whispers. "Did Gage tell you Ben went to the dance without you?"

I nod, choking on unshed tears. And even now it's difficult to rearrange the beliefs that I've held close to my heart for so many years. Benito's betrayal struck me deeply. I've been carrying it around for years.

"I'm so sorry, Skye," Zara says. "It's all my fault."

But it isn't. It's Gage's fault. And twelve years later, two grown women are still feeling shame over things that he did.

Zara and I look at each other, and our faces hold twin expressions of pain.

THIRTY-NINE

Benito

IT'S three in the morning when I tiptoe into my darkened apartment. There is no one in the living room since my sister went home hours ago, after Skye had insisted she was fine and just needed sleep.

I don't want to disturb Skye's rest. So I lock up my gun and then remove most of my clothing in the bathroom. My face in the mirror looks tired, but that's really okay with me. We spent the last few hours booking Sparks and Gage and collecting evidence. Sparks had several firearms in his home, one of which was unlicensed. And Gage had all that cash he won't be able to account for.

The unrelated felonies are piling up. Now we just need to nail 'em on the bigger charges.

The bikers who dropped the drugs off with Sparks got picked up, too. If I'm very lucky, they'll cooperate in the morning when their lawyers arrive. And the motorcycle shop owner, too.

Everyone lawyered up right away. So the investigation will drag out. But that's okay. We'll get there. I can be patient now that four criminals are wearing orange jumpsuits.

I can't cure drug addiction, but I can get unsafe product off the streets. It's not a bad day's police work.

When I'm ready for bed, I move quietly into the bedroom. Skye is sleeping on her side, her silky hair arrayed on the pillow. I slide into the bed, propping myself up on an elbow to look down at her.

I just spent ten minutes trying not to wake her up. But I can't stop myself from running a hand down her arm, just to feel the warmth of her body. I know she's okay. But I'm going to have nightmares for a while where I'm picturing Gage putting Skye in a headlock. Just the idea makes me want to hurl.

Skye shifts in her sleep, and then her eyes fly open.

"Easy," I whisper. "It's just me." I scoop her up and pull her close. "Sorry to wake you up. But I need to hold you. Are you sure you're okay?"

She nods, tucking her face against my shoulder. "I'll be okay. My mind is blown, though."

"He's finally behind bars."

"That's not why," she whispers. "Zara helped me figure something out tonight."

"Hmm?" I nose into her hair and inhale the sweet scent of her shampoo. I feel better already.

"The night of grad prom," she says. "Gage told me you took Jill Sullivan to the dance."

I yank my head up and look down at her. "What?"

"That's what he said when he came home. To explain why you never showed."

And I'm stunned. "You thought I just *abandoned* you?"

"He was very convincing. He gave details. And you weren't *there*, Ben! I couldn't think of anywhere else you'd be!"

"In jail!"

"I know that now," she says quietly. "I'm sorry. I shouldn't have believed him."

"Jesus. Don't apologize for something that fucker did. He's done hurting us. I just can't believe that happened." My mind is reeling as I try to remember all the events of that night. "Zara was supposed to explain."

"She feels terrible," Skye says, sitting up. "She saw Gage come home and talk to me, saw me get upset. She just assumed he'd told me he put you in jail."

I sit up, too, feeling twitchy again. "God, I should have clocked him tonight when I had the chance. But I wanted to be the bigger man."

"You are," she says, stroking my cheek. "But now you know why I kind of lost my mind today at the rental counter."

"Oh, *fuck.*" Jill again. "That's...*Jesus.*" Words fail me. I can't even excuse myself. Because everything Jill said was pretty much true. Except that Skye probably assumed we'd been carrying on for twelve years.

I let out an unhappy groan. "I don't know how to explain myself right now. Except to say that the Jill thing was casual."

"You don't have to explain yourself." She sighs. "I wish I could unhear it, though. I'll probably always wonder if I'm sexy enough for you."

"Yes! God." I wrap both arms more tightly around her. "I have it so bad for you."

"I'm just jealous," Skye grumbles. "Everyone has more experience than I do. And, fine—I spent the afternoon imagining that the secret sex room in your soul is a lot like Penn Station at rush hour."

This hits my funny bone, and I actually laugh. "It's not Penn Station. I guess it's more like a stop on a commuter rail line. Active but infrequent."

Skye snorts, and puts her face in her hands. "We really aren't the same. I don't want to crucify you for having a sex life. But it's hard for me to understand."

"I know," I say, putting a hand on her knee. "I get it."

"Do you?" She lifts her perfect chin and studies me. "It took a lot of trust for me to go there with you. To get so..." She clears her throat.

"Naked?" I suggest.

"Vulnerable," she corrects. "And naked. It's kind of the same thing for me. I was feeling pretty good about us. And then along comes Jill with her request for, uh, your handcuffs."

And now I might die of embarrassment. *That was just a one-time thing. That was her idea.* These denials are right there on my tongue. But they're not actually the point. "Skye, I need to show you something. Come here." I get up.

"Is it your handcuffs?" she asks drily. "I'm not up for that right this second."

"No, it's better." I kneel on the bed and gather the comforter around her. "Put your arms around me." When she does, I scoop her off the bed, comforter, sheet and all.

"Where are we going?"

"You'll see in a minute. Hold on."

Skye is not a petite girl, which I love. But it does make the grand gesture more difficult. She has to cling to me carefully so that I can carry her through the bedroom doorway and out into the living room. I cross to the sliding glass door. "Open that, will you?"

She fumbles for the latch and then slides it open. The screen door, too. "What's out here?"

The deck boards of my balcony are freezing under my feet. It isn't balcony weather, which is why we haven't come out here before. But this is important. "Look."

Skye swivels her head and then gasps. "It's here? The same chair?"

Sure enough, our double-wide deck chair is the only furniture on my balcony. "It's the same one. I couldn't ever stand the thought of getting rid of it." I bend my knees and set her down on it. "Move over."

She scoots. I close the door behind us. And a few seconds later we're sitting side by side on the deck chair, the way we always did before. Skye pulls the covers around us and puts her head on my shoulder. "It's like time travel, Ben. This is amazing."

"No, it's better." I wrap my arms around her and squeeze. "I never got to hold you like this, even though I wanted to."

"I wanted you to," she says. "But everything was so complicated."

She's right, it was. We weren't ready to be the kind of couple I wanted us to be. "We're here now. That's all that matters."

Skye hugs me even more tightly. I get a smile as she tips her head back against me. "My God, the stars!" It's a clear night, and the moon has already set. The great, dark bowl above us glitters with the light of the milky way. "I forgot how bright and beautiful they are in Vermont."

We're quiet together for a moment, and I stroke the soft skin of her arm. "Honey, I wouldn't have fooled around with Jill if I'd known there was a chance you'd come back to me. I'm not going to try to explain it. Casual sex has always been easier for me than for you, I expect."

"I know. It's okay." She kisses my chin.

"The point is this—I spent many more hours sitting on this chair wishing you were here with me than I ever spent in her bedroom. Or anyone else's for that matter. With you, there's no such thing as casual. The fire I feel for you won't ever go out. "

Her response is to lean in and kiss my neck. Slowly. Leisurely. Soft lips caress my skin. And a warm tongue tastes me.

I make a low groan as my body responds to her, as it always has. And always will. "If you keep doing that, we're going to have to finally christen this chair."

She smiles against my skin. Then she slowly licks the edge of my mouth, and I can't wait anymore. I turn my head and claim her mouth in a real kiss.

And now my teenage fantasies come to life. This is it right here—Skye is kissing me on our chair. Her hot mouth teases mine. Then she moves on to worship my neck, and then my chest after I shrug off my T-shirt to encourage her.

I'm living my best life as she kisses her way across my pecs. I wind her hair around my hand and sigh. It's hard not to whisper all the dirtiest desires in my heart. Skye is exploring me at her own speed, and I don't want to push her. But my dick is aching as she runs a thumb slowly down my abs, and then skims her knuckles along the sensitive skin of my lower belly.

I try not to gasp as she reaches inside my boxers for my cock, and then swipes her tongue across the head. I make a hungry sound, though. Who could help it?

Blue eyes flick upward toward mine as she tentatively slides me inside her mouth. "J-Jesus," I stammer, clenching my legs. "That's...ungh."

When I was eighteen, I'd thought about this every day. Several times a day. I never once expected it could actually happen. Her tongue strokes my shaft, and the pleasure is almost too intense.

"You kill me, you know that?" I say in a strangled voice. "You're all I need."

She releases me and lays her face on my hip. "Even if I don't know what I'm doing?"

"Like I care. Does anyone, really? Come up here and let me kiss you."

Skye moves. To my great excitement, she kicks off the flannel shorts she's wearing to reveal nothing beneath them.

My fantasies are living large tonight. Eagerly, I kick my boxers off, too.

She straddles me, and I pull the comforter up around her shoulders. Then I lift the T-shirt she's wearing off her body.

"It's cold," she yelps.

"Come closer. We'll keep each other warm." I take her mouth in a kiss that goes wild right away. We are nothing but heated mouths and thrusting tongues. My erection is trapped against her soft body. We're cocooned together in the cool night, and I've literally never been happier. "Fuck, honey." I fill my hands with her breasts and moan. "Let me go find a condom, before I burst."

"I'm covered," she breathes, kissing me again. "Don't go *anywhere*."

My balls tighten with excitement. It's unlike me not to be cautious about unprotected sex. But I've been very safe up until now. And Skye's eagerness is like a gift she gives both of us. If this is the moment when my love—and her bravery—burn through all her fear, then I'm going to let it happen.

"You are so amazing to me," I whisper between kisses. "Come here and let me love you."

She lifts her body, and I line myself up. And then her slick heat is enveloping me as she takes me inside. I let out a groan so loud that it probably startles the owls in the trees. There is nothing between us at all. Not even twelve lost years. Our mouths lock together without missing a beat. And, slowly, we begin to move against each other.

The chair creaks. I have to concentrate on holding myself in check. The breathy sounds she makes as she rides me are practically enough to bring me to climax. Forget the slide of her breasts against my heated skin and the pulse of my happy cock.

I'm such a goner.

Then something on Skye's right snags her attention. She looks down at me again, and I lift my chin for a kiss. She smiles, and it's almost bashful.

"You good?" I pant, my fingers fanning out on her perfect ass.

"Yes. But..." She glances to the side again, and then quickly returns her gaze to mine. "I can *see* us."

"Oh." My lust-addled brain takes a second to catch on. "Our reflection?" The lights are out inside the house, so I suppose the sliding glass door might behave like a mirror.

"Yes." She pauses, her hands in my hair. "It's..."

"Hot?" I guess. Then I chuckle. "Do you not like it?"

"No, I *do* like it." She squeezes her eyes shut and then opens them again. "Is that weird?"

"Fuck, no. Sit up." I lever us both into a sitting position, and I put one foot down on the deck. "Look now."

Skye turns her head toward the door, and I fill my hand with her breast, knocking the comforter away. Then I lean down and take her nipple into my mouth, while my hand skims every inch of her skin that I can reach.

She gasps, and her body clenches around me.

"That's right," I whisper, kissing her neck. "There's nothing more beautiful than you when you're turned on." I roll my hips, and she wraps her arms around me.

But I can't do my best work when I'm sitting on the edge of the chair like this. "Lay back, honey." I nudge her off of me. It hurts to lose her, but it's only temporary. I arrange her on her back, her head on the comforter at the wrong end of our chair.

She covers her breasts against the sudden chill.

"Look now," I order, covering her sweet body with mine. I hook an arm under one of her thighs and then fill her. We both groan. "Watch," I pant, moving inside her.

It's exquisite. I bite my lip just to feel a pinch of pain. "Wrap your legs around me," I beg. When she does, I steal a single glance at the glass door to see what Skye sees.

And it's a mistake. The view of our coupling makes me suck in a breath. Skye's long legs are clutching my body, and her chest is heaving. Her breasts bounce as I fuck her.

"Got to come, honey," I say through gritted teeth. If not now, then soon. I can't take the sight of all that beauty underneath me. I close my eyes and lock all my muscles in one last desperate attempt to stave it off.

That's when Skye moans and clutches me. I grind against her and she cries out. For me. And I almost let out a yell of victory as I chase my own joy.

FORTY

Skylar

WAKING up is hard to do.

It didn't used to be difficult. In New York I bounce right out of bed and scurry off to work. But there are a couple of factors at play here in Vermont.

First, I was up 'til all hours having porch-chair sex.

Second, Benito's warm, naked body is pressed against mine in the bed. He's hit the snooze button twice already. But neither of us can let go and get up.

"Urgh," he says, his face in the pillow.

"Yeah," I agree with a sigh. "But I'm going to shower now. I have to prepare for the press conference."

"Dere-mugh-been-perf-m-phone," he says.

"What?"

He turns his face away from the pillow, and I get today's first view of his warm brown eyes. "There are seventeen messages on my phone. I guess I'd better get to work, too."

Neither of us moves.

"Count of three?" I suggest.

"One," he says.

"Two."

"Two and a half." He grins.

"I love you." It just falls out of my mouth.

Benito's eyes get soft and hazy. "I love you, too, honey. Always have."

"I know it's complicated. I have this job in another city. I probably have to go back to it soon. But..."

He holds up a hand. "We'll figure it out. Not this morning, but eventually. It'll all work out."

"Okay," I say softly.

"It won't be easy for me to get a job in New York," he says. "I've got an awfully fractured resume for a narcotics officer. Short stints everywhere. But I could try. Or I could beg the DEA for my job back, with a transfer to the New York office. They'd probably say no, and the hours would suck but..."

"Benito?" I can't even believe my ears.

"Yeah?"

"You'd leave Vermont for me?" That doesn't even make sense.

He props himself up on an elbow. "Baby, I would. It wouldn't be the best career move, but I wouldn't even hesitate. Career isn't everything."

I'm speechless.

His phone is not, though. It chirps on the bedside table with a new message. "Hold that thought," he says. "Or hit the shower? I know you need a few hours to get ready." He pinches my hip.

"You don't appreciate my efforts," I say, sitting up.

"Oh, honey I *do*," he purrs. "But the coffee is waiting and..." His eyes narrow.

"What?"

Still frowning, Benito crawls toward me in all his naked glory. "Jeez." He places a gentle hand over the bruised spot on my collar bone. "God, I hope I didn't hurt you last night when we were..."

I cover his hand with mine. "I'm fine, tough guy. Now answer your messages."

Rolling away from him, I take myself into the bathroom. Because I do need a nice long time to do my face. He's just going to have to learn to live with it.

———

Forty minutes later we arrive in the coffee shop, but there's a problem. "Someone is on our sofa," I grumble as we wait to order.

Benito chuckles. "Shoulda gotten ready faster, baby. You know I could clean up all the crime in Colebury in the time it takes you to paint that stuff on your face."

"Really? Because I think it just took you twelve *years* to clean up all the crime in Colebury."

He makes a disgruntled noise. "All the crime in Norwich, then."

"I plan to be on camera today. That takes extra makeup."

He gives me a heart-melting smile. "You'll let me mess up that lipstick later, right?"

Someone makes a gagging sound, and I realize it's Zara. "You going to order or just stare at each other like goobers?"

Whoops! I turn my attention to Zara, who looks exhausted. "Don't you ever get a day off?"

"She won't take one," says Roddy the hot baker. "Not until Audrey comes back from maternity leave."

"But she should," says Audrey, appearing in the doorway to the kitchen, the baby in a carrier on her chest. "I swear—having a newborn is easier than running a coffee shop."

"Can I hold him?" I blurt out. Just seeing those chubby legs dangling from the carrier fills me with the need to give them little squeezes.

"Sure!" she says. "I'll bring him over once you sit down."

We order our coffee and bagels, and once again Zara tries to prevent Benito from paying.

"Look," he says. "Get over yourself. Why are you doing this?"

"The better question is why are you fighting it? Everyone grumbles when I don't give 'em free stuff and now you're grumbling that I want to? Which is it?"

Ben shakes his head at his sister. "You've been weird ever since Skye turned up."

"Well." Zara puts her hands on her hips. "I always thought it was my fault you guys weren't together. I'm the one who texted you when Gage pulled us over. And now I know it's even worse. If I'd actually explained to Skye why you weren't there..." Her eyes get red as she passes us two mugs of coffee.

"Holy Toledo," Audrey says. "Nothing makes Zara cry. Where's my camera?"

"She's just tired," I insist. I really don't want Zara to feel bad about this. "Let's all caffeinate so we're ready for the hearing later. And the press conference. Would it be weird to throw an indictment party? Is that a thing?"

"Let's make it a thing," Audrey says. "Which hors d'oeuvres go best with criminal prosecution?"

Roddy whips out his phone. "Cop party..." he says as he taps on the screen. "A donut theme! Well done, internet. And don't forget the handcuffs."

I make a noise of irritation, and Benito chokes on his sip of coffee.

"The handcuffs are too much?" Roddy asks. "Sit down somewhere. I'll fix your bagels."

Benito drops a twenty on the counter. "No backsies." Then he puts a hand on the small of my back and guides me toward a different couch, because ours is still taken.

We're eating terrific bagels with bacon cream cheese when Audrey sits down next to me. "Are you still game to hold him? I could run in back and mix up a batch of biscotti for Zara."

"Sure!" I set down my mug. "Let's snuggle, Gus."

Audrey places him in my arms, and he looks up at me with dark blue eyes.

"Hello!" I say softly. "It's nice to see you again. Have you been well?"

He answers by closing his little starfish hand around a lock of my hair, and giving it a tug.

"He just ate, so he should be cheery. Back in a jif!" Audrey says before sprinting away.

The sofa depresses beside me as Benito scoots in and looks down at the baby. "He can't take his eyes off you."

"Where else would he look?" I stroke his soft little chubby cheek, and he opens his mouth in surprised pleasure.

"She's mine, little dude," Benito teases. "Find your own girl."

Now that he mentions it, the way the baby is fingering my hair does seem a little possessive. I hope he's doing that just to put Benito in his place.

"You like babies, huh?" Benito says, wrapping an arm around me. "I never knew that about you."

"Sixteen is a little young to be excited about babies. But I love babies." Gus gives me a thousand-mile stare with his little blue eyes. He looks sleepy. And if he was unhappy, I'd know. "Babies are very honest. They lay it all out on the table. They tell you exactly how they're feeling."

"Yeah? I can do that. How's this? I can't wait to have babies with you."

My body actually jerks a little at this revelation. I'm still not used to this version of Benito—the one who says he loves me and takes me to bed. "Okay, wow. How many are we talking about here?" The truth is that having a baby with Benito is a fantasy so lovely that never once have I allowed myself to consider it.

"Five is a nice number, don't you think?"

I make a choking noise of surprise, which alarms little Gus. His eyes widen and then narrow.

"It's okay," I whisper. "This man is full of crazy talk. Five is a very high number. Doesn't three sound more reasonable?" This whole discussion is blowing my mind. Benito as a daddy? I can't imagine a better father. If he guards a child even half as well as he takes care of me, that will be one lucky kid.

"It's not so many," he says, nuzzling my ear. "We can practice making them right after work."

"You need practice?" I tease. But my nipples tighten at the idea.

"Nope," he whispers. "Twins run in my family. Just a warning." He kisses my neck.

That's when my phone begins to ring in my bag, and Gus looks around with big blue eyes, as if to ask, *Aren't you going to get that?*

"Benito, could you grab the phone?"

With a sigh, he gives up on his public display of affection to grab the phone and hand it to me. "The caller says McCracken," he reports. "Please tell me his name is Phil."

"Nope, it's John. There's nothing funny about this guy. Hello?" I say, answering it.

"Copeland! The van..." I hear static as the connection cuts in and out. "…Brattleboro. We'll arrive… press conference. Write my… ready to brief me."

"Wait, what? Who's in Brattleboro?"

"I'm…" More static. "…cover the drug bust. Goddamn this connection!"

Maybe my boss is actually in Vermont? Where else would he have such terrible cell service? "*You* want to cover the story?" I shout, trying to catch up.

"Hell yes! It's big…" More static. "The flow of opiates has changed direction."

"True. But that's *my* story."

And then the line goes dead.

For a moment I just sit there with my phone to my ear, trying to make sense of that call. Why would McCracken come all the way to Vermont?

Baby Gus gives my hair a tug and makes a noise of impatience. So I click off my phone.

"Everything okay?" Benito asks, taking the phone from me.

"Just the usual bullshizzle. I think my boss just mansplained my own story to me. And he may or may not be on the way to Vermont."

"That sounds complicated." Baby Gus lets out a squawk of agreement.

"Yeah."

"My brother picked up your rental car last night. It's right outside." He pecks me on the cheek. "Do you need anything before I run off to work?"

"No, I suppose not," I admit. "Will you be at the press conference later?"

"Yep." Benito stands up and then lifts the baby out of my arms. "Guess what, little guy? You have to go back to your mama now." The baby blows some bubbles with his tiny lips, and Benito grins.

My ovaries dance a little jig at the sight of the two of them.

"I believe it's my turn to hold him," Roddy the hot baker says as he joins us. "Hand him over."

As Benito passes Gus to Rod, I glance around the coffee shop. All the women are watching with dreamy little smiles. And I swear there's estrogen rising around us in a mist. There's nothing like two hot guys holding a baby.

"Off to work," Benito says, offering me a hand. I let him pull me up off the couch. "I'll look for you at the press conference. I'm off to pick up my dress uniform from the cleaners. And get a haircut."

"You have a dress uniform?" I squeak. Now there's a pleasant image I hadn't considered before.

"Yeah," he says, his eyes amused. "Shiny buttons and everything. I'll let you peel it off me later."

"Oh my." My lady bits give a little shimmy at this idea. So I don't even have the urge to step back when Benito leans in, brown eyes full of desire. He closes his eyes at the last second and kisses me right there in the middle of the coffee shop. And it's such a good kiss that I have to wrap my arms around him and return it.

Public display of affection doesn't usually sit well with me. Then again, I'm not usually the one who's lip-locked to a hot guy in the middle of a coffee shop. The rest of the world recedes as Benito's lips stroke mine. And then his tongue comes out to play...

"This is a family establishment," Zara says from somewhere nearby. "Benny cut it out. Mrs. Blake is fanning herself."

I force myself to gentle the kiss, and Benito steps back with a frustrated sigh. "I'll see you later. We'll break in more of my furniture."

"Stop right there." Zara hooks an arm through his and tugs him toward the door. "I do not want to hear the details."

"Fine. But let's just say that old deck chair is sturdier than it looks."

His sister rolls her eyes. "I already knew that."

"Wait." Benito stops cold. "What?"

Zara bites her lip. "Never mind. Forget I mentioned it."

"That's *my* sentimental chair. Don't tell me you actually..."

She gives him another shove toward the door. "It was just the once. Go catch some bad guys, would you? Bye!"

He gives her one more grumpy look. But I get a wave and a smile.

Then he's gone, leaving me with nothing but half a bagel and a silly grin on my face.

"You two are endlessly amusing," Zara says, picking up Benito's empty plate. "More coffee?"

"No thanks. I have to prepare for the press conference." Whether my boss shows up or not, you couldn't keep me away from news about Gage going to jail.

"Good luck out there. Did you know your news piece ran on Green Mountain Public Radio this morning?"

I pause on my way toward the door. "What? Really?"

"Yep." Zara lifts a tray of dirty crockery. "I think the story is going to be big. I loved the part where you asked Misty Carrera what Gage was like as a neighbor." She chuckles. "I always did like that kid. She said, 'You know how sometimes when a guy is arrested his neighbors say, I had no idea? Well this isn't that guy. We all knew he was a criminal.'" She laughs again. "God, this is a good day. My mother is going to erect a statue in your honor. Stop by later and tell me what happens at the press conference, yeah?"

"Sure," I agree.

It *will* be a good day. I run out to the rental car and climb in.

FORTY-ONE

Skylar

EVEN THE WEATHER is on board for today's events. The sun is shining down on the steps of the Vermont State Police headquarters as the news trucks roll up one after another.

Zara was right. This *is* a big story. When I checked the headlines a minute ago, I found Vermont's biggest drug seizure on all the national news outlets.

And? They're all quoting WBTV news coverage. This has got to be good for my résumé, right? I'll bet Lane Barker will give me a reference now, even if my own boss won't.

I'm waiting when the WBTV van arrives. The door opens and Lane climbs out and inhales deeply. "I love the smell of criminal prosecution in the morning! Did you get some sleep?"

"Some. You?"

She shakes her head. "I was up all night making sure my station is on top of the scoop you handed us. You've got hero status in our office, now."

"It's true!" Jordy crows as he climbs out behind her. "First the penis and now this! You're a woman of many talents."

I wonder if that penis video will follow me for my whole life. But there's no time to worry about it now. "Here," I say to Lane. "I grabbed two copies of the press release."

"Ooh! A hand-out," Jordy says, snatching the paper from Lane. "That's very formal. Very big city. This case must be huge."

"It is!" I crow. "And we got there first." I always thought I'd be celebrating my first big scoop with my own boss. But life is funny that way.

"Look, about that." Lane measures me with her cunning blue eyes. "Thank you for that well-timed call last night, and the excellent on-camera work."

Uh-oh. "But?"

"But I can't use you for the story this morning. Your station threw a fit. Your boss is a real piece of work."

Well, crud.

"We would love to have you continue to report the story for WBTV. But we can't feature you while you still work for him. He was very clear about that. That's the only reason Jordy is here this morning. I would never step on your toes…"

"No it's fine," I say quickly. "I completely understand. You guys have been nothing but great." It's true, even if I'm disappointed.

Jordy is speed-reading the press release while the cameraman positions his tripod.

I step out of the way while Lane Barker presses a phone to her ear. "Jordy, they want to cut to you in sixty seconds."

"No problem," he says. "I'm ready for the intro."

It's fun to watch people I like do this job. Lane counts down and then points at Jordy, who smiles into the camera. "A crowd has turned out here at the state police headquarters to hear the police commissioner unveil preliminary charges against two drug traffickers arrested last night in the largest drug seizure Vermont has ever seen.

"The state of Vermont will charge the suspects with the sale of fentanyl, possession of fentanyl, and possession of a regulated drug. But this is only the beginning. Sparks and Gage will likely be brought up on federal charges as well. The recent surge of overdose deaths is likely due to the shift toward pure fentanyl shipped from China through Canada. Stay with us as the commissioner makes his statement. Now, back to Jack on the news desk."

"You're clear," Lane chirps. "Nice, kid."

The cameraman grabs his equipment and moves into position to capture the commissioner's statement.

"Skylar!" someone shouts.

I whip around and see McCracken pushing through the crowd to reach me. He's sweating through his shirt already, in the usual fashion. "What are you doing here?"

He makes a noise of irritation. "What do you mean? It's a big story."

"Sure it is. But..." I glance over his shoulder and see Rocco the cameraman lumbering in our direction. "I've done a great job of reporting it so far. You could have just sent Rocco if you want the story so badly."

He wrinkles up his bulbous nose. "Gimme the press release, sweetheart. I don't have time to discuss this."

He reaches for the copy in my hand, but I jerk it away. "Not so fast. I want this story. I told you I was working on it. I know everything there is to know about it. You don't get to steamroll me on this."

"Christ. We'll credit you on the web article. But after that stunt you pulled last night? Emily Skye can't just show up on another station's newscast. That's some bullshit right there. Where is the loyalty? And moonlighting is not allowed under your contract."

He's right about that, except for one thing. "They're not paying me. I was just helping out the station *who helped you*. Where is the gratitude?"

"Good point, sister," Lane says with a cackle.

McCracken casts an anxious glance toward the podium. The police commissioner will arrive at any moment. "Gimme the damned press release, Skye. Or you're fired."

"You can't fire me," I snap. And then I *really* snap. "Because I quit," I say, taking a step back. "Find your own copy of the press release. Find someone else to do your job for you."

"Not funny," he snarls, stepping forward and grabbing my wrist in his sweaty hand.

"Hands *off* her," barks a voice that I know and love.

While I love it when Benito turns up to rescue me, it would be convenient if that weren't so often necessary. So I yank my wrist away from McCracken to show him that I can hold my own. I tuck the press release behind my back like a petulant child. And then I finally turn to look at Benny.

Wowzers. Benito in a green dress uniform is not to be missed. Since I saw him last, he's had a haircut *and* a clean shave. Suddenly my poor little heart is conflicted. Was Benito hotter with his mountain-man scruff and too-long hair? Or is he hotter like this—with the strong line of his jaw that I remember so well contrasting with the crisp white shirt. The deep-green wool of the uniform makes his skin glow.

The effect is dazzling—like looking into the sun. "Those are shiny buttons," I say stupidly.

"Damn," Lane Barker sighs from somewhere nearby. "He can shine my buttons any day."

"Is there a problem here?" Benito asks. The hard edge in his voice is unmistakable.

"No problem at all." McCracken laughs uneasily. "This is just a little joke, officer. She's holding my story hostage."

This man will never learn. "I am *not* your little joke. And it is not your story. It's never going to be your story. And I'm never working a day for you ever again."

"This is your boss?" Benito snorts. "Great management skills, apparently. Listen, I'm going up on that dais." He points at the podium. "If I see you touch her or even speak to her again, I will interrupt the press conference to personally come down here and kick your ass."

"Uh. Okay," McCracken says. "I don't want any trouble."

"Then find somewhere else to stand," Benito says through clenched teeth.

Finally, McCracken begins to back away from me.

"My god," Jordy breathes. "Your boyfriend is hot when he's angry."

It's true. But he's hot all the time. And he *is* my boyfriend. I've never had one of those in my whole life. Not really.

"Are you okay?" Benito asks.

"Just fine," I squeak.

He pecks me on the cheek and then walks away, while a hundred pairs of eyes watch him.

"Did you really just quit your job?" Jordy asks.

"Yep." My heart is thumping inside my chest. But it's true. Enough's enough.

He offers me the microphone.

"What's that for?"

"The follow up. You can cover it. It's not moonlighting anymore."

I'm speechless. "But it's yours now."

"Nah." He shakes his head. "She who scoops it, hoops it."

"That is not a saying," Lane Barker snorts. "But it should be. Go ahead, Skye. It's okay."

I close my hand around the microphone just as the commissioner takes the stage. "Last night between the hours of seven and eleven p.m., two dozen of Vermont's finest arrested four men during a drug transfer..."

My eyes scan the podium, landing on Benito as he stands beside his boss with the other officers. He's the most handsome out of all of them.

I've just quit my job. I'm going live on-air in a matter of minutes. But all I can think about is skimming my lips across Benito's clean-shaven jaw. And taking him back to bed.

For the first time in my life, it's a struggle to get my mind out of the gutter.

So this is how the other half lives.

FORTY-TWO

Skylar

THREE WEEKS later I'm in my happy place. Well, one of them anyway.

It's a Sephora store. One at a time I'm opening and testing each new lipstick shade. The back of my hand is beginning to look like I have a peculiar rash. But this is what I do when I need a bit of soothing.

I've just come from a job interview at a small-time cable sports network in lower Manhattan. I hated it on sight. It's another version of *New York News and Sports*, only with worse ratings and bigger assholes in charge.

Even worse—I think they're going to offer me a job. And I don't have any idea what I'll say.

When Benito put me on the train to New York last week, I'd just finished a round of interviews in Vermont. Aunt Jenny—who's visiting the city at the moment—had FedExed me my best suit and heels. I'd printed a fresh batch of résumés and passed them around Burlington like seeds in the wind.

But so far I don't have an offer. I had some great conversations, but it's a really small news market. Nobody has an opening right now. That's why I deigned to visit the sports network today, and why I'm taking two more New York interviews tomorrow.

It's nice to get interviews. After breaking the drug-bust story in

Vermont (and after my penis episode—I guess I'll never know which was more influential) it was suddenly easier to attract the attention of producers and editors.

But. I was really hoping to be offered a Vermont job. Benito wants me to be there with him. And I want that, too. But I need to work. If not in Vermont, then here.

The problem is money. I've helped Rayanne hire a lawyer to defend her against the charge of leaving the scene of an accident. It's possible that the charges will be dropped, or that she'll be able to plead down the sentence to community service.

But her lawyer costs more than three hundred bucks an hour. And I also helped with her bail money.

It's not a good time to be jobless. And—let's face it—producers will only remember my big scoop (and my penis) for about ten seconds. If I don't get a job now, I'll fade into obscurity again.

Obscurity is lovely, but not when you're poor.

After uncapping another lipstick shade (pretty petal!), I test it on my hand. I won't be buying anything today. Or anytime soon. But Sephora is where I go when I need to think bright, happy thoughts. To paraphrase Audrey Hepburn, nothing ever goes wrong at Sephora.

Here's a fun fact—there is only one Sephora in the whole state of Vermont. And it's inside a J.C. Penney. That's what Benito is asking of me if I move up there.

And I'll do it. I really will. I'm just not sure when.

My rent is due in nine days, which further complicates the decision. Even though my apartment is a bargain for New York, it's still a wad of cash. If I pay another month's rent, it will drain my savings account.

I need a plan. Fast. I can either pack up my life and teleport myself to Vermont, where I have no income, or I can try to get a job here until something closer to Benito comes along.

"Is there anything I can help you with? Do you have any questions?"

I look up to find a stunning young African American woman addressing me. Her makeup is perfectly applied, and she wears an apron sporting about thirty makeup brushes in various sizes and textures.

Part of me wants to ask if they're hiring.

"No thanks," I say with a smile. "I love your lashes, though." They sparkle subtly in a dark blue color.

"Thanks! The shade is called Midnight Sensation."

"I'll check it out."

I won't, though. And when she moves off to help someone else, I snag a tissue and wipe off my hand. It's time to meet Aunt Jenny for some pricey sushi that I can't really afford. But it was her idea. And she might insist on treating because she's going back to Florida tonight.

It's odd that she picked sushi, though. Not exactly Jenny's favorite.

I leave the store and maneuver my way across the street and through Union Square park. It's super crowded. Wall to wall bodies. I could really live without these crowds. A month ago I thought of Vermont as a hell on earth. But now it's growing on me. Nobody jostles you in Vermont.

The sushi restaurant is on a quiet street, though. I step inside and scan the tables for Jenny's silver hair. But she isn't in here.

"Can I help you?" asks the hostess.

"Table for two for Copeland?"

"Right this way." She gives me a smile, and beckons for me to follow her from one sleek room into the next. Wow, Jenny picked a cool restaurant. If only I weren't broke, I might really enjoy it.

I walk past a teak wall carved with modernist fishes and scan the diners' heads. Jenny's silver hair does not pop into view. But then a man turns around in his seat, and my stomach flips.

Benito. He's here?

He rises, smiling. "Hi honey. Thank you for meeting me for lunch."

"How...?" I'm speechless. "Jenny...?"

He grins. "She was in on it. I called your house phone last night and she picked up."

"Oh!" is all I manage to say before he steps closer to me and kisses me. "Ahh," is all I can say after that. *Benito.* He smells like pine trees even in New York. And he looks even better. His scruff is grown out again.

And I never could resist that smile.

"Sit," he says, guiding me into my chair. The hostess leaves us with menus. "How was the interview?"

"Fine." I wrinkle my nose, because the interview is the least interesting thing in the world if Benito is sitting across from me. "How are *you*. Is Speakeasy opening on time? Did they get the liquor license sorted out?" I've become very invested in the Rossi family events. We finally had dinner with Benny's mom—twice. And we also went out to eat with May and Alec at the Worthy Burger. The pickles were just as good as promised.

Benito doesn't answer. He picks up my hand from where it lays on the table, and kisses my palm. "I miss you. So much."

"Me too." That's just a given. "Did you catch any bad guys this week?"

"Mm-hmm," he says, kissing my palm again, his scruff tickling me. "But let's talk about your job."

"What job? That's the whole problem."

He holds my hand between both of mine. "I know you think so. But I'm not so worried. Let's order some fancy sushi and talk about that. Have you eaten here before?"

I shake my head. "It looks lovely. But I should probably be eating a food-truck falafel instead."

"I came all the way to New York to tell you not to worry about money. Well—that's not really true. I came all the way to New York because I haven't kissed you in over a week. And to tell you not to worry about money."

"Why? Money is a pretty big problem right now."

"Yes and no." He releases my hand and picks up his menu. "Tell me what to try. I want everything."

We each order different dishes, so we can taste each other's. And then Benito asks me again how the interview went.

"It went fine, okay? I think they're going to offer me a job. Which means I have to find a different job quickly so I don't have to say yes."

"You didn't like them?"

"Not even a little. It's a total bro atmosphere. My interviewer wore a backward baseball cap and a baseball T-shirt reading 'Frat Boy.'

And his assistant offered to pose for me if I wanted to draw *his* penis."

Benito closes his eyes. They remain closed for a long beat, as if he's summoning the will not to turn into the Hulk and smash things.

"I'm not going to take it," I say with a sigh. "Even though I could really use the paycheck. Maybe one of my interviews tomorrow will work out. I know you don't want me to take a job in New York."

He props his chin in his hand. "See, I do want you to. But only if it's your dream job. If you told me right now that you have an amazing opportunity in Manhattan, I'd be really happy for you."

"Oh." That's the most generous thing anyone has ever said to me.

"But—and I really am begging, here—please don't take a job you really don't want. You and I have been kept apart before. By a horrible man, and by shitty luck. I came here to tell you that I don't want money to be one more thing that keeps us apart. I don't care about money."

"I don't really either." This is *mostly* true. I do have a weakness for fine cosmetics. "But I'm ready to go into debt if Rayanne needs me to. And I need a job to make sure it's not all a huge disaster."

Benito nods. "Okay, let me ask you a question. If you weren't worried about paying Rayanne's lawyer, what would you be doing right now?"

"Oh, that's easy. I'd be feeding you a super-quick lunch in your apartment so we could have a nooner." And my neck heats only a little after this confession falls from my mouth.

He blinks once. "Honey, I'm still not used to you saying things like that. But I *strongly* approve."

I smile at him, feeling pleased with myself. I've become a lot less shy with Benito. It's easier than I thought, because every time I surprise him in bed, his look of gratitude is so swift that it makes me want to take those risks.

"Okay." He clears his throat. "We're definitely revisiting that idea later. But right now I'm talking about work. If you didn't feel so much pressure to find a job, how would you be viewing the whole thing?"

"Oh." That's a fun question. "I'd probably be in Vermont, pitching some freelance stories to New England magazines while I wait for a full-time job to open up. And I'd be begging the TV stations to put me on their sub lists, so I could get a foot in the door."

"So why not do that?" he asks. "We can live cheaply if you don't have to carry a New York apartment."

"Freelance is *really* unpredictable. I could make three thousand dollars one month, and three hundred the next. That's just too much uncertainty."

"We won't starve," he argues. "I wouldn't ever let that happen."

"I *know* that," I say a little too sharply. "But I don't always want to be the girl whose problems you have to solve. It's like high school all over again."

"Not even a little." He leans forward in his chair, his dark eyes boring into me. "You missed something very important."

"What?" It's hard to miss my pathetic bank balance.

"That I need you, too."

"Oh, but—"

He holds up a hand to silence me. "I need you near me. I need to come home to you every night, eat dinner in my kitchen, and hear about your day. I want you in my bed, and in my life."

Well. If he puts it that way...

"If you have a really excellent, life-changing reason why that can't happen in Vermont, I'll listen. I'll relocate. But a short term cash-flow problem isn't a good enough reason, Skye."

"I see." And as I'm sitting here in a sushi restaurant I'm learning something important about myself. It's actually harder for me to open up to that kind of love than it is to get naked with him.

But I want to try.

FORTY-THREE

Benito

SKYE IS LOOKING at me across the table with soft eyes. I want to kiss her so badly, but I'm just going to have to wait. I am very patient— but only up to a point.

"I could take out a mortgage," I offer. "If Rayanne's legal battle gets really expensive."

"You don't have a mortgage?"

"It's small. I only borrowed a little to put in that kitchen, and that fancy shower stall." I wiggle my eyebrows at her, because we've had an awful lot of fun in that shower.

She smiles. "That was a great investment. But I don't want to you to mortgage your home for Rayanne."

"Well, I don't want you to mortgage your life for her, either. Would she do the same for you?"

"*Ben.*" Her face falls.

And I realize I'm being unfair. Love isn't always logical. "I retract the question. It doesn't matter. I admire your generosity. But I'm greedy for my share of you." I extend my legs under the table and capture her feet between mine. "Please think about it. When you go to those interviews tomorrow, take it all in. Ask yourself where you want to spend your days, and with who."

"I will," she promises.

That's when a waiter appears to set down several plates full of decadence in front of us. And he brings me a Japanese beer and a glass of wine for Skye.

"Wow," she says, admiring the food on her plate. She has a dish made from raw salmon and avocado. It's shaped like an elaborate flower. "So beautiful."

"We're celebrating," I tell her.

"What are we celebrating?"

"We're celebrating the fact that we're sitting in the same place having lunch together. It's something I plan to celebrate as often as I can."

"Me too," she says, lifting her chopsticks. "I like the way you're thinking."

I give her feet a squeeze under the table and then dig in.

It's a great meal. There aren't a surplus of stellar sushi restaurants in Vermont. But I don't tell Skye. I'm still working on selling her on the place.

A young waiter comes to refill our water glasses and check on us. "Is everything to your liking?" he asks.

"It's wonderful," Skye says, giving me a smile.

"Lovely," he says. And then, "Nice penis, by the way."

"Thank you," she and I both say at once.

The guy shakes his head and walks away smiling, but the couple at the next table gives us really strange looks.

"Do you think people will ever stop saying that?" I ask my date.

"Nope," she says, pinching a bit of mango between her chopsticks. "It's just that I don't care anymore."

"That's my girl." I take a sip of my beer. And my cop senses tell me that the couple sitting beside us is still eavesdropping. "Are you ever going to show me your penis?" I ask Skye. "I mean, everyone else has seen it."

"Well, sure," she says, licking her lips. Her eyes dart to the side. It's just a flicker, but I can tell that she knows exactly who I'm baiting. "I'll show it to you tonight. If you ask real nice."

I make a comical growling sound, and Skye cracks up.

In my peripheral vision, I see the freaked-out faces of the couple at the next table.

Five hours later we're lying in her bed, our sweat cooling from the first of what I plan to be many rounds of loving tonight. I have to go back to Vermont in the morning, so every minute counts.

I met Aunt Jenny after lunch. She's a fun lady, and only half as pushy as my own mom. But now she's off to JFK for her flight home. I swear our clothes came off before her taxi even made it onto the Triborough Bridge.

Now I groan happily as I roll over, but my knee smacks into the wall. "Ow."

"I'm sorry," she says. "This is a small apartment."

She's not lying. "And a small bed." It's a double and mine is a king. "Not that I'm complaining." I'm about as satisfied as a man can be right now.

"I'm still a little afraid to impose on you with my money troubles," she says. "But I'm going to do it anyway."

My heart lifts immediately. "Really? Don't tease me," I say, kissing her neck. "I want you to come home with me so bad. We'll rent a U-Haul. Tomorrow."

She laughs. "Can I have a few days? Jeez. My whole life is in this tiny apartment. And I need to show up for those interviews tomorrow. If I don't show my face, I'll burn those bridges."

"Fair enough," I grumble. "Can we move you soon?" I lift my head and look around the little bedroom. "You don't have much furniture."

"I don't care about the furniture. Yours is nicer. But I have a lot of shoes."

This makes me laugh into the pillow, and I don't even know why. I'm just giddy. I can't wait to finally move my girl into my apartment and lock the door on the whole damn world.

"You know, I think it's time," she says.

"For what?"

"For me to show you my penis video."

"Really?" I pick up my head again. "You don't have to. I was just trying to freak out that other couple at lunch."

"I know, and that was super fun." Skye smiles at me. Her cheeks are rosy, and her hair is mussed. My blood stirs again. Already. Because I don't think I'll ever get enough of her looking like that. "But it's not such a big deal anymore. Let me get my phone."

She slides out of bed and crosses the tiny room while I ogle her naked body. But when she gets into bed again a moment later, there's a crease in her forehead.

"Problem?"

"No, not exactly. I have an email from Lane Barker. It's kind of cryptic. 'Call me. I have something for you, but it's not exactly what you want.'"

"Are you going to call her?"

"Of course," she says. "I hope it's not the traffic and weather, though."

"I'm pretty sure we don't have a traffic report in Vermont, honey. Unless a herd of cows gets in the road, it's pretty rare to have a traffic jam."

"Good point."

"Call her."

"Not yet. Fair's fair." She taps on the phone to bring up a YouTube video. Then she hands it to me.

The screen fills with a shot of Skye in a sleek dress in midnight blue. She looks as poised and comfortable as if she's speaking to Jenny in the living room. "Take care in the Lincoln Center neighborhood today, as construction continues to disrupt traffic southward toward Columbus Circle..." As she speaks, she's drawing a diagonal line where Broadway meets the park.

Now, Broadway is a thick street. Nice and thick. And—holy crap —Columbus Circle makes a perfect scrotum. The first gurgle of laughter escapes my chest, but I choke it down.

"No, it's okay," real Skye says. "Let it out. Even I can find it funny now."

But I keep my cool until she draws a mushroom shaped cap on the problem. Broadway is *very* excited. And I howl. Who could help it? "Oh h-honey," I gurgle. "That's..."

"Magnificent, I know. If you handed me a sketchbook and a fresh box of markers, I don't think I could do as good a peen right now if I tried."

"M-me neither." I giggle. "Jesus."

Skye gives me a kiss on the nose. Then she takes her phone out of my hand.

I roll my face into the pillow to try to compose myself. But for several long minutes, the little tremors and aftershocks keep shaking me. I want to punch every guy who ever laughed at Skye. But Jesus Christ, that's a funny video.

She comes back into the room a minute later to find me smiling at the ceiling. I take one look at her freaked-out face and sober instantly. "What's wrong?"

"Well, my mind is blown. Again. I called Lane Barker. And there is a job for me—but not one I interviewed for."

I sit up fast. "What is it? They're creating a traffic job for you?"

She grabs my chin. "You're hilarious."

"Well, tell me."

"It's radio. Green Mountain Public Radio needs someone to fill in on the news desk while one of their hosts is on maternity leave. The person they had backed out."

"Public radio," I say slowly. "They don't do fluff. You might like it? Not as sexy as TV, though. Is that an awful idea?"

Her face breaks slowly into a smile. "It's a *wonderful* idea. I'll never have to worry that they only want to put my cleavage on camera. The executive producer is a woman. They share some content with WBTV."

"So this is a good thing?" I'm a little confused.

"It's amazing. Yeah, it's only a temp job. But it's a foot in the door. Lane seemed to think that this sort of stint leads to a permanent job pretty often."

"Baby, really?" I grab her and hug her. "You're going to take it?"

"I so am. And they want me to start as soon as I can get up there."

"That's amazing. That station is big in Vermont, you know. Everybody's in their car a lot because it's so rural. I can listen to you while I wait to arrest bad guys." I palm her smooth knee, and then relax against the pillows. "So can we just get a U-Haul and move you to Vermont now?"

"Pretty much," she says. "I don't want to wait anymore."

"Me neither. But I can think of one major problem with your cool new job."

"What's that?" She's already distracted herself by running her knuckles up and down my happy trail.

"You can't draw any male genitalia on the radio."

"As far as you know." Skye snorts. "Don't forget that I'm uber-talented."

We both start to laugh until I have to kiss her again.

————

Thank you for reading Fireworks! Join Sarina's mailing list to hear about more new titles.

Acknowledgments

Dear readers,

Next time I have an idea for a book that requires an understanding of law enforcement, please remind me of my inadequacies.

I was shored up by Vermont prosecutor Heidi R. Thank you for your wisdom! And thank you to Sergeant Lisa F. for taking all my questions. You were both invaluable. And all the law enforcement errors made herein are entirely my own fault.

As always, thanks to Edie Danford and Jo Pettibone for your editing prowess. I gave you some extra errors to find this time. You're welcome.

Thanks to Sara Eirew and Sarah Hansen for another great cover!

And thanks to Vermont for giving me such a rich landscape to write. And thank you readers, for making the True North series a bestseller! I owe you big.

Love,
Sarina

CPSIA information can be obtained
at www.ICGtesting.com
Printed in the USA
LVHW031625211019
634863LV00013B/1327/P

9 781942 444688